T0008564

PRAISE FOR

THE BAKER'S MAN

"Combine four parts love, two parts excitement, a dash of humor, and a pinch of magic and you have Jennifer Moorman's delightful *The Baker's Man*. Moorman's sweet, heartfelt confection will please anyone looking for a charming, witty, utterly delectable read!"

—LAUREN K. DENTON, *USA TODAY* BESTSELLING
AUTHOR OF *THE HIDEAWAY* AND *A PLACE TO LAND*

Jennifer Moorman's *The Baker's Man* is a teaspoon of love, a dash of magic, and a whole heaping cup of southern charm. Anna's legacy of unconventional romance and luscious baked goods is a treat from start to finish. Perfect for fans of Amy E. Reichert and Jenny Colgan.

—AIMIE K. RUNYAN, BESTSELLING AUTHOR OF *THE SCHOOL FOR
GERMAN BRIDES* AND *THE MEMORY OF LAVENDER AND SAGE*

"*The Baker's Man* is a charming recipe of magic, romance, friendship, and the importance of staying true to yourself.

—HEATHER WEBBER, *USA TODAY* BESTSELLING
AUTHOR OF *MIDNIGHT AT THE BLACKBIRD CAFÉ*

"*The Baker's Man* hits my sweet spot with mouthwatering baked goods and an enchanting romance. Jennifer Moorman's scrumptious tale has all the magical ingredients: best friend banter, small town drama, and the mysterious arrival of the perfect man!"

—AMY E. REICHERT, AUTHOR OF *ONCE UPON A DECEMBER*

THE
BAKER'S
MAN

THE BAKER'S MAN

A NOVEL

JENNIFER MOORMAN

HARPER MUSE

The Baker's Man

Copyright © 2023 Jennifer Moorman

All rights reserved. No portion of this book may be reproduced, stored in a retrieval system, or transmitted in any form or by any means— electronic, mechanical, photocopy, recording, scanning, or other—except for brief quotations in critical reviews or articles, without the prior written permission of the publisher.

Published by Harper Muse, an imprint of HarperCollins Focus LLC.

This book is a work of fiction. The characters, incidents, and dialogue are drawn from the author's imagination and are not to be construed as real. Any resemblance to actual events or persons, living or dead, is entirely coincidental.

Any internet addresses (websites, blogs, etc.) in this book are offered as a resource. They are not intended in any way to be or imply an endorsement by HarperCollins Focus LLC, nor does HarperCollins Focus LLC vouch for the content of these sites for the life of this book.

Library of Congress Cataloging-in-Publication Data

Names: Moorman, Jennifer, 1978- author.
Title: The baker's man : a novel / Jennifer Moorman.
Description: Nashville : Harper Muse, [2023] | Summary: "This enchanting and whimsical tale of friendship, love, and the power of baking dreams into life will open readers' eyes to the magic all around them"-- Provided by publisher.
Identifiers: LCCN 2022039080 (print) | LCCN 2022039081 (ebook) | ISBN 9781400240470 (paperback) | ISBN 9781400240494 (ebook) | ISBN 9781400240500
Subjects: LCGFT: Romance fiction. | Novels.
Classification: LCC PS3613.O575 B35 2023 (print) | LCC PS3613.O575 (ebook) | DDC 813/.6--dc23/eng/20220928
LC record available at https://lccn.loc.gov/2022039080
LC ebook record available at https://lccn.loc.gov/2022039081

Printed in the United States of America

23 24 25 26 27 LSC 5 4 3 2 1

To Daddy and Ma, my family and friends, the Mystic Water Book Club, and all my rock star readers who have supported this dough-boy dream for years and kept my hope alive, my spirit lifted, and my heart filled with joy.

Magic is believing in yourself. If you can do that, you can make anything happen.

—Johann Wolfgang von Goethe

PROLOGUE

THE OLDER GENERATION OF TOWNSPEOPLE IN MYSTIC WATER, Georgia, still talked about that night in late July when the south-bound train carrying sugar cane and cotton was late because the on-duty conductor had eloped instead of going into work. Two hours passed before anyone realized the train hadn't pulled out of the station, and it took another two hours before a substitute conductor could be found.

So, four hours later than usual, the train barreled through Mystic Water, blasting its horn at every crossing and waking everyone from a deep sleep. The train brought with it an intense summer wind that swept over the town, uprooting half the willows along Jordan Pond. It plucked sunflower petals and created twirling yellow tornadoes. It caused the sleeping birds such anxiety that they erupted into twilight birdsong and didn't stop until about the time Bea's Bakery opened for business.

Nobody slept that night, not with the train and the wind and the birds. More than half the town showed up at the bakery the next morning in desperate need of a cup of Bea's Give-Me-a-Jolt Java, and that's when they saw him—Joseph O'Brien—looking like a man who'd climbed out of an Irish novel, broad shouldered, red haired, and green eyed. He was working behind the counter alongside the bakery owner, Beatrice, like he'd been born to be her partner.

Some said he jumped from the southbound train. Others said he appeared like magic. Everyone agreed they'd never seen a man look more in love with any woman than Joseph did with Beatrice.

CHAPTER 1

PEANUT BRITTLE

Bea's Bakery offered cure-alls in the form of pastries, chocolates, cookies, cakes, cupcakes, and specialty drinks. Everyone in Mystic Water depended on Beatrice O'Brien to soothe their pains, give wings to their hopes, and spark their passions. Bea's Bakery supported the town's needs like columns supported the Parthenon. Her doors were always open, figuratively, no matter the time of day. Everyone knew they could call Beatrice after hours, and she would have exactly what they needed: a twilight brownie for stargazers, a tropical white chocolate tart for those needing a vacation, or a peppermint dark chocolate cookie for settling an uneasy heart. They didn't even always have to call Beatrice; sometimes she would show up on their doorsteps with the answer to a question they hadn't yet asked.

Delilah Gill swore that one midnight, Beatrice brought over a batch of sea salt caramels that changed her life forever. Delilah never revealed how she was altered, but the folks of Mystic Water had their suspicions, especially after Delilah moved out of her mother's basement, finished her law degree, and became the judge of the local court.

Beatrice offered love and happiness to the whole town until she was eighty-five. One Saturday morning rainstorm clouds, smeared gray and gloomy, gathered in the sky, refusing to pour. Mystic Water suffocated beneath a humid summer haze that clung to the skin like syrup. When the doors to the bakery refused to open, the townspeople gathered outside, confused and unsure how to go about their days without treats or coffee or the famous Saturday morning brownies. Beatrice's son, Charlie, finally opened the doors with slumped shoulders and defeat in his eyes.

For three weeks after Beatrice's death, no one in Mystic Water could look at chocolate without feeling the drag of sorrow. Coffee tasted bitter on the tongue. Shoppers in the Piggly Wiggly glared at pastries.

Then news of Beatrice's granddaughter returning to Mystic Water blew through the town like a honeysuckle wind, sweet and nostalgic.

Anna O'Brien, a hometown girl, had moved away to attend the Institute of Culinary Education in New York City. While she was a student, she worked as a baking assistant in a fancy downtown hotel, and following graduation, she was promoted to sous pastry chef. Mystic Water locals spotted Anna in town only on major holidays, when she was seen wearing a robin's-egg blue apron and laughing behind the bakery counter with Beatrice. She hadn't lived in Mystic Water in at least five years, but the front page of the *Mystic Water Gazette* alerted everyone that Anna would be returning to her Georgia roots, reopening the bakery, and following in her grandma's footsteps.

Opinions divided the town. Half said they would refuse to even try her creations when the time came because they feared the disappointment would be too great to bear. Their doubts were as plentiful as fireflies in July; there was no way a girl trained in NYC could satisfy their traditional Southern palates.

The other half prayed the ability to create delectable treats ran in Anna's blood, which hopefully hadn't been diluted by her brief stint up north. Within days of reopening the bakery, Anna quieted the doubters and validated the optimists with her grandma's well-loved recipes. Within a month, she'd charmed everyone with her own creations, and after two years of waking before dawn, sweating through south Georgia summers with the bakery ovens blazing, and using enough sugar to sweeten even the bitterest disposition, Anna reestablished Bea's Bakery as a wellspring of joy and deliciousness.

When people ate what Anna O'Brien baked, they smiled wider, laughed louder, and left the bakery she'd inherited with more confidence than when they arrived. Her chocolate chip cookies made Jordan Hillman propose to Julie Farmer on their fourth date. Her OREO brownies caused Roger Jackson to think he could dance the Charleston like he had in the '40s. One sip of her Saturday morning hot chocolate made everyone a good neighbor. People in town swore Anna could make anything better than the original, and they were right. It was a skill she'd been honing since she was big enough to stand on a step stool and help her grandma in the kitchen.

While most children spent their after-school time watching

cartoons and their summers flying kites and playing pickup games of baseball, Anna spent almost all her free time helping at Bea's Bakery. Anna had a superior sense for knowing how to combine ingredients and flavors into delicious creations. She also had an unusually strong sense of smell, which gave her an incredible advantage for pairing ingredients in a way that enhanced the eating experience. Each treat she made engaged the eyes, the nose, the tongue, and every pleasing nerve in the body.

A spatula and a whisk became extensions of Anna's hands. Beatrice special ordered Anna's first apron with #1 Baking Assistant embroidered in looping white script across the watermelon-pink bib. As Anna grew, her aprons did too, and by the time she finished high school, she had a rainbow assortment, each one with a different phrase stitched on it, hanging in her closet.

It was a natural step after high school for Anna to continue her culinary education, so she attended a local junior college and earned an associate's degree in business. If she wanted to one day own a bakery, she needed a solid foundation of skills to keep it running. Beatrice had shared management and leadership knowledge with Anna through the years, and she learned best with hands-on experience, but Anna's parents insisted she have a formal education. No daughter of theirs was going to skip out on college. Anna's mama, Evelyn, believed good Southern girls needed to follow certain "rules," and although receiving an acceptable education wasn't in the top slot, it definitely held a spot in the top five.

Evelyn resisted Anna's desire to attend culinary school, but not because she felt it was an unsuitable path for her daughter. The school of Anna's choice was located in New York, and according to Evelyn, no decent Southern young woman up and moved that far north on purpose. But Beatrice had been the main supporter of Anna attending the Institute of Culinary Education because it was the top-ranked culinary school in the nation. Knowing she could brag about her daughter attending *the best* caused Evelyn to relent, but she made Anna swear she would move back to Mystic Water after graduation.

It was obvious to everyone that Anna had a special talent for pastries and baking, and her grandma knew there was much more for Anna to learn and see outside of Mystic Water. Although Anna believed she would most likely take over Bea's Bakery one day—because that's what everyone assumed would happen, especially her mama—Beatrice encouraged Anna to blaze her own trail, even if that meant never returning.

Anna had followed her grandma's advice. She excelled at the institute and received the award for Most Likely to Succeed, bestowed by classmates and instructors who believed she would make a name for herself. After graduation she continued to expand her skills while working with one of the most prestigious pastry chefs in New York City.

Every time they talked, Evelyn asked when Anna was moving back to Mystic Water and often texted random updates about townsfolk.

Susie Callahan had a baby boy. Named him Patrick.

When are you moving home?

Derek Dunes bought the old Farmer house. Have you booked a moving van yet?

Anna learned to respond with a heart emoji and nothing more. During phone calls, Anna sidestepped the question by saying she was still receiving on-the-job training and Beatrice could handle the bakery perfectly well without her for a bit longer.

In truth, Anna wasn't ready to move back to Mystic Water. She had plans, the seed of which had been planted by Beatrice before Anna even moved to the big city. Working as a sous pastry chef at the hotel required long hours, and some days were so exhausting she'd stumble into her tiny apartment and collapse onto the bed fully dressed, sleeping the night away without moving until her alarm beeped the next morning. Every little bit of money that didn't go to living expenses was tucked away for Anna's one-day dream: owning her own beachside bakery. She didn't reveal this desire to anyone, especially not her mama, who would have flipped her lid if she thought Anna wasn't coming home.

That beachside bakery dream came to a full stop the Saturday morning Anna received a phone call from her daddy, Charlie, letting her know that Beatrice had passed away peacefully in her sleep. He asked Anna to come home for the reading of the will and for the funeral, understanding she might not be able to stay much longer than that. But Anna knew in an instant her life in the city was ending. Her daddy might have been okay with her returning to New York, but there was no chance her mama would be. Anna had a good idea of what her mama expected: Anna would move home and run Bea's Bakery. Maybe Anna expected the same of herself because *What will happen to the bakery?* ran on a loop in her mind.

She sobbed her way through packing up the few things she owned in her apartment, cried when she turned in her notice at work, and blubbered her good-byes to the few friends she had in the city. Then she rented a car and made the two-day trip south to Mystic Water, blasting her grandma's favorite songs through the Bluetooth connection and crying into multiple bags of Doritos and bottles of Coca-Cola.

Most of her heartache came from the loss of her beloved grandma, her number-one supporter and one of the kindest, most loving people she had ever known. A sliver of the heartbreak was caused by letting go of the dream she'd been cultivating for years. At least she would still be able to bake and share her passion with others. It might not look the way she'd envisioned it, but when did life ever look the way anyone imagined?

During the reading of the will, Anna learned she had inherited not only the bakery but also a hefty chunk of money along with a handwritten note and a hand-carved lockbox with a key.

For opening your own place one day, no matter what anyone says. Follow your heart and forge your own path, sweet girl, and sell this place with my full permission if that's what *you* choose. Bea's Bakery was always my dream. It doesn't have to be yours—not if your sights are fixed somewhere else. Open the box only when you need to. You'll know exactly when you do, and you'll know what to do with it. I love you.

Even without Anna telling her, Beatrice had known where the girl's heart was taking her. Anna hadn't shown anyone the letter, not even when her mama demanded to see it. Evelyn relented only when Charlie firmly asked her to leave Anna alone with her grief. After the funeral, Anna hesitantly asked her parents if they thought the bakery should be sold. Evelyn launched into a full-blown monologue about all the reasons that suggestion was absurd. Didn't everyone know, including Anna, that she was always going to take over the bakery? It was Anna's responsibility, Evelyn declared, and her duty as a devoted granddaughter to continue the O'Brien legacy.

Guilt crept into Anna's heart as her mama's words pinched against her skin. Anna pictured herself standing in the bakery kitchen, watching her grandma pull fresh chocolate chip cookies out of the oven, the scents of vanilla and melted chocolate permeating the space. Bea's Bakery had been Anna's special place, a haven where she could let loose and create. With grief rolling her shoulders forward, Anna couldn't bear another loss. Closing the bakery forever felt like a betrayal of her grandma's hard work. No matter what Beatrice's letter said, Anna couldn't turn her back on her family—not now, and not with her mama's piercing gaze staring holes straight through Anna's forehead, daring her to disagree.

So Anna packed away her dream and hid it with Beatrice's letter, the locked box, and its key on the top shelf of her bedroom closet, then forgot about all of them.

Two years later an October-afternoon sun eased its way toward the horizon and turned the sky outside Bea's Bakery the shade of caramelized sugar. Anna leaned her hip against the counter, watching the last of the shoppers flitter down Main Street on the way to their cars. Evening customers shuffled into Mackie's Café, beckoned in by the scents of flank steak marinated in a merlot reduction and rosemary mashed potatoes that would melt in the mouth. Looking over her shoulder, she smiled at the calendar tacked to the wall. The red heart she'd drawn around today's date marked the two years she'd spent loving Baron Barker.

Her cell phone vibrated in her apron pocket. She fished it out and accepted the call with a smile. Before she could even say hello, one of her best friends, Lily Matthews, burst into a conversation as though they'd been talking long before the phone rang.

"I know you love surprises, but I also know you love to plan, and guess what Jakob just told me about Baron? They were having lunch today, and Baron said he has a *big surprise* to share with you. Jakob wouldn't say what the surprise is, but I think *we* know, don't we? It's about time. How long has it been? Three years—"

"Two."

"Yes, two, that's right, which is long enough, isn't it? Are you ready? What are you wearing? Tonight, I mean, not now. Baron told Jakob he was seeing you tonight. Are y'all going out? Mackie's Café?"

Lily stopped long enough to inhale, and Anna's eyes darted to the clock on the wall. The bakery officially closed in ten minutes.

Anna passed through the wide, arching doorway that led to the kitchen. "I'm making dinner for him, taking it over to his place." The aroma of crushed garlic, fresh tomatoes, and bubbling parmesan cheese and béchamel sauce filled the room. Anna was baking lasagna bolognese, Baron's favorite, for their anniversary dinner. The prepared garlic bread sat on the counter, waiting to be toasted beneath the broiler. She'd even carefully wrapped a bottle of their favorite vintage wine.

"You think this is it? It *is* our two-year anniversary today."

"Then, of course, it's happening. We always knew he'd ask you. How could he not? He's been crazy about you since the first time he laid eyes on you. This is it, Anna. He's going to propose. I just know it."

Anna's free hand flew to her heart. It palpitated as if she were about to take a flying leap from the high dive into the country-club pool.

"Are you there?" Lily asked.

"Yes. I'm just . . . trying not to freak out." Anna lowered her hand and rested it against the cool stainless steel countertop. She inhaled a slow, deep breath. Her cell phone beeped in her ear, notifying her of another call. She glanced at the screen. "Baron's calling. I'll call you back tonight—unless we get carried away with all the excitement."

Lily squealed. "Don't forget to call me! I don't care what time it is. I want all the details."

Anna swapped calls. "Hello?" Excitement quickened her pulse.

"Hey, Anna-Banana," Baron said. "What time are you coming over?"

Anna's heart pounded a *rat-a-tat-tat* against her ribs. "As soon as the bakery closes. I can be there in about twenty minutes. Does that work?"

"Perfect. I have a surprise for you."

Anna squeezed the phone in her hand and closed her eyes. "Yeah? Can I get a hint?"

Baron laughed. "No way. See you soon."

"See you soon," Anna repeated, and Baron disconnected. She danced a jig around the kitchen and shoved on a pair of oven mitts. She tapped a happy rhythm on the countertop and then opened the oven. Melted cheese oozed and bubbled, and she let the scent wash over her. She held out a mittened hand, pretending to gaze at an excessively large diamond ring on her finger. "Marry you? Why, of course I will, my darling!" she said in a melodramatic Southern-belle accent.

Anna slid the lasagna into an oven-safe bag and covered the garlic bread with aluminum foil. She'd broil it at Baron's townhouse. She hurried upstairs to the second-floor apartment above the bakery to change out of her work attire. She'd already laid out a knitted dress the color of ripe plums, black leather booties, and her favorite pair of silver hoop earrings. She tossed her hair up into a messy but intentional bun, letting a few pieces of her auburn waves frame her face.

Downstairs, she grabbed the bottle of wine and the chocolate sweets she'd wrapped up earlier along with the lasagna and bread. Then she bundled herself into her car and drove across town feeling as though a trapped hummingbird were fluttering in her stomach.

Baron lived in an end-unit townhouse he had, until recently, shared with his brother, Brody. The exterior was a combination of stones in an assortment of browns ranging from tan to sepia. The woodwork was stained a dark chocolate, creating an overall masculine and imposing facade. Numerous times, Anna had tried to convince Baron to at least put plants on the front porch to break up all the brown. He always reminded her he was a class A plant killer. Not to mention his travel schedule for work left very little time for keeping anything alive and thriving, especially plants.

She hiked up the brown-brick stairs to the small front porch, her arms loaded with dinner and dessert. The door was unlocked, and with careful maneuvering, she managed to turn the knob without dropping dinner on the welcome mat she'd bought him when he moved in.

When she didn't see Baron in the living room or kitchen, she called up the stairs, "I'm here."

"Just got out of the shower. I'll be right down," he said.

Brody had decorated Baron's living room. It held an L-shaped couch with a solid pinewood frame and stainless steel feet. Its low round arms and stiff-pillow back, along with the button tufting on the seat, boasted a trendiness that Baron definitely did not adhere to. The meteorite-gray armchair with a black metal frame and the oval-topped distressed aluminum coffee table had also been left behind by Brody when he moved. Baron had hung a few artistic poster prints from his travels in Hawaii and Malaysia but had added very little else to the downstairs aesthetic.

Baron's minimalistic style spoke of his dislike for having too many possessions—because too much stuff inhibited picking up and moving at a moment's notice—and also his townhouse's use as more of a stopping place in between work and travel sites. As a travel marketer and adviser, he spent four to five days of every week, sometimes more, traveling all over the world. Baron's company sent him to scout out a destination area, participate in local or resort activities, and get a feel for the place and its surroundings to better market and sell packages to their clients.

Since landing in Mystic Water two years ago, Baron's work-related travel had been mostly contained to the United States, so he was often home for a long weekend, when he and Anna could hang out after the bakery closed. Over the few days they were able to spend together each month, Baron always had ideas for how they should fill their time. He'd convinced Anna to do all sorts of activities she never would have tried on her own, like bungee jumping, indoor skydiving, and rock climbing.

When she could get someone to cover for her at the bakery, they'd taken day trips. They hiked through most of the Georgia state parks, kayaked the Oconee River, and learned to salsa at a well-known studio on the Georgia-Florida line. Anna liked to think Baron challenged her to try new things and take adventures that at first seemed scary, while she calmed him and kept him grounded and mostly reasonable. A part of Baron, though, could never be tamed—it was something a little too wild—but she appreciated that about him. No one would ever describe Baron as dull, not with that megawatt smile and twinkle of mischief in his eyes.

The kitchen in Baron's townhouse was nearly as bare and lacking in personality as the other rooms, but Anna didn't really mind. Baron's vivacious personality filled a room as soon as he entered it, and once he was present, she stopped noticing how generic and empty his townhouse seemed. How it felt like a place where *no one* ever lived—a home without a heart.

Anna put the lasagna on the stove top and turned on the broiler. Then she slid the garlic bread into the oven. She pulled plates and glasses from the cabinets before opening the bottle of wine. By the time she heard Baron bounding down the stairs, the table was set, and she had his favorite music—jazz—playing on the Bluetooth speaker in the kitchen.

Anna grabbed the bread from the oven and switched off the broiler. A breeze blew stray pieces of Anna's hair into her face.

For a few seconds, the napkins on the table fluttered like butterflies. The scent of the ocean filled the air.

Within seconds, Baron stepped into the kitchen. His tall frame cast a long shadow across the tiles, and as always, his blond hair was disheveled, as if he'd spent the day sailing or surfing. He grinned and scooped Anna into a hug before she could even say hello. Baron squeezed her and kissed her neck, and all at once she was overwhelmed by the smell of a wind blowing across the sea and the strength of his arms tight around her, feeling as if she'd be blown miles and miles away from shore if he weren't holding her to the earth.

When he returned her to her feet, she steadied herself and exhaled. "Well, hey to you too," she said.

"It smells like an Italian feast." With his hands resting on her hips, he leaned down and kissed her. He glanced over her shoulder at the bread and then noticed the set table. "What's with all the great food? You trying to win me over?" He winked.

Anna's smile faltered. "It's our anniversary. Two years."

Baron's eyes widened, and then he winced.

"You forgot." If he'd forgotten their anniversary, did that mean his proposal today was coincidental?

"I'm a jerk," he admitted. "I forgot. You know I'm not good with dates. But one of us is a decent human being. It smells great, like everything you make." He smiled, cupped her face, and kissed her again. "I say we eat, and then I'll share my surprise."

Anna's stomach dropped. She tried to catch it before it busted through the floor but failed. She glanced at her left hand and managed not to look nervous as she smiled. "I can't wait to hear it."

She served squares of lasagna onto their plates, and her

hands trembled. Baron noticed her struggling to cut through the bread, so he offered to help. "You doing okay?"

Her laugh squeezed out in staccato bursts. "Long day." She willed her heart to calm down. "But I'm happy to be here now . . . for the surprise."

Baron poured two glasses of wine, and once they were seated, he said, "Let's toast to new beginnings."

This was it! Anna clinked her glass against his, and they both took a sip. Baron slid his fork through the lasagna, took a bite, and moaned. "You make the best lasagna in the world. If you didn't already own a bakery, I'd tell you to open a restaurant."

"I wanted to make your favorite," she said as she glanced down at her plate. How could he eat when she could barely keep her body from fidgeting?

"You're the best." Baron shoved another few mouthfuls of lasagna and bread into his mouth before he put down his fork. "You aren't eating. You must be more excited than I am. I thought I could wait until dessert to tell you, but let's just do this now." Baron pushed away from the table and turned his body to face hers.

Anna lifted her napkin from her lap and placed it beside her plate. Her heart pumped so wildly she could barely breathe. She patted her messy bun and adjusted her earrings, anything to keep her hands busy. Baron reached out and grabbed both her hands in his, and she held her breath.

Baron's grin widened. "I got the job," he said.

His words made no sense in relation to what she'd been expecting, so she stared at him without responding.

He chuckled. "You with me, Anna-Banana? I got it. The job in California."

Anna's brain kicked into gear, and she pulled her hands out of his. She recalled a conversation they'd had months ago about a large travel agency in California that was looking for experienced marketers and people willing to globe-trot to find the most elite destinations for clients. But the conversation, like most with Baron, had been all over the place and full of what-ifs and maybes and one-days. He hadn't talked about the job in California as though it was even a consideration, merely a stream-of-consciousness piece of information.

"The long shot, possible dream, never-gonna-happen *job*?"

Baron slapped his palms against his thighs. "Yes! You were paying attention. They emailed me two days ago, asked for an interview, which I did yesterday, and by this morning, they offered me the job."

Anna's heart fell into her plate of lasagna, and he continued.

"The agency is flying me out tomorrow for two weeks in Napa Valley so I can acclimate to the way things are done. They want me to start within the month. I'll find an apartment while I'm there and take in the sights. I'll need to put this place up for sale. God, can you believe it? Two weeks in California, in Napa Valley no less. While I'm there, I'll tour a few vineyards, maybe go to the beach." When Anna still said nothing, Baron stopped smiling. "Aren't you excited?"

Anna pressed her lips together and leaned back in the chair to avoid doubling over with disappointment. She wished Lily hadn't called her. Now she felt deflated when she should be excited for Baron. He was obviously over the moon about this new opportunity, even if it was on the opposite side of the country from her.

"It's great," she said, her voice as flat as naan. "It sounds like a once-in-a-lifetime opportunity."

Baron reached out for her hand. He twined their fingers together and tugged her up and out of her chair. "What's wrong, Anna-Banana? I thought you'd be happier."

"I was, I mean, I am. It's great. Really. Really great. You're leaving tomorrow?"

Baron brushed the auburn hairs from her face, and she closed her eyes and inhaled slowly, breathing in the heavy scents of garlic and baked cheese competing with the bitter smell of lingering ocean water. "I'll pack tonight, and I'll drive to the airport in the morning. This is a big deal for me. You know that."

Anna nodded. "It's a great opportunity," she said and tried to smile, but it felt broken on her face.

"Hey, I'm sorry I forgot it was our anniversary. I'll make it up to you when I get back, I promise. I wish I was better at this sort of thing because you deserve that." Baron pointed one finger to the side of his head and made circles in the air. "There's all this stuff going on in there all the time."

Anna swallowed. She stared down at the brown sugar trapped beneath her fingernails. She felt as if a peppermint had lodged itself halfway down her throat. Baron rubbed his thumb across the top of her hand, and the movement distracted her, eased the tightness in her chest, but not enough. She took a step backward. "I'm really happy for you," she said. "I know how much you'll love it. The travel, the fun, the future. I guess I just thought that if this sort of life change came up, there would be more *we* in your plan."

"More what?" he asked and shoved his free hand through his damp hair.

"Us," she answered, motioning to the space between them. "There doesn't seem to be any *us* in your future in California.

I . . . well, I don't know how I fit in. I hoped that you would have wanted me to be a part of it somehow. Lily called today and said you told Jakob about a surprise you had for me, and since it's our anniversary, she assumed it was a ring . . ." Anna stopped.

Baron's mouth fell open, and for a long, uncomfortable minute, he said nothing while Anna chewed on her bottom lip and thought about hiding beneath the couch cushions. She hadn't meant to mention the ring.

"Wow," he said and let go of her hand. He rubbed the back of his neck and stared at the table full of uneaten food and wine. "I thought you'd be excited about all of this. I didn't know you thought I might ask you to . . . You love it here, don't you? Don't you love this town?"

"This is where I grew up. It's a great town, but I don't have to live here forever," Anna said.

"You want to leave Mystic Water?"

Anna stared at her fork teetering on the edge of her plate. Hadn't he ever listened when she told him she wanted to open her own bakery somewhere else, start over somewhere new? She'd often felt trapped in her hometown because *someone* had to take over her grandma's bakery, and she'd had no other choice—not really. "This isn't about Mystic Water. This is about you taking a job in California. And I'd be . . . *here*. Did you not think about what would happen to us?"

Anna might have laughed off the entire misunderstanding if Baron hadn't looked so horrified at the idea of being engaged to her and so completely unaware of what his sudden move across the country would do to their relationship. She looked at him, feeling her insides splintering like peanut brittle.

"I'm sorry," he said, but he didn't sound apologetic. He

sounded like a man woken from a deep sleep. "This all happened so fast. I don't even know what it's going to be like out there. Life is going to change for me. You know I love you, but ever since I got the offer this morning, my mind has been full steam ahead on next steps to get me out there and prepared for the job. You're the first person I wanted to share it with, but I didn't think about what that would do to us."

"You didn't think," she repeated. "And the first person you told was Jakob, not me." When Baron continued to stare at the table, she added, "I'm going home." Tears tightened her throat and pricked at her eyes. She needed to get out of there before she made a complete fool of herself and sobbed into the lasagna.

Baron reached for her. "Don't go," he said. "Stay. Let's finish our dinner. You worked hard on it."

Anna shook her head. "I think it's best if I go home. You can cut the lasagna into sections and freeze it. It reheats well." Anna grabbed her half-full glass of wine and downed it. Then she walked to the door. With her hand on the doorknob, she hesitated. A part of her had hoped he would argue, hoped he would refuse to let her leave so they could sort out this sudden weirdness. But clearly he wasn't going to fight for her. Clearly the idea of marrying her had horrified him so completely he had nothing else to say. Anna opened the door and rushed out.

CHAPTER 2

RUM CAKE

ANNA LEANED HER FOREHEAD AGAINST THE STEERING WHEEL. She fought the tears, but they gathered in her chest until she felt like she was choking. "You win," she whispered as they rolled down her cheeks.

She grabbed her cell phone and texted Lily: Tonight was a bust.

After tossing the phone on the passenger seat, she reversed out of Baron's driveway and drove home, steadily wiping away tears. The weight of disappointment and confusion hunched her shoulders. "Walking on Sunshine" came on the radio, and Anna glared at the dashboard display.

"That's just cruel," she said as she turned off the music. Anna struggled to process the evening that had started as a celebratory anniversary dinner and ended with an unraveling relationship. Baron was moving across the country, leaving tomorrow to look for a place to live. Did that mean they were breaking up? Did he want to try long distance? Did *she*?

Anna unlocked the bakery and dragged herself inside. She

shuffled through the dark rooms until she reached the kitchen and flipped on the lights. Her cell phone pinged with Lily's response: What happened?!? Anna texted that she'd talk to Lily tomorrow and turned off her phone. She wasn't in the mood to talk about how her two-year relationship with Baron had crumbled to cookie dust, that he hadn't even thought of asking her to go to California with him. The only thing Anna was in the mood for was being alone and eating cookie dough straight from the container.

She hefted a five-pound tub of homemade double chocolate chip cookie dough from the cooler. With an ice-cream scoop, she shamelessly doled out a healthy portion and promptly shoved it into her mouth, chewing slowly and trying not to drool on her knitted dress. Then she grabbed a small saucepot from the rack and heavy cream from the cooler. She warmed the cream over medium heat, and while she waited for it to come to an almost boil, she dumped dark chocolate chunks into a glass bowl. As soon as the milk heated through, she poured it over the chocolate. Using a fork, she whipped the chocolate nearly to death, whipped it until the chocolate ganache clung to the tines and refused to let go.

Anna licked the fork and tossed it into the closest sink. She grabbed a wooden spoon and dipped it into the ganache. She opened her mouth wide and crammed the spoon inside. Chocolate collected in the corners of her mouth. She licked her lips, and like a gingerbread cookie whose legs had been snapped off, she sagged to the kitchen floor, still holding the spoon in her hand.

Two years. Two years she had spent loving Baron Barker, encouraging him, partaking in every spontaneous adventure, supporting his every whim, even his three-week desire to write a Pulitzer Prize–winning western novel while staying at a dude ranch in Montana. Baron's latest adventure would take him across the country to one of the most-successful travel agencies in the nation, and he had made no plans for her to go with him—hadn't even thought of adding her to the equation. She squeezed her eyes shut, wrapped her arms around her bent legs, and sobbed into her knees.

Half an hour later, Anna was still sitting on the floor when she heard someone walking down the steps from her upstairs apartment. She felt a jolt, as if she'd been injected with a shot of espresso. The dark, nutty scent of coffee filled the space. She lifted her head and looked at the clock.

"Anna," Lily called as she crept down the stairs. "Anna . . . are you down here?"

"Unfortunately." She groaned, stretching her cramping legs out onto the cold tiles and letting her arms fall to her sides like limp noodles.

"Where?" Lily asked as she walked straight past Anna toward the darkened front room of the bakery. Her fluorescent-pink sweater made her look like a glow stick against the shadows. "I've been calling and texting you. Why are you ignoring me? I thought something terrible had happened, so I came straight over. I've been knocking upstairs at the apartment door. I thought you'd fallen asleep, but you know I couldn't go home until I made sure you were okay, so I used my key. What are you doing down here? Baking?" Lily paused at the archway and stared into the darkness. "What did Baron say? What happened? Do you hate the ring? Where *are* you?"

Lily rounded the island and stopped so quickly she pitched forward, her blond curls spilling over her shoulders. She placed her coffee mug on the island. "What in the world are you doing on the floor?"

Anna blinked up at her, feeling the sting of more tears in her eyes.

Lily rushed over and squatted beside her. "What's wrong? Is the ring ugly? Did he give you his grandma's hunk of junk? I'm sure we can convince him to get you something better." Lily eyed the spoon in Anna's hand and the half-empty bowl of solidified chocolate on the floor beside her. "Is it that bad?"

"He didn't ask me anything, Lily," Anna said, wiping her eyes with the back of her hand. "He's leaving tomorrow. Said he's going to find a place to live. They want him there before Thanksgiving."

Lily's brows furrowed. "Whoa, back up. Where is he going? Who wants him where before Thanksgiving?"

"California," Anna mumbled, considering whether she wanted to jab the spoon back into the ganache and eat the rest. "He accepted an offer for his dream job *across the country*, and he didn't even think about what that would mean for us. In fact, he didn't think about us at all. I want to be happy for him because I *know* it's a big deal, but . . . I'm sad for me."

Anna could see the wheels spinning in Lily's mind, working overtime to catch up. "He took a job? In California? When did this happen? Did you know he was looking for jobs out there?"

"Not really," Anna admitted. "He mentioned it once a few weeks ago. They offered it to him this morning, and he accepted.

No discussion with me. No questions about what I'd think about living in Napa Valley, soaking up the sunshine and eating grapes . . ."

"Okay, so he didn't ask you to marry him tonight, but surely he's going to California to find a nice place for y'all to live. He wants to scope it out first, find the right place. Then he'll come back for you."

"No," Anna said. She closed her eyes and sighed. "He could have asked me to go with him, but he didn't. I think it's over. When I mentioned an engagement ring and that I thought we would go together, he looked like I'd sucker punched him. Honestly, he was so flabbergasted I would have laughed if I hadn't wanted to cry so badly. Plus, he forgot today is our anniversary. I made his favorite meal and those stupid little chocolate turtles he loves." Her bottom lip quivered. "I don't even know if we're broken up or not. It can't possibly work, can it? Him there, me here? It's a gazillion miles away."

Lily sat down beside Anna and pressed her back against the bottom oven. "Well, this really sucks."

They sat in silence for a few minutes. Then Lily said, "No, we're not going to sit here and feel sorry for you. If Baron doesn't know how awesome you are, then he's a world-class idiot." She stood and pulled Anna to her wobbly feet. "You clean this place up, then go upstairs and take a shower. You've got chocolate all over your face, and that might be cookie dough in your hair. Did you eat dinner? Or is this . . . your go-to meal?" Lily held up both hands. "No judgment here. I just need to know if I should order food."

Anna shook her head. "I lost my appetite at Baron's, and I doubt it'll return anytime soon."

Lily huffed. "I'll see about that. Let's get upstairs, and I'll order pizza and drinks. I refuse to let you spend your anniversary alone and swimming in this pity pool. And turn your phone on. If, by chance, your mama calls tonight, she'll have a conniption if she can't reach you."

Anna nodded, but she felt like a puppet whose strings had been severed. Lily headed for the stairs. With one foot on the bottom stair, she looked at Anna and said, "I'm really sorry. I have half a mind to call Baron myself and give him the business. What a complete jack—" She clenched her jaw and released it before starting again. "But I won't. Let him spend the next two weeks thinking about how much life sucks without you."

Anna's apartment above the bakery was small, a one-bedroom, one-bathroom, cozy space that always smelled like fresh chocolate chip cookies and warm vanilla cake. Cookbooks spilled from the bookshelves in her living room and found their way to the coffee table, beneath the table lamp next to the overstuffed couch, and to the bay window, where they leaned against the panes as though waiting for the moonrise. A vase of white daisies bloomed on the windowsill in the kitchen where the walls were painted a soft shade of vanilla buttercream. Oatmeal cookies snuggled quietly on a glass-domed cake plate on the antique, petite table for two.

Tucked onto bookshelves, stuck to the fridge with magnets, and displayed around the apartment were trinkets from all the times Anna spent at Wildehaven Beach with her family. Wildehaven Beach, located on the southern coast of Georgia, was a short car ride from Mystic Water. Every summer Anna's grandparents would close Bea's Bakery for two weeks and take a much-needed vacation to a beachfront condo, and Anna always accompanied them. Some of her favorite memories were of building sandcastles with Beatrice, beating Grandpa Joe at Putt-Putt, and eating treats from the local beachside bakery while sitting on the pier. Anna's parents also enjoyed taking short weekend trips to the beach throughout the year, so she felt as though Wildehaven Beach was a home away from home.

A painting of a sailboat with its sails lifted by a summer wind as it coasted through blue-green waters had caught her eye at a local beach gallery and now hung in her living room. A cobalt-blue miniature sailboat sat between a cookbook on Southern cakes and a flavor thesaurus. Postcards from the beach decorated the front of the stainless steel refrigerator, and half a dozen photographs of her and her family at the beach were scattered through the apartment.

The beach and baking themes stretched into Anna's bedroom. Her queen-size bed was a marshmallow affair of soft blues and white with a riot of feather pillows in different shapes and sizes. An octopus-print pillow cuddled close to one stitched with a pair of dancing cupcakes wearing sneakers and polka-dot-wrapper skirts.

Anna stepped out of the shower and secured a towel around her body as she shuffled into her bedroom. After she pulled a comb through her wet hair, she tugged on a pair of pajama pants decorated with pink and aqua cupcakes and a matching aqua tank top. She tugged a sweatshirt over her head as she shivered in the cool air. Then she sat on the edge of her bed and sank into the down comforter. What would a life without Baron look like? He hadn't exactly *broken up* with her, but it was clear their lives were moving in different directions. How drastically would her life change? Her weekends would be freer, but her weekdays would look much the same. She would receive fewer texts, but he hadn't been the greatest texter either.

Her day-to-day routines wouldn't change much in his absence, but she had plugged him into every mental and emotional aspect of her life. Even though they hadn't seriously talked about their future—there had been no ring shopping or Pinterest wedding board making—she *had* imagined his life knit with hers. But she fit only into his present, which was ever changing. He smiled at her from a picture on her dresser, his blue eyes shining, and an evening breeze drifted through the open window, toying with her damp hair. Anna shivered again.

A knock sounded at the front door, and Lily's voice combined with a man's muffled voice. The pizza had arrived. When Anna walked out of her bedroom, Lily was placing a large pizza box on the kitchen counter along with a two-liter bottle of Coca-Cola.

Anna twisted her hair into a knot before jamming two chopsticks into it. The aromas of roasted hazelnuts and supreme pizza quickly filled the small space and gave Anna a shove of energy.

"Dinner's here," Lily confirmed. "I made a pot of coffee. Want a cup?"

"No thanks. I'd be up all night," Anna said, thinking she might not be able to sleep well, anyway, with the way her mind was racing, intent on repeating her conversation with Baron and wondering if she could have done or said something different, something better.

Lily pulled down plates from the cabinet and got out three glasses. She opened the silverware drawer. "Fork or no fork?"

"No fork." Anna slid out one of the kitchen chairs and sat. "Do you think this was bound to happen?"

Lily flipped open the pizza box, and looping ribbons of steam rose from the roasted vegetables and melted cheese. "Baron moving to California?"

"No. I mean us not working out. Was this inevitable? Because he's so—"

"So Baron? Because he's all over the place, literally and figuratively?"

"And I'm so . . . boring?"

Lily frowned deeply. "You are *anything* but boring. Dependable? Yes. Responsible? Yes. But boring? Never. You're stable, and Baron"—Lily sighed—"has never been." She dropped a slice of pizza onto a plate and handed it to Anna.

Anna picked at a mushroom and stared at the indention it had made in the cheese. "You're not surprised this is happening then."

Lily slid another piece of pizza from the box. "I *am* surprised," Lily admitted. "I'll be honest. When you and Baron started dating, I didn't think it would last because of *him*, not because of you. He was just a click above being a bum. Albeit a good-looking bum, but he was a total couch surfer."

An unexpected laugh crept up Anna's throat, and she defended Baron. "He wasn't a bum. He worked freelance, and he'd been backpacking across Malaysia and Thailand for a year. He was crashing with his brother here until he found his own place."

"Yeah, yeah, I know, but he never intended to *stay* in Mystic Water," Lily argued. "Until he met you, and then it was like *bam*, he couldn't leave. Remember how he kept saying he was probably going to be moving soon? After a few months with you, he stopped saying that. Then he bought his brother's place when Brody moved. That's when I believed he was really going to stick around. So, actually, I *am* surprised by this. And disappointed in him."

Anna rubbed her temple, then pointed at the glasses on the counter. "You got out three—" Her cell phone illuminated on the kitchen table, and she snatched it.

"Is it Baron with an apology?" Lily asked.

Anna shook her head. "It's Tessa. She says she'll be right up."

Lily nodded. "I texted her, told her we were having a girls' night and you needed us."

Tessa Andrews was the third part of their best-friend trio. Anna, Lily, and Tessa met while hanging from the monkey bars during fourth-grade recess and hadn't stopped hanging around one another since. Even through college, moving away, and eventually all finding their way back to Mystic Water, they had stayed close and involved in one another's lives.

Anna's brow wrinkled. "Didn't she have a date tonight with Tommy Carpenter? I hope you didn't make her leave early. They might have been having a nice time."

Lily chuckled. "Tommy the taxidermist? You're kidding, right? He's a nice guy, sure, but he's an odd bird. You know he likes to show girls his collection of dead animals, don't you?"

Anna's eyes widened. "He does not. That's just gossip."

Lily shrugged. "Ask Tessa. She'll set the story straight. Oh, and I also told her we needed booze tonight, specifically rum."

Tessa knocked on the door and Lily flung it open, making an exaggerated "come in" motion with her arm.

Anna groaned. "You can't be serious. I have to be up at five a.m. to start baking. I haven't had rum since that horrific incident in twelfth grade when I yakked on Becky Johnson. She *still* hasn't forgiven me. She calls me Anna O'Barf to this day."

Tessa closed the door behind her and laughed. "Man, that was awful. Why was it so *green*? Hey, y'all." She put a bottle of rum and a bottle of wine on the counter. She was dressed in a scarlet long-sleeved honeycomb-knit shirt paired with fitted jeans. Her straight shoulder-length brown hair still held some curl from her date night. She kicked off her black ballet flats by the door. "This was unexpected. I love girls' night. We haven't had one in weeks. Thank you for helping me graciously end my date with Tommy."

Lily cocked an eyebrow. "Did he show you the wild boar? Was it everything you hoped and more?"

Tessa rolled her eyes. "The peacock was kinda pretty."

Lily pointed at Anna. "Told you! He takes his dates on a tour of his dead things."

Tessa eyed the pizza but didn't pick up a slice. Lily dropped ice cubes into the glasses, then she poured in the rum until the ice cubes rose to the tip-top before splashing in the soda like a garnish. She grabbed three colored straws from Anna's stash on the counter and gave the drinks a quick stir.

"I only want rum in my Pirate's Booty Bundtlettes," Anna said.

"Those are one of my favorites," Tessa said. "The ones with coconut flakes, white chocolate, and drizzled in a rum syrup, right?" She rubbed circles onto her stomach. "I could eat half a dozen of those."

Lily snorted as she laughed. "I think you have. At the Fourth of July festival this year. Isn't that when Danny Lincoln saw you scarfing them down and was impressed by your appetite and asked you out?"

Tessa groaned. "He's such a good kisser too. If he wasn't so into LARPing, I would have stuck that one out for his kisses alone. But when he insisted I learn Elvish so we could communicate exclusively with *his people*, I had to end it."

"He made those pointy ears look sexy," Lily teased. Looking at Anna, she added, "I promise you won't be barfing on the homecoming queen after a few glasses of rum and Coke." She handed Anna a glass. "You can add any leftover rum to your next batch of cakes. Humor me tonight, please. I haven't felt good all day, and I need a breather. And *you* definitely need something to take the edge off."

Tessa took the drink from Lily and they clinked their glasses together. "No more than two for me. I have a seven a.m. house showing tomorrow for a client who wants to see the place before work, so I gotta get home at a decent time sans hangover in the morning." She met Anna's gaze. "Lily said you needed us. Everything okay?"

Anna swirled the straw through the ice cubes in her cocktail and took a hesitant sip. Her face scrunched up. "Holy guacamole, Batman, this is strong." She put down the glass and motioned for them to follow her into the living room, where she sagged onto the couch. Anna grabbed a pillow decorated with an oversize bright red apple filled with the words Big Apple NYC, the only remnant from her New York City days. She squeezed the pillow against her chest. Better to get everything out in one breath. So, without stopping for a response, she blubbered out the evening's events, ending with the three best friends sharing the strongest rum and Coke Anna had ever had.

Tessa read Lily's expression before speaking. "Well, that just dills my pickle," she said, finishing off her cocktail. "I can't believe him. Up and moving away like, 'Oh, I'm just a hop and a skip away.' No, you're actually *not*, Baron. You're more than three thousand miles away. It's not like he doesn't travel a ton anyway, so why does he have to move? Can't he do the job from here?" Her eyes widened. "Wait, maybe he's going to find a place to live and then tell you to come out there! But then . . . you'd be leaving us."

Anna shook her head, and Lily confirmed she had suggested the same possibility. "Y'all didn't see his face. Me going with him or meeting him later hadn't crossed his mind."

"Lord, have mercy. I'm so sorry," Tessa said. "I'm almost speechless."

Anna's lip twitched up in one corner. "Almost."

Tessa grinned and reached over to give Anna's hand a squeeze. "Well, I *can* talk a gate off its hinges."

"You and me both," Lily said with a laugh.

"One of the many things I love about you both," Anna said. "Thanks for coming over. I know I'll get through this, but it helps to know I don't have to do it alone."

Tessa huffed. "I wouldn't be surprised if he comes back singing a different tune, wanting you to join him. He's not going to like a life without you. I can guarantee that. Who would? Not me."

Lily raised her empty glass. "I'll second that! Who needs a refill?" She pointed at the TV's screen saver. "Turn that on. I already have a movie cued up for us."

"*Pet Sematary*?" Anna said once the TV screen illuminated with the paused movie. "No way, José. You know I hate horror movies. I'd rather burn a batch of cookies and sell them to children."

Lily brought Anna's cocktail and pizza into the living room. Then she made Tessa and herself another drink while Tessa placed the pizza box on the coffee table. Lily lifted the cake dome, then scraped the oatmeal cookies onto a plate and added them to the buffet.

"First of all," Lily said, "it's impossible for you to ruin a batch of cookies. Second, we're not watching something sappy like *Sleepless in Seattle*—"

Anna's hands clasped together. "I love that movie."

Lily took a healthy bite of pizza. Mozzarella cheese stretched from the slice to her lips. "Yeah, I know, but we're not watching that tonight."

Tessa made a fish face and sucked her cocktail through a bright yellow straw. "She has a point."

"You're right." Anna reached for her slice of pizza and took an unenthusiastic bite. Watching a romantic comedy was probably a rotten idea. Her cell phone illuminated next to the pizza box, and she grabbed it. "It's a text from Baron."

Lily shoved her blond curls out of her face, and she and Tessa both asked, "What's it say?"

"'Will stop by tomorrow on way to airport.' And that's it." Anna pressed her lips together. A salty wind blew through the open kitchen window and slammed shut the top of the pizza box. Anna rubbed her hands up her arms.

"Nice, Baron, real nice. So eloquent," Lily grumbled. "He's an idiot, Anna. He'll come around. He knows you're one of a kind."

Baron was her best friend aside from Lily and Tessa; how

was it possible that she felt this great divide between them now? Anna felt like she was trying to swallow two pirouette cookies whole, and they were logjammed in her throat. She walked to the kitchen. Grabbing the window sash, she stood on her tiptoes and slid it closed. While Lily started the movie, Anna rejoined her friends on the couch and, ignoring the straw, tilted back her glass of rum and Coke and drained half of it.

After the movie, Anna insisted on turning on all the lights, and when she glanced at the door that led to the staircase going down into the bakery, she thought of turning on the shop's lights too. No need to let something undead creep around the bakery unseen. Tessa forced herself to go home, hating to leave what might turn into a slumber party, but she couldn't afford to miss her appointment or show up looking bedraggled. She promised to stop by the bakery tomorrow to check in.

Anna stood in the kitchen, finishing her third glass of rum and Coke, and rubbed her temples. She blinked a few times to see if the room would come into better focus. "I think I'm toast."

Lily grabbed the last oatmeal cookie and giggled. "You were toast an hour ago, and was I right or was I right? No homecoming barfing. Speaking of gross ideas, let's talk about *Pet Sematary*. Who would you bring back from the dead?" Lily shoved the cookie into her mouth.

Anna shuddered. "Are you insane? No one. Didn't you see what happened to the little boy? What about the freaky little cat?"

Lily wagged her finger at Anna. "Come on, play along. Would you bring back Elvis? Maybe Tom Sawyer?"

"Tom Sawyer wasn't even a real person."

Lily giggled. "I bet he was cute, though."

"And incredibly underage for you. He'd be twelve or thirteen."

"Yikes!" Lily agreed. "I'll stick with Jakob."

Anna closed the pizza box and carried it to the kitchen. "Besides, you can't bring people back to life, not physically at least."

"Too bad you can't bring back the perfect man for yourself. Someone like Cary Grant or Paul Newman. Or better yet, too bad you can't *make* one."

"I thought Baron was the right guy for me," Anna said with a heavy sigh. "Maybe I just wanted him to be. Maybe I was forcing it." She tried three times to fold the pizza box in half and shove it into the trash can.

"Like you're forcing that pizza box?"

Anna frowned and left it on the counter.

Lily propped her legs on the coffee table. "With your baking skills, you could make someone even better than Baron. Someone just the way you wanted him to be."

Anna shook her head and laughed weakly. "I wish." But she wrinkled her forehead in thought as she sat on the couch and curled her legs beneath her. "Grandma Bea used to tell me she made my grandpa out of dough."

Lily snickered. "Sounds like something she'd say. She could make anything. Like you."

"I *loved* when she'd tell me the story of how she made him," she said, leaning her head back on the cushions and closing her eyes. "I used to hop up on the back counter in the kitchen when everyone was gone for the day and she was closing up. She'd warm up a chocolate chip cookie for me and pour a big glass of chocolate milk. Then I'd beg her to tell me the story. She must have told me a million times, but she always acted like she was telling me for the first time. When I inherited all her cookbooks, I found his recipe in the back of one of them."

"*His* recipe?"

Anna rolled her head to the side to look at Lily and immediately regretted it. Her brain sloshed around like hot cane syrup inside her skull. She put both hands on the sides of her head to steady the swaying room. "The recipe with the ingredients for how she made Grandpa Joe. How much flour, sugar, that sort of thing. And the secret ingredient too."

Lily snorted into her fourth rum and Coke. "What was the secret ingredient?"

Anna shrugged. "No idea. Every time I asked about it, she changed the subject." An image of a locked box and its key sitting on a shelf in her closet popped into her foggy mind. "You know . . . Grandma left me a few things besides the inheritance money. A lockbox and a letter. She said I'd know exactly when to open the box and what to do with it."

Lily sat up and put her glass on the coffee table. "What was inside?"

"I never opened it."

"Why not?"

"I haven't needed it, and she said not to open it *until* I needed it."

"How can you possibly know if you need it if you don't even know what's in it? It could be full of ancient artifacts or jewels."

Anna laughed. "Seriously, Indiana Jones? Ancient artifacts?"

"Where is it now?"

"In my bedroom closet."

Lily's brown eyes widened. She jumped up from the couch, swayed on her feet, and clutched her stomach. "Whoa, bad idea." She blinked rapidly, and once she regained her balance, Lily reached for Anna and dragged her to the bedroom.

Lily flung open the closet doors. "Let's break it open."

"I have the key."

"You have the key," Lily repeated dully. "How could you not have opened it? Weren't you curious?" She tucked her unruly curls behind her ears.

"She said not to open it until I knew it was the right time. But when I say it out loud now, it sounds super lame. Why *didn't* I ever open it?" Anna stood on her tiptoes and pulled down the box. She had taped the original letter and the key to its top. "In my defense, with the funeral and trying to figure out how to run the bakery, I forgot about it."

Lily bounced onto the bed. "Well, bless your heart. You are such a rule follower. Have you ever stepped out of line?"

"Yakking episode, twelfth grade. Real low point in my life." Anna shrugged. "Otherwise, no. I prefer to stay in the lines."

Lily laughed. "Open it!"

Anna gently removed the taped letter and set it aside on her nightstand. She detached the key from the tape and crawled onto the bed beside Lily. She slid the key into the keyhole. "Wanna guess what's inside? Dead Sea Scrolls? Or maybe a crystal skull?"

Lily snorted and then hiccupped. "Open it before I jerk a knot in your tail!"

After she released the lock, dense energy pulsed from the

box, through the key, and into her fingers, vibrating the bones in her hand. Her heart pounded in fierce, rapid beats, and she wished she hadn't drunk a third glass of rum and Coke. Her head felt full of cotton candy.

When Anna flipped open the lid, she saw a yellowed, bulging envelope with her name written across the front sitting atop granules that sparkled like golden sugar caught in the sunlight.

"Wow," Anna breathed. She removed the envelope and popped the fragile seal. Inside were folded pages of a letter written in Beatrice's cursive handwriting. "She wrote this to *me*?" Anna put the letter on her nightstand, then reached out to touch the glittering substance, but Lily slapped her hand away.

"Don't touch it."

Anna pushed her hair from her face. "Why not?"

Lily leaned forward to examine the contents. "What the hell is that stuff? My heart feels funny. Why is it all sparkly like that?"

"It looks lit up from the inside. Maybe it's a special kind of sugar."

"Locked in a box?" Lily scoffed. "Why would anyone lock up sugar?"

A crazy idea started forming in Anna's mind. The golden sugar twinkled and beckoned to her. She felt a prickle skip down her spine, and the granules whispered to her. *Use me. Take me.* "Do you think . . . Is it possible *this* is the secret ingredient?" She stuck her fingertips into the granules and felt a rush of warmth rocket up her arm.

Lily stared, transfixed. "You might be right. Where would she get this stuff? I doubt she ordered this off Amazon. Black market?"

A chuckle echoed up Anna's throat. "The black market of baking? Doubtful." Anna lifted the letter. "Maybe the answer is in here."

"Do you really think Grandma Bea made your grandpa out of that stuff? I mean, it sounds pretty ridiculous," Lily said, laughing, but it sounded forced, and the air around them smelled like bitter coffee grounds. "Maybe we're drunk. Maybe the rum was spiked with something."

Looking down at the brilliant grains, Anna began to seriously question her grandma's story. "It sounds far-fetched, but what if it's possible?" She closed the box. "You're right. We've had too much to drink. Let's go to bed."

Anna tried to stand, but Lily grabbed her arm. "Wait. I have a *great* idea. Let's go downstairs, and you can make a man with this fairy sugar because if anyone can make a delicious man, you can."

Anna giggled but she stopped when she realized Lily was serious. Suddenly an image of Frankenstein's monster flitted through her brain. An oversize stomping giant with a scarred, stitched face made from the body parts of corpses. The image lifted a moldy hand and waved. She grimaced and blinked away the vision. "Bad idea. No, *terrible* idea."

Lily squeezed her arm. "You look like you're going to be sick. Come on. Get the sugar and let's make your man. I'll grab the rum."

Anna tried to smooth out the creases on her grandma's recipe. In her neat, cursive script, Beatrice had written:

JOSEPH O'BRIEN

Notes on the basics: Flour, sugar. Only the best ingredients. Quarter to half cup of confectioners' sugar to make him just sweet enough, but not too much. Salt to complement the sweet. A good balance is essential. High-quality yeast. Vanilla extract because it goes well with just about everything. Royal icing to make him stick and never wander away. A pinch here and there of favorite herbs or spices (basil, oregano, anise, cinnamon, turmeric). Warm water, not too hot or you'll create a scalded man, angry and hard to live with. High-quality olive oil for helping him move through life with ease, never getting stuck or losing pieces of himself. Knead the dough just long enough—very important. Kneading too long will make him hard and unbendable, like a rock in the stomach. Kneading not long enough will make him soft—too weak, too pliable, a moldable mess in anyone's hands. Not a good man. Creativity, dreams, love: crucial ingredients, always.

Ingredients

¼ cup confectioners' sugar, more or less if needed

2¼ teaspoons yeast

3 cups all-purpose flour

1½ cups warm water

1 teaspoon salt

2 tablespoons of favorite herbs or spices

A couple dabs of royal icing

1 teaspoon vanilla extract

1 tablespoon secret ingredient

2 tablespoons olive oil

A dash of creativity
A pinch of dreams
A shimmer of love

Directions

In a large bowl, combine water, sugar, and yeast. Let sit for five minutes until yeast foams and releases its pungent odor. Next add flour and salt to the bowl. If desired, add herbs and spices. Use a wooden spoon to gently combine ingredients. Add royal icing and vanilla. Combine and add secret ingredient. Make sure to incorporate the ingredient throughout the dough. Finally add olive oil. Toss the dough to coat. The dough will be slightly sticky but manageable with your hands. Lightly flour hands and counter. Knead for an acceptable time. No rising time needed, as secret ingredient enhances the finished product well enough. Press dough into a heart shape, approximately two inches thick. Bake for fifteen minutes at 425 degrees Fahrenheit. Make sure to give him a name before you close the oven door. After fifteen minutes, turn off the oven, but do not open it. Leave dough in oven for at least two hours, longer if needed.

Anna looked at the ingredients scattered across the counter. Lily sat on the island and snickered while she talked about what kind of man she would make if she could bake worth a lick. She debated with herself about what her boyfriend, Jakob, would be made of. "Whiskey or bourbon? Marshmallows—no, s'mores. Beef jerky . . . sour apple Blow Pops . . ."

Anna wrinkled her nose. "Jakob sounds gross."

"Hey!" Lily protested.

"This is stupid," Anna said in a huff. "I'm tired, and I'm going to have a righteous hangover in the morning, which is going to be here, oh, in just about five hours. And these are the most random ingredients I've ever heard of for a dough recipe. No way this is going to work."

Lily pointed the nearly empty bottle of rum at her. "Make the man, and make sure he's hot. It'll make Baron so jealous. I'm kinda looking forward to that part of this whole shenanigan. Besides, if it doesn't work, we'll just gorge on the dough boy later." Then she snorted and burst into another round of giggles.

Anna rubbed her eyes and preheated the oven. "Man, this ranks way up there on the list of stupidest things I've ever done."

She grabbed a large bowl. The recipe directions were ordinary enough, but the combination of ingredients, such as royal icing paired with strong herbs or spices and vanilla extract, was bizarre. Using yeast but not allowing for proofing time went against Anna's instincts. If the secret ingredient didn't work, then Anna's dough ball would be denser than Lori Beauchamp's Christmas fruitcake, which Mystic Water townspeople regifted every year.

Anna poured lukewarm water into her bowl and added a half cup of confectioners' sugar, hoping the result would be a somewhat romantic man. She scooped yeast from its oversize glass jar and sprinkled it over the sugar-water mixture. After allowing the yeast to bubble and foam, Anna tossed in two cups of all-purpose flour followed by a cup of whole-wheat flour. She hoped the combination would give him an even skin tone, and the completely absurd fact that she was actually giving this recipe so much thought had her grabbing the bottle of rum and taking another swig. She tossed in a teaspoon of sea salt so he might love the ocean too.

"What will make him good and wholesome and kind?" Anna asked aloud.

"Chocolate?" Lily said, finishing off the bottle of rum.

Anna dropped in a palmful of dark cocoa powder. She added the leaves from three sprigs of rosemary because it was her favorite herb and because its woodsy scent would hopefully make him a lover of the outdoors. If she was making the most absurd recipe ever, why not go big with her additions? So she added a pinch of cinnamon because the season called for it, and then she sprinkled in cumin to give him a spicy, smoky edge.

Anna added a cashew-size glob of purple royal icing to the mix to make him loyal, then poured in a teaspoon of vanilla extract. She dipped a tablespoon into the sparkling, golden sugar. When she leveled it with her finger, warmth spread up her arm until it reached her head, where it tugged her lips into a smile. She added the special ingredient and shoved her hand into the dough to incorporate everything. Rather than olive oil, Anna poured canola oil into the bowl because he needed to be able to withstand the heat and not break down when life became too hot or too complicated.

She flipped the dough ball around a few times in the bowl to ensure the oil coated the dough. Then she plopped the dough onto a floured board and began to knead. When the dough had just enough elasticity, she patted it into a heart shape as directed and put it on a baking stone.

As an afterthought, Anna rolled out a piece of white fondant. She let her mind wander over a list of possible names before scribbling on the fondant rectangle with an edible black-ink marker.

> Dearest Elijah,
>
> I don't know that soul mates exist or that true love finds everyone, but I've heard anything is possible. I'd be willing to give love another try if you are.

Anna shoved the note into the dough like a sail on a boat. She opened the oven, slid the baking stone and dough gently inside, and closed the door. Then she wiped her hands on her apron.

"Bedtime," she said.

Lily was tilted over on the island at an awkward angle, the bottle of rum dangling from her fingers, too close to the edge. Her curls blanketed her face.

"Hey, Sleeping Beauty," Anna said, poking Lily in the ribs and taking the bottle. "Let's get you up and into bed. I can't possibly carry you."

"Call Jakob," Lily said, pushing herself into a sitting position and nearly tipping off the island.

"I'll text him and say you're sleeping over," Anna said. "You can drive home in the morning."

Lily shook her head, releasing a wave of curls in her face. "I can't sleep without my super-special-squishy pillow and my white noise machine." She pointed a finger at Anna. "No, not even if I'm totally hammered. I'll toss and turn and be *more* of a mess in the morning."

"It's late, Lily," Anna argued.

"Call him," Lily said. "He doesn't care. Promise."

Half an hour later, the bread was baked, and the oven was

off with the dough heart waiting inside for its big reveal. Jakob retrieved Lily with a sleepy grin, and Anna turned off the lights in the bakery. After returning the locked box to her bedroom closet and tucking the letter into her nightstand drawer, she drank an enormous glass of water, took two ibuprofens, and collapsed onto her bed without even pulling down the sheets.

CHAPTER 3

MORNING GLORY MUFFINS

ANNA GROANED AND ROLLED OVER. SUNLIGHT SLIPPED THROUGH the slats in the plantation blinds and lined her face. Her head pounded like a drum corps was working out the kinks in its routine just behind her eyes. She stretched her arm out, and her hand fell into an indention left behind on the pillow beside her. Had Baron slept over? Her thoughts moved slower than blackstrap molasses, but Baron's name triggered a memory from last night, which almost revived her tears. Baron had most definitely *not* slept over, and he might never be in her apartment again.

Anna grabbed the pillow and pressed it over her head to block the sunlight and the rush of memories reminding her of all the good times she'd had with Baron. The fabric smelled like pine and rosemary, which she would have found strange if she hadn't felt as if someone swapped her brain for pie weights.

She sat up as slowly as possible, afraid of making any sudden movements. When she inhaled, she breathed in the smell of warm donuts and their sugary, sticky glaze and melted choco-late. That was the moment she realized her bedroom was entirely too bright, and not just because she had the hangover to end all hangovers.

Her eyes darted to the clock on her nightstand. It was six forty-five a.m. Anna gasped, and a shooting pain pierced her left temple. She groaned and doubled over.

She tried to fling herself out of bed, but the sheets tangled around her legs, and only the top half of her body lurched over the bedside, so she dangled there like a caterpillar half out of its cocoon. Within seconds, the sheets pulled away from the mat-tress, and she fell, smacking her forehead on the wood floor.

Anna lay there with her cheek squashed awkwardly against the floor and her body folded over, unable to move. She was going to have a goose egg on her forehead for sure. She inhaled deeply and cracked open one eye. Why did her room smell like donuts? Anna gathered herself up off the floor and began a herky-jerky rush to get ready. The bakery would be opening in less than fif-teen minutes, and she hadn't even started a single treat.

She brushed her teeth while pulling on a pair of jeans. Deciding cutesy casual would have to do for today's attire, she tugged on a blue, vintage-style Smurfs T-shirt and slipped on a pair of white leather sneakers. There wasn't time for makeup, but she washed last night's misery off her face and applied extra moisturizer because she looked about as dried out as a prune. As soon as she got the day's treats going, she'd down a cup of coffee and then drink water only for the rest of the day to rehydrate her body.

Pulling her fingers through her tangled hair, she hurried down the stairs to the bakery. As she neared the bottom of the staircase, the drippy, sweet scents of baking intensified. She'd left the dough she and Lily had concocted in the oven overnight. Did it have that strong of an aroma?

Anna grabbed her apron from the hook and turned in a full circle, trying to decide where to start as she tied it around her waist. Her gaze stopped on a sheet tray sitting on the island. It was crowded with both glazed and chocolate-covered donuts. She reached out a tentative finger, and the chocolate came away, warm and gooey, on her fingertip. Her mouth fell agape.

"What the—"

A man walked out of the back room carrying a canister of powdered sugar. Anna screamed and stumbled backward, tripping over a ten-pound bag of flour. She landed hard on the bag and slipped off the side as a powdery cloud puffed over her like fog, dusting her hair and clothes.

The man chuckled and put the canister on the island. He held out his hand to her.

"What are you doing?" she asked in a voice that was unnaturally high-pitched and much too dry. She fanned the flour cloud away.

"Making donuts. It's Wednesday. Isn't that donut day?" he asked, seeming genuinely confused.

"No, *here*. What are you doing *in here*?" She was afraid to stand up. Would anyone hear her scream? How had he gotten inside the bakery? Why would a thief break into the shop and bake for her?

The man continued to stand in front of her with his hand held out, and Anna took a good look at him. He was at least six feet two, taller than Baron. His eyes were Caribbean blue, and his skin was the color of light brown sugar. His sandy-brown hair was cut short but still long enough for Anna to run her fingers through. Her hands twitched, so she clasped them together in her lap.

His grin was lopsided, and his mouth was full of impossibly straight white teeth. He was undeniably handsome, but that didn't mean he wasn't a psycho who liked to bake donuts. He wore one of her larger plain-white aprons, which she kept on hand for catering events. But beneath the apron she could see a red shirt that looked exactly like Baron's University of Georgia T-shirt. His blue jeans were at least an inch too short, and his flip-flops looked an awful lot like the pair Baron left at her place just in case he needed a spare. He had written his name in all caps on a sheet of paper and slid it into the clear pocket on the front of the apron. It read: Eli.

Anna's eyes opened as wide as jumbo jawbreakers, and she covered her mouth with her hands. She shook her head as if to shake away the image before her. Her eyes drifted to the oven where she'd left the heart-shaped dough the night before. The baking stone was drying in the rack beside the sink. The baked loaf was nowhere to be seen, unless . . .

"Elijah?" she whispered through her fingers.

"Yes?"

Anna scrambled to her feet. "Whoa, this can't be happening. This is *insane*. The rum was tainted. Maybe it was full of hallucinogens. Maybe I'm tripping out right now. Maybe I'm having an exceptionally vivid dream. You're not real. You *can't* be."

She stepped too close to him, and her senses overloaded. She smelled rosemary and cinnamon, spicy chocolate and melted sugar. Looking away from his clear blue eyes was difficult. Anna wanted to back away from the stranger in her kitchen, but a million invisible gossamer threads connected the two of them, tangled them, wove them together. She sucked air, heady and sweet, into her lungs. Her lips tingled, and she felt an over-powering urge to touch him.

"You feeling okay?" he asked. "I let you sleep in this morning. Of course, I couldn't wake you even when I tried an hour ago." He grinned, and Anna's mouth fell open.

"You were in my *room*?" She wiped her sweaty palms down the front of her apron. *Oh no, no, no.*

Elijah chuckled. "I slept in there, didn't I?"

A strangled sound bubbled up her throat. "You slept with me?"

Elijah laughed, wrinkled his brow, and a timer dinged across the room. He walked over to one of the ovens and opened the door. "Cookies are done. I chose peanut butter cookies for today's cookie du jour. And I made Morning Glory Muffins. I know you wanted to change up Wednesday's muffins, something in addition to the usual blueberry. I think they turned out well. Wanna try one?"

With Elijah across the room, Anna could breathe normally again. She shoved her hands into her hair, and when she tried to pull them free, some of her fingers stuck in the tangles. She pressed her palms to her thighs and dropped her head between her knees.

"You okay?" Elijah asked.

Anna shook her head. "I think I'm going to pass out." Black spots leaped in front of her eyes, and her next pull of air was full of the woodsy scent of wet pine trees in the fall.

Elijah put his hand on her lower back. "Hey, why don't you go upstairs and lie down? I can handle things down here." His hand moved to her shoulder blades.

Heat zinged up her spine, pulsing from his fingers against the fabric of her thin T-shirt, warming the skin beneath. Anna jerked upright so quickly she lost her balance. Elijah steadied her. The heat from his hands made her feel as though her insides were melted butter; her knees turned into Twizzlers. She stumbled out of his grasp. Someone knocked on the front door. Anna peered out through the archway that led to the shop. Frances Dotson cupped her hands around her eyes and pressed her overly made-up face to the bakery's glass door.

"It's seven," Anna said.

"I can handle things this morning," Eli assured her. "A lot better than you can handle your rum."

His grin sparked heat low in her belly. The knocking grew louder. Anna rushed to open the shop and glanced at the display cases. Every shelf was filled with treats, minus the last open spot, where the donuts would slide in.

"Good morning, Mrs. Dotson," Anna said with a frazzled smile. The crisp October morning air rushed into the front room.

"You're never late," Mrs. Dotson said, pursing her merlot-red lips.

"First time for everything," Anna mumbled, throwing a quick glance toward the back room. "Bit of a hectic morning."

Elijah emerged holding the tray of donuts, and he smiled and waved. "Good morning. Fresh donuts."

"Oh my," Mrs. Dotson said in a breathy voice. "New help, I see."

"He's hard to miss," Anna agreed.

"Ain't that the truth." Mrs. Dotson raised her penciled-on eyebrows at Anna. "What are you doing with your hair? New style? I'm not sure it's working for you."

Anna turned and looked at herself in the hanging mirror behind the counter. A pitiful sound escaped through her parted lips at the sight of her unruly auburn hair. One side of her hair was out-of-control wavy and not in an attractive way, as if she'd pulled last year's Halloween wig out of the bottom of a trunk. The other side was a tangled mess, half straight, half unfortunate.

"There are no words for this hair," she said.

"My thoughts exactly," Mrs. Dotson said, clucking her tongue. "Introduce me to your new helper."

Anna blanched. "No!"

"Pardon me?" Mrs. Dotson asked, arching her dramatic eyebrows. She opened her mouth to say something else, but Anna dashed away, grabbing Elijah by the arm and dragging him into the back room.

"Are we dreaming?" Anna asked, mostly talking to herself. She retied her apron and wiped her hands down her front.

Elijah leaned casually against the island. "Do you usually dream of Mrs. Dotson? I know I don't. The purple eyeshadow just doesn't *do* it for me."

Anna gasped. "How do you know her name?"

Elijah grinned. "Are you *that* hungover?"

Anna shook her head and then ransacked a drawer until she found a rubber band. She whipped her hair into a messy bun and pointed her finger at Elijah. "Where did you get those clothes?"

"Your closet, where else?"

"You must be joking," she blurted. Elijah *was* wearing Baron's clothes. "How did you get here this morning? Did you crawl out of the oven?"

Elijah lifted one eyebrow. "What is up with you this morning?"

"Humor me!" she nearly shouted.

"I woke up and walked down the stairs," he answered.

Anna pressed her fingertips to her forehead and closed her eyes. She inhaled and exhaled several times. "This can't be happening."

The bell on the counter began to ding over and over again. "Are you planning on serving me this morning? There's a line forming, Anna," Mrs. Dotson complained.

"Be right there!" she shouted. "You stay back here this morning. Don't come out. At all."

Elijah frowned. "But"—he peered over her head at the front of the shop—"there are five people in line now, and who's going to get the coffee going?"

"I will," she said in exasperation. "Just *stay back here.*"

Anna ran out into the shop and attended to Mrs. Dotson, who always ordered the same thing on Wednesdays: two glazed donuts, one lemon bar, one red velvet cupcake, and a Diet Coke to go. Anna waved a harried good morning to the other customers.

Mrs. Dotson paid and grabbed her bag. Before she walked away, she leaned over the counter, her five gold necklaces swinging forward, and called, "Excuse me, sir, but I'd like to welcome you. I'm Frances Dotson."

Elijah poked his head around the archway, and Anna's legs became cement. The entire line of customers shifted so they could see the stranger in the back room. A lopsided grin tugged Elijah's mouth up to the left, and he stepped out of the back, all broad shouldered and easy on the eyes. He held out his grizzly-bear-size hand to Mrs. Dotson.

"A real pleasure, ma'am," he said in a decidedly Southern accent. "I'm Elijah, but you can call me Eli. Anna can call me anything she wants."

Anna gripped the countertop. Mrs. Dotson cut her gaze over to Anna but didn't release Eli's hand. "Is that so? I imagine Baron would object."

Eli winked at her and leaned forward conspiratorially. "What he doesn't know won't kill him, and Baron is on the Naughty List at the moment."

Anna wobbled and mumbled, "This is very bad."

Eli stepped over to her and put his hand on her lower back. Her blood surged hot, and all the clean air was replaced by the smell of caramelized sugar.

"I didn't know Anna was looking for new hires. I haven't seen any advertising. How did you end up working here, Eli?" Mrs. Dotson asked.

Without removing his hand, he ushered Anna behind the cash register so she could help the next customer, and Eli stepped aside so he could speak with Mrs. Dotson.

"Anna and I went to the Institute of Culinary Education in New York together. We met in our Breads and Other Yeast-Raised Doughs course. Our baking and pastry styles are nearly identical, but nobody can bake like Anna," he said, smiling over at her. "I'm passing through town, between jobs, so what better way to spend my time than with Anna? She's letting me crash here for a while. Hopefully a long while," he added.

Anna's hand hovered over a Morning Glory Muffin as she turned to look at Eli. She knew he was lying, but it sounded so natural, and even more than that, it sounded like he *believed* what he was saying. When the truth of that sank in, her hands began to shake. If Eli was truly something she created last night, then he was like a newborn. He didn't have a past, a family, a history *at all*. Yet there he stood, telling Mrs. Dotson they'd gone to the institute together. She had to get him away from the customers. She had to hide him somewhere, *anywhere*, until she could figure out what to do with him.

Anna bagged four muffins and handed them over to Mr. Jones. "Will that be all?" she asked. She reached out to grab Eli, but he slipped away and headed straight for the coffee urns in the corner behind the counter.

"Better keep an eye on him," Mr. Jones said as he handed her exact change.

Eli carried the first urn to the back room, and he made sure to smile at Anna when he passed. "I'm sorry, what's that?" she asked.

Mr. Jones leaned toward her, and his readers slipped down his nose. "I said you better watch that one," he repeated, pointing toward the back room with an arthritic finger. "If he can charm old lady Dotson, then he'll be charming all the ladies in town by the end of the week. That includes you," Mr. Jones said with a playful smile.

"Me?" Why did her voice sound like she was doing an impersonation of Minnie Mouse? "I have a boyfriend, Mr. Jones. You remember Baron." She *had* a boyfriend. What she and Baron were now was as murky as burned butter.

Mr. Jones waved a dismissive hand and grabbed his goodie bag. "Just the same. That one has his eyes on you."

As Mr. Jones walked off, it dawned on Anna that she'd given him baked goods *made by Eli*, and she hadn't even taste tested anything. *What am I thinking?* But that was the main problem; she *wasn't* thinking clearly.

The bakery door opened and brought in the smell of burning logs and charcoal on a grill. Anna's eyes fell on Thomas Harper, the junior college's biology professor and Jakob's first cousin. Thomas and Jakob were not only family but also good friends and golfing buddies, and Baron played with them sometimes when he was in town. Thomas was also a bakery regular on his way into work most days. He would notice a new employee, especially an exceptionally handsome one, and it was highly probable he'd have questions. Questions Anna might not be able to answer. Anna normally enjoyed her morning conversations with Thomas, but Eli added a whole new dimension to everything. Thomas smiled at her before falling into the back of the line.

She could hear Eli moving around in the back room and hoped she could get through the remaining customers before he reentered the front of the shop. However, just as Thomas stepped up to the counter, Eli walked out carrying a coffee urn.

"Good morning," Anna said. "Want your usual bear claw and Italian brew?"

A deep line creased between Thomas's dark brows. "Who's that?"

"Hmm?" Anna asked innocently, but she felt a wave of heat roll over her as Eli passed behind her. She tried to hold her smile steady for Thomas. "New *temporary* employee."

Thomas toyed with the gold band on his left hand. "What happened to the young girl from the college? Josie, wasn't it?"

"Took a few weeks off for midterms and then fall break. Your usual?" she asked again.

Thomas's smile was tight, and his eyes followed Eli's movements. Was Thomas being overprotective of her or Baron? He didn't yet know that Baron was ditching her for the Pacific Ocean and picturesque, rolling hills covered in vineyards.

"I haven't seen him before. Does he live in Mystic Water?" Thomas said, watching the movement over Anna's right shoulder.

Before Anna could answer, she felt Eli's hand on her back. Her mind fogged over, and her heart pumped thick, hot blood down to her toes. She couldn't focus on anything except the feel of his hand against her. Her bottom lip drooped.

Eli held out his other hand to Thomas. "Eli," he said.

"Thomas Harper. One of Anna's regulars."

"Dedicated. I like that. How are you? Italian brew to go, right?" Eli asked, handing over a paper coffee cup with a lid. He removed his hand from Anna's back.

Thomas took the offered cup and thanked him, but Anna blinked and saw confusion in Thomas's dark eyes. "Do you live in town?" he asked Eli.

The air was rimmed with the smell of burning leaves, and Anna coughed. She grabbed a bear claw from the display case and wrapped it.

"For now," Eli answered.

"One bear claw to go," she interrupted, struggling to inhale a full breath. "See you next time."

"I think I'll sit awhile," Thomas said, and he thanked Anna for the pastry. He pulled out his cell phone as soon as he sat and started texting someone.

"Sure. Great. Sit for as long as you like. I'll just be here . . . baking or losing my marbles. Probably both," she babbled.

No one else was in line, so Anna scurried to the back room to fill a glass with ice water. She splashed some of it on her face and blindly reached for a towel to dry off. She gulped down half of the frigid water.

"He's territorial," Eli said much too close to Anna's ear.

She yelped and tossed the rest of her water straight into the air. It rained all over the countertop, and she and Eli danced out of its path. Eli's hand was on her arm, and she wiggled away from him.

"Stop doing that," Anna said, pressing her back against the wall. The sight of his smile tugged something deep in her stomach.

"Doing what? I thought we were having a conversation," he said.

"Stop *touching* me," she said. "I can't think when you do that."

Eli took a step closer. Her hands fell to her sides, and her too-wide green eyes watched him.

"That doesn't sound so bad," he said, and his voice was thick like caramel.

Anna's heart pounded, and she pressed her hands to her chest in case it burst out. "I feel like I'm having a heart attack." Eli took another step toward her, and she made the mistake of looking up at his face. His blue eyes undid her, so she darted away from him, putting the island between them. "You stay on your side."

Eli tipped up his chin and laughed loudly. It echoed through the back room and out into the bakery, and Anna's heart leaped. The front door opened, and the bell jingled. A briny breeze blew through the shop. Tiny piles of powdered sugar tornadoed across the island. A man's voice said hello to Thomas.

"Lord, help me, it's Baron," she whispered and scrunched up her face. "Someone stick a fork in me. I'm done."

"I'll help him," Eli said, moving toward the archway.

Anna jumped in front of him like a ninja and held up her

hands, ready to karate chop him if needed. "No way, José," she argued. "You stay here. *Please.*"

Eli held up his hands in surrender. "I'll stay put, but only because you said please."

Anna exhaled and stepped through the archway. Baron stood at the counter, staring at the pastries in the display case. "Hey," she said, feeling like a pound of jumping jelly beans was ricocheting around in her stomach.

He looked up at her with sleepy eyes. She couldn't read his expression, and she fought the urge to jump over the counter and wrap her arms around him.

"Donuts look good," he said.

"Want a few for the road?"

Anna was already sliding open the glass door when Baron reached across the counter and grabbed her hand. He gave it a squeeze, and she squeezed back. "About yesterday," he began, "I still don't know what to say. I had no idea you wanted to . . ."

"Wanted to what?" she asked, unwilling to help ease the awkwardness she heard in his words. She needed to hear him say it, to hear him say again that he hadn't thought of her, of *them.*

He released her hand. "That you wanted to go with me, that you wanted to get *married*," he said too loudly. "We've never had a serious conversation about it."

Anna frowned, and her face reddened. She could see Thomas's attention locked on them. "We've never had a serious conversation about much of anything," she admitted. "How could we have, when you're always gone?"

"That's not fair," he said.

"It's not about fairness," Anna said in a voice only loud enough for Baron to hear. "We've been together two years. Lots of people our age get married after dating for less time." Her throat felt thick with tears. She willed herself not to cry.

"And you want to get married?" he asked.

Anna wished his voice didn't sound so strained, so tight. "Yes. Maybe. *I don't know.* I know I love you. I wanted to be with you."

Baron grabbed her hand again and twined his fingers with hers. "I love you, Anna-Banana. Wait, what do you mean *wanted* to be with me?"

Anna sighed and closed her eyes. She inhaled the faint smell of the ocean; it seemed a thousand miles away. "You're leaving, and I'm staying, and you didn't even once think that I might want to go with you."

"For this two-week trip?" he said.

"No, not *this* trip, Baron," Anna argued in a whisper. "But afterward. You're moving to California. You're leaving me. That will make us past tense." Anger pushed aside the tears.

"I don't want to break up," Baron said.

"What *do* you want?"

He hesitated. "I . . . I don't know."

"There's your answer," she said, unable to mask her disappointment. He didn't even know what he wanted. Perhaps he never had. "If you wanted me, you'd know. Go to California, Baron. Get settled into your new life, but I need a break."

"For how long?" he asked, sounding worried for the first time since their conversation last night.

"For as long as I need—"

"Hey, Eli," Thomas called from a table for two near the windows, "could I get a refill?"

Like the surprise crouched in a jack-in-the-box, Eli sprang

through the archway and strode toward Thomas's lifted cup. Baron turned his entire body to watch Eli walk across the room.

"Who the hell is that?" Baron asked without lowering his voice.

Eli walked behind the counter and filled Thomas's cup. "Hey, man," he said to Baron with an easy smile. "I'm Eli, a college friend of Anna's. I'm helping out around here for a while, and she's letting me crash at her place." He motioned with his head toward the upstairs apartment. He carried the coffee to Thomas and returned to Anna's side.

Baron said nothing, and Anna wished so hard for a black hole to appear beneath her feet and swallow her. A vein throbbed in the center of her forehead. Baron looked at Anna, asking her questions with his eyes, but her mind was full of nothing but the wind blowing straight through her ears.

"Is that a joke?" Baron asked Eli when Anna blinked at him in silence.

"Which part?" Eli asked, leaning casually against the back of the display case.

Baron's eyes narrowed. The bakery door opened, and a bone-cold wind flooded the room and blew the loose hair from Anna's face. Thomas walked out whistling the theme song from *The Good, the Bad and the Ugly*.

"Anna, what the hell is going on? I've never even heard of this guy, yet he's *staying* with you? You live in a one-bedroom apartment—"

"It's a good-size bedroom. Plenty of room," Eli said. He nudged Anna with his elbow as though sharing an inside joke. She gawked at him. Baron squared his shoulders, and the air in the room sizzled like an electrical storm full of heat lightning.

The bell jingled again. Tessa stepped into the bakery with one hand clamped onto the strap of her brown leather crossbody bag and one hand lifted into a wave.

"Good morning," she said. Her royal-blue peacoat was buttoned all the way to the top, and she'd wrapped a navy scarf around her neck and shoved it down between the lapels of her jacket. Her smile faltered when she caught sight of Baron at the counter.

"Welcome to the circus," Anna responded.

Tessa stepped up next to Baron and gave him a tight-lipped smile. "Hey, Baron, I wasn't expecting to see you here. I heard you were on your way out of town. Something urgent. Like a last-minute decision made without consulting anyone who might need to know the plan." Only then did he turn and look at her. "Congratulations on your new job *across the country from Anna*. Must be bittersweet for you—"

"Tessa," Anna said in a warning voice.

Her comforting smile for Anna was genuine. "Sorry, I'll just order and leave you to what I hope is a conversation full of groveling—I mean, sincere apologies. You know, putting things right before up and moving without warning—"

"Tessa—"

Tessa's gaze slid to Eli, and her focus shifted instantly. "Well, hey there," she said and tossed a questioning gaze toward Anna. She flipped her hair over her shoulder and stepped closer to the counter. "New hire? Hi, I'm Tessa."

"Eli. Nice to meet you, Tessa. I've heard a lot about you," he said, extending his hand in greeting.

Tessa's surprised expression lifted her eyebrows. "You have?"

"He just blew in from out of town last night to stay with Anna," Baron said. "Is that why you left my place early?"

Anna's mouth fell open in shock. "You *know* why I left early."

Tessa looked at Anna. "Last night? Must have been late. I didn't leave until eleven."

Anna shook her head. "Eli wasn't here last night. Lily stayed over until after midnight. You can ask her."

"He said he's crashing at your place," Baron sniped. "I assumed the slumber party had already started."

"Slumber party," Eli said with a wide grin. "I like the image that conjures."

Baron's jaw clenched.

"He's staying with you? Upstairs? Do you even have a pullout couch?" Tessa asked.

"Nope," Eli confirmed. "Queen-size bed."

"Lord, help me," Anna whispered when Baron's face reddened.

"Who *are* you?" Tessa asked Eli. "A crazy handsome cousin? A brother we never knew about? As long as you and I aren't related, I'll be happy."

Eli laughed, and Tessa shifted closer to the sound.

Anna's head throbbed. "Tessa, we can catch up later, okay?"

Tessa nodded. "You better call me, or I'll phone stalk you." She pointed at the display cases. "I'll take two peanut butter cookies, a chocolate-covered donut, and a Morning Glory Muffin, please. If you want to toss in your cell number," she said to Eli, "I can send you some real estate options if you're looking for a place to rent."

Eli filled a bag of treats for Tessa, and Anna rang her up. Tessa threw one more scathing look at Baron, then skittered out the door, letting in a smoky wind on her way out.

"Don't you have a plane to catch?" Eli asked, pushing away

from the display case and stepping so close to Anna their arms touched.

Baron's cheek twitched, and his jawline jutted out when his teeth clenched. Anna could count on one hand the number of times Baron had lost his temper. Even though his temper was a quick but explosive outburst, she wanted to stop the conversation before it derailed. She slapped her hand to Eli's chest and demanded, "Get in the back now." When he didn't budge, she glared at him. "*Now!*"

Eli pressed his hand over the top of hers for a few seconds, and her vision blurred. Then he turned and disappeared into the back room. She exhaled loudly and turned to Baron.

"What the hell is going on, Anna?" Baron asked.

"Nothing. He's just . . . passing through," she answered, using Eli's lie because what else could she say? She couldn't admit she *made* him last night out of flour and the fairy sugar her grandma had locked away in a box. Anna almost laughed, wondering how Baron would react if she said, "I baked him, and voilà, he's a real boy!"

"Passing through," Baron repeated flatly. "And apparently staying in your apartment. When were you going to tell me about him?"

"He just showed up, first thing this morning," she said quickly. "He's harmless." Her stomach tightened. Was he? "And I was going to tell you." Eventually.

Baron shoved his hand through his hair. "I'm leaving the state, and a stranger is staying with you. This is fantastic news," he said sarcastically. "I don't like him."

Anna walked around the counter and touched Baron's arm.

He visibly relaxed. "He's a friend," she said, even though *friend* didn't quite seem like the correct word to describe Eli. "You're going to miss your flight if you don't get going."

"What about us taking a break?" he asked, reaching out to tuck an unruly piece of hair behind her ear.

Anna's chest tightened, and she pressed her lips together. "This trip will give you some time to think about us. But for now, we need to take a break."

Baron didn't argue. His eyes drifted to the archway. "What about him? How long is Frankenstein going to be staying with you?"

"Frankenstein?" Anna's stomach rolled, making her feel like she'd eaten too much raw cookie dough. She glanced over her shoulder, but Eli wasn't standing there.

"He's huge."

"A few inches taller than you," she said with a slow smile, and Baron pulled her into a quick hug. "I don't know how long he'll be here. Not long?"

"Not long sounds like a good answer to me," he said and kissed the top of her head. He stepped away and exhaled. "I'll call you when I land."

Anna nodded. "Be safe."

She watched indecision ripple across Baron's face. He didn't seem to want to leave, but she assumed that had more to do with Eli waiting in the back room than it did with him wanting to stay with her. A part of her still wanted him to stay, to tell her that he couldn't imagine moving across the country without her by her side. But he turned and walked out. Anna watched him until he rounded the corner and disappeared.

Sadness settled over her, as heavy as a wool blanket in the rain. Her shoulders sagged. She'd spent two years building a life on a foundation made of piecrusts. What was she going to do with Eli? He couldn't possibly stay with her in her apartment, which suddenly seemed much too small to contain the two of them.

Eli startled Anna when he lurched out of the back room with crossed eyes, rod-straight zombie arms, and his right leg dragging behind him. His bottom lip looked like it was being pulled by a fishhook. "Master," he moaned, "I am here to do your bidding."

Unexpected laughter bubbled up her throat so quickly she nearly choked on it. "What are you *doing*?"

Eli laughed and straightened up. "I'm being Frankenstein."

She couldn't help but laugh again, despite the fact that her life had turned into a train wreck. "You mean you're Frankenstein's monster, unless you're trying to be Igor." She tried to sidestep around him, but he blocked her entry into the back room.

Eli pointed to his chest. "No. Me, monster. You, Anna."

She snorted and poked him in the chest. "No. You, idiot. Me, hungover." She skirted around him, feeling the heat from his body reach out and encircle her, beckoning her closer.

Anna walked into the kitchen and saw the baking stone she'd used last night. She lifted it slowly in both hands. A darker stain marred the surface of the beige stone—a stain in the shape of a heart. Electricity danced across her skin. Static filled her ears. If the golden sugar in the box was actually the reason for Eli's existence, then it made sense that Beatrice had locked it away. Now Anna was a modern-day Pandora, and what she'd done couldn't be undone.

She glanced over her shoulder. Eli leaned casually against the archway, his arms crossed over his chest, watching her with his too-blue eyes and a smile. Looking at him, she found herself unable to deny the truth: Eli was hers.

CHAPTER 4

MUDSLIDE COOKIES

THE REST OF THE AFTERNOON WAS A CIRCUS OF ACTIVITY. More women than Anna had ever seen in her bakery flocked to the store as though she might be giving away free samples from the Fountain of Youth. For the first hour or two, Anna wondered what was drawing half the town's women in for donuts or éclairs or dark chocolate truffles. When she finally noticed the way everyone seemed completely enchanted with Eli's good looks and affable manner, she understood. Even the men in town, with the exception of Baron and Thomas, were charmed. He talked about sports with the jocks, music and literature with the inspired. Anna spent most of the afternoon sweating like a pig in the back room, baking and trying to keep the display cases stocked.

At least baking was a distraction from the hollowness Baron's thoughtlessness had created. It was also a distraction from Eli, from the way she wanted to touch him and feel the vibration that rushed up her arms and the thrilling roller-coaster drop of her stomach.

She carried a warm tray of freshly baked Mudslide Cookies to the display case. Eli stood beside a table of four women, all giving him their rapt attention, and laughed. One of the women reached out and playfully swatted him. A twinge of jealousy twisted Anna's stomach, and she looked away. Was the attraction a side effect of the secret ingredient? Did every woman in town feel the same magnetic pull to Eli? Did he turn them to pudding too?

Anna closed the display case and groaned. Deciding whether her feelings for Eli were abnormal or real or manufactured was the least of her worries. She had a man, who had sprung up fully formed from a ball of dough, and she had no idea how she was going to explain his existence at all, let alone figure out what to do with him at the end of the day.

Two hours later, when the bakery closed and she and Eli had cleaned and put everything away, her stomach was in such a tightly wound knot that she felt as if she'd been spinning too long on the merry-go-round.

Eli hung his apron on the hook and rubbed his hands together. "Finally," he said. "You've been working like a machine today. Ready for a relaxing evening?"

Anna wanted to say something, but she was afraid if she opened her mouth, she might pull a repeat of the twelfth-grade rum incident. Her eyes drifted toward the steps leading to her apartment. Was she really going to let Eli go upstairs with her tonight and stay over? Lord, what would her mama say? What would *anyone* say? She hadn't responded to Lily's or Tessa's texts with anything more than, Busy day, I'll text later. Now it was later, and she still didn't know how to respond. To anyone.

"You're really worn out, aren't you?" Eli said. "Running a

bakery is no joke, and if I can be honest, you make it look easy, but I know it's not. I know they've asked a lot of you to stay and do this day after day. At least now you have an extra pair of hands to use any way you need." Eli crossed the room and untied her apron, pulled it over her head, and hung it on the wall. "How about you take a bath, and I'll make dinner?" He motioned his head toward the staircase.

As soon as he touched her, all the confusing, conflicting thoughts and fears in her head melted. She felt warm all over, like she'd already slipped into a drawn bath. Eli untethered something inside her, and her body seemed to float above them, looking down at the only two people in the world.

Eli grinned. "Your eyes just glazed over," he said. "Was it the bath idea or me cooking dinner?"

Or the idea that he had an extra pair of hands that she was free to use in whatever way suited her fancy? This was a slippery mudslide of a slope she was on. He stepped away from her and turned off the lights. Anna blinked a few times.

"Both," she said quietly, and because she had no idea what else to do, she climbed the stairs to an apartment that she could already imagine bursting apart if Eli continued to touch her. Walls would not be able to contain the energy that surged when he came too close.

Anna stood awkwardly in the open area comprising the living room and kitchen and listened to Eli's footsteps on the stairs. He walked straight past her and into the kitchen. He rummaged through the pantry and then looked through the refrigerator.

Anna could do nothing but stand in the living room breathing in the scent of winter pine and hot chocolate.

Eli finally stopped and looked at her. "Go take a bath," he said and made a shooing motion with his hands. "I won't burn down the place."

"Is this weird? This is weird, right?" she blurted.

"Me making dinner?" he asked, sounding sincerely confused.

"You in my apartment. A *man* in my apartment other than Baron."

Eli placed a cast-iron pot on the gas range. "Would you rather I was Baron?"

The question startled her, but not as much as the truth. "No," she admitted. "I just haven't had any—"

"Gentleman callers? No other suitors entertained in here?" he teased.

Anna chuckled. "This isn't the 1800s."

"Frankly, dear Anna, I don't give a damn," he said and struck a dramatic pose.

A playful feeling stirred in her heart. He was paraphrasing a quote from her favorite novel. "Sir, you are no gentleman."

Eli's grin called her closer to him. "An apt observation, and you are no lady."

Anna sighed dramatically. "I love that book."

"I know," he said. "Now scoot. Let this gentleman caller get dinner going."

Anna obediently walked into her bathroom, but how could she relax in the bathtub when there was a stranger cooking in her kitchen? She sat on the edge of the tub and winced as she pulled the rubber band from her tousled hair. Her auburn waves tumbled down around her shoulders. Eli didn't feel like a stranger. In fact, he felt *too* close, too much a part of her core. She skipped the bath and opted for a quick shower.

By the time she finished drying and straightening her hair and changing into her most chaste pajamas, she was tempted to drop onto her bed and sleep for a few hundred years. The entire apartment smelled spicy, and when she left her bedroom she found Eli grabbing bowls from the cabinet. She paused in the living room and watched him.

"Spying on me?" he asked without looking at her. He ladled what looked like chili into the bowls. The scents of cumin and cayenne swirled around him.

Anna walked toward him. "How did you know I was here?"

He glanced over his shoulder. "The air feels different," he answered, grabbing two spoons and bringing the bowls to the coffee table. He motioned for her to sit, and she curled up on one end of the couch, hoping to put distance between them.

She thanked him when he passed her a bowl. She cupped her hands beneath it and warmed them. "How so?"

Eli brought a box of saltines and two cans of Coca-Cola to the coffee table and sat beside her on the couch, causing her to slide so close to the armrest she was nearly sitting on it. She couldn't risk touching him, not when her defenses were weakening due to the sleepiness that crept in at the corners.

He scooped a spoonful of chili into his mouth. He swallowed and answered, "It's easier to breathe, like a sigh pulled from way down here." He tapped his stomach. "Plus you smell sweet, like sugar cookies and cupcakes."

Her breath caught in her throat. It was a ridiculous sort of compliment, but it made her feel warm and gooey like a cookie straight out of the oven. She tried to readjust her position on the couch, and her knees bumped Eli's legs. He patted his thigh.

"Stretch your legs out," he said.

Her eyes widened. A warning alarm blared through her brain. "I'm comfortable," she lied.

Eli balanced his chili bowl in one hand and grabbed one of her legs, and then the other, with his free hand. Before she could argue, her legs were stretched across his thighs, and within seconds, she felt the white-hot pulse of Eli's warmth radiating up her legs and causing her entire body to tingle. She could barely breathe, let alone *think*.

"Eat up," he said. He popped the top on his Coke can and took a big gulp.

She shoved the spoon into the bowl, distracted. She filled her mouth too full and then spent the next few seconds trying to figure out how to chew without food spilling out. When she finally swallowed, she said, "This is my favorite chili recipe."

"I know," he said and grinned at her. He passed her a cracker.

She stared at the salt granules on top of the cracker. "How do you know?"

He shrugged. "I know lots of things about you."

"But *how*?" she asked again. The chili revolted halfway down, and Anna rubbed her fingers across her chest in an attempt to fight off the heartburn. Did the fact that she created him give him an insider's guide to her memories, to her thoughts and desires?

"Because we're friends," he said and ate another spoonful of chili. He put his bowl down on the coffee table and rested his hands on her shins. "Don't you know a lot about Lily and Tessa?"

Anna inhaled sharply at the mention of their names. "You know them?"

Eli cast a questioning gaze her way. "I saw Tessa today in person, remember? But they're your best friends, and you've talked about them a lot."

Only problem with that explanation was that she hadn't talked *to him* about them ever. Anna shoved the cracker into her mouth to avoid having to reply. If he had access to her memories, did that mean he also had top-secret clearance for her more deeply buried dreams and desires? Did he know that being near him was driving her bananas in a way she'd never experienced? She'd been attracted to Baron, but it had evolved over time; their attraction was not this intense. Anna didn't believe in instalove, though she enjoyed reading stories about it. Was this magnetism a side effect of her creating him? Did that mean it wasn't real?

As if reading her mind, Eli put his hands on her legs, and rational thoughts fled the scene. Anna felt the uncontrollable urge to reach out and touch him. Eli took the bowl from her hands, which was a mistake because her fingers began to twitch, itching to find out what his skin felt like. Would he feel real? Would she be able to feel his heartbeat? Would she feel a pulse at his wrist? Against his neck?

When his blue eyes locked on hers, she could feel her hand lifting. Even though she knew she should jam it beneath the couch cushions, she couldn't stop the movement. And then her fingertips were against his cheek, tracing the shape of his jaw line, slipping down his neck. Eli reached up and grabbed her hand, and a volcano exploded inside her. Her vision tunneled, and she couldn't inhale enough air into her lungs. She felt herself leaning forward, her eyes closing, wanting nothing more than to experience Eli up close.

The Turtles' ringtone "Happy Together" blared from Anna's

cell phone in her bedroom. Her eyes jerked open. "Baron," she gasped. She jumped up so quickly her forehead slammed into Eli's, knocking his head into the back of the couch. He groaned, and Anna scrambled over him. "Sorry."

The cell phone vibrated off the dresser. She snatched it from the air before it hit the floor. "Hello?"

"Hey, Anna-Banana," Baron said, sounding almost relieved to hear her voice. "Took you a while to answer. I thought I might miss you."

Her pulse throbbed against her temples. Had she almost kissed Eli? "I was in the other room, eating dinner. Had to run for the phone. How are you? You made it safely, I guess. Easy travel day?"

"Long travel day," he said. "But, yeah, I'm here. It's a hotel near the office. I'll go in tomorrow morning, get a tour. Some of my coworkers are going to show me around town afterward. How was your day?"

Anna sat on the edge of her bed. "Super busy day. I'm lucky I had help—"

"Eli?" Baron said, and his voice chilled by degrees. "He still staying with you?"

Anna's stomach fluttered. "Yes."

"What's he doing?"

"As in now? He's eating." Baron's Q&A stirred irritation in her, which surprised her. Since he wasn't interested in a future with her, his jealousy over another man felt like sandpaper against her skin.

"Is he sleeping in your bed? With you?"

Anna scowled. "Of course he isn't going to be sleeping with me."

"Lock your bedroom door when you go to bed."

"Seriously, Baron?" Anna responded. "He's not like that. Let's change the subject because this is pointless." An evening wind drifted in through her open window, causing her hair to tickle her face.

"You should see where I'm staying. It's a boutique hotel, real fancy. They leave sugar cookies in the lobby. Nothing like yours, but better than nothing," he said. "The view from the room is incredible. Nice room too. King-size bed, walk-in shower. The agency really set me up right."

Anna sighed. "Sounds really nice. I guess they'll keep you busy while you're there—"

"Hey, I gotta go. My car is here. I'm meeting some of the team for dinner and drinks."

"Oh, okay. Well, don't miss your ride."

"I'll call you later," Baron said. "Or text. Depends on how much time I have. And hey . . . I miss you."

"I miss you too," she said as a conditioned response. In truth she felt empty.

"Talk to you soon."

Anna stared at the phone. Guilt, viscous and raw, churned in her stomach like boiling simple syrup. She dropped onto her bed, arms splayed at her sides. Less than a minute ago she'd been a breath away from *kissing* Eli. She draped her arm over her face and groaned. When she inhaled, she breathed in the rich scent of Eli, all dark chocolate and passion. Anna pushed herself up on her elbows. He leaned against her bedroom doorjamb.

"I can't do this," she finally said when the silence dragged on too long.

"You don't have to," Eli said as he stepped into her bedroom. "You told him you were taking a break."

"I mean, I can't do this," she said, waving her hands in front of her. "I've been with the same guy for two years, and we just broke up. I'm not ready for . . . whatever *this* is. You're doing something to me, and it's messing with my head."

"What do you want me to do?" He sat beside her on the bed.

Anna slid away. "Just stop what you're doing. I can't *think*."

Eli's smile faded. The air around them shifted. Anna held her breath.

When Eli spoke again, his voice was low. "I can't stop," he said seriously. He moved his hand across the bed until their fingers touched. "Can you? Tell me you don't feel it too, and I'll try to give you what you want. I'll leave right now."

Could he really leave? Was he free like everyone else to do as he pleased? The thought of Eli walking out the door made her mouth go dry. He wrapped a finger around one of hers, and she looked down at their hands.

"Do you want me to go?" he asked.

She hesitated for a few seconds and then shook her head. The sight of his slow smile had her holding her breath.

"I'll give you some space," he said. "I can respect that. I'll bring your dinner in here."

"I'm not sure I can eat," she said.

Eli nodded. "It's been a long day. Why don't you get into bed, grab yourself a book, and I'll clean up."

Eli hopped off the bed. Anna shoved the extra pillows off the bed and scooted farther up until she lay on her pillow and stared at the ceiling. She didn't have the mind for reading tonight. She'd probably end up staring at the same page for hours. Her thoughts were stuck in a pinball machine. Eli couldn't possibly stay, but she couldn't bear to send him out the door. Where would he go? What would he do for money? *How* would he get anywhere without transportation? He was wearing borrowed clothes and living off memories that weren't even his own. Anna squeezed her eyes closed. It was worse than that; she didn't *want* him to leave. Even now she wanted him to walk back into her room just so she could feel the intensity that rippled off him and washed over her.

A few minutes later, with the bedroom lights turned off, Anna listened to Eli pull a quilt from the linen closet, settle on the couch, and dial the radio to a local station turned down low. As tired as she was, she couldn't fall asleep. Knowing he was in the other room kept her awake and listening.

At nearly midnight, Eli stood in her doorway and whispered, "You awake?"

She swallowed. "Yeah."

"You're supposed to be sleeping," he said. "Want me to tell you a story until you fall asleep?"

Anna pushed herself up on her elbows. "Are you joking?"

Eli jumped onto the empty side of the bed and nearly bounced her straight off the side.

"I would never joke about bedtime stories," he said. "What would you prefer? Suspense, horror, adventure, happily ever after?"

Anna knew she would never have a chance of falling asleep now that Eli was inches away from her, filling up her room with the smell of rosemary and pine. "Definitely not horror."

Eli rolled onto his side and faced her in the darkness. "Once upon a time—"

"Are you making this up, or is this a real story?"

"All stories are real if someone believes in them. Now, hush."

Anna listened to Eli tell a story about a young boy who woke up in a strange land. She stayed awake long enough to learn he met a beautiful young girl, but Eli's voice calmed her in a way she hadn't expected. She drifted off to sleep just as the girl told the young boy she needed his help.

CHAPTER 5

HUNKA BURNIN' LOVE CAKE

ANNA DREAMED OF LYING ON THE GRAY-WHITE SANDS OF Wildehaven Beach, the sun warming her skin, a breeze blowing in from the ocean. She could feel Baron beside her, so she moved closer to him and pressed against his side. The moment felt suspended by perfection and ease. In the distance, someone began singing "9 to 5."

Anna mumbled, "Keep it down." But the music only grew louder and louder until she found it too irritating to ignore.

"Time to get up," a male voice said.

Anna's eyes opened. She was in her room, not on the beach with Baron. Dolly Parton sang from the cell phone on the nightstand. Anna's arm and leg were draped over the man in her bed, who was most definitely not Baron. Her whole body tensed.

"For the record, that was all you," Eli said in a deep, sleepy voice. "My hands are under my head. You, on the other hand, are all over me and making it difficult for me to behave."

Anna quickly rolled over, flopping out of the bed. Embarrassment caused her cheeks to burn hot. She looked at Eli stretched out on top of the covers, his long body barely fitting in her bed. He wore only a pair of Baron's boxers, which looked a little too tight, a little too short, and a whole lot too enticing. The sight nearly short-circuited her brain. Anna rubbed her hands down her face and dragged herself into the bathroom. She pressed her palms and forehead against the closed door. She felt as though someone had shoved her into a cotton candy machine.

The wood of the door warmed beneath her hands, and somehow she knew Eli stood on the other side.

"I'm not trying to make this worse for you," he said, his voice muffled by the door.

"Are you sure? Because I'm . . . fragile." And she didn't know why she couldn't control how she felt about him, why she couldn't tamp down the attraction that simmered perpetually.

"No one would ever describe you as fragile," Eli said. "Vulnerable?"

"How about weak and defenseless against your charms?"

Eli chuckled. "Nothing happened."

Anna flung the door open. "A man I'm not dating slept in my bed," she argued. "That's *something*."

"It's not like it hasn't happened before," Eli countered. "The Pie Monger slept in your bed after y'all worked for hours to finish that catering project to land his externship. He wouldn't have been accepted if you hadn't helped him."

Anna's mouth dropped open. She'd forgotten about Joey "the Pie Monger" Plummer from the institute. Eli's recall of *her* memories unsettled her. "I didn't like Joey like that. Sleeping in my bed with him was like sharing a room with a brother, if I had one."

"And sleeping in a bed with me *isn't* like that?"

Eli stood before her in the borrowed pair of boxers, and her concentration wobbled. She took a step backward into the bathroom and rubbed the back of her neck. "Nope."

"I'll sleep on the couch from now on. Try to pretend I'm the brother you never had."

Anna grimaced. "If I had a brother, I definitely wouldn't feel—" She stopped herself from finishing the statement with *this intense desire.*

Eli smiled slow and easy and stepped into the bathroom. "Wouldn't feel what? Like you wanted to plant a big fat one on me?"

"I thought you weren't trying to make this worse," she said, shoving him out of the bathroom. "Now, stay out. I have to get ready. Then I'll figure out what to do with you."

He smirked. "I have a few ideas about what you can do with me."

Anna closed the door in his face.

"I'll meet you downstairs," he said. "It's cupcake day."

"I know what day it is, Eli!"

The whole apartment seemed to expand with the sound of his laughter.

Anna tried to focus on making sure the bakery's treats were prepared before the customers arrived at seven a.m. With Eli's help, she finished baking, icing, cutting, and arranging with plenty of time left over to hang out, which Anna tried to avoid by cleaning the windows and organizing an already organized pantry.

When the first customers arrived, Eli was right by Anna's side, and she couldn't help but notice what a great team they made. Before long, she was smiling and laughing with him and the customers. During a midmorning lull, Eli sat down with Mr. Silverstein, who always ordered six different cupcakes on cupcake day and ate each one in turn, relishing them like guilty pleasures. He swore the cupcakes kept him curious and happy for an entire day.

While Mr. Silverstein worked on the key lime cupcake with lime cream cheese filling, he and Eli discussed the town's up-coming Fall Festival, which would occur a week from Saturday. Anna took this opportunity to slip into the back room unnoticed. She grabbed her cell phone and crept into the large freezer. She wedged the door open with a wooden spoon.

First she texted Tessa: Sorry for not calling yesterday. The bakery has been slammed, and I needed some time to sort through everything that happened with Baron. I'll call later.

Anna then dialed Lily's number. Lily answered on the fourth ring, out of breath and sounding frazzled. "Hello?"

"Hey," Anna whispered, "do you have a minute?"

"A couple. I got in a shipment of clothes that I need to tag," Lily said. "You okay? You were stingy with your words yesterday, almost cryptic. But I wanted to give you space. Tessa and I agreed that if we didn't hear from you today, we'd stage a friendtervention—"

"I'm okay, sort of. Let me preface this entire conversation with the fact that I know this is going to sound insane. Something happened the other night after you left—"

"The rum night?"

"Yes, the rum night—"

"You didn't barf on Becky Johnson, did you? Kidding!" Lily laughed at her own joke. "Did you have a righteous hangover the next morning?"

"Yes, I had a hangover, but that's not—"

"Did Baron call? Have you heard from him today?"

"No, I haven't. This isn't about—"

"Tessa said you have a new employee, a man. Did you tell me you were hiring? I don't remember that. She said he's crazy cute. Actually, she said he's more delicious looking than your Hunka Burnin' Love Cake. Why didn't you tell me about him?"

"She came into the bakery yesterday," Anna explained, her frustration growing, "and it was a madhouse, so I didn't have a chance to call either of you. Lily, will you zip it for two seconds and let me talk?" Anna sighed in exasperation. "The new worker is Elijah, the man I made with the magic sugar in Grandma Bea's box."

Anna held the phone away from her ear because Lily's laughter was piercing. When Lily finally stopped laughing, Anna said, "I'm serious."

"Ain't no way you're serious," she said, still chuckling. "Your bread dough is your new worker? Anna, when is the last time you slept? Have you been pulling a few all-nighters?"

"Lily, get yourself over here, okay? I need you."

"I can't leave the shop now," Lily argued. "I have this shipment to go through."

"I don't care. Ask Amanda to work the register. I need you—"

"What are you doing in here?" Eli asked.

Anna released a strangled yell and bungled the phone so badly it looked like she might be trying to teach herself how to juggle. It bounced out of her hand and off blocks of frozen butter before ricocheting into her forehead. She leaned down, retrieved the phone, and hung up on Lily.

"Taking inventory," she said, rubbing her forehead.

"Is that code for taking a supersecret phone call?" he asked.

He reached out and smoothed her long hair with his hand, pressing cold strands against her neck. Anna tingled. Eli looped his fingers around hers, and she didn't immediately pull away. He was right-out-of-the-oven warm against her cold skin.

"If you stay in here much longer, you're going to be a Popsicle."

Anna hurried past him, shoving her cell phone into her back pocket. The front door opened, and October air swirled into the shop, bringing with it the smell of pumpkin pie and apple cider. Eli went to help the customer, and she was grateful for the moment alone.

She gathered her thoughts. How could she make Lily believe her? How would Lily react? The front bells jingled again. She rubbed her temples and walked through the archway. Lily rushed into the shop wearing a fuchsia sweaterdress and brown boots. Her blond curls corkscrewed more than usual and framed her face like a wild mane. Her eyes locked on Eli, and she came to a full stop. He smiled at her.

"Wow," Lily said. She tossed her blond curls over her shoulder and let her expression go all soft and dewy. Anna marched over to Lily and grabbed her arm.

"Lily, this is Eli. Eli, this is Lily," Anna said, then she dragged Lily to the back room.

"*Gorgeous* is not an adequate word for that hunk of manliness out there," Lily said. "He's a sex god. Honestly, I know you might still be upset about breaking up with Baron and not ready to date just yet, but I'd say give this rebound a try—"

"Keep your voice down," Anna scolded. "Lily, focus. On *me*."

"Okay, okay." She closed her eyes and inhaled slowly. "If this was an excuse to have me check out the new help, then thank you. Now, can I take him out to lunch?"

"Lily!"

"You're in a foul mood today."

"Listen to me," Anna hissed through clenched teeth. "That man out there is the product of our night of rum. Remember? We came downstairs, and while you drank yourself into oblivion, I created a recipe. I added the sparkly stuff we found in the box, and when I got up the next morning, Eli was here in the bakery."

Lily frowned and twisted a blond curl around her finger. "I don't understand what you're saying. Your new hire showed up early for work when you had a hangover? Did he throw out the bread dough without asking?"

Anna whispered even though she could hear Eli talking to someone out front. "That guy out there came out of one of these ovens. I made him."

"Are you high right now?" Lily asked.

Anna clenched her teeth together so tightly a vein bulged in her forehead. "On what, Lily? Life? Insanity? You don't believe me? Go out there and ask him where he went to high school. Ask him where he went to college. Maybe ask him what his last name is, and then come back here and tell me. I don't think he has any memories of his own. But how could he? It's like he sprang out of nowhere. *I made him* with the secret-ingredient recipe."

Lily looked doubtful, but she left Anna standing in the back room. Anna could hear Lily talking to Eli, and she heard them laughing. But when Lily returned to the back room, she wasn't smiling. She wore an expression like someone had given her day-old coffee laced with spoiled milk.

"He definitely went to college with you in New York, which I find disturbing because you never mentioned him before now," Lily said. "How did you not date him when you were there? He clearly thinks you're the cat's pajamas. But he wasn't as quick to tell me where he went to high school. When he came up with a name, it was Mystic Water High, and he's our age, which means he would have been in our class. Obviously, he's lying—"

"He's not lying," Anna said. "Those are *my* memories. Eli thinks he went to college with me because *I* went there. I created him, Lily. He has no memories of his own. Of course he would say he went to our high school—*my* high school."

Lily chewed her bottom lip. "Did you name him Elijah Guittard?"

Anna shook her head. "Just Elijah."

"He's chosen a last name for himself."

Anna repeated the last name, and realization prickled over her skin. She walked over to a shelf and pointed to a ten-pound box of dark chocolate. "Guittard? Like the chocolate maker? He named himself after chocolate."

Lily laughed. "Anna, what kind of game are you playing? This is crazy. You know that, right? Okay, game over. Tell me what's really going on."

Anna reached out and grabbed Lily's hands. "I swear I'm telling you the truth." Anna felt Lily's hands tremble in her own.

"But that's impossible," Lily whispered.

"Somehow the impossible became possible."

"You can't go around creating people!" Lily said. "Was your grandma magic? Are *you* magic?"

Anna wrung her hands together. "I have no idea what this means. And I'm scared out of my mind—until he walks into the room, and then I can't think of *anything*."

"What do you mean?"

"He casts some kind of spell over me. My mind feels empty but full of him. Full of *us*," Anna babbled.

"You think he's evil?" Lily squeaked. "Like dark magic or something? I saw this movie once about—"

Anna shook her head. "No." She leaned against the island. "It's not like that. He doesn't feel evil at all. He seems good and kind and wholesome. I think if anyone is bad, it's me. This is serious, Lily. Remember what happened to Victor Frankenstein? He lost his freaking mind."

Lily pressed both palms against the island. "I need a minute." She pulled in a few deep breaths. Then she paced the back room while she rambled. "First of all, Victor Frankenstein made a man out of used body parts—gross. Being followed around by a gigantic, stitched-together man would make anyone go insane. I get tired of Jakob sometimes when he won't give me space. But as far as I can tell, Eli is all one piece. Second, Eli isn't exactly a monster that's causing people to try to torch your bakery. He's absurdly good-looking, and he seems to have the hots for you. What are you going to do? How did this happen? I feel like I've eaten bad Chinese food. Have you told Baron? Tessa? Have you told anyone else? Not that they'd believe you."

"I've only told you," Anna said. "And I don't plan on telling anyone else. Not until I figure out what to do."

"Where is Eli living?"

"He's staying with me."

"Are you bonkers? You're letting that dough boy live with you?"

The temperature in the room rose, and Anna breathed in the smell of melting sugar.

"Please tell me that I'm the dough boy," Eli said and grinned.

Lily squeaked and stood behind Anna as if she thought Eli was dangerous.

"We're out of double dark chocolate chip cookies. Mrs. Rogers just took the last dozen. Want me to get started on a new batch?" he asked.

Anna grabbed Lily's arm and tugged her forward. "Actually, Lily is going to take you to buy some clothes. I'll make the cookies. I know you didn't bring much on your trip here, and she has the afternoon off. She volunteered to help out."

The bell on the front door jingled again. "Hold that thought," Eli said and left the kitchen to assist the customer.

Lily's eyes widened. "I can't leave Amanda at the shop all afternoon." She mouthed, "You can't possibly leave me alone with this freak show."

Anna frowned. "I told you the rum was a bad idea," she mouthed. "You owe me."

Lily dragged one finger horizontally across her neck.

Anna shook her head. "The worst he'll do is charm the pants off you, but don't even entertain that thought." Then she added, "*Please.*"

Lily huffed. Eli returned and leaned against the archway, smiling at them. Anna felt Lily relax beside her. Eli's smile could stop wars. Anna walked past him and opened the register. She counted out a handful of cash.

"Here," she said, shoving the money into Eli's hands. "Yesterday's pay for working."

Eli pushed the money back. "You don't have to pay me."

"You're not working for free," she argued. "I think they'll arrest me for that." She held the money out to him, and he took it, holding her hands for a few seconds. When her thoughts started leaking out of her ears, she tugged her hands away.

Lily adjusted her dress. "If we're not back in a couple of hours, send out a search party. You know I have a locator on my car, right? If anything happens, the police can find me."

Anna exhaled loudly. "You're going *shopping*."

Lily responded with a glare.

Eli wiped a smudge of flour from Anna's cheek, causing her to sigh in a completely inappropriate way. Her body arched toward his like they were two magnets sliding across the floor. "We'll be back," he said to her. Then he looked at Lily and said, "Anna and I have dinner plans. We'll definitely not be out for long." He crossed the room toward the door.

Lily stared bug-eyed at Anna as Anna lifted her fingers to her cheek. Lily gave her a look that said, *We're going to discuss this later*, and they were out the door, leaving behind an afternoon wind that brought in cherry-red maple leaves.

CHAPTER 6

DARK AND STORMY GANACHE

BLUSTERY AFTERNOON WINDS BLEW IN SWOLLEN STORM CLOUDS. The muggy air dampened everything as the town waited for rain. Anna closed the bakery at dusk, and she checked her phone for messages. Tessa had texted earlier in the afternoon, reminding Anna to call her for the scoop on Eli, but she'd received nothing from Baron. She was surprised by how little she felt, like a hollowed-out bread bowl—mostly air and empty. Maybe she'd needed this break more than she realized. Maybe she'd been the one holding them together all this time, and the stress had pressed her tuile-cookie thin.

Anna pulled up her go-to baking playlist on her phone, connected it to the Bluetooth speaker in her apartment kitchen, and turned up the volume. At first she closed her eyes and swayed her hips to the music, letting her anxiety and worry melt away. By the second song, she was bouncing around the kitchen, arms in the air, tossing her hips around like she hoped to win an award for most spastic dancer. But the chaotic happiness made her feel alive and free of everything.

Her apartment door swung open, and the scent of ripe cherries burned her nose. Anna had no time to stop her dance-a-thon and turn down the volume before her mama stood gawking at her.

"What on earth are you doing?" Evelyn O'Brien asked.

Anna lowered the volume and tried to smooth down her shirt to press out the wrinkles. "Mama . . . I was . . . dancing," Anna said breathlessly.

"Is that what you call it?" Evelyn asked. "Looked like a woman possessed."

"You're not far off," Anna muttered. "You should knock, you know. I never barge into your house without knocking."

"I have a key. Why would I knock?" Evelyn glanced around the living room as though she expected to see someone. Her styled blond hair rested against her shoulders in a perfectly soft curled-under bob, hair no doubt sprayed in place. Simple gold hoops dangled from her ears, and the modest scoop of her dress's neckline allowed for a short gold necklace adorned with a tiny pearl pendant. Her khaki long-sleeved dress fell to her knees, and she completed the ensemble with thick wool tights and tall black boots.

Evelyn's sense of style was immaculate, always appropriate for every occasion, and nearly the opposite of Anna's. Anna had inherited most of her daddy's traits, both personality and looks. Evelyn was a delicate Southern flower, the leggy blond beauty of teenage dreams, someone to be called upon for etiquette and design advice. Anna was the girl to organize the pantry and host the bake sale. With her wavy auburn hair, love of graphic tees, and penchant for never skipping dessert, Anna didn't look or act much like her mama. One thing they did share was their rigid rule-following tendencies. Evelyn tried to instill in Anna many Southern traditions and genteel manners, but the one that stuck was her need to be obedient and responsible. Anna had grown up more frightened of her mama's disappointment than anything else. Making her parents proud had always been at the top of her list, and so far, Anna hadn't failed them as a daughter.

Evelyn straightened magazines on the coffee table and sat on the couch. "Besides, what would I interrupt? A baking session?" She smiled at her daughter. "Come and sit. I have exciting news."

Anna dropped onto the couch. Exciting news from her mama usually had to do with a benefit or charity event, the ladies she played tennis with, or mild Mystic Water gossip. "How's Daddy? He didn't come by for his cookies this afternoon."

"He's finally agreed to let me redo the kitchen. I had him looking for a specific tile this afternoon. But you'll never guess who called me today. Charlotte Clarke." Evelyn paused for effect. When Anna didn't fill the silence, Evelyn huffed. "The Clarke House? That gorgeous historic Victorian on Dogwood? I *know* you know the one. You practically begged me to drive you by there every Halloween and Christmas. Well, she's selling it."

This was her exciting news? Anna tucked her legs beneath her on the couch and spun her hair into a loose bun. She slid the ponytail holder off her wrist and secured her hair in place. "That's interesting," Anna said to let her mama know she was listening, even if the information wasn't riveting.

The Clarke House was one of the older homes in Mystic Water, and her mama was right. It was a stunning showcase of architecture and class. The craftsmanship was enough to make a lover of historical homes swoon, and the original embellishments and woodwork warranted bragging rights. It was a three-story Victorian beauty with most of its original splendor intact, including original glass windows, some stained for pops of color. The yellow-and-white exterior paint and landscaped front yard reminded Anna of a springtime gingerbread house nestled among pink dogwoods, azaleas, and lavender. Although Anna had never seen the rose gardens in the backyard, townsfolk talked about them as if they were sacred spaces.

If Anna had the ability to sketch out her dream home, she would have drawn the Clarke House. As children, she, Lily, and Tessa had often walked the sidewalks on Dogwood Avenue, ogling the historic homes and pretending they'd grow up to live in one. For as long as Anna had been alive, Charlotte Clarke had lived in the house, raising her family and then welcoming in her grandchildren.

"I hope someone who loves old homes buys it," Anna said. "It's a beautiful piece of history."

Evelyn's smile widened and she patted Anna's knee. "Charlotte knows you've always loved it, and she's agreed to let you make an offer before she officially lists it on the market."

A laugh burst out of Anna. Evelyn looked affronted, and Anna's laugh died off. She cleared her throat and asked her mama, "Is this a joke?"

"Do I ever joke?" Evelyn asked.

"Fair point."

"Tessa is representing Charlotte as her Realtor," Evelyn said. "You'll make an offer, of course. Opportunities like this are rare, and you could finally move out of the bakery."

Anna's mouth was as dry as if she'd thrown a handful of flour onto her tongue. "I like this apartment, and that house is huge, not to mention expensive."

Evelyn folded her hands together in her lap. "This is a shoebox, honey," she said. "And not a place you live in forever. You have plenty of money to cover a substantial down payment with the inheritance money your grandma left you."

Words from Beatrice's last letter to Anna about the inheritance money came to her mind. *For opening your own place one day, no matter what anyone says.* The money was for Anna's dream bakery, and she hadn't touched it in two years. She'd let it sit and accrue interest in a money market account. But her mama didn't know what the letter said, didn't know the money wasn't intended for a down payment on a house. Now that Anna owned Bea's Bakery, maybe the money didn't have to be used for opening her own place one day. Her heart twinged. Anna thought she'd buried the dream of a beachside bakery, but apparently, she hadn't buried it deep enough because that seed was still sprouting just below the surface.

Evelyn continued, "I think Baron would love the Clarke House too. It's big, yes, but a wonderful space for a growing family."

Melancholy slipped into the room, swirled around Anna, and settled beside her on the couch. She glanced toward the kitchen, where quiet music drifted out of the speaker. Journey's "Don't Stop Believin'" sounded more like a plea than a rock anthem. "Baron was offered a job in California, and he's moving," Anna said, unable to look at her mama. "He's there right now for a two-week introduction of sorts."

Evelyn sat up as though electrocuted, displacing the air in

the room like an approaching tornado. "You're thinking of leaving Mystic Water? You can't. You belong here. I won't stand for it. This is your *home*."

Her mama's words, confident and demanding, twisted in Anna's stomach in a new way. In the past Anna had always been respectful of her mama's opinions, sure her mama knew what was best. But her mama's assumptions, formed without discussion, were disconnected from the truth.

Anna opened her mouth to explain, but her mama stood and paced the living room.

"I know you love Baron, but how could he ask you to leave? He has a perfectly good job now. He's gone half the time anyway, which I have never approved of, by the way. What kind of man leaves his girlfriend alone all the time with no one to care for her?"

"I'm hardly a defenseless woman, Mama," Anna said. "I can take care of myself without a man."

"What's in California that he can't do here?" Evelyn asked, her voice rising. "This town needs you. What would happen to the bakery without you? It's been here for more than fifty years, and I'm not going to let it close down on my watch. It's a part of this town, part of its history. What would people say? They loved your grandma, and they love this bakery. *You* love this bakery. I can't believe he'd expect you to up and desert your family and all we've built here."

The room stank like cherries forgotten in a summer sun. Anna stood and rubbed her stomach. She felt nauseous and clammy. "He didn't ask me to go."

Evelyn's eyes widened. Her pink, glossed lips parted, but nothing came out. Then she pressed her hand to her pearl pendant. "Oh, honey, I'm so sorry."

Anna tried to swallow but couldn't. Her mama's pity undid the last of her resolve. She shrugged as if to say, *It doesn't matter*. But it mattered so much she felt suffocated by her crumbling plans. She wasn't sure which was worse now: her mama's disapproval or her pity. Anna hadn't known her mama objected to Baron traveling all the time. But now it was clear her daughter wasn't even competent enough to keep together a lousy relationship. Evelyn opened her arms, and Anna stood and closed the short distance between them. Evelyn wrapped her arms around Anna.

"You know I don't like to speak ill of people," Evelyn said as she rubbed Anna's back. "It isn't polite, but he's an idiot for not asking you to go."

"Mama, you were just mad when you believed he *had* asked me to go." Despite the ache in her body, she smiled against her mama's shoulder.

"Of course, you can't go with him, but I'm indignant that he didn't ask," Evelyn said and pulled away from Anna. "You've followed that boy around for years and supported all his nonsense whims. Like the time I nearly had a heart attack when he took you rock climbing and said you didn't have to wear a helmet."

"Mama, we wore helmets—"

"Not the point!" Evelyn argued. "He said they were optional, and he made *you* optional all the time. You were just sitting here waiting for him to come home every weekend like a sweet little girl, but I've always thought you were too good for him. You need a solid man. A good man who knows how special you are—"

A bolt of lightning lit the entire apartment. Thunder rattled the windows, and books leaped off the shelves. The front door flung open, and Eli rushed inside. He dripped rainwater onto the hardwood.

"Barely made it," he said, dropping shopping bags on the floor and rubbing one hand through his wet hair. Glittering water droplets flew through the air. "One more minute and I would have had to swim from the car."

His drenched clothes adhered to his body as if he'd taken a shower fully clothed. Evelyn stood rigid beside Anna. Eli noticed Evelyn and smiled. Anna dropped her head back and stared at the ceiling. Could the timing be any worse?

Eli walked over to Evelyn. "You must be Mrs. O'Brien." He held out his hand, and Evelyn hesitated before shaking it. "I'm Eli Guittard. It's a real pleasure to finally meet you."

Evelyn's eyebrows rose on her forehead. She looked at Anna for an explanation.

"Mama, this is Eli, and he's a—a friend from New York. We met at school. He's helping me at the bakery for a while. You know Josie is off for a few weeks, so I'm grateful for an extra pair of hands."

Evelyn smiled her pageant best, but her eyes scrutinized Eli. "From the Institute of Culinary Education?" she asked. "How lovely. We didn't meet many of Anna's friends from New York—"

"You didn't meet *any* of them," Anna corrected.

"Yes, well, our visits were always preplanned with sightseeing, weren't they?" Evelyn countered. "It's nice to meet you, Eli. Anna must really trust you to let you help at the bakery. She takes her job seriously. She's worked very hard to establish herself in Mystic Water and run a successful business."

"Yes, ma'am," Eli agreed. "She's the best at what she does."

Evelyn hummed in her throat and tossed a curious look at Anna. "Is this temporary while Josie's out? Will you be staying in town long, Eli?"

Eli looked at Anna. "As long as Anna needs me, I'll be around."

When he smiled at her, Anna couldn't help but sigh. She shoved her hands into her pockets because all she wanted to do was trace the outlines of his chest muscles with her fingers.

"Is that so?" Evelyn asked in a voice that skirted the edge of shock. "Where are you staying, Eli? I hope you're not paying too much for a short-term lease. I know a few people who are renting out houses or small duplexes at affordable prices. I'm sure they would be willing to work out a month-to-month lease with you."

Eli smiled. "That's kind of you, and I'll keep it in mind. I'm staying with Anna at the moment."

Evelyn's brown eyes bulged like popovers, and Anna feared she might have to shove them back into her mama's head. "Eli, would you give my daughter and me a minute alone?"

Eli grabbed his shopping bags and headed for Anna's bedroom. "I'll jump in the shower. Nice meeting you, Mrs. O'Brien. I hope to see you again."

When the bathroom door closed, Evelyn rounded on Anna. "Have you lost your mind? You're letting a grown man stay in your apartment? This place is barely big enough for you."

"Mama, it's only for a little while." Anna grabbed a kitchen towel and started drying Eli's puddle and trail of water.

Evelyn fisted her hands on her hips. "How well do you know him? Does Baron know he's staying here?"

"Yes, Baron knows." Anna didn't bother adding that Baron was displeased about her houseguest too. Having her mama and Baron on the same team was more than she could stomach at the moment.

"I can't imagine he's okay with it. I'm certainly not."

On her hands and knees, Anna wiped away the last of Eli's wet footprints. She stared up at her mama. "I'm sick of caring about what Baron thinks. Need I remind you, you recently referred to Baron as an idiot? I'm not sure either of us should give much weight to his opinion. And I'm a grown woman. I can offer a friend a place to stay if I want. It's my choice."

Evelyn's lips pressed together as she prepared her argument. "It isn't proper. What will people say? You have *a man* staying with you, and he's not even your boyfriend, which still would be inappropriate even if he *were*."

Anna threw the wet towel into the sink. "Mama, I don't care what the town thinks. It's my business, my life."

"He's too handsome to stay with you," Evelyn argued.

Anna was so shocked she laughed.

"Don't you laugh at me, young lady. He is, and you're a beautiful woman. Things happen between boys and girls."

"Mama," Anna said in exasperation. She filled the kettle with water and set it on the stove. She needed to busy her mind or else she would be tempted to think about the "things" that happened between boys and girls, with her and Eli playing the leading roles.

"You have a stranger living in your apartment," Evelyn said evenly. "And people will talk, believe me. They'll talk about anything and everything, and the more a story gets around, the wilder it gets. And you're okay with that? Who are you, and what have you done with my good daughter?" She stared at Anna with her dark eyes and shook her head. "I think you need to remember that this is your home; it matters what the people here think about our family, and you have a responsibility to us and to yourself." Evelyn walked to the door. When she opened it, the raging storm winds gusted into the apartment, fluttering book pages and bringing in the pungent scent of sulfur.

"Mama . . ."

"Think about what you're doing. I'll call you tomorrow." Evelyn grabbed an umbrella from the stand next to the door. She opened it and walked out into the rainstorm.

Anna swan dived onto her bed and screamed into her pillow. Thunder growled outside her windows, and dishes rattled in the cabinets. The dark and stormy night raged, aligning its intensity with the tempest roaring through her heart. Anna rolled over onto her back and hugged the pillow against her chest like a life preserver. Eli stepped out of the bathroom; steam crawled along the ceiling. She turned her head and looked at him. He wore nothing but a towel wrapped around his waist. Anna smashed the pillow over her face, but she could still smell a hint of melting chocolate.

A few minutes later, the mattress shifted beneath his weight. Anna lowered the pillow and hazarded a glance. He was now fully dressed in a T-shirt and jeans, and his blue shirt matched his eyes perfectly.

"You okay?" he asked.

"Better than I was ten minutes ago. Show me what you bought with Lily."

He opened a shopping bag and grabbed the folded clothes inside. "You want to talk about it?"

Her brow wrinkled, and she propped up on her elbows. "About what you bought?"

"About what went down with your mom before I got here."

Anna shook her head. Thoughts of Baron, Eli, the Clarke House, and her mama sank together in the mire of her mind. "Let's see what you found."

Eli laid his clothes on the bed. Lily was a professional fashionista. Her exemplary taste shone as Anna sorted through Eli's finds—an assortment of T-shirts, long-sleeved shirts, a sweatshirt, and a second pair of jeans in a lighter wash. She smiled at him. "Your pants fit." What she didn't add was that his jeans now fit so well, she had trouble not staring at him.

Lightning zigzagged outside her bedroom window. Eli pretended to model the jeans he wore, which were now long enough for his tall frame. He shared the contents of the other bags, which included boxers, socks, tennis shoes, and his own pair of flip-flops.

Rain assaulted the windowpanes, and Eli returned to the bed. "I thought you'd look more alike, you and your mom," he said. "I knew she was blond and tall, but I thought in person, I might see more similarity. You must look a lot like your dad."

Anna thought it was odd that Eli wouldn't know what her daddy looked like. Maybe some of his memories were blurry, like looking at an image through water. Anna nodded. "I do look a lot like my dad, who looks a lot like my grandpa. The people who knew Grandpa Joe tell me I look exactly like him. Should it bother me that people think I look like a man?" Anna teased, causing Eli to chuckle. "Grandpa was Irish." Or at least that's what they'd told everyone.

Anna lifted a lock of her hair. "Red haired and green eyed. Fortunately for me, my hair is more auburn than flaming red."

"People can't call you Carrots," he said. After a long pause, he added, "Your mom was pretty burned up about something."

He reached out and hooked a finger around one of Anna's. She closed her eyes and sighed. His touch filled her with warmth, like being wrapped in a bedsheet just out of the dryer. She lay back on the bed and stared at the ceiling. Holding Eli's finger seemed to anchor her, calm the jumble tangling inside her.

"Lord love her, but my mama is intense. She has all these *ideas* about who I should be," Anna said, surprised by her candidness.

"Is she right about who you should be?"

"I used to think so," Anna said. "Most of her ideas work for me. She wants me to be successful, hardworking, confident, and capable."

"All things you are."

She looked at him and relaxed into the gentleness of his gaze. "You know she has never *once* asked me what I wanted to do with my life? She always assumes. The only reason she supported me moving to New York was because it was temporary and would give me a better understanding about how to be successful running Bea's Bakery. She never thought I would do anything else or *be* anywhere else."

"And she never asked," Eli echoed her words. "Do you miss New York?"

Anna closed her eyes. "Not really," she said. "It was fun for a while but too noisy for me. Too busy. If you stood on a street corner in New York City for too long, you'd get run over by someone or a lot of someones. If you did the same here, someone would stop and ask if you needed help." She smiled at him. "I guess I like a slower pace."

"You love it here?"

"I do love Mystic Water," she said. "It was a great place to grow up."

Eli shifted closer to her on the bed. "I sense there's a *but* there."

She rolled her head to the side and looked at him. How did he know exactly what to ask? How did he know all the places to start digging and dig deep? Did Eli already know her feelings? Did he already know what she would say because she'd created him from her own consciousness? "But I never wanted to come back here and live forever."

"Yet here you are," he said as he leaned onto his side.

Anna felt drawn to him. She wanted to curl up against him and press her face against his chest. When he slipped his hand into hers, she knew it would be a mistake to move any closer to him. A fire sparked low in her stomach and sent flames of heat to every nerve.

"Grandma Bea died, and someone had to keep the bakery running. It was the right thing to do."

"But not what *you* wanted to do." He rubbed his thumb over the top of her hand.

"I love working in the bakery and being a part of Grandma Bea's life," Anna said and tugged her hand out of Eli's grasp. Touching him shoved aside the chaos in her mind and set her at ease, but the strong pull she felt for him needed to be dialed down a few dozen notches.

"She'll always be a part of you no matter where you live," Eli said.

Anna rolled off the bed and walked to the window to watch the fierce rain slap the panes. Curiosity struck her, and she looked at him. "Do *you* miss New York?"

Eli sat up and slid to the edge of the bed. He shrugged. "Sometimes. I got used to the noise, got used to falling asleep to the honking and the constant rush of people, so when I left, I missed it. That sounds weird, I know, since most people complain about it." He rubbed the back of his neck and sighed.

Realization trickled down Anna's body like goose bumps. "I never got used to the noise." Eli *didn't* share every thought or emotion with her. Was he . . . changing? Becoming more separate from her? She risked another question. "What did you want to do after graduation? Open a bakery?"

He chuckled. "Wasn't that everyone's answer in pastry school? Nah, you remember that deli near Central Park where they served the Nova Scotia salmon on pumpernickel?"

Anna's hand went to her heart. "I loved the salmon and egg on their house bagel."

"That's my kind of place," Eli said. "That's what I'd like one day. Neighborhood sandwich shop. Small, intimate, where everybody knows your name."

"Sounds like a bar," Anna teased, then she sobered because Eli's dream was nothing like her own. It was as if his life had started with her, but he was branching off on his own. What did that mean? Would he not be forever tied to her? Why did the thought of not having him around fill her with an ache that rattled through her bones? "Where would you want to open it?" She paused to swallow the tightness in her throat. "Back in New York?"

Eli stared off for a few seconds. "I'm still figuring out that part." Shifting the subject back to her, he asked, "If you don't want to stay in Mystic Water forever, why don't you make plans for something different?"

Anna shook her head. "This town needs me," she said. "They need this bakery."

"Those sound like your mom's words, not yours. I think everyone would survive without your chocolate cake. People adapt."

"The town loves this bakery almost as much as they loved Grandma Bea. It's what they want—to have it open and me running the place, keeping it alive."

"Maybe I should ask you what your mom never has. What do *you* want?"

Anna fell silent. After a time, she said, "I used to dream about a beachside bakery, like the one we used to go to in Wildehaven Beach. I want to step outside every day and hear the sound of waves rushing the shore."

"And drag your feet through the sand?" Eli asked.

She smiled at him. "Yes."

"I have a thing for the ocean too," he said. "It calms me, like you do."

"But how can I leave Mystic Water?" she said.

"You're not trapped here, Anna. You can leave anytime you want. Just like I can. You're free."

How could she possibly leave Mystic Water? What would her parents say? What would happen to Beatrice's legacy? Not to mention, what would she do with Eli if she left town? She didn't even know what she was going to do with him now. Anna pulled clothes from her dresser and headed toward the bathroom to shower.

"You're right," Eli said when she didn't respond. "No one would ever forgive you, and the beach is a lousy place to live. Hurricanes are bound to strike. Wildehaven Beach is probably a dump these days. Entirely too much sand and sun."

Irritation flared inside Anna. She pointed a finger at him. "You've never even been there," she argued. "Wildehaven Beach is beautiful. It's the perfect seaside town, and the bakery is on the boardwalk right on the beach."

Eli tapped the side of his head. "I have a mental picture in here. I don't remember it being that great. If you had a bakery at the beach, you'd never be able to keep sand out of the food. Your cookies would be gritty, but maybe beach bums like dirt in their food."

Anna glared at him. "You have no idea what you're talking about."

Eli leaned lazily back onto the bed. "You must really like the place."

"I love it," she said, crossing her arms over her chest.

"Maybe you should move there," Eli said.

"Maybe I will."

When he grinned at her, Anna realized he'd been pulling the truth out of her. In her frustration, she threw her clothes at him. Eli laughed and tossed the clothes back at her. He spun her underwear around his finger and smirked.

"You might need these."

Anna's face burned. She crossed the room faster than a

breath and snatched her underwear from his finger. Then she marched into the bathroom and slammed the door. She pressed a hand to her chest and felt her heart pounding beneath her fingers. She'd never admitted to *anyone* how much she wanted a beachside bakery. Now that the truth had been released, she felt unable to pull it back in.

CHAPTER 7

BLUEBERRY HAND PIES

ANNA GRABBED A HANDWRITTEN RECIPE BOOK OFF HER SHELF, then hustled down the stairs into the bakery, hugging the collection to her chest. The kitchen smelled of hazelnut and sugar cookies. A couple dozen cookies were cooling on racks, and Eli was bent over, looking into the oven. He stood when he heard her enter.

"Stop letting me sleep in," Anna said. "I can't get used to waking up so late. I'll never recover."

His hands dwarfed a pink mug as he cupped it. "Hey, don't blame me," he said. "I heard your alarm go off, and I got up. You turned it off and fell back asleep. I thought maybe you needed an extra day off."

"A midweek day off . . ." she said wistfully. She pointed at his mug. "Coffee? Is there enough for me? I need a double shot of espresso today."

He nodded and sipped. "I made hazelnut vanilla. No espresso yet, but I can make you a cup."

"I don't like the flavored brews." She laid the book on the island. "I want to make the blueberry hand pies today, using Grandma Bea's dough recipe in here, but I want to add blueberry powder to the dough for an added punch of flavor." She pointed to his mug. "I prefer coffee's natural flavor. Why do you like hazelnut vanilla if I don't?"

Eli chuckled. "I'm only allowed to like what you like?" He moved across the room to stand near her. The warm aroma of hazelnuts and cream swept over her, and she inhaled.

She looked up at him. "Aren't you?"

He laughed again, and the front bell jingled. He walked out of the back room and wished good morning to the first customer of the day. Anna released a shaky breath.

"Grab the sugar cookies out of the oven, will you?" Eli called from the front. The bell jingled again.

Anna removed the sheet tray from the oven and placed the hot cookies on cooling racks. Then she brought the cooled sugar cookies to the display case. "Seriously, you need to wake me up next time," she whispered.

Eli waited for the customer to leave before he refilled his coffee. "I can get things started without you. You tossed and turned all night. I thought you could use the rest."

"How would you know that?" she asked. As far as she was aware, last night Eli had kept his promise to sleep on the couch.

"I heard you."

Anna watched Mr. Jones park in front of the bakery and climb out of his burgundy Lincoln. "My mind was all over the place last night, and I'm not used to having someone stay at my place." She smoothed her hand down her hair and thought of Baron. He hadn't called or texted again since he'd arrived in California. Maybe that was to be expected, but his complete willingness to let her go without a fight unrolled a dull sadness inside her.

"What about Baron?" Eli asked.

Anna turned to look at him, surprised by the way Baron's name sounded acidic on Eli's tongue. "We mostly stayed at his place. He said it was easier."

"He said that because he's selfish, and he always did what was better for him. He knew you'd agree to whatever he asked because that's what you do. You like to make it easy for everyone else, and takers keep taking as long as you're giving for free." Eli looked away from her and greeted Mr. Jones.

Anna felt the urge to defend Baron, but the truth of Eli's words stung. Together they prepared Mr. Jones's usual order, and she watched Eli closely. He was different, edgier. Mr. Jones left, and Anna busied herself with furiously wiping off the clean tabletops. She didn't want to admit that Baron was self-centered because then she would have to admit that he'd never put her first. She would have to admit that she'd settled for less than she deserved and two years of her life had been wasted on someone who'd never wanted to commit to her. Anna sighed heavily and stared out the front windows. Wet maple leaves lurched across the street in the October wind.

She knew Eli was behind her when she breathed in the spicy scents of chiles and chocolate. She squared her shoulders but didn't turn around.

"You're mad," he said. "I'm sorry."

"For what? The truth?" She laughed, but her throat was

tight, and the sound squeezed out, pathetic and broken. When Anna pushed past him, Eli grabbed her arm.

"What I said hurt your feelings," he said. "I'm sorry for that."

Anna wiggled out of Eli's grasp. The air in the room chilled her skin, and she shivered as she walked away.

"He's an idiot," Eli said.

Anna finally turned to look at him. "Knowing that doesn't make me feel any less dumb."

"Dumb?" he asked, sounding stunned. "Why would *you* feel dumb?"

"You've been here all of two days, and you've managed to accurately assess why the relationship was never going to work—something that took me two years to realize, and I only see it now because I was forced to. I thought we could make it work, and if I loved him enough, it would all be okay somehow. And I ignored all the things I didn't like about our relationship."

"It's not dumb to love someone and have hope they'll change," Eli said.

He walked to her, and the magnetic pull between them intensified. If she'd been wearing roller skates, Anna knew she would have zoomed straight into his arms. She wanted to be wrapped up in him, to hear his heartbeat, to have him eradicate the hollowness and sadness.

The front door opened, and Evelyn walked in looking tailored and classy in a silky cream-colored blouse paired with navy slacks. A Burberry plaid scarf looped around her neck and matched her tan leather purse. Anna wondered for the millionth time how such a beautiful, flawlessly manicured woman could have a daughter like her, who was presently wearing a pair of jeans and a red long-sleeved shirt advertising Coca-Cola.

"Good morning," Evelyn said. She adjusted her diamond stud earrings. "Charlotte is going to let us have a look at the house this morning. Grab your purse, and let's go. Tessa is meeting us there."

As the fog shifted in Anna's brain, she babbled a few incoherent words in surprise. Then she said, "Mama, I can't leave the bakery right now. I have work to do."

Evelyn nodded toward Eli. "You have help. Eli, you'll be fine for a couple of hours, won't you, dear? You can run this place without Anna, right? I doubt she would have hired you if you weren't capable, don't you agree?"

"Yes, ma'am," he answered. "Anna, it's fine. I have everything under control. I know the schedule for today."

"I can't leave Eli alone in the bakery," Anna argued.

"What am I gonna do, eat all the brownies?" Eli teased. "I'll try not to blow up the place."

Anna faced Eli so her mama couldn't see her face. "I don't *want* to go," she whispered. "She wants me to buy a house."

Eli's eyebrows raised. "Does it have two bedrooms? We could move in together." He winked at her.

Evelyn cleared her throat. "We're wasting time, Anna."

"Go," Eli encouraged. "You won't be long, and until then, I'll take care of everything."

"I'll meet you in the car," Evelyn said and walked out.

Anna grabbed her purse and tossed her car keys onto the kitchen island. She ripped a flap off a box of butter and scribbled her cell number on it. Eli stood in the doorway and watched her.

"Don't forget the blueberry hand pies, and don't overwork the dough. You might need to chill it for longer than usual. Can you do that?"

"I promise I won't get too handsy," Eli said. "Unless you say please."

Anna's blood pumped hot, and Eli inched closer. The torn flap of the butter box hung loosely in her hand, and her lips parted.

"Forgive me?" he asked, taking the paper from her hand and touching her fingers.

"For what?"

"My comments about Baron."

Hearing Baron's name snapped Anna back into the present. She put distance between her and Eli and made a dismissive hand gesture. "Don't worry about it."

"Is that a yes?"

She heaved a sigh and wanted nothing more than to ask him to just hold her until she didn't feel so tangled up inside. But thinking of Eli holding her caused a whole new set of problems.

"Of course I forgive you. I have to go. My mama is about as patient as a three-year-old waiting for cookies to bake. You call me if you need *anything*. If there's an emergency, you know my car is parked in the back," she said. She hurried out into the front room, but she stopped abruptly at the front door. "You know how to drive, right?"

Laughter burst out of Eli. Anna stared at him and smiled. She wanted to stand there and hear that sound again and again. It loosened the tension in her chest.

"Get out of here," he said. "You have about five seconds before your mom calls you from the car."

Anna hesitated and then rushed out.

A low wrought iron fence separated the Victorian garden of the Clarke House from the sidewalk. Anna pushed open the gate and walked up the stone pathway leading to the house. She loved the square mansard tower, the lacy trim, the bay window.

The carved wooden front door with inlaid glass panels opened. Tessa stepped out and onto the porch. "Good morning." She tugged at the bottom of her soft gray suit jacket. The blue blouse beneath added a splash of color that paired well with Tessa's coloring.

Anna again wished she had put more thought into her clothes today, but waking up late and in a panic about the bakery had shoved style out of her mind. Plus she spent most of the day with her clothes hidden behind aprons, so worrying too much about whether she was a fashion fail never seemed worth it. "Hey, Tessa. That blue looks great on you."

"Is that your way of apologizing for not calling me sooner?" Tessa smiled. "And thank you. I'm so excited you're going to put an offer on this house." She pulled Anna into a quick side hug. "I've always thought this house suited you. I told Mrs. Evelyn it *looks* like you. It has that gingerbread-house, sugary-wonderland feel, doesn't it?" Tessa gave Evelyn a hug while wishing her good morning.

"I'm here to *look* at the house," Anna corrected, "not buy it."

Confusion flickered in Tessa's eyes. She tucked her hair behind her ears. "Mrs. Evelyn said you were interested in purchasing it."

Before Anna could argue, Evelyn ushered everyone inside. "Let's have a look at the house, Tessa," Evelyn said. "No reason to spend all our time on the front porch in this chill."

The foyer's ceiling was high and arched. A hook was mounted

high along the main archway, left behind from the days when a kerosene lamp lit the entryway, Tessa explained. Thick, decorative crown molding traced the top of every wall. They stepped into the parlor, and Anna oohed over the original iron mantel and fireplace. She smoothed a hand over the cool iron mantel top. Sunlight poured in through the bay window as Tessa pointed out other features.

The sitting room had been turned into a library with built-in shelves. The thick, wavy antique glass on the windows made everything on the outside look like a dream. Anna walked to the windows and pressed her fingertips to the glass. The trees swayed against the blue sky, giving off the appearance of a wonderful watercolor world waiting for her on the other side.

"The kitchen is this way," Tessa said. "I know that's the most important room to you. Mrs. Clarke recently updated all the appliances."

Anna and Evelyn followed Tessa down the hallway. Stained glass transom windows invited rainbow light into every room. The house smelled like warm gingerbread and sweet icing.

"All the furniture is negotiable too," Tessa said. "You can decline the offer and furnish the house with your own style, but many of these pieces are antique, and Mrs. Clarke is willing to sell them for bargain prices that you'll never find online or at auction. The bed in the primary room alone is worth almost seven grand. Think about it." Tessa stopped at the doorway to the kitchen and ushered Anna and Evelyn in first.

"Wow," Anna said as she walked in.

A vase of white daisies had been placed on the counter. The size of the kitchen was unusually large for an older home. Anna assumed that at some point in its history, the owners had decided to expand their cooking and eating area. The expansion alone made the house worth buying. There were two stainless steel wall ovens. The double refrigerator had been faced with a walnut panel so it blended with the cabinets, as had the dishwasher. Anna walked through the kitchen, her fingers brushing the cabinets and appliances. The almond-colored enamel gas range was shiny and wide with four burners, a large burner in the center, and a removable grill top. There was a warming cabinet set into the bottom and two smaller ovens. A lot of simultaneous baking could be done in the kitchen.

Tessa clapped her hands together and smiled. "I *knew* you'd love it. It's gorgeous. Look at the light in here. And the walnut cabinets. I'd *die* for a place like this."

Anna examined the farmhouse sink. She ran her fingers over the wide basins. "You love your condo. All that white shiplap and matchy-matchy neutral-tone design."

"I do like understated classy," she admitted. "And it's easy to decorate when everything is the same color. To change with the season, all I have to do is add colored pillows." Tessa pressed her palms against the smooth granite countertop. "But this place is perfect for a family."

Anna frowned. "I'm not moving in here with my parents." She stepped into the breakfast nook. Spring roses would bloom outside the kitchen windows. Anna imagined hanging a hummingbird feeder right outside so she could watch for their fluttering wings.

Tessa worried a button on her jacket. "I just meant eventually . . . with Baron maybe?"

"Baron is gone," Anna said and walked out of the kitchen. Her mama called her name, but she kept walking. She felt irritated with herself for being mean to Tessa. It wasn't Tessa's fault Baron had ditched her for a more exciting life. Did she need to remind herself that it was *her* idea to take a break? "It's not like it was going to work long term anyway," she mumbled to herself. Anna had dreamed of being in this house with Baron, but those dreams were swept far away, carried out to sea.

The wide spiral staircase was half suspended from the ceiling and curved like a seashell as it rose to the second floor. Anna grabbed the walnut railing and climbed. She peeked into the first bedroom, which was obviously the primary room. Light reflected off the cornflower-blue walls, and a large canopy bed dominated the center of the room. Anna walked through the ensuite bathroom, admiring the tiles and claw-foot tub. On her way out of the room, she paused.

For a moment, she pictured herself curled in the gigantic bed, flipping through a cookbook. Then, without anyone else living in the house, her imagination turned her into a lonely spinster listening for the sounds of footfalls that never came. The vision shifted, and Eli bounded into the room, wearing his boxers and holding a plate of freshly baked cookies. Anna's heart stuttered and then rocketed into high gear.

"Get ahold of yourself," she grumbled, blinking away the image.

The second room was smaller and painted lavender. Sunlight slipping through the lace curtains cast intricate designs on the hardwood floor. A queen-size bed positioned between two large windows was centered across from an antique dresser with an oval mirror. The final bedroom had soft yellow walls, a twin bed covered in a cream-colored quilt, and a walnut dresser with a large framed mirror. There was another full bathroom in the hallway, and Anna admired the octagonal black-and-white tiles.

When she reached the end of the hallway, she stepped into the tower room. The small room had no useful purpose. It was much too cramped for a bed or even a table. The ceilings were low, and anyone taller than Anna would have to hunch. Two long windows allowed in plenty of sunlight. She noticed a slender door on the opposite wall. Anna opened it and revealed a narrow wooden staircase.

The door at the top opened onto the flat surface of the roof—the widow's walk. Anna stood in the sun and inhaled. She smelled lavender and pine. She couldn't imagine anywhere more perfect to live than this house. Except she wanted to pick it up and move it to Wildehaven Beach. A gull cried, and Anna smelled ripe cherries.

"What are you doing up there?" Evelyn asked from the bottom of the stairs. "Come down here."

Anna met Tessa and Evelyn in the second-floor hallway. "What do you think?" Tessa asked. "Isn't the primary bedroom dreamy? There's so much light in this house, and I know how you like windows. Having the first offer is a big deal because this house will go fast. These historic homes rarely come up for sale, and when they do, they're gone lickety-split."

"Why don't you ride with Tessa to her office and look over the contract?" Evelyn asked. "You can walk to the bakery as soon as you're done."

"Mama—"

"Go," Evelyn said and patted Anna on the arm. "Nothing is binding. Look it over and see how you feel. I think you'll realize it's perfect for you. I need to run. I left your dad at home with the contractor, and they're probably sitting on the back porch talking about football. I'll never get my kitchen finished." Evelyn hugged Anna and Tessa, leaving behind the whispery scent of her magnolia-blossom perfume.

Anna followed Tessa downstairs, and they made another pass through the kitchen. There was no doubt the house was incredible, but did Anna sincerely want to move into the Clarke House as a single woman in a town where she never wanted to settle down? Sure, she'd dreamed of living in a house like this when she was younger, but the dream had included a family and kids. And those childhood dreams existed long before she moved away, experienced a different life in the city, and started forming new dreams.

Tessa opened a door that led to a glassed-in back porch. There was a full view of the glorious gardens that would be a riot of color in the spring. Stone pathways curved through the yard and disappeared behind boxwood hedges. Pruned rose bushes would sprout new growth, and the sleeping wildflowers would burst into life in the warmer months and bring in butterflies and bumblebees. Tessa opened the door to the backyard and stepped outside. Anna followed.

Tessa cleared her throat. "I didn't mean to upset you earlier about Baron," she said. "I guess I keep thinking he'll come back and change his mind. That he'll decide to stay here with you."

Anna rubbed her fingers over the leaves of an unruly rosemary bush. "I don't think it's going to play out that way." She looked at Tessa. "He's doing his dream job, or at least one of them. And I'm not sure him changing his mind is what I want."

"You don't want to get back together?" Tessa asked. "After

two years? I'm not happy with him for doing this, but after that long, surely there's a way to work through it."

"That's the thing, Tessa," Anna admitted. "I don't want to work through it. I got so used to him being gone all the time, and this doesn't feel much different. But shouldn't it? Shouldn't I miss him and *want* him to come home and be with me? I don't."

"I'm surprised you're not sadder," Tessa said. "When Lance Waller broke up with me after six months, I was a wreck for a whole week. I can't imagine if we'd been together two years. I really thought you and Baron were going to stay together, get married, and settle down in a place like this." She motioned to the Clarke House.

"Isn't that the story all little girls are taught to want?" Anna said with a small smile. "Find a guy, marry him, have babies. Happily ever after."

"I prefer the ones about the princesses with all the jewels."

"And a golden carriage."

"No doubt," Tessa said and laughed. "He can keep the glass slippers. Those seem like a disaster waiting to happen."

"You're right, though," Anna said. "I *should* be sadder, but I feel mad at myself for not seeing that he and I weren't ever going to take the next step. I let things get comfortable. I never made him sit down and talk seriously about a future. With him traveling all the time, it was easy to put the conversation off, and maybe that prevented me from having to face the truth or get too serious myself."

"I should thank you," Tessa said.

"For what?"

"For stealing Baron away from me so he couldn't destroy my heart," she said, nudging Anna with her elbow.

"I did *not* steal him," Anna argued, but Tessa was smiling.

When Anna had returned to Mystic Water a little more than two years ago for Beatrice's funeral, Baron had been in town less than a month, crashing at his brother's house between jobs. Tessa had spotted Baron at the Piggly Wiggly and struck up a friendship, which she hoped would turn into a passionate love affair. She and Baron were friendly and had gone on a few chaste dates, and when Anna returned, Tessa dragged her grieving friend along on a dinner date. Baron took one look at Anna and nearly forgot Tessa's name. In her defense, Anna had no interest in dating Baron, who seemed like a wild card even then, but he'd slowly convinced her to agree to a date. Tessa had stepped aside, but not without pouting for a couple of weeks. Now it was a joke between friends that Anna was a boyfriend stealer.

Anna turned and walked toward the house. Thinking about how Baron was able to leave her behind so easily sucked some of the light from the day and blew a bitter wind across the yard. She pushed her long hair over her shoulders. "How's your mama?"

Tessa tugged at her jacket. "She's doing better and had her last treatment this week. She keeps asking about you and Lily, wanting to know when y'all will stop by."

Anna nodded. "Any time she wants us to. When she feels like having company, we'll swing by, and I'll bring over her favorite dessert."

Tessa smiled. "She'd like that. When are you going to tell me about the hot tamale working at the bakery? It's like he came out of nowhere."

"He kinda did," Anna agreed.

"Seriously, give me the scoop," Tessa said.

"What do you want to know?" Anna opened the back door

and walked inside. She didn't have a lot of information to share about Eli, and of the little bit she did know, she couldn't share it all with Tessa. She hated to be dishonest with her best friend, but the fewer people who knew the truth, the better.

"What's he doing with you?"

Anna stopped abruptly. "He's working for me."

Tessa tucked her hair behind her ears. "Where did he come from? Did he just move here? How did he know you were hiring if you haven't advertised?"

Anna hesitated. "We went to college together in New York. He stopped through town on his way to . . . on his way *through*, and he saw I needed help. Or I *mentioned* I was down a person with Josie on break, so he volunteered to stick around for a week or so to help out."

Tessa's forehead wrinkled. "That was nice of him. I guess he's got the extra time to make a stopover here. So he's not planning on staying long?"

Again the idea of Eli leaving squeezed the air from Anna's lungs. "I don't actually know how long he'll stay."

"He must have gotten a room at Whippoorwill Inn," Tessa said. "Although it's kinda expensive to stay in a B and B for a few weeks. I could ask around to see if anyone is interested in renting a room temporarily."

"He's, uh, staying with me. On the couch, of course."

Tessa gasped. "With you? Why, you little minx. What will your mama say?"

"She already knows, and she said a lot."

"Lord love a duck, I bet she did," Tessa said. "How well do you know him? You feel okay about him sleeping at your place?"

"He's harmless," Anna said, but as soon as the mental image

of him walking out of the bathroom in nothing but a towel surfaced, she knew those words were untrue.

Tessa walked through the downstairs, turning off lights. "Is he married? Dating anyone? Has he fathered any children he doesn't take care of? People are asking."

Anna laughed, but the back of her throat burned as though she'd swallowed whole chipotles slathered in adobo sauce. "He hasn't even been here a week, and people are already sharking around him?" she said. "He's single as far as I know." Anna felt a strong urge to say Eli was *hers*, and the ferocity of the thought surprised her.

Tessa locked the front door. They climbed into her Toyota Corolla, and Tessa turned on the radio. "I can't believe he's single. He's really good looking."

"He is," Anna agreed, and she noticed Tessa hadn't stopped smiling.

Tessa parked in front of Andrews Real Estate Agency, and she and Anna climbed out of her car. The real estate office took up the bottom floor of one of the oldest brick buildings in downtown Mystic Water. The front room had a modular white sofa, two armless orange chairs, a circular metal coffee table with wooden legs, and two ficus trees. The largest wall had been painted primary blue, and an oversize colorful painting of the local downtown park dominated the wall. The office also had a conference room, a break room, and two personal offices.

Tessa's mama had started the business years ago, and she put Tessa to work when she was a teenager, doing odd jobs like filing, answering the phone, and sorting the mail. Tessa accompanied her mama to houses, rentals, and plots of land, learning everything about real estate and how to help people find just what they needed. After college Tessa continued working with her mama, and during this last year of her mama's treatment, Tessa had been running the business mostly on her own, successfully so.

Tessa's spacious office boasted a wide window with plantation blinds. The decorating style was contemporary with white walls, two framed abstract paintings of black-and-white faces, and an acrylic desk. Two white chairs faced the desk, but no other furniture was in the room, making it feel unfinished and lackluster. The oddest item in her office was a misshapen, lumpy doll that sagged on the desk like it no longer had the energy to sit up straight and watch the world.

"Do you ever think of adding color in here?" Anna asked.

"Lily said the same thing just the other day," Tessa said, "only she compared it to a sanitorium. Sterile and bland. I've been thinking about painting, just haven't gotten around to it. After we had that pipe leak and the crew came in and repaired and replaced drywall, they covered most of the walls with primer paint. I've been so busy this last year that stopping to paint my office fell off the to-do list."

"You could hire someone."

Tessa reached for a sticky notepad, one of the few spots of color on her desk. She jotted down a note and held it up for Anna. "Done." Her note read, *Hire a painter*.

Anna picked up the doll on Tessa's desk. Although it was old, it didn't look loved on and threadbare the way favorite stuffed animals did after years of being dragged around and slept with.

The doll's yarn hair hung unevenly around her face, and her button eyes were a faded blue. A pink heart had been sewn onto the doll's orange dress, but a zigzagging line of black thread divided the heart in half. Her bumpy body seemed stuffed full of cotton balls and knots of yarn.

"Why do you keep this poor little thing here?"

Tessa sat at her desk chair and motioned for Anna to sit down. "Grandma Mildred stitched her for me when I was little," she said. "She thought it would protect me."

"From what?" Anna asked. Tessa reached for the doll, and Anna handed it over.

"From a broken heart, I think," Tessa said. "She wasn't quite right in the noggin. Did I ever tell you that?" When Anna shook her head, Tessa continued, "She was a sweetheart, don't get me wrong, but she was strange. She used to talk about your grandma sometimes."

"She did?"

"They were best friends when they were younger, but . . ." Tessa rubbed her thumb over the doll's heart. "But they had a falling-out over a guy. Grandpa Joe, actually."

Anna shifted in the uncomfortable chair. She'd never heard this story, and she hadn't known Tessa's grandma and Grandma Bea had once been best friends.

"What happened? Did your grandma like Grandpa Joe first?"

Tessa sat the doll on her desk and propped it against a coffee mug that said Everything I Touch Turns to SOLD. "This is the part where it gets strange. Grandma Mildred swore that your grandma made a man for her and then stole him."

Anna's entire body stilled. An icy chill swept through the room. "Made a man?"

"Out of dough," Tessa added.

Anna made a squeaking noise in her throat.

"I know," Tessa said and chuckled. "Totally absurd, right?"

"Yeah . . . totally absurd," Anna repeated. Goose bumps rippled over her skin.

Tessa shrugged. "Like I said, she was such a loving person that we overlooked the fact that she might not have had all the crayons in her box." Tessa pointed at the doll. "It made her happy to make these hideous little dolls and give them to us as protection charms. So, like any decent granddaughter, I kept it. When she used to visit me at the office, it made her giddy to see that I'd kept it here, and even now that she's gone, I don't have the heart to toss it. Anyway, enough make-believe stories, let's talk about real life." Tessa opened her laptop, and her fingers zoomed across the keyboard.

Anna pressed a hand to her stomach. So Beatrice had made Grandpa Joe for Tessa's grandma Mildred, and it had backfired? Beatrice couldn't have known that if she created a man, he would show up loving *her*. Was that attraction automatic? Could Grandpa Joe have chosen Mildred instead? Anna's mind drifted to Eli. Was he bound to her because he *couldn't* choose someone else? But even that morning he'd been making decisions that weren't the same as Anna's. His choice in coffee was insignificant, but what if bigger changes were possible? Then Anna remembered the letter tucked away with the secret ingredient in the locked box. Maybe it held answers.

The printer started spitting out paper, and Anna's mind

refocused on Tessa. "Here's the paperwork on the Clarke House." She passed the papers to Anna. "It's a basic agreement. Should you decide to place an offer, you would need to put down earnest money. Mrs. Clarke wants at least a month to move out. As I mentioned, she's willing to negotiate on any of the furniture. It's a standard contract, nothing too quirky, but you can read through it and let me know if you have any questions."

Anna's cell phone rang. She fished it out of her purse. "It's Lily. Hello?"

"Hey," Lily said in a strained voice. "Are you at the bakery right now?"

"No, I'm at Tessa's office."

"What are you doing there?" Lily asked. "Are you looking for a house? Oh, are you trying to find a rental for Eli? Listen, I need to talk to you both. How long are you going to be there?"

"You sound a little stressed. Are you okay? I should be back at the bakery in less than ten minutes. We're wrapping up here."

"Can I meet you at Tessa's? Will you wait there for me? I can come right over."

"Sure." Anna disconnected. "Lily's on her way over. She sounds weird, sorta strung out."

"Too much espresso?" Tessa asked, and Anna shrugged.

Anna flipped through the paperwork. Because of her inheritance money, she had more than enough for a down payment on the house. Her mortgage would be affordable. Mrs. Clarke only wanted a grand for earnest money, and Anna could do that without dipping into her inheritance. Anna leaned back in the chair and placed the paperwork in her lap. She absentmindedly braided her hair and stared at the top page. She never dreamed she'd have an opportunity to live in the Clarke House. She could sign the paperwork right now, but accepting one dream meant forfeiting another. If she used the money for the house, she wouldn't be able to chase the dream of opening her own bakery on the coast. Maybe it was time to let the bakery dream go.

"What's stopping you?" Tessa asked.

Anna looked up. She hesitated. "It's a big decision."

Tessa leaned forward on her elbows and toyed with a ballpoint pen. "Here's what I suggest. You put down the earnest money to let her know you're interested, especially since she agreed to let you make the first offer. I know you like the house, but buying one is a big deal, so think about it. You don't have to sign the contract today."

Anna nodded. Tessa's advice made sense. Maybe in a few more days Anna could sort through the mess that was her life. She didn't know how she would be able to work out the problem of Eli in a few days' time, though. Anna sent the earnest money electronically from her bank to Tessa's real estate account.

The front door of the office opened, and within moments, Lily appeared in the doorway. "Are you buying a house? What is going on here?" Lily asked, pointing at paperwork in Anna's lap. She plopped down in the chair beside Anna. Her manic energy vibrated off her and landed on Anna. Anna rubbed her hands up her arms. Lily's eyes were puffy, and she rarely went out without at least a light application of makeup. Today she wasn't even wearing lip gloss, and there was a sad slump to her shoulders. Lily looked like she hadn't slept in a day or two.

"I haven't bought a house. Not yet. The Clarke House is for sale, and I just sent earnest money," Anna explained.

"I *love* that house," Lily said. She dropped her purse on the floor beside her chair. She wiggled out of her coat. "It's hot in here. Is anyone else hot? I've been sweating all day. What made you decide to buy a house, and such a big one? Are you thinking of moving in with someone?" Lily looked pointedly at Anna.

"Mama's idea," Anna said.

Lily's mouth formed a small O. "Well, that makes a heckuva lot more sense. You can get your earnest money back, can't you, if you change your mind?"

Anna and Tessa both nodded.

"You okay, Lily?" Tessa asked.

Lily averted her gaze and continued, "Tessa, how can you stand being in here all day? This place is like a hospital room. Would it kill you to paint—"

"Lily," Anna interrupted. "Did you have something you wanted to tell us?"

Lily wrung her hands together, and anxiety rippled through the room. Anna and Tessa glanced at each other. The silence lingered, then Anna's cell phone rang.

"I'm sorry," Anna said and winced when she saw the bakery was calling. "I have to answer. Eli is alone at the bakery."

"Eli," Tessa said in a dreamy voice. "Anna told me all about him."

Lily snapped her gaze at Anna. "She did?"

Before she answered the call, Anna blurted, "I didn't tell her much." She sent Lily a look that said she hadn't told Tessa everything. "I don't know that much about him."

"She told me only the important things," Tessa said. "He's single. Can you believe that?"

"I can, actually," Lily said.

"I gotta take this." Anna accepted the call. "Hey, Eli, is everything okay?"

"Hey!" he said. "How's the house? All you dreamed it would be?"

"The house is great. Is something wrong?"

"Nothing's wrong, so don't panic," Eli replied, "But Mrs. Shirley's luncheon is today, and I've already started on the cupcakes—she needs four dozen—and the bakery has been slammed, so I'm low on treats. I hate to call you back from whatever you're doing, but I won't be able to restock *and* get the cupcakes to Mrs. Shirley by one. I'm sorry."

"Dadgumit, I completely forgot, and it's not your fault. Keep the display cases filled, and I'll be right there." Anna disconnected. "I am so sorry, but I really have to go. Four dozen cupcakes have to be delivered today by one, and Eli is drowning." She touched Lily's arm. "Can this wait?"

Lily sighed. "Yeah, it's fine. Nothing's going to change between now and when we talk. Go ahead. We can catch up later."

Anna rubbed her temples. "You sure? I'm sorry to bail out. I can stick around for another few minutes."

"I'd rather not rush this," Lily said. "Go on. I can tell y'all later."

"You can tell me. I'm not going anywhere," Tessa said. "We'll update Anna later."

"I promise to call you as soon as I'm done for the day." Anna stood. "I'll meet you anywhere, and we can talk." She looked at Tessa. "Thanks for showing me the house." She shoved the paperwork into her purse, said a swift good-bye, then hurried the few blocks to the bakery, wondering if she'd done the right thing by sending the earnest money so quickly. Also, what kind of news had caused Lily to look so weary and unlike her normal bubbly self?

CHAPTER 8

LADYFINGERS

ANNA PUT AWAY THE LAST OF THE CLEAN DISHES AND GLANCED at the clock. She had one more hour to get through before she could fall face first onto her bed. Her brain felt like a water balloon ready to burst. She'd barely delivered Mrs. Shirley's four dozen cupcakes on time. She'd sped straight across town, praying for only green lights and no stray dogs. Mrs. Shirley had given her the side eye but thankfully still paid her the agreed-upon amount.

The rest of the day had been a blur of colors and people, like watching confetti swept up in a windstorm. There was a constant flow of customers into the bakery, and many people she'd never seen set foot on her black-and-white tiles. On one hand, she was thankful for the business. On the other hand, she couldn't help but wonder if their patronage had more to do with Eli's charm than with her creations.

Eli avoided her all afternoon. Sure, they'd been swamped, but she could count on one hand the number of times he'd made eye contact with her. His distance only intensified her confusion. She sighed and thought of the Clarke House, of the earnest money she'd put down so easily. She could still change her mind and ask for her money back, but was backing out the best decision? Or was moving into the Clarke House the right step? Anna couldn't quite picture herself living in that grand Victorian alone. She looked at Eli and tried to imagine him in the house with her, but her mind clouded over.

She grabbed replacement napkins from the back room and carried them to the front. Eli was helping the last customer in the shop, and she felt his eyes on her back. When the customer was gone, he spoke.

"What are you putting in your cookies?"

"Which ones?" she asked. The display cases were nearly empty. She wondered whether she should bake more, but it was too close to closing time. Any stragglers could take whatever was left.

"All of them," he said. "These people can't get enough."

Anna looked at him. "I think it's *you* they can't get enough of."

Eli laughed. "Me?" He leaned against the counter and crossed his arms over his chest.

"You and your enchanting personality. You've charmed the whole town," Anna said. She sighed and looked out the windows.

"But not you?"

His words startled her. She wanted to argue and say he had charmed her the most, but the front door opened. As soon as she saw Tessa, she realized she'd forgotten to call Lily.

Anna met Tessa halfway across the bakery. "Is Lily okay? It's been a madhouse today. I was going to call once I closed. What was her news?"

Tessa glanced over Anna's shoulder and waved at Eli. He

waved in return. Then she whispered, "It's not my news to share. You'll have to ask her. It wouldn't be right for me to tell you. Anyway, I just finished for the day myself, and I wanted to ask Eli a question."

During all their years of friendship, Tessa had never known a secret about Lily that Anna didn't. The idea made her skin feel prickly.

Tessa toyed with her hair and walked toward Eli. "Is there any chance you're free tonight?" she asked him.

Anna's mouth fell open.

Eli glanced at Anna and shrugged. "What's happening tonight?"

"I've been thinking"—Tessa turned to look at Anna as if she was seeking support—"that I should paint my office. Anna and Lily have been telling me for weeks that it's unsightly, and it's time I did something about it." She refocused her attention on Eli. "Instead of hiring someone, I thought maybe I could paint it, but I've never painted before. Do you think you could help me with it? I bet you're handy. You look handy. And it shouldn't take long, maybe a couple of hours? I can buy dinner. And wine, too, or beer. Whatever you prefer."

"Wine? To paint an office?" Anna babbled. Her body wouldn't respond. She wanted to walk over to Tessa and tell her to back off, but she just stood and stared like a goldfish floating in a plastic bag at the fair.

"Sure," Eli said. "I've been told I'm handy. And Anna needs some space, so this is a good time to give it to her. What time do you need me?"

Anna shook her head, but no one was looking at her. She hadn't told Eli she needed space.

Tessa bounced twice on the toes of her black flats before composing herself. "If you're free now, I'd love to have you go to the hardware store with me. We can look at paint samples together." She looked at Anna and smiled wide enough to park a full-size sedan in her mouth. "Can you let Eli go early today?" Her hazel eyes pleaded with her best friend.

"Okay," was all Anna could say.

Eli untied his apron, dropped it off in the back, and left the bakery with Tessa. The room stank of burned caramel, and Anna pulled her cell phone from her pocket. No missed calls. No texts. She called Lily and reached her voice mail. A tidal wave of loneliness and confusion crashed over her as she stood in the silence.

After closing down the bakery for the day and trudging upstairs, Anna thought Eli had been right. Maybe she did need some time alone. After showering away the day's sweat and breathing in the orange scent released by the shower steamer, her body started to relax along with her mind. Beatrice always had wisdom to offer Anna over a plate of brown butter blondies or slices of her red velvet cake. What would her grandma tell her now? That thought triggered Anna's memory of Beatrice's letter, which she still hadn't read. She opened the nightstand drawer and removed the bundle of folded pages.

Anna lay sideways on her bed and held the yellowed parchment. She turned on her bedside lamp as nightfall blanketed Mystic Water. Tiny white daises bordered the edges of the powder-blue stationary. Anna rolled onto her back and read.

Dearest Anna,

I hoped to one day tell you this in person and explain the strange gift bestowed on our family many, many generations ago, but I can feel my time here is ending, and your dreams are just beginning to grow. Rather than weigh you down just now when you are on the verge of discovering the path for your own life, I'll leave this story for you. When the time is right, you'll find it and learn the truth that has been waiting for you since you were born.

Our family's gift is so old no one quite remembers when or how it all began. All I can do is tell you what was told to me by my mother when I was sixteen—a story, I'm sure, that was told to her by her mother when she became of age.

Our family is the keeper of an enchanted substance. To me, it is like sugar. Others have called it powder, sand, and even fairy dust. No matter what you call it, its power doesn't change, and the power it contains must be protected and respected. Our family's gift has the power to create. "Create what?" you might ask. Anything the pure heart desires.

Our family has always had cooks, bakers, and medicine women. These professions are the perfect vehicle for using the substance, and this special gift chooses the next person in the family who will guard it. Once in a lifetime, the keeper of the gift is allowed to use it. There are no rules other than this—it can only be used once by the keeper. How and when the keepers use the gift is up to them.

My mother created a house when the family home burned down after a tragic fire. Her aunt created a bridge that gave her family access to a fertile farmland on the other side of a wide river. Even I created with it, and that is why I wish

I could tell you this in person. These stories are difficult enough to believe on their own, and on paper they might read like fairy tales, but I hope you will feel the truth of it in your heart.

You are the next keeper of our family's gift. I hope you will use it well and that it will lead you toward happiness. Guard it, protect it, and always follow your heart. It will never lead you astray.

Anna pressed the parchment to her chest and trembled beneath the paper. She looked over at her closet, which contained a locked box that housed the centuries-old family gift. Would she have chosen a different path if she'd known about the power and purpose of the secret ingredient? Would she have agreed to make a man out of dough? Too late now. That cat was out of the bag and presently spending time with Tessa. Anna kept reading.

My best friend, Mildred, came into the bakery one day during the afternoon lull, and her eyes were so wild I felt sure she'd spent another night with insomnia. Since her breakup with Clayton Barnes, she'd been suffering a great deal. I tried to console her and help her see that there would one day be another man for her, but she wept like a woman who had lost the great love of her life. Someone, her mother I'd guess, told her she was past her prime and men would find her too old to marry. This wasn't true, but Mildred believed her mother knew best.

Mildred moped at the counter and said she wished I could just bake her a man. I hesitated, but only for a few seconds.

Mildred was my dearest friend, and if there was a chance I could help her find true love, how could I say no? I swore her to secrecy and told her about our family's gift.

Mildred doubted at first, but as soon as I brought out the box of glowing golden sugar, her eagerness could barely be contained. She said she wanted me to create a man and that she trusted me to come up with the perfect recipe. I had doubts almost immediately. What if I failed her? What if the man wasn't perfect for her? What if the recipe didn't work at all? But Mildred begged me to at least try.

I only agreed to the plan so she would leave the bakery because I knew the after-school children would be coming soon. She said she would come back that evening, and she and I would make her a man.

Anna assumed they made Grandpa Joe that night. She felt sorry for Mildred, who'd wanted a man of her own to love, but that wasn't how the story went. Grandpa Joe ended up with Beatrice, and although Mildred eventually married, she harbored her bitterness for Beatrice until she died. Anna wanted to read more, but her stomach growled.

After making herself a grilled cheese sandwich oozing with two American cheese slices on smashed-flat, buttered white bread, she curled on the couch and wondered about Eli. What were he and Tessa talking about? Would she ask questions he couldn't answer? Would she get him drunk on wine and find out he could kiss like a dream? Her stomach knotted, but she shoved the sandwich into her mouth. She grabbed her cell phone and dialed Lily's number for the umpteenth time. The call went straight to voice mail. Anna didn't leave another message, and she debated sending another text. Maybe Lily was busy, or maybe she was upset with Anna for not taking fifteen minutes to be a good friend and listen to her news.

Anna did what she always did when she was upset. She baked. As she stirred the batter for double fudge caramel brownies, she reread the contract for the Clarke House. She plucked a postcard from Wildehaven Beach off the fridge and rubbed her thumb over the glossy image. She let her mind wander to what it would be like to have a bakery at the beach, one like the bakery she and her grandparents had frequented every summer. A smile formed on her lips, and she heard the distant call of seagulls.

How could two dreams be so far apart? She never doubted she had done the right thing by returning to Mystic Water and taking over Bea's Bakery, but now she wondered: *Who* had it been the right thing for? Buying the Clarke House and settling down sounded like the logical next step for her, but why did she still feel so restless? Why wasn't she jumping at the chance to own her dream house? Something was holding her back, and Anna was afraid to start digging too deeply. If she dug too far into the foundation, the whole flimsy structure of her current life might come tumbling down.

Anna poured the brownie batter in a greased baking dish and slid the pan into the oven. Then she sat at the table and used her finger to clean the remaining chocolate from the bowl.

After Anna had eaten three brownies, drunk a tall glass of chocolate milk, and become bleary eyed, she finally decided it was time to call it a night. Eli hadn't come home, and it was nearing ten p.m. She was tempted to call Tessa to see how their evening was going, but what if Tessa answered out of breath and giggly like a teenager in the back seat of a car on Look-Off Pointe? She climbed into bed with a stomachache and fell asleep listening for the sounds of Eli's footfalls on the stairs.

CHAPTER 9

BANANA PUDDING

ANNA AWOKE BEFORE HER ALARM CLOCK WENT OFF AND TIP-toed to her bedroom door. Eli was asleep on the couch, one arm thrown over his head and both legs dangling off the edge of the cushions. He didn't look comfortable at all. She should offer him her bed, and she'd take the couch until they could figure out better living arrangements. Maybe she *should* buy the Clarke House, and Eli could have his own bedroom there. The second bedroom was roomy with a lot of light, and he could choose his own paint color. He had joked about living there with her, but that was before he spent an entire evening with Tessa. She didn't even want to entertain what they'd spent the night doing because it made her sick to her stomach. Was this how Mildred felt when Grandpa Joe chose Beatrice?

Anna changed for work and glanced at her cell phone. No missed calls or texts. Baron was taking "the break" seriously, but could she blame him? She hadn't texted or called him either. This was the longest they'd gone without contact in months. She pictured Baron wandering through vineyards, smiling in the sun.

In Anna's mind, a Californian woman meandered beside him, and they shared jokes about travel and spontaneity. Anna felt as though she'd eaten a spoiled egg. She crept down the stairs and eased the door to the bakery shut. This time she would let Eli sleep in.

She started the coffee and turned on the ovens. Saturdays meant a hodgepodge of chocolate treats—chocolate peppermint cocoa, chocolate flavored coffees, éclairs, tarts, turtles, truffles, cookies, fudge, and mini lava cakes. Chocoholics came in on Saturdays to indulge. Anna put on a small pot of hazelnut vanilla coffee especially for Eli. While she was whipping up a batch of fudge, he came down the steps.

"I'm late for work. Does this mean I'm fired?" Eli asked with a sleepy grin. He grabbed his apron from the wall and looped it over his neck.

"Possibly," she said. She grabbed the small carafe and poured him a cup of coffee. "Good morning."

Surprise flitted over Eli's face, then he smiled at her. Her chest expanded, and she sucked in a sweet, sugary breath. In these moments, Anna could pretend Eli was just a man who had walked into her bakery and not someone who'd stepped out of her oven in the middle of the night. He seemed so real—so real she wanted to run her hand down his arm to see if touching him still made her tingle. Did he make Tessa tingle too? She cleared her throat.

"How was last night?" Anna said, returning to the fudge on the stove. "I didn't hear you come in."

"I used my stealthy ninja skills," he teased. "It was fun. Tessa's a nice girl. She has terrible taste in color, though."

Anna's shoulders relaxed. So he thought Tessa was a nice

girl, not a super-sexy woman. Guilt piggybacked on Anna's relief. Tessa was one of her best friends, and it was completely selfish of her to want Eli if Tessa was interested. She poured the fudge into a square ceramic dish. "Tell me she didn't choose gray or high-gloss white."

"Orange. Gumdrop orange." Eli checked the list of today's treats, then gathered ingredients for the turtles. He lifted two glass jars. "Cashews or pecans?"

"I like where your mind is going," Anna said. "Let's go with cashews and—"

"Top them with flaky sea salt?"

Her smile stretched across her face. "It's like you read my mind."

"We can call it Turtles by the Sea," he said with a wink as he returned the pecans to the shelf.

"What color is gumdrop orange?"

"It's 1980s bright. I'd bet it glows in the dark."

Anna shook her head. "Weren't you supposed to help her pick out a color?"

Eli held up his hands in surrender. "There's only so much a man can do when a woman makes up her mind."

"Does it look like the Great Pumpkin, Charlie Brown?"

"Why yes, Linus, it does." Eli drank from his mug.

Anna chuckled. It felt good to share easy conversation with Eli again. She tested the peppermint cocoa. The rich, dark liquid warmed her tongue and put a shine in her green eyes as she swallowed. She sighed. "I would live inside this if I could."

"You and Willy Wonka."

Anna set her mug in the sink and gathered ingredients for the truffles. Today she thought she'd make a variety filled with dark chocolate, raspberry, peanut butter, or almond cream. "I wish he was real."

"I bet you wish you had a golden ticket too," Eli said.

Anna looked over her shoulder, and they shared a smile that made her insides feel hot and gooey like the center of a fresh cinnamon bun.

Tessa called midmorning and asked if Anna could leave the bakery long enough to have lunch with her mom and Lily. Anna had just enough time after the call to whip up Mrs. Andrews's favorite dessert, banana pudding. At a quarter till noon, Anna stepped out of the back room to see Lily and Tessa talking to Eli. Tessa looked like she'd been riding the Ferris wheel at the fair, all rosy cheeks and glossy eyes. In contrast, Lily had subtle shadows smudged beneath her lower lids, and her blond curls spiraled out of control, barely contained by a pink headband.

Anna cradled the banana pudding in her arms and joined them. "I'll be back in an hour or two," she said to Eli. "Call me if you need anything."

Tessa touched Eli's arm. "Anna, you have to swing by and see the office. Eli was so much help." She cast a sweetheart's gaze at Eli and added, "If pastry-chef life doesn't work for you, you could start a career as a painter."

"I'll keep that in mind," he said.

Lily didn't say anything, and she wouldn't meet Anna's gaze. "He said you picked a nice, bright color."

"October Orange," Tessa said. "I think it's actually called Tangerine, but October Orange sounds better."

Lily made a strangled noise in her throat and said, "I'm going to get some air."

Eli tossed a thumb over his shoulder. "Those cookies won't bake themselves. You ladies have fun."

"I hope to see you soon," Tessa said as Anna followed Lily outside.

"You okay?"

Lily shook her head. "I've been pukey all morning. No offense, but the smells in the bakery were making my stomach turn."

"That's not good. Why don't you go home? Tessa and I can go to lunch. You probably shouldn't be around Mrs. Andrews if you're not well."

Lily saw her reflection in the bakery windows, and she tried unsuccessfully to pat down her hair. "It's not contagious. It'll pass."

Tessa leaned on the door and slipped outside. "Eli is so great, Anna. He's not like other guys."

"I wonder why," Lily said cryptically, and Anna narrowed her eyes, but Tessa seemed oblivious. They climbed into Tessa's car and drove to the Andrews home.

After months of treatment, Carolyn Andrews's skin was pale and pulled too tightly over her thin frame, but her hazel eyes were alert and bright, and her smile was easy. She sat in the airy sunroom, which was filled with midday October sunlight and warmth. The tropical plants flourished, and the gray, overweight house cat lounged beneath Carolyn's chair.

Anna followed Lily and Tessa into the sunroom but stopped

when she noticed a familiar face in a set of photographs on a sideboard. Anna put down the banana pudding and lifted the frame. "Is this Grandma Beatrice?"

Carolyn motioned for Anna to bring over the frame. Reading glasses hung from a silver chain around her neck, and she lifted them onto the bridge of her slender nose. "Yes, and that's Mildred, Tessa's grandmother. My mother-in-law, may she rest in peace."

Beatrice and Mildred stood with linked arms, both smiling widely at the camera, looking like two best friends caught in a moment of joy. "I didn't know they were friends until the other day," Anna admitted.

"Yes, they were very close. Childhood friends, I believe," Carolyn said. "But they had a falling-out. This is one of the few remaining pictures of the two of them, and they look so happy, don't they? I hope you girls always stay close and don't let men drive you apart." Carolyn handed the frame back to Anna so she could return it to the sideboard. "Men certainly aren't worth losing friendships over."

Once everyone sat at the round table, Carolyn said, "My three favorite girls. I'm so glad you were all free for lunch today. It's been too long. I made chicken salad. Tessa, do you mind grabbing the lunch from the kitchen?" Carolyn adjusted herself in the chair. "Lily, you look peaky today. Are you working too hard at the boutique?"

Lily patted her unruly curls. "I'll be okay. I haven't been sleeping well. Work is good, though. Steady, but not too many long hours."

"Have you tried chamomile tea?" Carolyn asked. "Add a bit of whiskey to really settle the mind." Anna and Lily both looked surprised, but Carolyn raised a finger to her lips and winked. "You can take the girl out of Tennessee, but you can't take Tennessee out of the girl. My excuse is that at least it's weaker than the moonshine my daddy used to make."

"I usually prefer coffee," Lily said. "But I haven't been able to drink it for the past few days."

Anna felt a twinge of guilt. She and Lily still hadn't talked about whatever was troubling her, and something was definitely wrong with her best friend.

"I heard Baron took a job in California," Carolyn said.

Anna resisted the urge to sigh. "Yes, ma'am."

"I was sorry to hear that," Carolyn said. "You two have been together for a while, and I know how much it hurts to break up. We can always learn lessons from relationships. Baron helped you try new things, and you kept him grounded. I'm not surprised that you've decided to move on, though. I know you'll find a man better suited for you, if you want one. Baron wouldn't have been a good fit for Tessa either."

Lily's head popped up. "You knew about her liking him first?" She glanced at Anna.

Carolyn smiled and stared out the window as though recalling a fond memory. Her short dark hair was shot full of gray now, and it was impossible to miss the frailty in her movements. "You know Tessa has always been a little boy crazy."

Anna and Lily chuckled. "We like to say she's eager and open for new opportunities," Anna said.

Carolyn laughed. "That's a gentle way of saying she is easily distracted by shiny things. Baron was this handsome, adventurous boy, so full of life and energy. Tessa has a way of finding new people as soon as they arrive in town. It's like she has an internal sonar that leads her straight to them. From the first moment she saw Baron, she was crazy about him. She'd never smiled so much in her life. Well, not since the boy before him, of course."

"But they weren't really *dating*," Lily said.

"*Not yet* is what she kept saying, but she had high hopes. But you came home, Anna, and he could see nothing but you." Carolyn folded her hands together on the table. "But that's the way life is, full of unexpected entrances and exits. I know you'll miss him." She patted Anna's hand. "But he was much too flighty for you. He was lots of fun, I'm sure, but I'm surprised you tolerated him for so long," she added with a flick of her wrist. "I imagine a different kind of man for my Tessa too. Someone who keeps her on her toes, who challenges her, but I don't believe he's found her yet." Carolyn lowered her voice to a whisper. "She mentioned a new employee at the bakery, and I could hear in her voice that she's interested. Is he a good guy?"

"He's the perfect guy," Lily answered, but under the table she poked her finger into Anna's thigh, meaning, *He's perfect for you.*

Carolyn shrugged. "Only time will tell." She glanced over her shoulder at the covered dish on the sideboard. "Would it be too much to hope you've brought banana pudding?"

"Just for you," Anna said with a smile that felt stiff. She couldn't swallow past the jawbreaker-size knot in her throat. Lily could be wrong. Eli might be the perfect man for Tessa. Tessa wasn't shy about putting herself in front of him, and Eli was definitely taking notice.

Tessa breezed in with sandwiches, chips, and homemade lemonade on a tray. The conversation stayed light and easy, but Anna's mind kept drifting between Eli and her future. She felt stuffed full of questions yet starving for answers.

CHAPTER 10

PEACHES AND CREAM PIE

ELI LOOKED RELAXED WHEN ANNA RETURNED TO THE BAKERY after lunch. The display cases were still half stocked, and the OREO cake she'd made that morning was half gone beneath the glass dome on the counter. Anna had barely stepped onto the black-and-white tiles when Tessa barreled in behind her, nearly smacking her with the door.

"Oh, sorry, Anna," Tessa said. "I was on my way into the office, and I had a great idea. Let's all of us go out tonight. Maybe Fred's Diner? Lily said she and Jakob could go."

Anna noticed that Tessa was only looking at Eli. He turned his blue eyes on Anna. "We don't have any plans, do we? No cakes to make, no parties to prep for?"

"Are you including me?" Anna asked.

Tessa giggled—*giggled like a teenager*—and smacked Anna on the arm. "Of course I'm including you. Both of you."

"I'm in," Eli said, and Tessa's grin stretched so wide Anna worried her face might split apart like a plastic Easter egg.

"Easy there," Anna mumbled. Then she nodded and said, "Me too."

"Let's meet at seven." Tessa looked at both of them. "No complaints? Awesome, see you then. I can't wait!" She touched Anna's arm. "Thanks again for coming over today. It meant the world to Mama. Gotta run. Have a great day, you two." Then she rushed out of the bakery as fast as she'd rushed in.

"Did you feed her Pixy Stix for lunch?" Eli asked. "She's really excited about something."

Anna knew exactly what Tessa was excited about: more time with Eli, and he didn't seem to have objections. "How did we do today? Did you win over any new customers? As if there is anyone left in town who hasn't been by to see you." Anna eyed the half-empty cases. "Maybe I should whip up a few more batches today. We normally sell out of the peanut butter truffles first." She counted the remaining truffles in the case. "I'll bake another two dozen of the triple chocolate chip cookies too."

"The éclairs were a big hit," he said. "People couldn't quit bragging about how good they were." He smirked at her.

"You made the éclairs."

"I know."

Anna rolled her eyes and went into the kitchen. She knew Eli had followed her when she breathed in the scents of spicy chocolate and warm, sticky sugar. She watched him gather the tools they'd need to start the truffles and cookies. He looked real enough, solid and human, and her mama was right—he was too handsome. She hadn't wanted to admit it, not even to herself, but she *liked* Eli . . . a lot. And she didn't want him to be anywhere but in the bakery with her.

Anna wasn't dense. She knew Tessa was very interested in Eli. She hadn't seen Tessa this giddy over a boy since David Newman moved to Mystic Water in the sixth grade. Tessa was excitable about every new dating prospect, but her eagerness about Eli was next level. But wasn't Eli Anna's? Hadn't she made him because Baron was a jerk? Baron, whom Tessa had also been very interested in. The words *boyfriend stealer* rose up like indigestion in her chest.

Eli mashed his finger between her eyebrows, pulling her from her thoughts.

"Stop thinking so hard," he said. "You're going to wrinkle your face permanently."

She smacked away his hand, but she was smiling and losing herself in his too-blue eyes.

Fred's Diner was located on the edge of town where the streetlights thinned, and its glowing neon sign beckoned locals and travelers alike. It was the epitome of an all-American diner. The classic menu offered everything from hamburgers ten different ways to chicken fingers to hot dogs with or without cheese and chili. There was country-fried steak, a double-decker tuna melt, and loaded french fries, just to name a few of the crowd favorites. They also served malts and shakes, apple pie à la mode, and a banana split large enough for a party.

When Anna and Eli arrived, Fred's Diner was already packed with the Saturday-night crowd. They found the others sitting in a semicircle booth for six in the far back corner. Tessa's face lit up as though someone shone a flashlight down from the ceiling. Anna imagined a speech bubble appearing above Tessa's head saying, "He's here! He's here! He's here!"

Tessa wore a carnation-pink shirt and matching lipstick. It complemented the rose undertones in her dewy complexion. Her excitement brought out a youthfulness that made her eyes bright and eager. Tessa looked at Eli and patted the red vinyl beside her. Eli slid in, and Anna sat beside him on the end. Jakob and Lily were across from them in the half circle.

Jakob Connelly, Lily's steady boyfriend for the past four years, leaned casually against the back of the booth with his arm hooked around Lily's shoulders. He oozed calm with a healthy dollop of sex appeal. Jakob's dark hair looked as if Lily had been running her hands through it, but he still managed to look presentable and clean in a pressed button-down shirt and khakis. The dimple in his left cheek reminded Anna of a mischievous little boy. His affable nature had always made him one of the most popular boys in school, and he was mostly oblivious to the stares he incited from women on a daily basis. Jakob welcomed them, but Lily appeared to be lost in her own thoughts, barely acknowledging their arrival.

Anna introduced Eli and Jakob with slight apprehension. Jakob was good friends with Baron; would Jakob feel weird about Anna being with Eli? Her worries were unfounded. Jakob apparently thought Eli was Tessa's date and said as much, which caused Anna to sag against the booth. She needed to pull herself together and be happy for her best friend, but her stomach ached with the realization that Eli wasn't interested in her.

Jakob quizzed Eli on his sports preferences and realized they had a lot in common, which shocked Anna because she knew very little about sports. Yet another indication that Eli was morphing into his own person with his own likes and dislikes. Jakob and Eli spent the first few minutes sharing their opinions on quarterbacks and fumbles and biased referees, laughing and talking to each other like they'd been friends for years. The more Eli talked, the more Anna's neck prickled. How could he possibly have that kind of knowledge? Was he absorbing the world like a sponge?

The waitress bustled over for drink orders, and Anna ordered a root beer float. Tessa ordered a Long Island Iced Tea, and Jakob ordered a beer.

"I'll have what he's having," Eli said.

Jakob nudged Lily. "What about you? Want a beer too?"

"No!" Tessa blurted, looking startled at her own outburst.

Lily narrowed her eyes at Tessa and then looked at the waitress. "Just water for me."

Jakob's expression turned serious. "Still not feeling good?"

"I don't want to push it," she said, and he squeezed her shoulder. "I'll be fine."

Anna tapped her foot against Lily's shin. "You okay?" Anna mouthed when Lily looked. Everyone was busy looking over the menus.

Lily discreetly shook her head and mouthed, "Later."

They all ordered greasy diner fare, and Anna sucked down her root beer float, wishing she'd ordered something stronger. Tessa had touched Eli at least a hundred times, and now Tessa's hand was propped on his forearm while she talked. Tessa had also turned into a laughing machine. Eli was suddenly the most hilarious person on the planet. When he could, Jakob tried to get a word in.

Jakob nursed his beer, and when Tessa paused after

describing a recent mold problem affecting real estate in the area, Jakob took the opportunity. "So, Eli, you work at the bakery? Tessa mentioned you're on your way to another job that's starting soonish. Pastry chef, I assume, like Anna?"

Eli swirled the beer in his bottle before taking another sip. "Actually, I haven't decided what I want to do next. I'm between jobs right now. I have a soft spot for pastry, but I was just telling Anna the other day that I've always wanted to own a sandwich shop. A classic deli with a side of gourmet options. We loved that deli in New York, didn't we?" he asked, leaning into Anna's arm.

Vanilla ice cream dribbled onto Anna's chin. She snatched a napkin from the dispenser and wiped her face.

Eli shrugged. "Maybe a combination deli and bakery, where people could have a meal and enjoy desserts too. A place near the ocean."

Anna felt like someone had pushed her beneath the broiler. Her skin itched. Then a gust of cold, briny air blew her auburn hair from her shoulders. Eli was creating his own life full of his own dreams and desires. He was no longer just a man she had created.

"Could I order, say, alfalfa sprouts on seven-grain bread with the crusts cut off?" Jakob asked and finished his beer.

"I pegged you as a club sandwich kind of guy," Eli joked. "You come to my place, and I'll make you the best gourmet sandwich you've ever had."

Jakob clinked his beer bottle against Eli's. "Deal. And if you end up by the ocean, even better. Anna, didn't your family used to have a condo at Wildehaven Beach?"

In her periphery, Anna could see Eli watching her. "They didn't own it, but we did stay in the same place every year. It's a great beach."

"Heard they have an awesome bakery too," Eli added.

The food arrived, and Anna stared at her bacon cheeseburger. She wasn't sure she could stomach it. Tessa filled Eli's ears with descriptions about the myriad properties in town that would be perfect for his deli. She couldn't give him an ocean breeze, but she could give him a cheery location and a promise to visit every day.

Anna chewed a french fry and noticed Lily was pushing her country-fried steak around with her fork. Her skin was olive drab, and her spiral curls drooped. She moved her plate away and excused herself to the bathroom. Anna waited a minute and then followed.

Anna stepped into the bathroom, which housed two stalls and a single sink made of Carolina-blue ceramic. Lily flushed the toilet and emerged looking ashen and wobbly.

"You think you have the flu?" Anna asked.

Lily made a scoffing noise in her throat. "Hardly." She threw cold tap water into her face and washed out her mouth.

"What is it then? You look like you feel terrible."

"Thanks," Lily snapped. She dried her face with a brown paper towel and poked at the skin beneath her eyes.

Anna leaned against the wall. The room reeked of hot grease and roasted espresso beans. "What's going on?"

"It isn't a good time." Lily tried to walk past Anna.

Anna grabbed her arm. "Tessa knows."

"Because she had time to listen to me."

"That's not fair," Anna argued. "You know I had to go back to work. I called you, but you didn't answer, and you didn't respond to any of my texts."

"I was mad at you," Lily said. "And puking." Frustration rippled off her like summer heat on asphalt.

"I'm sorry, but I've had a lot going on too. We made a man a few days ago, and he's living with me, and I have feelings for him, and Tessa is clearly in love with him, and Baron hasn't called me in days." Anna's eyes slowly filled with tears, and she blinked them furiously. "My life is a mess." She felt as though she'd eaten marshmallow fondant and couldn't swallow.

"It's not all about you," Lily said. Tears sparkled in her restless eyes. "You're not the only one with big problems."

Anna gripped the edge of the sink to steady her legs. This was all wrong. She wasn't supposed to be fighting with her best friend in a bathroom that stank of yesterday's Philly cheesesteak and angst.

Then Lily's shoulders slumped, and she rubbed her hands down her face. "I'm sorry, Anna." She flipped the lock on the bathroom door to prohibit anyone else from entering. "I didn't mean to snap at you. I'll tell you what I told Tessa, and I swear if you react the way she did, I'll deck you and leave you on this sticky floor." She managed a rueful smile.

Lily exhaled the same moment Anna's cell phone rang in her back pocket. She reached to silence it and saw that it was Baron calling.

"It's Baron," Anna said, swaying on her feet.

Lily made a shooing motion with her hand. "Answer it. I'm not going anywhere."

Anna hesitated. "No, he can leave a message. You're more—"

"Oh for crying out loud, answer it and see what the idiot wants."

Anna obeyed and accepted the call. "Hello," she said.

"Anna-Banana!" Baron said, his words muffled by overpowering background noise. "It's been a minute . . . how're you?"

"I'm good," she said, turning up the volume on her phone. "How have you been?"

"Busy," he said. "I've been busy." His words slurred together.

Anna's eyes widened. She looked at Lily and mouthed, "I think he's drunk."

Baron continued, "It's been great. Busy, though."

"You mentioned that," Anna said. "Where are you? It's so loud I can barely hear you."

"The Electric Lounge," he said. "It's great. You'd love it. Drinks, dancing, lots of lights. The hottest dance club in town."

"I don't like dance clubs," Anna mumbled.

"Valerie! Over here," Baron shouted.

"Who's Valerie?"

"Hey, gotta go," he said. "Call you later."

"Okay, sure, call me—"

Baron disconnected. Anna stared at someone's marker scribbles on the stall wall. It read: "In case of emergency, call Candi." Anna wondered if Candi could heal the sick feeling seeping through every vein, scalding her from the inside. "He's at a club with someone named Valerie. I heard her laughing in the background. He's definitely drunk." Anna choked and leaned over to put her head between her knees. "That root beer float is burning its way back up. I think I'm going to puke."

"Maybe you're pregnant too," Lily said.

Anna popped up so fast she stumbled into the paper towel dispenser and cracked the side of her head. She looked at Lily with wide eyes. The light dimmed, and a burning October breeze, smelling of brittle leaves and dark earth set afire, wriggled beneath the locked door.

"You're pregnant?"

Lily nodded, looking as breakable and frightened as a porcelain doll dangling from a second-floor window. Anna pulled her into a hug and held on until Lily relaxed. "Does Jakob know?" she asked.

"No," Lily said. "I'm terrified to tell him. His mama will likely pull her dyed-blond hair from the roots. She'll debate whether to sew the scarlet letter to my chest. We're not married. We're not even engaged. It's so scandalous."

Anna shoved her cell phone into her back pocket. "First of all, Hester Prynne was married to another man when she had her affair."

"Who the hell is Hester Prynne?" Lily said, wiping at her tears.

"*The Scarlet Letter.* Never mind. Jakob adores you," Anna said, grabbing toilet paper from a stall and handing it to Lily. "We're adults, not teenagers. So you're pregnant, so what? It's a big deal, sure, but it's not the end of the world. Jakob would marry you in a heartbeat."

"He's about to make partner at the law firm. I don't want him not to get it," Lily cried. "They're so conservative there."

"That's absurd," Anna said. "They don't give a hoot about Jakob's personal life. This isn't the 1800s. He doesn't even have to tell them anything anyway."

Lily clutched Anna's arm. "What about the other night? I got so drunk on that rum." She looked sincerely stricken. "Do you think—do you think I harmed my baby? I would never forgive myself."

"Oh, Lily," Anna said and tugged her into a quick hug. Then she pulled away and made Lily look at her. "One night of rum isn't going to hurt your beautiful baby, okay? You'll make yourself sick worrying about that for no reason. From here on out, you can eat clean, stay away from anything harmful, and take the best care of your body that you can." Anna inhaled slowly. "We'll get you through this and figure out the best time to tell Jakob."

Lily wiped at her eyes. "Thanks for not reacting like Tessa. She freaked out so bad I puked in her office."

"You added a layer of color. An improvement," Anna said. "From what I hear the new color is intense."

Lily laughed, and the air in the room lightened. "Don't go in there. It's blinding. For hours afterward, everywhere I looked was streaked with orange."

"I'm glad you're not going to punch me and leave me on this floor because I think that gum has been there for at least a month."

"Longer," Lily said.

Someone knocked on the door. "Y'all okay?" Tessa asked.

Lily checked her reflection in the mirror and pinched her cheeks for color. She nodded, and Anna unlocked the door.

"Just peachy," Anna said as she opened the door. If peaches could be confused and scared and clinging to their best friends so they didn't drown.

CHAPTER 11

BLACK STICKY GINGERBREAD

THE NEXT MORNING ANNA SAT WRAPPED IN A QUILT, CRADLING a mug of hot chocolate, in the cubby of her apartment's bay window. She'd convinced Eli to sleep in her bed while she took the couch. It was eight thirty a.m., and he was still snoozing away in the comfort of a space that fit his tall frame. Lots of people took it easy on Sunday mornings, but Eli's sleeping late might have had more to do with the fact that he'd stayed out until nearly eleven p.m. helping Tessa. During dinner at the diner, Tessa had mentioned wanting to rearrange the furniture in her condo to improve the layout, and Eli had offered to help without Tessa's prompting.

Anna had been tucked in on the couch when he'd come home. She'd wanted to ask him about his evening, but he seemed out of sorts and exhausted when he finally shuffled through the door. He hadn't even objected to taking the bed from her. He thanked her and disappeared into the bedroom without saying anything else.

Anna placed her mug on a cookbook and picked up the contract for the Clarke House. She rested it on her knees and flipped through the pages. The logical next step would be to sign the papers and buy it. At least her mother would be thrilled, but a part of her heart still balked at the idea of using the inheritance money to stay put in Mystic Water. Beatrice had always encouraged Anna to follow her heart and answer its call. But these days it felt easier to comply with what everyone else wanted, keep them happy and satisfied and stuffed full of cookies.

When Anna closed her eyes, a memory of Beatrice and Grandpa Joe sitting on a boardwalk in Wildehaven Beach came to her. She saw them sharing a slice of key lime pie and looking for dolphins surfacing from the deeper waters. Even after all this time, the ocean breeze called to her like nothing else did. She missed those summers spent with her grandparents, when she felt as free as the pelicans sunning all day on the pier or bobbing with the gentle, rolling ocean waves.

Anna exhaled a breath against the cold windowpane. Then she drew a question mark into the fogged glass. She heard Eli rustling around in the bedroom, his bare feet on the hardwood. She turned to see him step into the living room.

His hair stuck out from one side of his head, and he had the sleepy, innocent blue eyes of a little boy. The scents of sugar and cinnamon filled the room.

"Good morning, Sleeping Beauty," she said.

Eli grinned and pointed to the window. "What's the question of the day?"

Anna glanced at the fading question mark on the pane. "What to do with my life."

Eli moved a few books so he could sit next to her in the bay window. "Is this about the Clarke House?"

Anna exhaled and fogged up the corner of the windowpane. She drew a frowny face. "Yes and no. It's not *only* about the house. Mama would be pleased as punch if I bought it."

"Because that would mean you're here to stay."

Anna nodded.

"She *would* love that," Eli agreed. "But what's right for you? What do you want to do?" He picked up her mug and sipped her hot chocolate.

"I already put down earnest money. I should buy it. It's a great house." She looked at him and resisted the urge to reach out and pat down his wild hair. "But what do I want? I'd like to buy the house *and* have a bakery at the beach. Not possible, though. I can't have my cake—"

"And eat it too?" Eli finished her hot chocolate. "You want more?" She shook her head. He walked into the kitchen and refilled the mug for himself. "Why don't you call Lily and drive to the beach? The bakery is closed today. Go breathe in the ocean air. Maybe it'll help clear your head."

Anna uncrossed her legs and stood. "I like that idea. I don't have any plans today." She folded the quilt and draped it over the chair. Then she grabbed her cell phone and called Lily.

"Good morning!" Anna said, already feeling her spirits rising at the thought of taking a day trip to the beach. "Any chance you want to take a drive to Wildehaven Beach with me?"

Lily groaned. "I wish I could," she said. "But this morning sickness is no joke. I still haven't told Jakob what's really going on. He thinks I have the flu, and he's taking his mother hen duty seriously."

"I'm so sorry," Anna said. "Does anything help with the nausea?"

"I've been eating ginger lollipops like a champ. They help a little. It'll get better as the morning goes, but not until closer to lunch probably," Lily said. "I don't want to hold you up. If you decide not to go today, I promise I'll go with you once this nausea passes, which I hope is sooner rather than later."

Anna told Lily she'd check in later and hung up. "She doesn't feel well today. Would you want to go with me?"

Eli looked surprised she'd asked him. "I'd love to." He caught his reflection in the oval mirror in the kitchen. "Whoa, look at my hair. Looks like I had a rough night." His laughter filled the apartment, and the room swelled with the joy of it.

"How *was* your night?" she asked, chuckling as he tried to smooth down the unruly cowlick.

Eli stopped laughing and rubbed the back of his neck. He stared at the postcards on the refrigerator and reached out to touch the one that read Wish You Were Here. "Not much to report. We moved her stuff."

"Until eleven p.m.? Did you rearrange her entire house?" Anna asked, still smiling.

Eli cleared his throat and shrugged. "Not really. We hung out for a while afterward, then I came home." He finished his mug of cocoa and put the mug in the sink. "I'm gonna jump in the shower." Eli passed her, and Anna caught a whiff of overdone cookies.

His shift in mood was obvious, and it appeared to be connected to his evening with Tessa. What had happened between them last night?

⁓ℰ⌒

Wildehaven Beach was approximately an hour-and-a-half trip down a two-lane south Georgia highway. Anna wanted to cook a quick breakfast before they left, but Eli suggested they stock up on convenience-store snacks for their road trip. She hadn't eaten junk food for breakfast on purpose since summertime days spent with Lily and Tessa growing up, but Eli convinced her it would be an adventure. After sharing a large bag of Doritos, a SNICKERS, a bottle of Coca-Cola, and Skittles, Anna and Eli were singing at the top of their lungs, and it felt good to let go of the stress for a while.

During breaks from singing, they talked about places they'd like to visit, their favorite foods, and movies they wished they'd starred in. Eli's answers didn't exactly match Anna's, and rather than finding the information disturbing, she was beginning to feel comforted by the fact that Eli was becoming his own man. Her worry over what to do with him lessened because it was clear that Eli was making his own decisions apart from her. She wasn't responsible for Eli's well-being, and maybe that meant he didn't feel obligated to be with her. Maybe he *wanted* to spend the day with her at the beach.

When they arrived in Wildehaven Beach, Anna parked behind the bakery, and they followed the sidewalk until it connected with the boardwalk. The breeze off the ocean was chilly, and Anna zipped her jacket all the way to the top. She and Eli stepped onto the boardwalk, and instead of going straight to the bakery, they walked toward the water. An older man tossed a bright green tennis ball to his golden retriever, while a young woman jogged down the beach. Otherwise, the beach was deserted. Gulls soared through the air like feathered kites and skittered across the wet sand, dodging the waves lumbering in. Farther out, a group of brown pelicans floated on the undulating waves like toy boats in a bathtub.

Anna untied her shoes, stuffed her socks in her jacket pocket, and rolled up her jeans. Then she bounced into the cold sand. It squished between her toes, and she shivered. Closing her eyes, she breathed in the smell of the ocean, all fresh salty air and new possibilities.

"Last one to the water has to drink chunky buttermilk," Eli challenged.

When she opened her eyes, he was already sprinting for the wet sand. Anna yelled, "Cheater!" But she laughed and followed him, pumping her arms like a steam engine and closing the distance between them. Eli reached the water first and kicked a spray of water in her direction.

"You're faster than I imagined," he said, bending over and sucking in cool air. "The intense expression on your face was intimidating."

Anna kicked water at him. "High school track team," she said. She pointed at his legs. "Slim chance of winning when I'm racing against those mile-long legs." She laughed and dodged a kick of water. "You cheated, so I'm not drinking chunky buttermilk."

Eli laughed. Then he turned and looked in the direction of the boardwalk. "Which one is it?"

Anna stood beside him, breathing in the scent that was purely his. She pointed straight ahead. "The one there on the end with the blue-and-white awning. Aren't the windows gorgeous? There's so much light all day, but he used heat-reflecting windows to keep out the summer heat."

Eli used his toe and wrote in the sand. Anna followed behind him, reading his words until the entire sentence was complete: *You could live here.* She grabbed his arm and pulled him toward the boardwalk.

"Let's go have a look," Anna said. "Mr. Cornfoot and his wife, Mel, might be working today. They've owned the place forever."

At the tap at the end of the boardwalk, Anna and Eli washed sand from their feet with freezing cold water. Anna jumped around and complained of the cold until her feet were nestled back in her socks and shoes. As they neared the bakery, she discovered that what she'd thought from afar was a sign advertising the day's specials was actually a For Sale sign. She stumbled a step and latched on to Eli's arm.

"Easy there," he said, covering her hand with his. When he saw her face, he asked, "What is it?"

"They're selling the bakery," she said and pointed at the sign in the window. A surprising surge of disappointment nearly knocked her over. Seeing the sign felt like a piece of her child-hood was breaking off and being washed out to sea.

"Let's go inside," Eli said. "We can ask about it."

Anna smelled fresh oatmeal raisin cookies before she even opened the bakery's door. Warm air rolled out to greet them, and a man popped his head out from the kitchen. His weathered face stretched into a smile.

Timothy Cornfoot was tall and lithe from years of playing tennis. His hair was nearly white with slight undertones of the dark brown he wore in his younger days. His eyes were a rich brown and inviting, reminding Anna of smooth dark chocolate. "Anna? Little Anna O'Brien, is that you?" he said, wiping his hands on his apron. "This is a surprise. We haven't seen you in quite some time."

"I had the day off today, so I thought I'd visit," she said. "It smells so good in here." She walked to the display cases and smiled. She tapped the glass with her fingertip. "Mr. Cornfoot makes the best cream-filled donuts I've ever had." She debated asking for one, but she was still full of Doritos and chocolate.

Timothy slid his hands into his apron pockets. "That's kind of you to say, Anna. But after forty years, I was bound to perfect something. How's your grandma doing? I haven't seen her for even longer. The bakery keeping her busy? Mel and I know how that is."

Anna's heart shuddered. Timothy didn't know, but how could he? They were miles away from Mystic Water, and small-town word only stretched so far. "She passed away two years ago. I've been running the bakery."

"I'm so sorry to hear that," Timothy said with deep sincerity. "She was a wonderful woman, but you know that. And you took over the bakery, did you? I'm a little surprised. Not surprised that you would end up baking somewhere, but the last time I saw Beatrice, she seemed sure you'd find your future somewhere else."

"She did?"

Timothy nodded. "I bet taking over her bakery means a lot to your family and to the town. We know how special small businesses are to the locals, especially the ones who have been around for decades. It's hard to let them go."

"I saw the sign. You're selling?" Anna asked.

"It's time," he answered.

"The cake is perfection," Melanie Cornfoot announced as she breezed out of the kitchen, infusing the serious conversation with happiness. She was a beautiful woman in her late sixties. Her hair fell past her shoulders, salt and pepper, and Anna thought she resembled Emmylou Harris. "Well, hello there. My word, is that Anna O'Brien? Get over here, you beautiful girl."

Mel came around the counter and pulled Anna into a tight hug. When she asked about Beatrice and Anna relayed the news, Mel squeezed her harder and longer. When she finally let Anna go, she noticed Eli. "Anna brought a friend. I'm Mel Cornfoot," she said to Eli. "Sounds like you might have already met my husband, Timothy."

Eli introduced himself. "I work with Anna in Mystic Water. I'm her assistant. Nice to meet you both."

"Can I get you two anything?" Timothy asked. "I have coffee or hot chocolate, and Mel's coffee cake is perfection, as she mentioned."

"I never turn down cake," Eli said. "And I'd like a hot chocolate, please." He pulled out his wallet and placed a few bills on the counter.

"He's more than an assistant," Anna said. "He can do everything I can, and his éclairs will change your life. Hot chocolate, please." While Timothy prepared two mugs, Anna looked at Eli and shook her head. "How can you possibly be hungry?"

"How can you possibly turn down cake?" he said.

Mel returned from the kitchen with a coffee Bundt cake on a mint-green cake plate. The room filled with the smells of warm vanilla cake, cinnamon, and walnuts.

Anna thanked Mel for the slice of cake even though she didn't have an ounce of space left in her stomach. Eli took a bite and closed his eyes. "This is amazing," he said. "Don't suppose you'd give me the recipe?"

Mel ushered everyone to a table, and Anna continued the earlier conversation. "Why are you selling?"

Mel sighed and reached for Timothy's hand. "It's been forty-two years," she said. "Long years full of highs and lows. I've never regretted the decision to spend my life doing this, but it feels like it's time to let it go and start the next chapter."

"We could work until our bodies refuse to take another step," Timothy agreed. "But why not spend the rest of our days doing all the things we couldn't do while we were here?"

"Are you sad to let it go?" Anna asked. "Do you feel like you're letting people down?"

Eli reached his arm behind Anna's chair and looped it around her shoulders. He gave her shoulder a squeeze. She glanced at him and knew he understood the root of her question. His kind expression warmed her.

"All change has the possibility to be sad at first," Mel said. "In order to start something new, you have to let go of something else. One thing has to die for something new to be born in its place, so, yes, there is some sadness in that, but also hope. Nothing can ever take away all the memories we've had here. What we created here never dies. We take all of it with us when we go. And the people we've served here will always have those memories too. Like you and your grandparents. We did hope to sell this place to another baker, but so far we've had no takers."

"We're giving ourselves another month," Timothy said, "to find a possible buyer who wants to run a bakery, but after that, we've agreed to sell the building to whoever comes along."

"And if we find a willing baker, we're leaving all of our recipes," Mel said. "I won't have time to make cake while Timothy and I are globetrotting. I'm planning on people making cake for *me*." She patted Timothy's thigh and smiled.

"Since we're here," Eli said, finishing off his slice of cake at record speed, "and we also love baking, want to show us around your shop? We have friends from college, and we could put out feelers and see if anyone is looking for a beach bakery."

"I like the sound of that," Mel said. "You and Anna can give me your expert opinion on the state of things around here."

Eli grabbed his empty plate and stood. "I'm right behind you."

Anna heard Mel describing their top-of-the-line appliances. The kitchen had been completely updated two years ago, and it was amazing. The industrial-size mixer alone was enough to tempt any baker to buy the place. The lucky owner could make dozens of batches of treats at once. Bea's Bakery still had most of the original appliances and was smaller in scale. Working in this shop would cut Anna's preparation time in half, if not more.

Anna looked out the window at the white-capped waves rolling onto the shore. The bakery wasn't the only thing she loved about Wildehaven Beach. She could smell the ocean amid the bakery scents. It settled around her like handfuls of thrown glitter, and her shoulders relaxed.

"I'll miss this place," Timothy said. "But it's time I kept my promise to Mel and showed her the world. We've been happy here, but I'm ready for a new adventure myself."

"Me too," Anna said honestly. She looked toward the kitchen just as Eli popped his head out.

"You coming? I'm already sold," Eli said with a huge grin, and Mel laughed from the kitchen. "Anna, *you* would fit in that mixer."

After Mel gave them both a tour of the kitchen, its enormous pantry, and the two walk-in coolers, she said, "You two should enjoy the sun today. Take a walk."

"Take Eli to Tucker's Pier," Timothy said. "Mel, why don't you pack them a bag of treats to go?"

"You don't have to do that," Anna said.

"Nonsense," Mel said as she slid open the display cases. "Eli, come over here and tell me your favorites." He bounded over, and they whispered among themselves as the to-go bag grew fatter and fatter.

Anna thanked Timothy and Mel for the treats, and she and Eli stepped outside into the cool October air. The sun warmed her cheeks, and she exhaled a restful sigh. Would every day at a beach bakery feel like this one—perfect and peaceful?

"Timothy and Mel are great," Eli said as he strolled toward the beach. He shifted the bag to his other arm. "I can see why you love this place."

"Aren't they?" Anna said. "You know I can't resist a bakery, and they used to let me hang out with them for hours. Before I knew it, Mel had me in the kitchen whipping up brownies. We had so much fun, and it gave my grandparents time to themselves." Anna smiled at the memory. She untied her shoes, and Eli passed her the bag while he took off his shoes. "Whoa, this thing feels like a bowling ball. If we eat all of this, we'll end up in a sugar coma."

"Is that a challenge?" Eli smirked.

Time folded in half on the return trip to Mystic Water, and before Anna knew it, they were home. She groaned as she hauled herself from the front seat. The sun crept low on the horizon, and deep blues painted the sky. The first of the evening stars twinkled. Anna shivered as she jingled her keys around to find the one to her apartment.

"I can't believe we ate all that," she whined. "I have the shakes."

"I can't believe *you* ate three donuts. I thought you were pushing it with the second one, but when you went for the third, I knew it was bad news." Eli laughed. "I bet you'd bleed sugar right now."

Anna glared at him. "This is all your fault. You taunted me with them. All the oohs and aahs. I had to test them."

"Testing requires a bite, not the entire pastry," he said.

"Do you want to sleep outside tonight? Maybe a little frostbite will do you some good."

Eli chuckled and followed Anna inside. They shut the door quickly to block the freezing air that tried to follow them. Anna turned up the thermostat, and the heat clicked on. Her cell phone rang, and she rustled around in her bag until she found it.

"Hey, Tessa," she said.

"You haven't responded to my messages," Tessa said. "I've been waiting for you all day."

Anna pulled the phone away from her ear and looked at the number of her unread texts. She pressed the phone back to her ear. "Sorry, I haven't checked my messages yet. We went for a drive today."

"Who?" Tessa asked.

"Me and Eli." Anna dropped her bag on the table and sat in a chair so she could take off her shoes.

"Where did you go?"

"Wildehaven Beach. I needed a brain break."

"Tell Eli I said hey."

Anna looked up at Eli. "Tessa says hello."

Eli rubbed the back of his neck and stared at the postcards on the refrigerator. Anna stood and poked her finger into his bicep. Still he didn't look at her.

"Can you go into your room for a minute?" Tessa asked, lowering her voice to a whisper.

"What? Why?" Anna asked. But she walked into her bedroom, leaving Eli watching her from the kitchen. "Okay, I'm in my room."

"Is Eli with you?"

"No, he's in the kitchen. Why are you being so weird, and why are you whispering?"

"I have to tell you something." Tessa's voice pitched high like an excited child. "Last night I kissed Eli or he kissed me or we kissed each other! It doesn't matter who started it, but it was wonderful and perfect, and I could have died. *Died*, Anna. It nearly knocked my socks off, which I wouldn't have objected to. I could have kissed him for days. No, years! Did he say anything about it? Did he mention it today when y'all were out?"

Anna's ears started ringing. The sugar in her veins pulsed thick and sickening. She went to sit on the edge of her bed and nearly missed. She caught herself before she dropped to the floor. Anna mumbled, "Uh, no, he didn't—"

"So he doesn't kiss and tell?" Tessa said. "A real gentleman. Wow, Anna, it was incredible. I wish you knew just how good it was because words don't do it justice. Oh, I'm getting a call from a client. I'll call you later!" Tessa disconnected.

After spending the day with Eli, getting to know him and

laughing with him, Anna had almost forgotten that her best friend was smitten with the same man. She pressed her hand to her forehead. She was acting like a terrible friend. Her feelings for Eli had gotten out of hand, and she needed to contain them, stamp them out.

The room filled with the scent of stale donuts and glazed sugar that had hardened and flaked like crackled paint. She looked up to see Eli standing in the bedroom doorway. She'd never seen that expression in his eyes before—guilt and uncertainty.

"You kissed Tessa," Anna said. It wasn't a question. Tessa wouldn't make up that whopper of a story, and even more than that, Tessa was so thrilled that Anna could feel the energy rippling through the phone line and electrocuting her in the heart.

Eli said nothing; he simply stared at her. The temperature in the room spiked, making Anna dizzy. Her brain rocked in her skull like a boat in a storm. "She said it was amazing," Anna babbled. "That she never wanted it to end. The best ever." Anna looked away from Eli's piercing gaze. She blinked at the floorboards. "I'm happy for you both. Tessa is a great person." The words caught in her throat as though they were connected to fishhooks that someone yanked.

"I'm going to take a shower," she said. When she stood, her knees buckled, and she wobbled sideways. Eli stepped toward her, but she held up her hand to stop him.

"I'm sorry," Eli said.

"Why?" she asked.

"Because I can tell you're upset."

She tried to laugh it off, but her bottom lip trembled instead. "Why would I be upset? You're free to do what makes you happy."

"As are you," Eli said quietly. His eyes pleaded with her to let him come closer, so she took a step backward. Being near Eli was too dangerous now. The idiot side of her brain wanted him to hold her and take away the sick feeling clawing its way out of her. But the rational side of her brain told her to redraw the friendship lines between them—the same lines she'd been assuring everyone else existed.

Anna rushed into the bathroom and shut the door. Then she trembled so badly her teeth chattered. She turned on the shower water scalding hot and sat on the edge of the tub until steam fogged up the glass.

Eli had kissed Tessa. This perfect man she had created by accident, this man who tugged at her heart in a way no one else did, had kissed another woman. And not just any woman—one of her best friends. Maybe she was all wrong. Maybe Eli had never been hers. He was changing, making his own decisions, and evidently deciding Tessa was the one he'd like to be with instead of her. She knew she should be happy for Tessa's excitement, for finding such a great man. But her heart squeezed so tightly in her chest she could barely pull in a breath. Instead of feeling happy for Eli and Tessa, Anna climbed into the shower, let the water beat against her cold skin, and cried into the blue-and-white tiles.

Anna's bedroom door was shut when she emerged from the bathroom. She crawled onto her bed and thought about Baron. She wondered what he was doing and if Valerie was filling his time in California. She'd set a new record for how to lose two guys in less than a week. Her insides felt hollow, full of nothing but the

October wind. She didn't exactly miss Baron. What she missed was the normalcy of her life a week ago—when she and Baron were still a couple, when he still lived in Mystic Water, and when she hadn't created a man who tempted her like nothing else. A man who was falling in love with her best friend.

Anna opened the nightstand drawer and pulled out the letter. She wondered if Beatrice had anything else to say about Mildred's man.

I never imagined the recipe would work. I don't know why I doubted the power of the gift because I knew it had worked for others. If I had known beforehand what the consequences of the recipe would be, how it would hurt Mildred, I never would have agreed to do it. But it's too late for us now. What's done is done, and Mildred hates me. I tried to apologize. I tried to make her understand this wasn't my fault. Even her mother sent me away anytime she saw me coming up their walk. Mildred was my best friend, but afterward, she wouldn't even walk on the same side of the street as me. At first I wondered what she told everyone because surely they wondered why we were never together anymore. I could only assume they thought it was because of Joe. A man was responsible for driving a wedge between two lifelong best friends.

During those first few weeks, I watched Joe sitting on the deck drinking sweet tea and reading the newspaper. I remember thinking he would have been perfect for Mildred. He was just her type, so doting and responsible. So predictable and kind.

How could I have ever known that Joe would not love Mildred? That he could love no one but his maker? His maker—me. I did not want a man. I did not dream of Joe. I had other plans for my life. There were places I wanted to see, but having Joe was like having a child. He became my responsibility, and he loved me dearly from the very first moment he saw me.

He was good to me, but he didn't set my heart beating like I dreamed of. At first I wasn't sure he loved me by choice. He knew nothing else, only that I was the one he chose to be with forever. Some nights I would lie awake and feel the reality of my life sitting on my chest like an avalanche. When Joe felt me slipping into this dark place, he held my hand and comforted me. But he never made me explain what I was thinking. Sometimes I thought he knew I did not love him the same way, and he was simply grateful I allowed him to be near me, that I allowed him to love me.

I missed Mildred so much during those early days with Joe. I would have traded him for her friendship again, but he would not have left me, and Mildred viewed him as tainted goods. I regretted listening to her and making a man.

Anna dropped her head back against the pillows. She was shocked to learn that Grandma Bea regretted making her grandfather. She had ultimately married Joe and had children with him. But had she ever been in love with him? Did she feel obligated to get married? Anna shared Beatrice's initial feelings of responsibility to her creation, but Anna felt sincerely attracted to Eli. She wondered if the difference was because Beatrice had attempted to make a man for Mildred, and Anna had made Eli for herself.

Anna stared at her bedroom door. Did the lingering effects

of creation cause her to have false feelings for Eli? His feelings for her were fading. Maybe it would be best to let Eli go, let him live his life with Tessa or whomever he chose. Anna rolled onto her side and looked at the darkness pressing against her windows. Eli had been a part of her life for less than a week. Letting him go should be easy, so why did that single thought make her forget to breathe?

CHAPTER 12

BEAR CLAWS

LATE THE NEXT AFTERNOON ANNA STOOD IN FRONT OF THE long piece of parchment paper she'd tacked to the wall in the bakery kitchen. Mystic Water's Fall Festival was happening in four days, and there was a lot of work to do to prepare for her usual booth and for the auction. Throughout the day, she'd added more desserts to the festival list, and now she added pumpkin pie to the list. It wasn't Anna's favorite, but it was one of the most requested desserts in the fall.

"I think you should add your grandma's coconut cake," Eli said from the doorway.

Anna and Eli hadn't spoken much all morning other than basic pleasantries. She wasn't sure how to act around him now, and he was careful to keep out of her way. Their attraction couldn't be ignored, but Anna refused to give in to the temptation because of how much she cared about Tessa and their friendship.

She didn't turn to look at him when he spoke, and she tapped the marker against the list. "It takes three days to make that cake."

Eli stepped into the kitchen. The air warmed, and she had a sudden craving for a warm cinnamon roll. She hazarded a glance his way. He looked so confident and calm. How was he adjusting to everything so easily when she felt like a toy car wound too tightly, ready to race off into disaster?

"But everyone loves it," he said. "You can charge more for it, and people will pay. You know Mrs. Davenport will buy one. Doesn't Mr. Heller buy two every year?"

Anna walked into the storeroom and tore off another long sheet of parchment paper. She tacked it to the wall beside the first one. Then she split the list into sections according to the days of the week. She started writing the baked goods beneath the day of the week they would need to be prepared.

"The festival officially starts Friday afternoon, but I never set up my booth that day. We're so close to the activities that we'll get a slew of people in here anyway, and I need Friday to finish up everything," she explained. "If we add four coconut cakes, they'll have to be started no later than Thursday and would need to be finished up by Saturday morning, but we're already swamped on Thursday. I have to cater Emma Haynie's birthday party Thursday at noon. I'll spend most of Saturday morning making last-minute touchups and setting up the booth. The festival starts at eleven a.m. and runs until the fireworks that evening. I don't see how we'll have time to add them."

Eli stood beside her, and she exhaled. He pulled the marker from her fingers. "Why don't we start the coconut cakes on Wednesday? Let's move the bear claws to Thursday. I'll do them in the afternoon while you're dropping off the party order. I'll have the coconut cakes finished by Friday, and they can sit overnight in the cooler. The flavors will have more time to meld, and they'll be even better for Saturday." He scribbled *coconut cakes—Eli* beneath *Wednesday*. Then he smiled at her and put his arm around her shoulders, giving her a quick squeeze. "And you're not doing this all by yourself. I'm here, and we'll get everything done together."

Anna couldn't help but smile. "Thanks." Just when she was becoming too comfortable with his arm around her shoulders, he pulled away. The bell on the front door jingled, and Eli walked out to help the customer. She felt his absence as if he'd been pulled away by a riptide, taking all the sweetness in the air with him. She turned and stared at the list. Then she began moving more items to the days-of-the-week sections. The next few days before the festival were going to be a madhouse.

She smelled ground coffee fresh out of the mill, and Lily bounced into the room holding a to-go coffee tumbler and wearing a lavender sweater, formfitting jeans, and her brown boots. Her curls were contained behind a headband with a silver, sequined flower on the side of her head.

"You look great," Anna said instantly.

"It's amazing what going from barfing all day to barfing only in the morning will do for you," she said and dropped her purse on the island. "It's like a switch flipped. That all-day nausea was killing me. Now I feel sick for about half an hour, and then the rest of the day I can almost forget I'm harboring a deep dark secret."

Anna knew Lily was trying to make light of her situation. "It's working for you. You look like the old Lily."

Lily smiled. She glanced at the lists and nodded her head. "I'm going to buy three dozen of the almond truffles. Make sure you make enough. Oh, pumpkin pie. Maybe I'll buy that too. I've had some weird cravings already." She looked at Anna. "On a scale of one to ten, how stressed are you about the festival?"

"Ten and a half?" Anna said. "At least I have Eli's help. He's completely confident we'll get it done." Anna added another item to the list.

Lily took the marker from her hands. She stood in front of the lists, blocking Anna's view. "I talked to Tessa," she said, looking serious. "She told me about her and Eli."

Anna closed her eyes and sighed. Couldn't she escape reality for five minutes without something reminding her that Tessa had stolen Eli's affection?

"How do you feel about it?" Lily asked.

Anna shrugged. "Not as happy for Tessa as I should be, which makes me feel like a real jerk."

"Because you like Eli too," Lily said. "You know we made Eli for you. Not for Tessa."

Anna suddenly felt the need to weep. She tried to blame it on stress and not sleeping well, but her heart felt as though it had a belt tightening around it. "We didn't even know what we were doing."

"But he's *yours*," Lily argued, keeping her voice down.

Anna shook her head. "He's making his own choices, and he's choosing Tessa." Her voice trembled. She needed to pull herself together. She couldn't be blubbering all over the place at work. "He doesn't want me, Lily. It's as simple as that. Baron doesn't want me either," she said, overwhelmed with self-pity.

"You dumped Baron," Lily argued. "And rightfully so. He would still be with you while living his best life in California, but we aren't playing that game." She dug through her purse, pulled out a set of keys, and jangled them. "You need a distraction. Tell

Eli to close this place down tonight. We're getting you out of here before you eat your way through the cookie dough tubs."

Anna wiped at her eyes. "Where are we going?"

"The Clarke House," Lily said. Anna opened her mouth to speak, but Lily continued, "You haven't officially told me anything other than you put down earnest money on the house, but I know you meant to tell me more. Mrs. Clarke is out of town until Saturday, and Tessa is quasi-housesitting for her. She goes over there at night to make sure everything is in order. I convinced Tessa to let us visit tonight under the guise that you're giving me a tour. She made me swear on my life not to break anything and, get this, not to throw a party. Can you believe that? What the hell, are we seventeen? Anyway, we're really going over there so you and I can have some time alone in a magical house." Lily smiled.

Anna felt so overwhelmed with gratitude she gave Lily a spontaneous hug. "Let me grab my stuff." When Anna returned from her apartment, Lily was telling Eli that she needed him to close the bakery without Anna. He agreed, and he looked up at her as she came down the stairs.

"Thank you," Anna said.

"Of course," he said. "When will you be home?"

"Late," Lily said. She motioned with her head for Anna to follow, and she walked out of the kitchen.

"Should I wait on you for dinner?" he asked. His blue eyes seemed to convey that he wanted her home with him.

Anna was tempted to tell Eli she'd love to have dinner with him. She wanted to sit and talk for hours, as they'd done during their trip to Wildehaven Beach. But she couldn't get the image of Eli kissing Tessa out of her head. It filled her insides with boiling oil.

"No," she said. "Don't wait up for me." Then she hustled after Lily. The wind slapped her in the face and turned her cheeks red, cooling the scald in her stomach.

After Anna gave Lily a tour of the Clarke House, she wasn't sure which of them was more excited about it. They settled into the brown leather sofa in the library, and Lily pulled her legs beneath her. She passed Anna her turkey on wheat and a bag of chips, then she unwrapped one for herself. "I've always thought this house would be amazing to live in," Lily said. "Remember how we used to drive by during the holidays when we were younger? She had so many lights strung like a fairy-tale house."

"On Halloween, she always had the best candy too," Anna added. She bit into her sandwich.

Lily nodded. "Hers was the only house Mama would let me eat the caramel apples from." She ripped open her bag of chips; a few jumped into the air and landed on the couch. Lily quickly tossed them back into the bag and brushed the evidence of crumbs from the cushion.

Anna's cell phone vibrated in her pocket. Baron's face lit up the screen with the incoming call. She laid the phone face down on the coffee table.

Lily looked curiously at her. "Don't you want to answer that?"

Anna shook her head. "Not really."

Lily settled back against the couch. "What made you want to drive to the beach yesterday?"

Anna swallowed. She rested her sandwich in her lap. "It was

Eli's suggestion. He thought going to the beach would clear my head."

"Did it?"

"Cleared it of everything but me and him," Anna said. "I forgot about the bakery, about Baron, about what do with Eli, and about Eli and Tessa. Everything faded away except us. We had the best time, laughing and talking. We even went to the bakery and talked to the owners." She tugged a piece of crust off her sandwich. "Then Tessa called as soon as we got back to Mystic Water, and the whole illusion shattered." Anna popped the crust into her mouth and chewed slowly. "They're selling the bakery."

"In Wildehaven Beach?" Lily asked.

Anna nodded. "They're retiring. They're trying to find someone who wants to run a bakery there before they just offload the appliances and then sell the building. It would be the perfect find for a baker because they already have everything you'd need, and the location is supreme." She gazed off at a shelf with books arranged by shades of blue. "Can you imagine working every day with that view?"

Lily's eyes widened. "You're considering it, aren't you?"

"Considering what?"

"Buying that bakery," Lily said. "I know that look in your eyes. You'd seriously move to Wildehaven Beach? You put down earnest money for this house. What is going on in that brain of yours?"

Anna sighed and leaned against the armrest. "I wish I knew. I'm all over the place, aren't I?" She snapped a potato chip in half and stared at the pieces. "Ever since breaking up with Baron and creating Eli, it's like my subconscious has decided to uproot everything, to seriously question what I'm doing with my life.

You know I never intended to move back here and run Grandma Bea's bakery for the rest of my life. After the funeral, I floated the idea that we should sell it, but Mama flipped out. She said if I didn't take it over, I'd be disappointing everyone and letting our family legacy die."

Lily huffed. "That's a bit extreme."

"You don't think she's right?" Anna asked sincerely. Lily had always loved Bea's Bakery too. They'd spent many childhood days learning how to bake and eating Grandma Bea's cookies. Lily's opinion about the bakery closing meant more to Anna than what the townspeople thought. "Was it self-centered of me to want something different?"

Lily put her sandwich on the coffee table. She opened her bottle of pink lemonade.

"Hell, no," she said. "I know the bakery has been in the family for years, but why is your mama so bent on making sure it stays open until the end of time? If she wanted you to grow up and be a baker, why can't you be a baker wherever you want? If Bea's Bakery closed, sure, people would be sad, but they don't stay sad for long, and it's not like your mama wants to run the bakery. It seems unfair that she'd expect you to do something she doesn't even want to do. She should support you regardless of where you end up. But, selfishly, I'm glad you came home. I missed you when you were in New York. And if you're seriously considering the bakery in Wildehaven Beach, I'll be sad for you to leave, especially now. My life is about to turn upside down."

"It's not like I'd never come home, and you know you could visit anytime," Anna said. Guilt crept from the corners of the room and coiled up her legs until it wrapped around her stomach and twisted.

"I know Wildehaven Beach isn't that far away, and I'd never turn down a weekend visit at a beach house." Lily smiled. "Let's forget the wrath of Evelyn for a minute and entertain this beach-bakery idea. What will you do about this house?" She reached for her sandwich again. "Somebody who loves it like we do needs to own it."

Anna shuddered. "Mama would be over-the-top furious with me. She might never speak to me again."

"She'll get over it," Lily said. "What do you want more? This house or the beach?"

Anna took a long drink of her Coca-Cola to try to wash down the uncertainty lodged in her chest. "I want them both."

Lily clicked her tongue. "Too bad. You can't have your cake and eat it too."

Anna nodded. "That's exactly what I told myself earlier. But I think I'd rather disappoint myself than disappoint everyone else. Mama's right. A lot of people would be upset if the bakery closed."

"They'll find a new place to get donuts," Lily argued.

"There's also the complication of Eli," Anna said. "He works here and has a job with me."

"Take him with you," Lily said seriously.

Anna's heart squeezed with the idea. "I'm not sure he'd go with me."

"Fine. Don't take him. What do you need him for anyway?" Lily asked, eating the second half of her sandwich.

"He bakes well," she said, avoiding eye contact with Lily.

Lily snorted a laugh. "I'm sure that's not the only thing he does well."

"Being around him makes me happy," Anna admitted. "I feel like I'm a stick of butter melting in the summer heat."

Lily's eyebrows raised. "Well, you don't say. She finally admits the truth about her feelings for the dough boy. Would you want to go without him? Would you be okay starting there on your own knowing he was here or somewhere else?"

Anna pressed her lips together. "I wouldn't like it because I do care about him, but, yes. I'd go without him. I can't spend my life waiting around for men to decide they want me to be a part of theirs."

"Dang skippy!" Lily exclaimed. "And if Eli's not your true love, then I know you'll find one, if that's what you want. And if you don't want a man, you don't need one to have a happy life full of chocolate chip cookies. You'd be at the beach, and you *love* the beach."

"I do," Anna said with a small smile.

"Here's another brilliant idea—because evidently I'm full of them tonight—if you don't buy this house, I think you should let me have it." Lily leaned her head back and funneled potato chip crumbs into her mouth.

The shock of Lily's statement halted Anna's sadness. "Would you want this place?"

"With Jakob? Of course. Who wouldn't want this house?"

"I'll let you have it, but only if you promise to deck it out in lights during the holidays and give out caramel apples at Halloween," Anna said.

"Jakob would have to be in charge of the lights. This time next year I'll have a baby to worry over." Lily glanced out the window. "That sounds so weird."

"When are you going to tell him?"

Lily toyed with one of her curls, wrapping and unwrapping it around her finger. "He's supposed to know this week if he makes partner or not. I'm waiting for the best time. I don't want to jeopardize his promotion by making him a stress ball. He'll want to tell his parents, and once his mama knows, I suspect the news will spread faster than wildfire."

Anna wrapped up the rest of her sandwich. "Are you nervous about how he'll react?"

"A little," Lily said. "I'm hoping he'll be excited, because I'm completely freaked out."

Anna reached over and gave Lily's knee a squeeze. "He loves you, Lily. I'd go so far as to say he's crazy nuts about you and adores everything about you. You know he wants kids."

"But we're not married. You know how old-timey some people are in this town," Lily said. "You think people will treat me differently?" Her watery eyes revealed her fears.

"What people? Stupid people? Hypocrites? Those people don't count. Only the people who know and love you matter. Think of the awesome sweets we'll have at your baby shower." Anna walked to the hall linen closet she'd inspected earlier. She pulled out two quilts. "Finish your sandwich, and let's wrap up and sit in the tower room. I think it's time for chocolate."

Anna and Lily curled on the floor of the dark tower room, wrapped in quilts that smelled like cedar. Lily had brought hot chocolate and travel mugs so they wouldn't have to use any of Mrs. Clarke's dishes. They sipped in silence for a while and stared out the long windows at the distant city lights. Stars appeared and disappeared as clouds rode the winds across the sky.

"Were you in love with Baron?" Lily asked.

Anna cupped her mug with both hands and stared at the lid. "I've wondered that a lot recently. My feelings for Eli, whether they're real or because of the secret ingredient, are so different from how I felt about Baron. It's made me realize that I loved Baron, but I wasn't head over heels for him, not even when we first met. It's nothing like you and Jakob. I can *feel* the love between you two when you're together. But even without Eli, Baron would still be leaving me for California. It hurts, but I think I'm more hurt from the disappointment. I miss him, but maybe I just miss the routine." She pushed her auburn hair behind her shoulders.

"And Eli? Are you in love with him?"

Anna closed her eyes, and an image of Eli floated through her mind. His smile made her catch her breath. "Tessa has feelings for Eli."

"That's not what I asked."

Anna looked at Lily and smiled wearily. "You have always been the one to drag everything out of me—never satisfied with my avoidance tactics." Anna glanced up at the stars. "It's possible I'm in love with him. Not that it matters now. He's chosen Tessa. But when I'm around him, I forget everything else. I feel so peaceful with him, and I don't want him to go. When I think of him leaving Mystic Water or me, I feel like someone is splitting me in half. But what if that's the magic?"

"What if it's not?" Lily asked.

"How would I ever know that it's real?"

"Does it feel real?" Lily asked. Anna nodded. "That's all that matters. You never talked about Baron the way you're talking about Eli."

Anna rubbed her hands down her face. She wanted to take

a twenty-year nap and wake up to find her life was settled and there were no life-altering decisions to be made.

"We're a sad little pair, aren't we?" Lily bumped her shoulder into Anna's.

Anna leaned her head on Lily's shoulder. "What am I supposed to do now?"

"Tell him," Lily said. When Anna started to protest, Lily continued, "I know Tessa likes him a lot, but you're in love with him, and I'm pretty sure if he knew, he'd pick you. I've seen the way he looks at you. The whole town has."

"Tessa would hate me," Anna said. "She'll think I'm trying to steal every man she likes."

Lily huffed, "Baron chose you, so not your fault. Tessa is a serial dater, anyway. She never has problems finding someone to take her out to dinner. As interested as she is in Eli, I don't think she'd keep pursuing him if she *knew* you were in love with him. Give Eli the option. Maybe he'll choose Tessa. At least he'll know how you feel."

What would Eli choosing Tessa instead of her feel like? Would her heart stop beating? Would she feel released from the magic? Anna sighed and finished her hot chocolate. "I'll tell Eli when you tell Jakob. Deal?"

"Deal," Lily said. "We'll tell them at the festival. That gives me less than a week to prepare myself for the free fall."

CHAPTER 13

SPICE KISSED PUMPKIN PIE

AT ALMOST MIDNIGHT ON THURSDAY, LINDA RONSTADT'S VOICE filled the bakery's kitchen. Anna pony danced around the island, moving her arms like a swimmer and tossing her hair around. She pointed at a pumpkin pie that refused to set up correctly and sang loudly, accusing the pie of being no good.

"Those are some strong words for a pie," Eli said with a huge grin on his face.

Anna gasped and clutched a hand to her chest. "You scared the bejeebers outta me," she said, turning down the music. Eli had gone out for a dinner date and movie with Tessa. At first Anna could think of nothing else but what they were doing. Then she made the healthier choice and refocused her energy on prepping for the upcoming festival. "I didn't hear you come in."

"I don't think you would have heard a firecracker explosion," he said, walking over to her pie. He poked his finger into the custard, and it sank straight through to the pie pan. "You're right. This pie isn't good." He licked his finger. "Tastes good if you like sweet pumpkin soup."

Anna shoved stray hairs from her face, leaving streaks of flour on her forehead. She grabbed the recipe and hopped up onto the island. Swinging her feet back and forth, she scanned the ingredients and frowned. "I added too many eggs. I don't think I've ever made that mistake," she said. "I'll start over in a few minutes." Now that she was sitting, fatigue made her limbs heavy and her eyelids droop.

"You need to go to bed," he said, sidling over to her. "It's almost midnight. I can make the pie while you get cleaned up."

Anna glanced at the clock. Where had all the hours gone? "You've been up as long as I have. It won't take long—another hour tops." She slid off the counter and yawned. "How was the movie with Tessa?" Anna had wondered what going to the movies with Eli would be like. Would he share the popcorn? Would they make space for both of their elbows on the armrest? Would he hold her hand? Before she could stop herself, she imagined being at a drive-in movie with Eli, cuddled up next to him while watching an action-adventure film. Never mind the fact that she hadn't been to a drive-in since she was six and there wasn't a drive-in theater within fifty miles.

"It was a chick flick. Tessa cried twice, and I ate a large popcorn by myself." Eli grabbed her arms and made her look at him. "Go to bed," he said. Then he pulled her into a hug for no reason. "You're wiped."

Anna sagged into him like a baby doll. He smelled like he'd been on a date, like movie popcorn and melting M&M's. She pressed her cheek into his chest and exhaled. "And the pie?" she mumbled into his T-shirt.

"I'll make it." He let go and turned her around, pushing her toward the staircase. "I don't want to see you again for a few hours at least."

She smiled sleepily over her shoulder. "I want to argue, but I'm too tired. Good night, and thank you."

"Sweet dreams," he said, and she dragged herself up the staircase. Tomorrow the circus of baking would start all over again.

Anna showered and changed into her pajamas. Eli was still downstairs in the bakery. She had almost passed that point when she could actually fall asleep, and the shower had revived her somewhat. She took Grandma Bea's letter out of her nightstand and carried it to the living room. Anna cracked open the door at the top of the bakery stairs so she could hear when Eli came upstairs to bed. Then she flipped off the main light, turned on the lamp, and settled herself on the couch beneath a quilt.

The shop went from being incredibly busy every day to being empty as a ghost town. People seemed to avoid it while walking through town. At night, Joe and I tossed out the goods that were only fresh for a day, and we saved the items we could still sell. After two weeks of doing that, I remember standing over the trash can and crying. That's where Joe found me one evening.

I told him I didn't know why people weren't coming anymore. He said we'd know soon enough, and as if someone had heard, there was a knock on the front door.

My good friend Mary Margaret knocked again, and I

unlocked the door. She and I stood in the darkened front room like fugitives. She spoke in whispers and eased, inch by inch, away from the windows until we were standing behind the counter.

She explained that Mildred had told the entire town I'd stolen her boyfriend. She'd filled everyone's heads with lies. Mary Margaret apologized for not coming by sooner, but she said Mildred had kept hawk eyes on her. Evidently the whole town was on edge because of the wildness they saw in Mildred's eyes.

I was indignant. I told Mary Margaret I hadn't stolen Joe. Joe had chosen me.

Mary Margaret understood. She said she believed me because it didn't make sense for Joe to have been Mildred's boyfriend when no one had ever seen him before they saw him in the bakery. She also said she and Mildred had gotten into a big argument because Mildred told her a cockamamie story about me making Joe out of dough like a common witch. Mary Margaret admitted that she feared Mildred was losing her mind. She said I should keep hope that people would return.

Mary Margaret pulled open the door and looked both ways before she rushed out of the bakery. Resentment flared in me like a gas burner. Mildred had pushed past personal and had chosen to destroy my business.

Joe was cleaning off the countertops when I returned to the back room. He looked up at me and gave me his most gentle smile. Up until that moment, I had not truly appreciated his support, his constant companionship. He had never once told me to snap out of my gloomy state, never once told me to get over losing Mildred's friendship for reasons he could not understand. Now when my hometown turned its back on me, he offered me a smile that said, *I'm here.*

I told him we were entering a war, and if it took me all night, I would bake sweets that would draw the town to me like bears to honey. Mildred wouldn't turn what I loved into something tainted and broken.

Joe grinned, and for the first time, I saw mischief flicker in his green eyes. He said he wouldn't let Mildred beat me either.

We stayed up until the wee hours of the morning mixing, molding, baking, and icing. Sparks flew from the ovens. The scents of chocolate and vanilla filled the air with a pink haze that slipped beneath the doors, and lights flickered on all over town. Sugary smells, warm, sticky, and sweet, floated from the kitchen and coated everything like a fine dusting of powdered sugar. Cupcakes sparkled on colorful cake plates, and cookies filled the display window like smiling faces.

Before we could unlock the door at seven a.m., a line had already formed. At least half the town rushed in with eager eyes and watering mouths. By noon, we had nearly sold out of everything. People bought faster than we could replenish our stock. That day Joe and I stood behind the counter, and I reached over and slid my hand into his. He gave my hand a squeeze, and I couldn't stop smiling.

Friday was ordered pandemonium—if there was such a thing. Festival setup was happening all throughout downtown and the nearby park. Music piped out of hidden speakers, and the sounds of people talking and laughing filled the streets. Running the bakery during usual hours and trying to make last-minute preparations for the festival left Anna feeling like she was trapped inside a spinning top. She hadn't sat down all day, and without Eli's badgering, she wouldn't have eaten either. Now after the bakery had closed for the day, the festival was in full swing. Colorful lights and echoes of happiness filled the air.

Anna crossed the last baked good—apple crumble muffins— off the list and smiled. She bounced into the front room and lifted her arms over her head like a cheerleader at a pep rally.

"We're done!" she said.

Eli looked up from the boxes he was packing for tomorrow. He'd labeled them according to what each contained and where it would be placed in the booth or at the auction. He smiled at her. "Victory is ours," he said. "This is my last box, and we can call it a night and celebrate the fact that we're going to bed before midnight."

Anna looked toward the bakery windows. She didn't have a direct view of the festival activities from her front window, but she could see multicolored tents lining the street and lights from the evening's events. White string lights stretched across the fronts of the downtown buildings. Gas lamps flickered, lighting the festival paths. Anna could just make out the outline of the live-music stage.

"What time is it?"

"It's after eight," Eli said.

Anna walked to the front windows. Stars twinkled, and maple leaves tumbled across the tops of the tents. Tomorrow she would join Mystic Water's Fall Festival as it became a colorful celebration of music, crafts, foods, and activities.

"You're going to love the festival," Anna said. "It's one of the best times to be in Mystic Water."

Eli folded the flaps on the last box and stretched his back. Then he walked over and stood beside her. "Want to order pizza and watch TV until we start drooling?"

Anna's heart fluttered. "You're not going out?" In Anna's mind, she expected Tessa to want to be with Eli every evening he wasn't working because that's what Anna would have wanted.

"I'm exhausted. I'd rather be a bum on your couch."

Anna leaned her head against his biceps for a moment. "We have to set an alarm *before* we start eating. I have a feeling that once we fill up on pizza, we're going to fade fast."

Eli chuckled. "You're in charge of the alarm. I'll be in charge of the pizza. Let's close this place down."

Eli ordered pizza, and Anna filled the claw-foot tub with water and lavender-scented bubble bath. When she eased into the water, the bubbles rose to her ears, and she draped her hair over the lip of the tub and sighed. She closed her eyes and soaked for a few minutes before she dried her hands and reached for the final pages of Grandma Bea's letter.

One day Joe brought home a guitar. He saw it in the pawn store window during his afternoon walk, and he said he felt lured in by the music he heard in his head. I laughed when he sat down at the kitchen table and tuned the strings. He hummed and twisted the knobs until each string sounded perfect.

I busied myself tossing dirty aprons and towels into the washing machine, but when Joe started strumming his fingers across the strings, I stopped, bent over with my hands hovering above the dirty laundry. I straightened slowly and walked into the kitchen.

Joe whistled and played a song I'd never heard before. He looked up at me, grinned, and made up words about me and the bakery. I asked him how he knew how to play the guitar because I don't have one musical bone in my body, and he shrugged. Said he felt it. My skin felt shivery as I realized that Joseph O'Brien was becoming his own man with his own talents and ideas. And still he was choosing to love me. That was something to smile about.

Love always,
Grandma Beatrice

CHAPTER 14

MANGO PASSION FRUIT TART

ANNA HAD RENTED TWO LARGE BLUE TENTS HOUSING LONG
tables in the front for selling the food and extra tables in the back
for storing the product not on display. Cupcakes spun on the
whimsical arms of holders shaped like trees. Pies sat in neat rows
and summoned people with their buttery, flaky crusts. Pairs of
cookies wrapped in plastic bags tied with aqua ribbons lined the
fronts of the tables. Eli hung a nylon sign with the words Bea's
Bakery, and it draped across the tops of both tents.

Anna hugged her arms around her chest and bounced on
her toes. "I think that's everything. People should start piling in
here within half an hour." She reached for her hot chocolate and
drank. It spread warmth throughout her chest and traveled to
her fingers and toes.

A cold north wind rushed down the streets. Anna's knitted
scarf flew into her face, and the sign flapped wildly before Eli
could tie it down tightly. Grandma Bea had always said a north

wind was a bad omen. It foretold coming storms, disaster, and sometimes violence. Anna shivered. What terrible thing could possibly happen tonight? She shoved aside the thought. The festival was going to be a fantastic time for everyone. She just knew it.

Eli stepped off the ladder and folded it. He grabbed his coffee. "You think the cold will keep people away?"

"Not the people in this town," Anna said. "I don't think a snowstorm could keep them out."

"Does it even snow here?" he asked.

She chuckled. "Hardly. We got a few flakes when I was in eighth grade, and people went bananas. They let school out early just so the kids could run loose, acting like they were gonna build snowmen and go sledding."

"Were you one of those kids trying to sled on a handful of snowflakes?"

"You bet I was," Anna said, recalling how she, Lily, and Tessa had tried to slide down a nearby hill on one of Beatrice's baking sheets. "Total disaster, but we still laugh about it."

"I would pay to see that," Eli joked.

Within the hour the downtown streets of Mystic Water were alive and packed full of people bundled in scarves, hats, and mittens. Steam rose from cups of coffee, hot chocolate, mulled cider, and buttered rum. Big band music swelled from the stage, and Anna bopped her hips to the rhythm. Vendors sold bratwursts, giant turkey legs, and kettle corn. Funnel cakes filled the air with the smell of hot vanilla, and blue and pink swirls of cotton candy bounced above heads like edible balloons. People walked by eating corn dogs, grilled cheese sandwiches enfolded in wax paper, and french fries in brown paper sacks dotted with grease.

As the day progressed, Anna brought out cookies and brownies to replace the dwindling supplies, and she refilled the cupcake stands. "We've sold more than half of our supply," she told Eli. "If sales keep up at this rate, we'll have to close down before the festival ends."

"That'll mean we can enjoy the rest of the night," Eli said.

"My thoughts exactly." She smiled at him.

Four young women giggled their way over to Anna. They cupped mugs of steaming hot chocolate and bubbled with a happiness that made their cheeks rosy and their smiles wide. She didn't recognize them as bakery regulars.

"Hey, y'all," Anna said. "See anything you like?"

The bright red-haired woman glanced over the offerings. "We're from out of town—road trip! And everyone keeps telling us we *have* to come and buy something from your booth. They swear your stuff is magical. I'm looking for a cure. I ate too many nachos—"

"Too many nachos?" the dark-haired woman laughed. "You cleaned out their supply. And I recall you trying to bite my finger off when I reached for one."

The redhead snickered. "Man, that cheese was good. What do you have that'll settle this stomach? Money is no object," she said playfully.

Anna lifted an aqua box stamped with an emblem of the bakery's logo. "Peanut butter truffles cure cheese overload. Eat a few of these, and you'll forget your rumbling tummy," she said with a smile.

"I could really use a good night's rest," the dark-haired woman said. "Crashing with these three nuts takes its toll on my beauty sleep."

Anna gave her two bags of double dark chocolate chip cookies. "Guaranteed to bring you peace and relaxation."

"What do you have to spur creativity?" the woman with long, curly hair asked.

"Something for laughter," the last woman added. Her hair was streaked with pink and blue that highlighted her fair skin and eyes. "We can never have enough laughter."

Anna motioned for the women to follow her to the far end of the table. "I call this the Black 'n' Blue," she explained. "It's a freshly made pie with blackberries and blueberries and a buttery double crust. I'd say one piece will do the trick, but if you find yourself in a creative lull, I'd add a scoop of vanilla ice cream on top." Anna picked up a dessert neatly wrapped in plastic and tied with a bow. "Laughter and delight are guaranteed with this Mexican chocolate cinnamon roll. You won't be sorry you bought this. In fact, you'll probably only regret not buying more than one."

The redhead squeezed in beside her friends. "I think we passed the ice-cream station a few minutes ago." She looked up at Anna. "We'll take three more of those rolls. Don't suppose you have a fork and spoon handy?"

Eli rummaged around in a box while Anna took payments for the desserts. Then Eli handed utensils to the woman. "We have a little bit of everything."

"I bet you do," the redhead said, and she winked at Eli. Then all four women giggled and walked off.

Eli shook his head and watched the women fade into the crowd. "Do people really think your sweets are magical?"

Anna shrugged. "If they believe it works, then it does. I know only what they've told me." She refilled her travel mug with hot chocolate.

"Do you believe in the magic?"

She paused for a second and stared at him. "Definitely."

"What's the most magical thing you've ever made?" he asked, and she coughed as she choked on her drink.

Tessa chose that moment to bound around the side of the tent. "Hey!" She waved at Anna and pulled Eli into a side hug. "I haven't seen you in days," she said to him. "Anna's been working you too hard."

Anna wanted to look away, but she couldn't stop staring at Tessa's arm wrapped around Eli, at the way she breathed him in and gazed up into his blue eyes. Eli draped his left arm around her shoulders and he gave her a squeeze.

"Hey, Tessa, how's the festival?" Anna asked, hoping conversation would distract her from their intimacy.

"It might be the best one yet," she said, dropping her arm but not moving away from Eli's side. "Mama felt like walking around today, so we've been taking everything in. There's so much more to see this year. Mama's resting in the park, listening to the band, so I told her I wanted to come by and see how y'all were faring."

"We've been busy," Eli said. A customer stepped up to the booth and ordered a slice of coconut cake.

Tessa lowered her voice. "Think you can let Eli slip away with me for a while later tonight?"

Anna wanted to keep it to herself that they might be done early at the booth, but she knew that was jealousy trying to tempt her into being a bad friend. She took the high road instead. "I'm sure he'd love to have a break, but we might sell out early and he'll be free to do whatever."

"I'd love to watch the fireworks with him."

Anna would too, but she smiled at Tessa's excitement. She

grabbed two wrapped brown butter blondies and handed them to Tessa. "Take these to your mama. She loves them. We'll see you in a bit."

Tessa made a squealing noise in her throat and squeezed Anna's forearm. "Thank you, thank you. I'll be back later." She bounced over to Eli and managed to touch him five different times while she explained she would check on them later.

Anna felt as though she'd eaten too many raw oysters. She and Lily had made a deal that she would tell Eli how she felt tonight. How could she tell Eli when Tessa was so obviously crazy about him? What kind of friend would she be? Just as her guilt was spiraling out of control, Lily and Jakob walked up.

Lily's arm was hooked in the crook of Jakob's elbow, and she carried a travel mug of coffee in her mittened hand. Jakob wore a down jacket and a black stocking cap pulled over his ears. He shook hands with Eli.

"It's dinnertime," Jakob said. "Lily isn't interested in the grease, but there's some pub grub calling my name. The Thirsty Whale has a booth in the park, and they've got the best fish and chips you've ever had."

Someone called Jakob's name. Thomas Harper crossed the path toward them and shook Jakob's hand. "We were just about to grab dinner from the Thirsty Whale's booth," Jakob said. "Want to join?"

"Sure," Thomas said. He nodded toward Eli and held out his hand.

"Good to see you again," Eli said, shaking Thomas's hand. "There are a few bear claws left if you want one."

"I'll save one for you," Anna said, "if you want it after dinner."

"Thanks, Anna," Thomas said, stepping closer to her. "Heard

about Baron moving to California." He touched her arm. "Are you closing the bakery?"

"Why would I do that?" she asked in surprise.

"Aren't you going with him? I figured you'd move and open a bakery there," Thomas said.

Anna made a scoffing noise in her throat. "I'm not moving, and if I open a bakery anywhere else, it's definitely not going to be in California."

"That's good news for the rest of us," Thomas said. "Bea's Bakery is a staple around here."

"I'm starving," Jakob said, interrupting them.

Eli looked at Anna and rubbed his stomach. He grinned at her. "Okay if I go?"

She was rendered incapable of saying no. "Go," she said. "I can handle this. Jakob's right about those fish and chips."

"I'll swap Lily for Eli," Jakob said, herding Lily to the front of the booth.

Eli grabbed his coffee mug. "You'll be okay?"

"I have Lily. What could go wrong?" Anna asked. Another powerful north wind blew through the streets. People grabbed their hats, and paper napkins tangled around ankles on their escape. Anna pressed her hands against the bags of cookies as if they might take flight and find new homes. Eli zipped his jacket and smiled.

"Don't blow away," he said. Then he followed Jakob and Thomas as they wove through the crowd. She watched him walk away until Lily tugged her arm.

"Tell me you didn't sell out of the almond truffles," Lily said.

Anna lifted a pink box with Lily's name written on the top.

"My treat to you. Two dozen almond truffles. Don't eat them all at once."

Lily grinned. "I can't make any promises." She opened the box and popped one into her mouth. She closed her eyes while she ate it. "Perfect," she said. "They always make me feel so stress-free. And speaking of stress, I'm guessing you haven't told him yet? Don't play dumb either. You know who and what I'm talking about."

Anna's shoulders slumped. "I don't think I can," she admitted. "I can't do that to Tessa."

Lily put down her box. Then she dragged Anna to the back of the booth. "You can't do this to *you*," she argued. "How do you think Tessa is going to feel when she finds out later that Eli has always been in love with you? You're doing her a favor by telling him the truth."

"You're operating under the assumption that Eli is going to choose me if I tell him how I feel," Anna said. "What if you're wrong?"

"I'm not," Lily said.

"But what if you are?"

"Then, fine, we'll know the truth. He'll go off and marry Tessa, and they'll live happily ever after, and you'll at least know you were honest and gave him an option."

Anna caught movement at the front of the tent.

"Could I buy a slice of pumpkin pie?" a young boy asked.

Anna smiled and helped him while Lily waited impatiently for her to return. When she finished with the customer, Anna crossed to Lily and lowered her voice. "Remember the letter we found that Grandma Bea wrote me? She explained all about the secret ingredient and how it's been in the family for generations.

She actually made Grandpa Joe for Mildred, Tessa's grandma, but it backfired, and he ended up loving *my* grandma instead. She wasn't even in love with Grandpa Joe at first."

"Say what?" Lily asked. "Tessa's grandma wanted the man Grandma Bea made?" Lily's eyes were wide. "History is repeating itself? Except . . . she didn't love him like you love Eli?"

Anna explained, "Not at first, and she thought Grandpa Joe only loved her because she created him," Anna said. "Eventually, she grew to love him in a romantic way. But I'm telling you all of this because . . . what if Eli is—or *was*—only attached to me because I made him?"

Another voice said, "What do you mean you *made* him?"

Lily and Anna jumped in unison. Lily squeaked and clutched Anna's forearm. Anna's heart leaped into her throat and cut off her air supply. If Anna had wanted to tell Tessa the truth about Eli, this would've been the last way she wanted it to happen.

Tessa stared at them with expectant brown eyes. Lily was the first to respond. She tried to chuckle. "She meant she made Eli his favorite dessert."

Tessa tucked her hair behind her ears and glanced around. "I heard what y'all were saying. Halfway back to Mama I remembered that she also loves your apple crumble muffins, and I wanted to get one, so I'm not here eavesdropping."

"Let's get you one of those muffins then," Lily said.

Tessa squared her shoulders. "You were saying your grandma made a man for Grandma Mildred. Were all her crazy stories true? Grandma Bea *made* Grandpa Joe?"

"How could that be true?" Lily asked, trying to laugh it off, but it sounded fake.

Tessa looked only at Anna. "The truth," she said.

The truth felt like an out-of-control, outrageously absurd thing that Anna could barely comprehend. "I, uh, well, we . . ."

Tessa looked at Lily and then back at Anna. "That's a start at least," she said. "And while you're telling me how this craziness is possibly true, do you want to also tell me about your feelings for Eli?"

"No," Anna blurted.

"No?" Tessa asked. "That's not an option. Let's start with the simple question. How could Grandma Bea have created your grandpa?"

"That's the simple question?" Lily mumbled.

"Don't make fun of me, Lily," Tessa said. "I deserve the truth. I can't believe y'all have been keeping this from me."

"It's not exactly a story I knew how to share," Anna said.

"You shared it with Lily!" Tessa argued.

"I was *there*," Lily replied. "Come to think of it, this might all be *my* fault."

Anna touched Tessa's arm. "Why don't we talk about it some other time? Your mama is waiting on you."

"Option two: we talk about it now. Grandma Mildred wasn't your typical grandma," Tessa said, "and we knew that. Even apart from the man-out-of-dough story, she was unusual, but if she was actually telling the truth, then that changes so much of what I thought about her." Tessa tightened the scarf around her neck. "It's hard to believe, though. *How* can anyone create a man?" She locked eyes with Anna and whispered, "Eli?"

When Anna didn't respond right away, Lily exhaled loudly. "Tessa, please don't flip out like you did when I told you my secret. I don't want to have to sedate you. But the story is true. All of it. Grandpa Joe and Eli were both created in Bea's Bakery."

Tessa pressed her hand to her chest and shook her head. "Are you serious?" she asked, leaning backward as though the reality knocked her balance askew. "How?"

Anna looked at Lily before answering. There was no going back now, no laughing the entire conversation off as a joke. "With magic sugar Grandma Bea left for me. She called it her secret ingredient," she said honestly. "I didn't think it would work."

"But it did," Tessa said, and her eyes shone in the strung lights. "No wonder none of us had ever heard of Eli." A wildness tainted her laugh. "And your grandpa only loved Grandma Bea because she made him. Does that mean if Eli has feelings for you, they're maybe not real? Is that why he's so attached to you? Because you made him? I was worried something was going on between you two, even after he kissed me, but this means he might actually want to be with me! Do you think I should tell him?" Tessa pressed her hands together over her heart.

Anna grabbed Tessa's forearms. "You can't tell him." Lily shook her head in agreement.

"Why?" Tessa asked. "That way he'll understand that his attachment to you is because you made him. He'll be free to love me the way he wants to."

Lily shook her head and stepped forward. "No, Tessa. You can never tell Eli the truth."

"You want to lie to him?" she asked.

"It's not lying," Lily argued. "You can't tell someone he's made from dough. He'll think you're out of your mind. It's better he doesn't know anything."

Tessa frowned. "I think we should be honest with him."

"For what purpose?" Lily asked. "So that you'll know you have all of his affections? You already do. You're already with him, so there's no reason to tell him anything. You don't want to hurt him, do you?"

Tessa frowned a moment longer, and then she said, "You're right. I really do think he cares about me, and I don't want to hurt him. I don't like being dishonest, though." She puffed air out of her cheeks. "Wow . . . this is unreal. How did y'all keep this a secret for so many days? I would have exploded."

"Oh, Anna has imploded already at least a dozen times," Lily said, giving Anna a small smile.

"Ain't that the truth," Anna said quietly.

Tessa smiled and pulled them into a hug so quickly Anna and Lily knocked foreheads. She whispered to them as if they were in a clandestine meeting. "This is so exciting. You created a man just for me. I don't even know what all of this *means*, but I feel all jittery inside." Tessa sobered slightly and added, "I definitely don't want to be like Grandma Mildred and have the whole town think I'm batty. Maybe it's best if this is our little secret." She looked at Anna and Lily, and they both nodded.

"I should get going," Tessa said. "Mama will wonder what happened to me. I'll grab one of those muffins before I go. How much?"

Anna flicked her hand to the side. "Take whatever you want. No charge."

Tessa thanked Anna and told them she'd be back before the fireworks. Anna wrapped her arms around her chest. The wind rushed through the tent and whipped her long hair around her face. Her teeth chattered.

"You have to tell him," Lily said.

Anna stared at the uneaten sweets. The lights dimmed and colors faded. "Why? You said Tessa has all of his affections."

"I only said that so she wouldn't go off blabbing to Eli that he's the dough boy," Lily said. "If he ever hears the truth from anyone, it should be from you."

Lily refilled Anna's travel mug with the last of the hot chocolate and handed it to her friend. "Now get up and put a smile on your face. You look like someone burned down your house. Jakob and Eli will be back soon, and we can't have you looking like that." She smoothed flyaway hairs away from Anna's face. "Speak of the devil, and he appears."

Jakob, Eli, and Jakob's parents, the Connellys, walked up to the booth.

"Look who I found," Jakob said to Lily. "Mom brought back a surprise for us from their trip."

Anna motioned for everyone to come behind the booth. Eli offered Anna a french fry from his cardboard boat that had been filled with battered cod. She declined and said hello to Jakob's parents. Then she made herself busy by straightening the displays. Eli finished his dinner while Jakob and Lily talked with the Connellys in the rear of the tent.

"You think we'll be done in an hour?" Eli asked, crumpling the boat and tossing it into a large city trash can.

Anna surveyed the tables and glanced back at the empty boxes. "It's possible," she said. "There's not much left to do, so if you'd like to go, I can handle the booth by myself."

"We started together, and we'll finish together," Eli said.

"Tessa wants to watch the fireworks with you," Anna said and then looked away from his gaze. When Eli didn't respond, she glanced over her shoulder to see him watching her. She tried to offer him an encouraging smile, but her heart wasn't in it, and only half of her mouth tugged up.

Jakob's voice pulled Anna's attention away from Eli. "They brought it all the way from Italy," Jakob said. "The sommelier a few tents over was nice enough to open it for us."

Jakob handed Lily a plastic wineglass. Lily's other hand unconsciously rested on her stomach. Jakob's father, Mr. Connelly, was distracted by a teenage girl with an overly excited border collie. The dog's leash had wrapped around the girl's midsection. She spun around in a circle and giggled, and the dog seemed to think it was a game. However, Mrs. Connelly's attention was on Lily.

Jakob toasted his glass against Lily's. "Here's to our future!"

Lily nodded. "Our future." She glanced at Mrs. Connelly while Jakob drank his wine. "This was so thoughtful of you."

"Jakob said you prefer sweet reds, and Vin Santo Rosso is one of the best," Mrs. Connelly said.

"You're going to love it," Jakob said.

"Why don't you finish off mine?" she offered, pouring her wine into his empty cup. "I'll give it a try later."

"What's wrong, Lily?" Mrs. Connelly asked.

"Nothing," Lily said, smiling and avoiding eye contact.

Anna recognized that look of panic just below Lily's stiff expression. She stared at them, trying to get Lily's attention as a distraction.

"Lily's had a virus for a week or so," Jakob answered. "She's been feeling better now." He looked at Lily. "But don't push it if you think this might bother your stomach. I'll save the rest of the bottle for when you're feeling 100 percent."

"I'm sorry to hear that," Mrs. Connelly said. "The flu?"

Jakob shrugged. "She refused to go to the doctor. She was throwing up off and on for a few days, but now she's only nauseous in the mornings."

Anna saw a sheen of sweat glistening on Lily's forehead. "You make it sound terrible," Lily joked. "I'll be right as rain soon."

"He makes it sound like morning sickness," Mrs. Connelly said. Then she leaned forward, and her dyed-blond hair fell across her shoulders, framing the creamy skin on her face. "You're not pregnant, are you?" she said in a playful whisper loud enough for the group to hear.

Jakob laughed and wrinkled his brow. "Mom," he said, "that's awkward. Next subject, please. How about this year's festival?" He nudged Lily with his elbow, but Lily didn't respond. She started trembling and couldn't seem to shake the chill that rippled over her. Jakob finally sensed something was wrong. "You okay?"

Anna had been unable to move until that moment. She made a motion to swoop in and save Lily, but Eli grabbed her arm. "What are you doing?" she whispered, trying to tug her arm free. He shook his head.

"It was a joke, dear. I wasn't serious about the pregnancy," Mrs. Connelly said and smiled with her bright white teeth. She adjusted her string of pearls. "I know my son wouldn't be so reckless, especially not in the middle of such an important promotion—" The tangled border collie butted its nose into the back of her wool pants, and she gasped. "Excuse me," she breathed out in offense to the apologizing teenager. Mr. Connelly tried to help untangle them.

Lily's cheeks flushed, and her eyes began to water. She looked at Jakob and said, "I'm sorry."

"For what?"

She motioned toward his glass of wine. "For not drinking the wine. I don't want to be rude about your mama's gift, and I didn't want you to find out this way," she said. She mouthed, "I *am* pregnant."

Anna gripped Eli's arm hard enough to imprint her fingers. Jakob's eyes widened, and he shook his head as if to loosen the words Lily had shoved into his ears. "You're what? How?"

Lily choked on a pitiful laugh. "I think the *how* is obvious."

"Whoa . . . you're . . . really?" Jakob said. An expression somewhere between a goofy grin and a look of panic filled his face. "How long have you known?"

"A week or so," Lily said softly.

Jakob touched her cheek, and his expression softened. "Why didn't you tell me sooner?"

"I was afraid," she admitted, "and I know you've been stressed about the promotion. I didn't want to add to it."

"You are *not* adding to my stress," Jakob said. "It's a lot, yeah . . . *a lot*, but—"

Unfortunately, Mrs. Connelly chose that moment to reenter the conversation. "What's a lot?" Mrs. Connelly asked, but no one was listening to her.

"Thank you for not freaking out," Lily said.

Jakob chuckled. "Oh, I'm definitely freaked out. I figured we'd eventually get to this point, but—"

"But not right now," Lily agreed.

He nodded. "I can't believe you're actually pregnant. You're sure?"

"Definitely sure."

"Excuse me," Mrs. Connelly said. "Did you say she's *pregnant*?" The judgment in her voice was as severe as the edge of a scalding blade passing through chilled cheesecake. Without waiting for a response, she stepped closer to Jakob. Her voice was low and stern. "Tell me you have not been foolish enough to get your girlfriend pregnant right in the middle of the biggest opportunity of your life. I hope you'll at least be intelligent enough to keep this mistake to yourselves until the firm makes their decision." The soft lines of her face faded. Her coral-colored lips were tight, casting deep lines around her mouth, and her jaw was rigid, as though she might be clenching her teeth.

"This isn't a mistake," Jakob said as tears rolled down Lily's cheeks.

"You meant to get pregnant *before* you're married?" Mrs. Connelly asked. "What will people say? It's inappropriate."

"I don't care what people say, Mom," Jakob said. "This is none of their damn business, and I'd appreciate *you* keeping this to yourself. Don't go off and gossip to your friends. My personal life is off-limits."

"You're my son," Mrs. Connelly argued. "Your life hasn't been *off-limits* to me since the day you were born."

"I'm serious, Mom," Jakob said angrily. "Back off for a minute, will you?"

Mrs. Connelly gasped. Then she stepped away and grabbed Mr. Connelly's arm. He appeared somewhat confused, but she dragged him away through the crowd.

Indecision filled Jakob's eyes. He rubbed both hands down his face. "Damn it," he swore.

Lily touched his arm, and he looked at her. "Go after her," she said softly.

"She's being such a snob," he argued. "I won't have her acting like we're a couple of stupid teenagers. She's—"

"She's your mom," Lily said. "Go talk to her, and try not to be angry with her. She grew up in a different time when this kind of thing was a much bigger deal."

"I don't *care* what people think," Jakob said.

"We shouldn't care about what people think," she agreed. "But we do care about your mama. Go on. I'll be fine."

Jakob pulled Lily into a tight hug, kissed her, and then hurried after his parents, calling out to his mama. Lily turned around and stared wide-eyed at Anna and Eli, who were unintentional witnesses.

Anna walked over to Lily and hugged her. "Go with him," Anna said. "He could use some support too."

Lily nodded and rocked on her heels for a moment. She tugged a curl and wrapped it around her finger. Then she inhaled and exhaled a shaky breath, looked at Anna one more time, and rushed off to find Jakob.

Anna watched Lily go, and she rubbed her fingers across her collarbone. Night began to fall. A group of children ran by with lit sparklers, leaving behind trails of falling stars.

CHAPTER 15

FIRECRACKER BUNDT CAKE

A WALTZ BEGAN TO PLAY FROM THE FESTIVAL BANDSTAND. "They'll work it out," Eli said.

Anna nodded. "I know. But I wanted it to be different for them when she finally told him. I hoped they could talk in private."

"Some things are better revealed out in the open."

Anna wasn't sure she believed him. Now that Lily had told Jakob the truth, Anna had to keep her end of the deal. Her heart fluttered so badly she wondered if she might pass out.

As soon as the sun set completely, the fireworks would begin. It wouldn't be long now. She would wait to tell him until right before he left to watch them with Tessa. That way if he full-out rejected her, Anna could fall apart in private.

Anna unloaded the few baked goods remaining in boxes, and she displayed them on the tables. Then she broke down the cardboard boxes with Eli's help. The temperature dropped slowly at first with the fading light and then quickly, chilling her cheeks and reddening her nose. Their breath puffed out in front of their lips in misty, white clouds.

"There's my girl," a man said.

Anna smelled green pine needles and freshly cut grass. She grinned.

"Hey, Daddy," she said. He stepped around the side of the tent with Evelyn behind him. Anna hugged him. "I wondered when y'all would stop by." She grabbed a bag of his favorite cookies and handed them to him.

"Looks like you've been ransacked," he said.

"We've had a good day," she answered. "Hey, Mama." Evelyn hugged Anna and then rummaged through what remained of the baked goods. "Daddy, this is Eli. Eli, this is my dad, Charles O'Brien."

Charles O'Brien was the opposite of Evelyn. Where she was wound tightly and pressed neatly, Charles was relaxed and casual. His friendly smile and quiet laughter set people at ease. Anna's daddy had always been a refuge from her mama's strictness. When Anna was a little girl, she and her daddy had often escaped to take hikes or sit in a fishing boat all day while Charles baited her hook and she spotted shapes in the clouds. He was the one to slip chocolates into her pockets and send her off to school when Evelyn packed Anna's brown lunch sack full of carrots and low-fat peanut butter on wheat bread.

"Call me Charlie," he said. "Nice to meet you. Evie said you went to school with Anna."

Eli nodded. "I did. Can't keep up with her, but I try," he said, smiling at Anna.

"That's not an easy task," Charlie said. "But don't give up just yet."

Eli laughed, and Evelyn asked if they were out of the walnut blondies. Eli helped search through the bags while Charlie pulled Anna to the side under the guise of telling her about the auction.

"I had to force your mama to stop bidding on your desserts," Charlie said with a sparkle in his dark eyes. "She was upsetting the townsfolk."

"Mama knows I'll bake her whatever she wants," Anna said and shook her head. She adjusted the black toboggan on Charlie's head because one ear was covered and the other stuck out like an elf ear.

"She can't help herself. It's her competitive nature. She's your biggest fan, you know," Charlie said. "I know it doesn't always seem that way."

"Because she seems like my biggest critic?" Anna asked.

Charlie chuckled. "That's her way of wanting the best for you," he said. Then he lowered his voice. "Even if she isn't always right. You remember what my mama told you, same thing she always told me: Follow your heart. People might not always agree, but they'll respect you for being brave enough to go your own way."

Anna's green eyes widened. A tornado of warm air circled around them, lifting Anna's hair from her shoulders. She hesitated and then smiled. "Thanks, Daddy," she said, feeling ten years old again and basking in her daddy's praise for a job well done.

"Charlie, we need to get going if we're going to find a good spot for the fireworks," Evelyn said, dropping the bag of blondies into her purse.

"Come have lunch with us tomorrow," Charlie said. "I talked your mama into making us fried chicken and mashed potatoes."

Anna laughed. "How in the world did you manage to convince her to cook with grease?" She hooked her arm through Charlie's and walked toward the front of the tent.

"I bribed her actually," he whispered. "New kitchen in exchange for greasy food at least once every two weeks." Charlie and Anna shared a conspiratorial moment of triumph.

"Eli, join us for lunch tomorrow if you're free," Charlie said. "Evie's cooking my favorite."

"I'd like that," Eli said as Charlie patted his back a few times.

"Be there at noon," Evelyn said and retied Anna's scarf around her neck before she and Charlie headed off to find spots to watch the fireworks show.

In the park, festivalgoers bundled up together on blankets and gathered groups of camping chairs in tightly knit areas. Firemen stood around the site where the fireworks would be launched and prepared for any stray sparks that might ignite trees or grass. The crowds on the streets thinned, and people huddled in clearings, already staring up at the stars dotting the midnight-blue sky.

Fear rose up like a beast within her. She couldn't tell Eli how she felt because she couldn't handle seeing his expression of guilt over wanting Tessa instead. He was a good guy, and she knew he'd feel bad about hurting her feelings. It wasn't like she'd never been rejected, but looking into Eli's blue eyes while he told her he was sorry for not choosing her was more than she could stomach.

"All done," Anna said as she lifted the last box into her arms. Best to make a breakaway while she could. "I'll carry this over to the bakery, and then I'll come back for the cardboard."

Eli took the box from her hands. He placed it on one of the back tables. "You don't have to take it right now. The fireworks will be starting soon."

Anna looked over her shoulder as if Tessa might arrive any second. She picked up the box again. "That's okay," she said. "You enjoy them. I can see the show from the bakery."

Eli shook his head and took the box from her hands. His fingers brushed hers, and her stomach tingled as though embers kindled inside her. "Stay here with me," he said.

Anna felt a rush like butterflies shivering inside her body, lifting her up, causing her chest to swell. She opened her mouth and exhaled.

"Eli," she said and paused. Words tangled inside her mind, and they struggled to find her tongue. The truth pulsed through her like a steady drumbeat. "Thanks for helping me," she babbled instead of what she meant to say.

"I like helping you," he said.

Lily had been brave. She'd spoken the truth to Jakob and took the risk, not knowing how he'd respond. Lily's courage gave Anna what she needed to attempt telling Eli how she felt. "Eli, I . . ." Her tongue dried and stuck to her teeth. She tried to swallow. When Anna looked up at him, she felt dizzy with emotion. She pressed one hand to his chest to anchor herself, but warmth spread up her fingertips, her arm, and burned up her spine. She felt his heartbeat beneath her hand.

Eli placed his hand over hers. "You what?" he asked, his voice low and expectant.

Anna blinked. "I'm in love with you," she whispered, her legs trembling. "I'm sorry. I know this is out of nowhere, and I know you like Tessa, but Lily said I should at least be honest with you about it. Tessa will be such a wonderful girlfriend, and it's okay if you don't feel the same way—"

Before Anna could finish, Eli leaned down, slid one hand onto her cheek, and kissed her. There was no hesitation in the kiss like Anna always encountered during first kisses. She knew without a doubt he wanted to kiss her, and once they started, she was captured, unwilling to stop. She arched into Eli, pulled toward him like a planet to its sun, and wrapped her arms around his neck. Anna felt her blood pumping through her limbs, felt her heart slamming against her ribs, felt the heat melting her like sugar. Eli slid one hand around her waist and held her against him.

The cold wind whipped past them, became caught up in their heat, and created swirling vortexes that collapsed a few tents down the street. Flames shot prematurely from the igniter and lit the wick of the first firework before anyone was prepared. It rocketed into the night sky and exploded, raining blue and green twinkling lights over Anna and Eli. The crowd clapped and hooted. More fireworks followed, echoing explosions that mingled with the collective sighs of the townsfolk, and Anna kept kissing Eli because she couldn't stop.

"What the *hell* is going on?"

Eli pulled away, and Anna swayed on her feet. Silver fireworks shaped like giant stars filled the sky and fell away toward the treetops. The smoky haze shifted in her brain, and she pressed her lips together, still feeling the burn of Eli's kiss. Two blurry faces came into focus.

"Baron," Anna said. All the sweetness pooling around her and Eli was swept away in the next assaulting wind, which left behind a rawness.

Tessa stood beside Baron, her mouth open in shock. Baron stepped toward them with his hands open, palms facing front.

"What the hell is going on?" he repeated.

"You're home early," Anna said. Yellow fireworks exploded in rapid succession and lit their faces with golden light.

"I wanted to surprise you," Baron said, not taking his eyes off Eli. "I didn't realize I'd be interrupting."

Electricity crackled off Baron, and the hairs on Anna's arm rose. Baron cursed under his breath, fisted his hands at his sides, and lunged for Eli. Anna jumped between them and used all her energy to shove Baron backward. Tessa grabbed Baron's arm and pulled him away from Eli.

"Baron, stop," Anna said. "*Please.*"

Baron shook Anna and Tessa off him, glared at Eli, then curled his lip at Anna. "I thought you said he was harmless," he said. "That looked like anything but." Then he stalked off.

"Anna, what's going on here?" Tessa asked with tears in her eyes. When Anna didn't respond, Tessa looked at Eli. "Does *anyone* want to tell me what the hell is happening right now?"

Anna cast a glance at Eli over her shoulder. White lights sparkled in the sky like glowing rain. He nodded his head once and walked to Tessa, holding out his hand to her. Tessa clung to him and let Eli lead her away. Anna chased after Baron.

Baron stopped on the corner a block over. He rested his hand against the lamppost and hung his head. That was the only reason Anna caught up with him. Her breath rushed out in hot puffs of air.

"Baron," she said. She saw his shoulders tense, but he didn't turn to look at her. "I'm sorry."

"You should be," he said.

On the next gush of wind, Anna smelled the salty sea. Baron turned and shoved both hands into his messy hair. He shook his head and kicked his shoes against the lamppost. A cluster of fireworks burst overhead, one inside another, each one bigger than the one before.

"You said he was your friend," Baron said. "You lied."

"I didn't lie," Anna said, hazarding a step closer to him. Anger and confusion hovered around Baron like smoke. Anna's body vibrated with uncertainty. "That was the first time anything like that has happened."

Baron threw his hands up into the air. "I'm so lucky to have caught the one-time event." His sarcasm burned her skin.

"I said I'm sorry. I know it doesn't make it better, but I can't change what happened," she said, already feeling the acrid sting of guilt in her throat. She pictured Tessa's shocked face and pinched the bridge of her nose. God, what a mess she'd made.

"I go out of town for a few days, and you move on right away? Did you even think about how this would make me feel? I thought we were taking a break to think things over, not so you could jump in the sack with that guy."

Tears stung Anna's eyes, and her heart thudded painfully against the cage of her chest. She pressed a hand to her breastbone. Like taffy stretched too far and too thin, she came apart in the middle. Flashes of red in the sky turned her tears to rubies rolling down her cheeks. Anger splintered inside her.

"Are you joking?" she asked, and the words sounded jagged and sharp. "You took a job in *California*. In case you didn't realize it, that's across the country from here. You never once thought about including me in that decision. You didn't care how it would make me feel. As far as I can tell, you're going to pack your bags and leave me, and that means our relationship is over for good."

Anna's words flew from her lips like poison-tipped arrows intent on piercing Baron in the chest. He took a few steps back under the assault and stared at her in disbelief. He looked like he wanted to argue her point, but he couldn't.

After a long pause, he said, "You're right." His voice was quiet, barely audible over the explosions of fireworks booming overhead and echoing down the streets. He looked up at her. "I didn't think of our future. I don't know what that means."

"It means we don't have one." The words caught in her throat and tangled around a sob. She wiped at her eyes.

Baron said, "I still didn't expect to come home to this."

"This won't even be your home for much longer," she said.

"No, it won't." He shoved his hands into his jacket pockets and walked away, leaving Anna standing alone in the flickering lamplight.

⌣

Anna walked toward the bakery, watching the fireworks paint the empty street in a throbbing kaleidoscope of colors. She wrapped her arms around her chest, trying to hold on to the escaping warmth. Releasing a shuddering breath, she fished the bakery's keys out of her pocket. Her fingers trembled, and the keys fell to the sidewalk. When Anna bent over to pick them up, she heard Eli's voice, and he sounded angry.

Anna straightened so fast she sidestepped off the curb. Eli strode up the street with Tessa struggling to keep up with him. She said something that Anna couldn't hear, and Eli stopped abruptly. Tessa slammed into his arm. The string lights flickered and popped.

"Tessa, please, stop following me. I mean it," Eli said.

Tessa grabbed Eli's arm. "Don't be angry with me," she begged. "We can talk about this."

Silver fireworks exploded in time with Anna's pulsing heart. *Boom, boom, boom.* Tessa's face was illuminated in ghastly light.

Eli pried Tessa's hand from his arm. "You've said enough," he said. "Don't follow me." His voice was resolute, and when he started walking again, Tessa stayed put and watched him go.

As Eli neared Anna, the asphalt grew hot beneath her shoes. Bulbs burst in the string lights, and half the street slipped into darkness. A stifling oven-hot wind slammed into Anna and filled her lungs with dry, burning air. Anna wasn't sure if Eli even saw her standing in the shadows outside the bakery until he stopped a few yards from her.

"Open the door," he demanded.

Anna unlocked the bakery, and Eli pushed inside ahead of her. She glanced down the street and saw Tessa still standing there. The fireworks finale filled the sky with burst after burst, pounding the night air like a hundred bass drums. Smoke covered the stars and twirled in the sky, caught in an unseasonable wind that created swirling, dancing pinwheels. She and Tessa locked eyes in the darkness for a few seconds, then Tessa turned her back to Anna and walked away. Anna stepped into the dark bakery.

Eli turned on the light in the kitchen, and Anna hesitated before following him. The entire room emitted a low hum that caused the pans to rattle on the shelves.

"Show it to me," Eli said.

Anna stood in the archway. "Show what to you?"

Eli's palms were flat on the kitchen island, and he stared at his fingers. "The magical sugar." Then he pushed away from the island. "Or tell me it isn't real. Just tell me that Tessa is a nice girl but a liar. She talks a lot, says things without thinking."

"Why would she tell you about magical sugar?" Anna said as her brain scrambled to find a solution while feeling like she was tumbling down a hill covered in thorn bushes.

"Doesn't the truth set you free?" he asked, his voice still angry and rumbling through the room like thunder. "She said it was only fair that I know the truth about you and me, about why I love you. She wanted to set me free." Eli's blue eyes met Anna's. "I need you to tell me she's lying."

A tremble started low in Anna's legs and shook her all the way to her scalp. Anna opened her mouth to explain, but nothing came out. She pressed her hands together to keep them from shaking, but her entire body vibrated like a tuning fork slapped against a tree.

Eli shook his head. "No, Anna," he said. "No, no, no. Don't tell me that you created me." He stormed over to the oven and flung open the door. "*In there.* Don't tell me I came out of *that.*" Eli's blue eyes were narrowed and flecked with anguish. He slammed his fist against the island. "I'm not some *thing,* Anna."

Anna's hands found her mouth. Tears spilled over her lids and rolled down her fingertips. "You're not a thing," she said when she lowered her hands. "You're not."

"Then what the hell am I?" he asked in a breakable, furious voice. "Did you *create* me?"

Anna could barely breathe around the splintering in her chest. More tears rolled down her cheeks. "Yes."

He clenched his jaw and shook his head, unwilling to accept her answer. "Show me the sugar."

Anna knew it wasn't a request. She stumbled up the stairs toward her apartment with Eli on her heels. She switched on the light in her bedroom and opened the closet door. Anna pulled down the locked box and held it out for Eli with shaking hands. He turned the key and inhaled loudly through his nose when he flipped open the lid. He shoved one hand into the sugar, and it shimmered on his fingers, skittered up his arm, and disappeared into his skin. He dropped the box onto the bed, scattering granules across her quilt.

Eli backed away toward the door. His blue eyes were wide and heartbreaking. Anna stood and held out a hand toward him. He seemed to look straight through her.

"None of this is real," he said in disbelief.

"That's not true," Anna argued.

"Why?" he asked. "Why did you make me?"

Anna swallowed and averted her gaze. "I was sad about Baron, and Lily thought it would be a good idea for me to make the perfect man for myself. We didn't think it would work."

Eli released a bitter laugh. "Tessa wanted to prove she was telling the truth by asking me questions about my past. Do you know what my entire past consists of?" he asked. "You. Just *you*." He pressed his fisted hands against his chest. "I have all this love for you, and it isn't even *real*. I don't even know what the hell I *am*." He dug a folded sheet of paper out of his pocket and tossed it onto her bed. "You wrote this, didn't you? Another lie?"

Anna reached for the paper. She unfolded a note written in her handwriting.

Dearest Elijah,

I don't know that soul mates exist or that true love finds everyone, but I've heard anything is possible. I'd be willing to give love another try if you are.

The letter looked like it had been folded and unfolded a thousand times. Her candy note written to a ball of dough had become a real love letter. She looked up at him and pressed the letter to her chest.

"I do love you, Eli," she said. Her throat closed tight with sadness.

His blue eyes began to water and shine in the light. "I'm not even human," he said in a voice so quiet Anna found herself leaning toward him. "You can't love a monster." He turned and walked out.

"Eli," she called.

Eli stopped, hand resting on her doorknob. Anna wanted to run to him, throw her arms around him, prove to him that her love was real. But Eli opened the door and walked out, saying, "Do us both a favor and let me go." Anna crumpled onto the hardwood and cried into her hands.

CHAPTER 16

CHOCOLATE CHIP COOKIES

ANNA GATHERED THE SPILLED GOLDEN SUGAR FROM HER COM-
forter in small handfuls and dropped it into the box. Then she
brushed the remaining granules onto the wooden floor, where
they sparkled like miniature jewels. She closed the box and
rubbed her fingers across the lid.

The tea in the red kettle whispered for a few seconds before
it became a loud whistle. She cradled the box in her arms,
walked into the living room, and placed the box on the coffee
table. Then she shuffled into the kitchen and grabbed the kettle's
handle as she turned off the burner. She poured the steaming
liquid over the peppermint tea bag resting in the bottom of her
mug. Anna bounced the tea bag up and down in the water and
crossed the small space to the bay window. She curled up, bringing her knees to her chest, and stared out the windows into the
night.

Festivalgoers ambled up the downtown streets on their way

to their cars. Their cheerful voices and laughter traveled toward Anna's window. She watched their shadows disappear around corners and heard their engines turn over, not a soul knowing the devastation she felt. Anna sipped her tea, musing that it might possibly flow out of the giant hole she felt had been shot through the middle of her body. She rubbed her right temple, trying to ease the throbbing behind her eyes.

She knew it was ridiculous, but as people passed by on the street below, she kept looking for Eli. She wondered if she would keep looking for him forever. A tear dropped into her mug of tea. Then another and another. Soon there were more tears in her mug than drops of peppermint tea.

Sunday morning dawned bright with a radiant October sunrise that mocked Anna's feelings. She dragged herself out of bed, thankful the bakery was closed for business, and showered in water hot enough to melt away years of her life. If only it could have dissolved the night before. Eli hadn't come home, which she'd expected. Still, she had hoped.

The apartment felt colder and emptier than it had in days. She needed to get her mind off herself, off her misplaced heart. Pulling a sweatshirt over her head, she decided one of the best remedies for heartache was baking. Downstairs she found a few boxes stacked on the kitchen island beside her keys. She'd completely forgotten to gather up the leftover goods and items from the festival the night before, but someone remembered. That same someone had locked up the bakery and left behind her keys. Eli? Or Lily?

She checked her phone, but there were no messages. Anna texted her mama to let her parents know she wasn't feeling well and wouldn't be over for lunch. She needed to check in on Lily today and see how the evening had fared. Hopefully Lily's had been better than Anna's. She wondered if Tessa had already told Lily what happened. When Anna thought of Tessa, remorse coupled with frustration left her feeling worse. Anna moped around the bakery, gathering ingredients for an OREO and peanut butter pie. She also started a batch of white chocolate macadamia nut cookies because Beatrice had sworn that cookies made any difficulty easier to endure. With her mind focused on mixing and baking, there was room for little else.

Anna texted Lily midafternoon after she'd made a variety of desserts for her one-woman sugar-rush buffet, and Lily revealed she knew about Tessa, Eli, *and* Baron. She also said she'd be over to see Anna later that evening. She first had to attend a Sunday family dinner "meeting" planned at the Connellys.

After skipping dinner and eating a slice of pie instead, Anna mindlessly flipped through her streaming options. Finding nothing of interest, she turned the TV off. She paced around her apartment, rearranged her cookbooks, and drank too many cups of tea. At almost eight p.m., someone knocked on the door. Anna's mind jumped right to Eli, even though she knew Lily was coming over. She flung open her apartment door, and Lily stepped through the doorway.

"Are you okay?" Lily asked, giving her a look of pity. Anna shook her head. "I want to talk about what happened, but before you say anything, you should know that Tessa is waiting in the car. She's confused and upset, and you might not want to talk to her, but we're best friends. All of us. This whole thing has spiraled out of control, and we need to fix this mess. I'm not losing the two of you over this."

Anna dropped onto the couch and folded in half, pressing her forehead to her knees.

"Everything is ruined. I screwed this one up big time." Tears tried to well in her red, swollen eyes, but she blinked them back.

"You have to fix this."

Anna sat up and wondered if she could take one more person's disappointment. Would Tessa yell at her? Accuse her of stealing her boyfriend? Lily must have seen the indecision on Anna's face because she sat down beside her on the couch. Lily shrugged out of her coat and unwrapped her scarf.

"We can work this out," Lily said. "But we're going to have to talk about it. This isn't worth ruining friendships." She glanced around. "Where's Eli?"

"He left," Anna said.

"When?"

"Last night," Anna said. "After I told him the truth, he left and told me to let him go. Said it was for the best. I'm not sure he'll ever speak to me again. I may never *see* him again." She closed her eyes and inhaled deeply. The thought of never speaking to him again left her with an ache too deep to rub away.

Lily shook her head. "He'll come back. This whole thing is forgivable."

"Is it?" Anna asked.

"Everything is," Lily said. "You can talk to Tessa and sort things out with her first."

Anna nodded. "Let's get this over with. Hey, what happened with you and Jakob? How was dinner tonight?"

Lily glanced into the kitchen. "Do you have coffee?"

"I have decaf in the pantry," Anna said.

"Decaf?" Lily curled her lip. "Why do they even *make* decaf? I need a jolt of something if I'm going to make it through this evening."

"Aren't pregnant women supposed to avoid caffeine?"

"Yes." Lily walked into the kitchen and opened the pantry. She pulled out a round tin of hot chocolate powder. "Chocolate in moderation is acceptable." She busied her hands while she talked. "Jakob's mama is . . . difficult. She thinks we've ruined our future. Completely melodramatic."

"I have milk and heavy cream in the fridge." Anna reached for her mug of tea. "What does Jakob think?"

"He thinks she's being over the top, but he's trying to smooth things over with her. His dad is completely cool about all of it. He's excited to finally have a grandchild. He gave me a hug before Mrs. Connelly gave him the evil eye." Lily shrugged, then put her mug in the microwave. "Jakob is more concerned about how I feel, which irritates his mama. So I told him to spend some extra time with her, help her feel special. I mean, I'm *pregnant* for crying out loud, and she's made this whole thing about her." She heaved a heavy sigh.

"She'll come around," Anna said. "If not now, then once that beautiful baby is here, she'll be bragging to the whole town about her grandbaby."

The microwave dinged. Lily stirred the chocolate powder into the milk. "I know. It still makes me sad, though. I wish his mama would be more reasonable." She blew across the top of the steaming cocoa before taking a sip. "Ready to start this party?"

Anna nodded. Lily texted Tessa, and Anna listened to Tessa's hurried footsteps coming up the stairs. She rushed through the door out of the cold night air, then stood in the living room with her hands clasped in front of her.

"Where's Eli?" Tessa asked.

"He's gone," Lily answered so Anna didn't have to.

"Gone where?" Tessa asked, her voice pitching high. She glanced quickly at Lily and then at Anna.

Anna shrugged. Tessa dropped into the chair. Tessa's mouth was so dry Anna could hear her swallow. Disappointment highlighted her frown.

Guilt expanded in Anna's chest, and she exhaled to release the building tensions. "I'm sorry, Tessa," she said. "I really didn't want to hurt you."

Tessa wrung her hands together in her lap. "Why would you kiss Eli?" she asked, and her voice wavered slightly. "You *knew* how I felt about him."

Lily pulled a mug from the cabinet and felt the side of the kettle. She dug a tea bag out of the pantry and dropped it into the mug. Then she poured the hot water from the kettle. She carried the mug into the living room and handed it to Tessa.

Anna lowered her gaze to the floor. "Because I have feelings for him too."

Tessa squeezed the mug between both hands and held it close. "I thought you had feelings for him because you made him." Anger pinched her voice. She stared into the tinting water. "You don't kiss someone your friend is dating."

Anna leaned forward, propped her elbows on her knees, and covered her face with her hands for a few moments. She massaged her fingertips across her forehead. "You're right. It was wrong of me and unfair to you."

"Tessa, Anna is well aware that she upset you," Lily said, "but she wasn't trying to hurt anyone. And you need to remember that we made Eli for *Anna*. She's had feelings for him since the beginning."

Tessa looked at Anna. "You should have told me," she said. Then she stared at the floor while she added, "I wouldn't have moved in on him if I knew you had a thing, but you acted like y'all were just friends."

"I know," Anna admitted.

Tessa straightened her shoulders. "You should know I have no intention of giving up my feelings. I think Eli cares about me, and we have something. I think you should back off."

Anna's eyes widened. Could she give Eli up to Tessa? Did it even matter now that he was gone? He'd been so angry with her.

Tessa sipped her tea and cleared her throat. "I wasn't trying to make the situation worse by telling Eli the truth." She sat her mug down and unbuttoned her coat. She slid her scarf from her neck and gripped it in her lap. "But you know how I get when I'm upset and start talking. I was so shocked to see y'all kissing, and Baron was there, and he was angry and wanted to fight, and Eli was trying to tell me what was going on between you two, and it just came out. He deserved to know the truth. He needed to understand why his feelings for you were confusing. I know you made Eli for you, but he and I were spending time together. He made that choice, right, to spend time with me?" She reached for her mug.

"He's not a puppet," Anna said. She leaned back onto the couch cushions. "He spent time with you because he wanted to." Because he had chosen Tessa. Then why had he kissed Anna like he never wanted to stop? A tiny flame smoldered low in her stomach.

Tessa tried to hide a small, relieved smile behind the mug.

She sipped her tea. "What you did isn't okay," she said. "I can see why you care about him, but my feelings for Eli are real, and I believe he wants to see where a relationship with me will go. I think it's only right and fair that you let him go."

Eli's words as he was leaving echoed in Anna's mind. *Do us both a favor and let me go.* She closed her eyes and nodded.

The three friends sat in silence for a minute. Lily folded her legs beneath her on the couch beside Anna. She drank from her mug, then asked, "What did you tell Baron?"

"The truth," Anna said. She finished her tea and pushed her hair behind her shoulders as she stared across the room at the brownies hiding beneath the glass cake dome. She recapped what had happened on the street corner with Baron.

The loss of Baron had become a dull ache. In her heart, pieces of him had been leaving for days. Only now with Eli gone did Anna realize how much space Eli had been taking up in her heart. With both men gone, she felt as hollow as a chocolate Easter bunny.

"It's over with him for good?" Lily asked. Anna nodded. Lily grabbed her hand. "I'm sorry."

"Me too," Tessa said.

When Anna looked at Tessa, she could tell Tessa's feelings were genuine. A small smile passed between them. The box on the coffee table caught Tessa's eye. She leaned forward and tapped her finger against the lid.

"Is this the box?" Tessa asked. "With the magic sugar?" Anna nodded. Tessa reached for the box and flipped open the lid. It sparkled and lit her face with dancing pinpricks of light. "It's beautiful." She smiled at the granules before closing the lid. "What are you going to do with it?"

Anna shook her head. "No idea. I thought of burying it. It's caused enough trouble." She looked at Lily. "Do you think it would hurt the earth to bury it?"

"You mean would the earthworms grow to gargantuan size or turn into mutants?" Lily grinned at Anna's shocked face. "I'm kidding. I doubt that would happen. But this is your family's gift. Do you really want to throw it away? Couldn't you just promise yourself never to use it again?"

"I can only use it once anyway," Anna said. "That's the one rule Grandma Bea mentioned."

Tessa returned the box to the coffee table. "Can anyone else use it?"

Anna shrugged.

"I don't think you should bury it just yet," Tessa said. "Think about it for a while and then decide. If you want to bury it, you should at least keep a little since it's special to your family."

Lily yawned and stretched her legs onto the coffee table. "The hot chocolate didn't give me the jolt I needed. I should probably go home, but I'm so comfortable right here." Lily pointed at the brownies. "Are those up for grabs?"

"There's also a pie, cookies, a cookies and cream mousse, and homemade butter pecan ice cream," Anna admitted. When Lily snickered, Anna added, "You know I bake when I'm upset."

"Thank God, for that," Lily said. "I'm sorry you've been stress baking, but it's a total win for the rest of us. And better than Tessa baking."

"Hey!" Tessa objected. "I can bake . . . frozen pizza and stuff." She wandered into the kitchen and opened the fridge to take out the mousse. She found a spoon, dug it into the speckled dessert, and slid a heaping scoop into her mouth. "We should have a slumber party tonight. We haven't done that in ages."

Lily yawned again. "Since I don't want to move from the spot, I'd say that's a great idea. Bring me a brownie, will ya?"

Anna stood and stretched her arms over her head. "I think I'm going to take a bath if no one cares. Feel free to find a movie we can watch. I'll be back in a bit."

Tessa pulled Anna into a quick but tight hug. "You're not mad at me, are you?" Tessa asked.

Anger wasn't the emotion Anna felt wrestling around inside her. The emotion was darker and bleaker. There didn't seem to be an easy way to describe how she felt, so she simply said no. Then she added, "I understand if you're mad at me for a while, but I hope you'll forgive me."

Tessa smiled. "It's already passing," she said, looking down at the box on the coffee table. "Such a small thing to cause so much chaos, but I think we can fix what's happened."

Anna lifted the lid just enough to see the shiny golden sugar inside. Sparkles danced across her face, and she closed the box with a sigh. "It can only go up from here, right?"

When Anna turned on the taps for the bathtub, she sat on the edge and wiggled her fingers through the steaming water. She thought of Eli on foot somewhere in town. Would he have walked far? Would he ever return? She sank into the water, draped her hair over the side, and closed her eyes. Even if he did return, she'd agreed to let Tessa have him. Losing Baron was going to be nothing compared to watching Tessa and Eli fall deeper in love every day. She shuddered in the tub.

Sometime later Anna jerked awake, startled to find herself reclining in cool water. After a few seconds of disorientation, she realized she'd dozed off while taking a bath. She shivered and climbed out of the tub, wrapping herself in a towel. The room smelled like baking bread, a mixture of rosemary, Italian seasoning, and a sprinkling of mozzarella. She dressed in pajamas and opened the bathroom door.

Anna found Lily sleeping on the couch, her head leaning against the back cushions and her legs still stretched on the coffee table. The living room felt humid and sticky. The odor of a hot oven hung in the air like low-lying storm clouds. Someone had put the mugs and dirty dishes in the kitchen sink. Tessa appeared to have gone home. The door to the staircase leading to the bakery was open. She stepped to the door to close it, but the lights in the bakery's kitchen were on. Anna heard someone moving around downstairs.

Her breath caught in her throat. Had Eli returned? She rushed down the stairs, nearly tripping over her bare feet as she stumbled down the last few steps. With a clear view of the kitchen, Anna gripped the railing on the staircase. Tessa was wiping flour dust from the island and looked up at Anna like a startled mouse. Grandma Bea's box rested on the island; its lid was flipped open, and the sugar glittered in the lights. Anna's eyes drifted toward the ovens behind Tessa. The red light on the top oven was lit, indicating it was in use.

"What are you doing?" Anna asked. She let go of the railing and stepped farther into the kitchen. When Tessa didn't answer, Anna pointed to the box. "What are you doing with that?"

Tessa tucked her hair behind her ears. "Don't be mad, okay? *Promise* you won't be mad." Tessa reached over and flipped the lid closed. "I had an idea."

CHAPTER 17

FLAMING CHERRIES JUBILEE

"Tell me you didn't use the sugar," Anna said in a strangled voice. She could tell from Tessa's expression that it was too late. She stared at the oven and felt a shiver run from her toes to her head, where it made her hair prickle and lift from her scalp.

"I did this for you," Tessa said, and Anna was surprised to see such excitement in Tessa's eyes because Anna felt an emotion akin to terror traveling over her skin. "I thought since you made Eli—and he's for me—that I could make *you* someone to love."

Anna covered her mouth with her hand and shook her head. She had no idea what would happen if someone else used the secret ingredient; Beatrice had left no warnings or list of consequences. Maybe no one else had ever tried something so foolish. Anna stared at Tessa with wide eyes before a realization struck her. She lowered her hand. "What recipe did you use?"

Tessa frowned. "I didn't have your recipe, so I used my mama's recipe for Italian bread from memory. Then I tossed in a few extra things." She glanced over her shoulder at the oven. "It smells wonderful, doesn't it?" Tessa's eyes were alive with anticipation.

No recipe. The stench of burning cheese, bubbling and charring beneath the intense heat, began to saturate the kitchen. "This isn't a joke, Tessa. You can't make a recipe using whatever ingredients you want. There's a science to baking, but this is next-level complex. How did you know how much of the sugar to add?" Anna moved slowly around the island toward the oven. She couldn't stop the anxiety growing inside her like an invasive vine. It wrapped around her stomach, then her lungs, then her heart. She tried to make her breaths deep and even, but her heart raced.

"I guessed," Tessa said with a shrug. "I dumped in a few handfuls." She looked disappointed. "I did this for *you*. I want you to be happy too."

Anna shook her head. "Look what happened when Grandma Bea tried to make a man for your grandma. Their friendship was ruined, and everyone thought your grandma was crazy. Me creating Eli almost ruined our friendship. This isn't right, Tessa."

"Just wait a little longer," Tessa pleaded. "Let's see what happens. He might be the most wonderful man you've ever known. Maybe he'll fix everything."

An idea occurred to Anna. There might still be a chance to repair the damage. "How long has the dough been cooking?"

Tessa glanced at the clock on the wall. "Ten minutes or so."

Anna exhaled. There was still time to stop Tessa's mistake.

Anna grabbed the handle of the oven, but Tessa snatched her hand away.

"Anna, *please*," she said. "Let's wait and see—"

The oven groaned and metal buckled as though something inside had become too large for the confined space. Anna grabbed Tessa's arm and pulled her away from the ovens. Smoke oozed out around the oven door and swirled in the air, creating dark clouds that hovered near the ceiling. The room stank of char. Without warning, the oven door burst open so violently it snapped from its hinges and slammed into the island. Tessa's fingernails dug into Anna's arm. They stood and stared, unable to move, transfixed by what was happening.

Through the smoke a malformed humanlike hand reached out and gripped the side of the oven. Black smoke billowed out, and something moved in the darkness, unfolding itself. The built-in oven dislocated from the wall on one side and jutted forward. Anna heard the grind and rasp of metal. Connecting pipes and wires snapped. A face emerged, and Tessa's scream caused a glass cake plate to shatter on the shelf. Blue shards exploded into the air.

Anna felt Tessa trembling beside her as her scream faded. The thing that emerged from the oven was no longer a ball of dough, but it wasn't a man either. It lurched sideways and gripped the only remaining rack in the hot oven. The doughy flesh on its hand sizzled, and the thing opened a slit in its knobby face, releasing a garbled, bubbling noise. It snatched the rack from the mangled oven and heaved it across the room, where it clattered into the storage room and sizzled against unused cake boxes. With a shrieking of metal, the oven pulled completely away from the wall and crashed to the floor. Anna knew gas would be billowing from the exposed, broken pipes in the recess where the oven had been. They needed to get out of the bakery.

The monster was tall but listed on uneven legs that looked like misshapen breadsticks with stumps for feet. It had two very human arms, but its hands were a combination of sticky, raw dough and fingerlike extensions. The body was lumpy like dough left uncovered overnight. Parts were hard and cracked like compacted mud in a dry riverbed, and other sections looked as though they would be tacky to the touch. The entire torso was flecked with bits of green. When it turned its hairless head, its black, deep-set eyes lacked proper lids, eyelashes, or eyebrows. Another horrible noise erupted from the slit in its face, and it lunged across the island for them, slamming into the box of golden sugar. The box careened off the island and smashed into the opposite wall. Tessa screamed again, and Lily's voice shouted from the top of the stairs.

"What's going on?" Lily hurried halfway down the stairs and stopped as she fanned smoke away from her face. "Is the bakery on fire?"

"Get outside!" Anna yelled over her shoulder. "There's a gas leak."

"What the hell is that?" Lily asked, staring at the misshapen creature pushing off the island into a standing position.

"Get out of here!" Anna repeated.

The monster yanked open a drawer in the island and pulled out a knife for cutting large blocks of chocolate. Anna tried to push Tessa toward the staircase where Lily stood, but the monster had quickly grown accustomed to its uneven legs. It pounced around the island with unnerving agility, and Tessa and Anna were forced back toward the ovens. Lily lifted a small canister of candy melts from a nearby shelf and tossed it through the air. Her aim was slightly off, but the canister crashed into the monster's shoulder, breaking off a piece of its back, and the monster stumbled forward and fell. Ovals of chocolate scattered across the floor as the canister shattered against the tiles.

Lily snatched two bottles of cooking oil from the shelf and flung them at the downed monster, one after another. The first bottle hit it squarely in the back and lodged itself for a moment in the doughy flesh. The second bottle missed it completely, bounced off the tiles, and burst open against the wall, sending a flood of oil across the floor. "Hurry," Lily yelled. "Get out while it's down."

Anna grabbed Tessa and pulled her toward the dining room so they could run out the front door. The monster lurched from the floor, and the bottle of oil popped out of its back. It leaned down, grabbed the bottle, and hurled it at Anna and Tessa. The bottle caught Tessa in the back of her head. She moaned and collapsed forward onto Anna, causing them both to fall. Anna's breath rushed from her lungs as Tessa's body pinned her to the floor. On her next inhale, Anna choked on the colorless gas that hovered over the tiles. The stench of rotten eggs filled her throat and caused her eyes to water.

Lily rushed to their rescue, and the only thing that saved them from the monster's wrath for a moment was the spilled oil. The monster's feet slipped, and it skidded into the wall, but it was quick to regain its balance.

"We have to get her off the floor," Anna said and coughed. "Gas."

Lily rolled Tessa off Anna and slapped Tessa's cheek, but Tessa didn't respond. The monster lurched around the island straight for them, sliding on slick, stumpy feet as it moved. Lily hooked her arms beneath Tessa's armpits and dragged her away. Anna pushed herself up and ran bent over toward the monster like a defensive tackle. She caught it in the stomach and felt her body press into its soft flesh. They slammed into the stove. The monster scrambled beneath her weight. Two of the burners on the stove clicked and flickered to life with low blue flames. The monster made the mistake of pressing its hands on the stove for leverage so it could push off and knock Anna to the ground. Both of its hands ignited. Anna stumbled away as the monster waved its hands in the air to extinguish the flames, but the fire leaped from its hands to its back and traveled to its feet, which quickly began to burn because of the oil slicking its body.

"We have to get out!" Anna shouted, scrambling to help Lily drag Tessa's body into the front room. "It's on fire, and there's a gas leak. If it gets too close to the flour sacks, they'll explode."

But it was too late.

The monster bellowed, throwing sparks like an exploding Roman candle. For half a second, the gas hovering over the tiles glittered as though hundreds of fireflies fought to escape with burning wings. With one great inhale, sound and air rushed toward the epicenter of the leak, and then an instant later, the gas whooshed into flames that roared across the floor of the bakery like a tsunami of fire. The force of the burst threw Lily off to the side. Anna's head slammed into a display case, and she crumpled to the floor, lying on her side in a daze, watching flames lick the walls and eat through bags and paper boxes. Tiny flames marched toward her, and she tried to move away, but her legs were slow to respond. When she opened her mouth to call for help, the air wasn't fit for breathing, and she coughed instead.

A massive hulking creature moved through the bakery. When it spun into view, the burning shape looked like a flame dancer. It crashed into the island, into the walls, into the staircase railing, leaving behind blazing trails that wrapped around everything and climbed the walls. Anna tried to sit up, but her head spun. The monster dropped to its knees, where it became a burning, bubbling mound dwindling to nothing.

Tessa lay in front of Anna with her body covered in pieces of melted chocolate. Flames jumped onto Tessa's clothes, and Anna reached for her, grabbing Tessa's arm. Anna tried to tug, but every time she breathed, she choked. A cry lodged itself in her throat. This was all her fault. Everything. She would lose *everything* tonight. Unable to keep her head lifted, Anna's eyes closed, and darkness swooped in.

CHAPTER 18

MOLTEN CHOCOLATE CAKE

A WINDOW SHATTERED SOMEWHERE IN THE BAKERY. MALE voices shouted and prodded Anna's mind awake. She heard the pounding of shoes against the tiles. Her body rose from the floor, and she dangled in the air, pressed against something warm and strong. Cold air rushed across her face and into her lungs.

"I have her. Grab Tessa," a man said.

Someone carried Anna at a quick pace. She coughed a few times before a solid, freezing burst of air filled her lungs. When she opened her eyes, a thousand stars glittered in the dark sky. She saw trees, and branches empty of leaves stretched across her vision.

"Eli?" she asked in a rasping voice.

He laid her on the crisp grass that poked into her pajamas like tiny toothpicks made of ice. "Lie still," he said, brushing her hair from her face. His hand lingered on her cheek.

"My head hurts," she said. Tears rolled out the corners of her eyes.

Anna felt a rush of relief at the sight of his blue eyes looking down at her face. She reached up to touch his cheek, but she heard Baron's voice. Then his face hovered into view, and Eli's was gone.

"Can you hear me? Are you okay?" Baron asked. "What happened?"

Anna suddenly pictured the jerking, burning monster as it destroyed the bakery's kitchen. She sat up and gasped. Pain shot through the back of her skull, and she doubled over. She clutched Baron's arm. "The bakery is on fire," she said. "My apartment." Anna saw a body beside her. Tessa. She reached for Tessa's still hand. Then she panicked at the sight of only Tessa. "Lily? Where's Lily?"

"Lily was in the bakery?" Baron asked. He looked up at Eli. "Did you see her?"

Sirens wailed in the distance, moving closer. People stood along the sidewalks, huddled together for warmth and comfort. Eli and Baron sprinted back toward the bakery. All eyes stared at the burning building lit from the inside with an eerie, flickering orange glow. Glass littered the sidewalk in front of the bakery, and smoke billowed out of the broken windows. Anna crawled over to Tessa, who was covered in Baron's jacket. She pressed her fingers to Tessa's neck. There was a steady pulse, and she wiped smudges of ash from Tessa's cheek. For a few seconds, Anna laid her forehead against Tessa's shoulder, thankful to know she would be okay. The night had shifted from heartbreaking to horrendous. Anna looked over her shoulder at the fire.

Anna stood and winced. Her head pounded, spreading an

ache from the back of her skull toward her eyes. She staggered up the street in the direction of the bakery. Baron stumbled out, bent over and coughing. He leaned against the next building and sucked in the cold night air. Suddenly, the flames roared, and the bay window in Anna's apartment shattered. Baron looked up and saw her. He ran toward her, grabbed her arm, and pulled her away.

"We have to stay back," he said. "The whole place is going up in flames."

Anna fought against Baron's strength. "No," she argued. "Lily and Eli—"

"He carried her out the back door," he said.

"Is she okay?"

"Her outfit has seen better days, but she'll be fine. I promise," he said, grabbing her shoulders and forcing her to look at him. "I promise."

Anna stopped struggling. Lily and Eli were safe. Her legs trembled, and she leaned against Baron. She saw tiny burns in Baron's shirt where sparks had leaped onto his clothes. He lifted her from her feet and carried her back to the grassy area. Baron lowered her to the ground, and Anna sat there watching as flames destroyed her life. A siren blasted through the night as a fire truck whipped around the corner onto Main Street. Firemen bustled out of a gleaming red truck and assessed the situation. They attached the fire hose to the blue hydrant and opened the nozzle full blast.

Eli appeared through the smoke. His arm was draped around Lily's shoulder, leading her to the grassy area. When Lily saw Anna, she tore away from him and ran to her best friend. They hugged tightly and shivered in the frigid air.

Lily said, "The blast knocked me out for a minute, and when I woke up, the fire had boxed me in. I yelled and yelled, but I couldn't see y'all through the smoke. And then I couldn't *breathe*. Eli appeared out of nowhere and snatched me up as if I were a doll." Her eyes drifted to Eli, who stood nearby watching Anna. "Are you okay?" Lily asked, looking Anna over. "Where's Tessa?"

Anna motioned over her shoulder, and they knelt beside Tessa. "She's okay. She has a pulse." Just saying the words made Anna's throat close. She shivered and stood, crossing her arms over her chest and watching the firemen combat the inferno.

"You're probably freezing in those pajamas." Lily slipped her arm around Anna's shoulders. Anna leaned against her. It seemed like the whole world was burning. Smoke blotted out the stars one by one. Main Street smelled like a catastrophe.

Anna started to say she was okay, but she wasn't. Ash floated through the air like snowflakes and caught in her hair. Her teeth chattered as the wind blew burned pieces of her life down the street.

"And the other thing?" Lily whispered.

"Gone. Burned up with everything else I hope. I don't know how anything could survive that."

Ambulances and police cars arrived on the scene. Policemen and EMTs spilled out of their cars, looking for victims. Baron ran over to meet them, and Anna watched as he pointed toward their small group crowded on the grass, clinging to each other just to make sure they weren't alone. Water battled the fire until only a sodden, charred mess—a great, gaping hole—remained where Anna's home used to be.

"We can repair buildings," Lily said as encouragement. "At least we're all okay."

Anna knew Lily was right, but when she stared at the remains of Bea's Bakery, her mind was blank except for one word: *gone*. She had no job, no home, no clothes, no food. The wind brought wisps of curling, ashy smoke and the horrible stench of burned plastic.

The EMTs immediately assisted Tessa, lifting her gently onto a stretcher. When they jostled her body, Tessa finally awoke. She called for Anna with a smoke-choked voice. The policemen approached and asked Anna to give details about what happened. She rested her hand on Tessa's arm while she explained the events leading up to the fire. She and her two friends had decided to make cookies, and the oven had malfunctioned, creating a gas leak. Anna and Tessa made eye contact, and Tessa mouthed the words *thank you*. Mystic Water would never know what really happened inside Bea's Bakery, and they would never know there had been a fourth body present in the fire.

They were lucky to be alive, the policemen and firemen agreed. The EMTs situated an oxygen mask over Tessa's face. She blinked up at Anna as tears filled her eyes. "It's going to be okay," Anna assured her. "It's going to be okay," she said again to assure herself. Anna gave Tessa's hand a squeeze as the EMTs pushed the stretcher into the ambulance.

An EMT began asking Lily questions and insisted she take a ride to the hospital so they could check her over. Lily refused. "I'm staying with Anna."

Anna turned and looked at Lily, at the defiance she saw in her friend's eyes. She walked over to the EMTs speaking with Lily. "You should go. Make sure you're okay. We breathed in a lot of smoke, and I'd feel better if I knew you and the peanut were okay," Anna said.

Lily's hand instinctively went to her stomach. "But what about you? Why don't you ride with me, and we can get checked out together?"

Anna's eyes drifted to the wreck of a building on Main Street. She rubbed the back of her head. "I should stay here and make sure the police have everything they need."

Lily sat down on the rear step at the back of the open ambulance. "Promise me you'll call the doctor in the morning if you're having any symptoms? Wait, where are you going to stay? Do you want to go to my place? Or call Jakob?"

Anna hadn't even thought that far ahead. Where would she stay? "I'll call my parents." Lily held out her pinky, and Anna almost smiled. She hooked her pinky around Lily's. "I promise I'll call the doctor in the morning if I need to." Anna pressed her lips together to keep them from trembling as Lily climbed into the back of the ambulance with an EMT, and the doors closed.

Anna walked up the wet street. Rivers of dirty water washed down the edges of the curbs and disappeared into the gutters. Anna bent down and lifted sopping wet papers. Underneath the soot and freezing water, Anna could faintly read the words of the contract for the Clarke House. The top edges were blackened and torn away. The contract hung limp in her hands, but she pressed it to her chest and squeezed her eyes closed.

She stood and inhaled a shaky breath, clenching her teeth to stop them from chattering. When she glanced around, she saw Eli in a crowd of people who'd gathered at the edges of the scene. Anna assumed they were late-nighters who had been lingering at the corner pub. She didn't see Baron anywhere. The crowd parted as the ambulances pulled away. Anna knew she should call her parents, but she looked at the burned shell of the bakery and realized her cell phone was lost somewhere in the rubble. Without thinking, Anna walked over to Eli. She stopped in front of him. She wanted to ask him to hold her, but she didn't have to. He enfolded her in his arms and pressed her against him.

"Thank you," she mumbled against his chest. "I'm so glad you came back."

"Not as glad as I am," he said, holding her tighter. He slid his hand down her hair and kissed the top of her head. His arms were streaked with soot.

"Everything is gone," Anna said, finally allowing herself to fully cry, not caring that they stood within view of people who were probably showering her with pity.

"It's going to be okay," Eli said as he stroked her hair, and Anna desperately wanted to believe him.

Time quickly slipped by, with people moving in soundless blurs of color. Anna felt she and Eli were frozen at the center of the activity as everyone else whirred past like people on a carousel. She could have stood in his arms forever, or at least until the shock wore off—which she felt might take forever just the same.

"Anna!" someone yelled. It was her mama.

Eli released his hold on her, and Anna turned to see her parents and Baron pushing through the crowd and around the emergency vehicles. Anna knew her mama must have been worried because she hadn't taken the time to properly apply makeup or make sure her hair was perfect. She still looked beautiful, however, and was the exact person Anna wanted to see. Evelyn wrapped her in a hug so tight Anna could barely draw a full breath. Evelyn stroked her back and pulled away just far enough to look at Anna's face. Her daddy wrapped both women in his arms and kissed the side of Anna's head. Then he pulled off his coat and wrapped it around Anna's shoulders.

"Thank the Lord you're okay," Evelyn said. "When Baron called, my heart nearly stopped. Your dad drove like a maniac to get us here. It's a miracle *we're* okay." Evelyn wiped Anna's dirty cheeks.

Anna looked at Baron, whose hands were shoved in his pockets, his shirt burned. "I thought you'd want me to call them," Baron said.

Anna nodded and her eyes filled with tears. "Thank you," she said and meant it. Baron had finally thought about what *she* needed. And at that moment she needed her parents more than anyone else. She wanted to nestle into the comfort they offered and lose herself. She wanted someone to tell her how to fix this terrible mess. But more than that, she wanted to lie down, close her eyes, and drift away long enough to ease the pounding in her head and the ache in her heart.

Anna heard her daddy thanking Baron and Eli, his voice flooded with gratitude. The police officers said they would call her if they needed anything else, and they expressed their sympathies. The firemen told her she would have to wait a few days before returning to the site because the rubble would likely still be smoldering from the heat of the fire even though it was freezing outside. The gas company was already working to fix the leak and prevent damage to other buildings, and the area was roped off for safety.

Anna walked toward Eli and slipped her fingers around his palm. "Do you—do you want to come home with us?" she asked, tearing up again. "You'll need a place to stay."

Eli shook his head. "Jakob is coming to pick me up. He said I could stay with him for as long as I needed. You go on with your parents. I'll be okay."

Anna squeezed his hand. "You sure?"

"Promise," he said, pulling her into one final hug.

Anna vaguely recalled being bundled into her parents' SUV and leaning her head against the window as they drove away into the darkness. When Anna shuffled through the front door of her parents' house, she breathed in the familiar scents of home—her daddy's soap, the lingering aromas of sweet tea and pound cake, the fresh tiger lilies her mama always kept in a vase on the entry table.

Anna leaned against Evelyn as they walked up the hallway to her bedroom, which looked exactly as it had when she was a kid. The pink-and-white striped walls and overstuffed duvet welcomed Anna. Her favorite childhood books adorned a white bookshelf, and the lacy curtains shivered when the heat kicked on. Evelyn folded down the duvet, and Anna lowered herself to the edge while her mama rummaged through the dresser for clean clothes.

"Here," Evelyn said, handing Anna a worn-out, oversize T-shirt with hearts and moons on it. "This should still fit. I'll get a glass of water and some pain reliever while you change."

Anna pressed the soft fabric of the T-shirt to her cheek. It smelled like home, like years of running up and down the hallways with bare feet, like laughing and painting fingernails with Lily and Tessa on Friday nights. Anna draped her ruined pajamas over the back of the desk chair and slipped on the clean shirt. She crawled beneath the covers and eased her head onto the fluffy pillow.

Evelyn returned with water and medicine. Anna took both

willingly and sighed as she lay down again. Evelyn opened the closet doors and searched for something before closing the doors. She offered a battered, one-eyed teddy bear to Anna.

"Buster?" Anna asked, and her voice cracked. She pressed her beloved childhood bear to her chest, wrapping her arms around him so tightly she almost wanted to apologize for crushing him. "I can't believe you kept him. You always complained about how dirty he was."

Evelyn pushed the hair from Anna's face, and tears shone in her eyes. "I'm not a complete monster," she said with a gentle smile. "I would never throw away Buster. You went on some grand adventures together. But that's probably why he's the dirtiest thing I've ever seen and also why he's been banished to the closet for all time." Evelyn leaned down and kissed Anna's forehead. "Get some rest." She switched off the bedside lamp. "We don't have to figure anything out tonight. Your dad and I will help you sort through everything. You won't have to do it all by yourself, okay?"

Anna had no doubt her take-charge mama would help her set the world right again. She was almost tempted to inform Evelyn she also had a broken heart, and if her mama could find a cure, it would be wonderful. "Thanks, Mama," Anna said, swallowing down her tears. "I love you."

"I love you. Very much," Evelyn said and closed the door.

CHAPTER 19

SUGAR COOKIES

ANNA ROLLED OVER IN BED. HER ROOM SMELLED LIKE HER daddy's breakfast coffee blend. Her mind registered that it was Monday, and she assumed Eli had gotten up early to make a pot of coffee for himself. But her bedroom was brighter than it should be against her closed eyelids. Had he let her sleep in again? She blinked open her eyes and stared at pink-and-white striped walls.

Anna bolted upright, and the bed sheets pooled at her waist. Reality rushed in along with memories from the night before. The back of her head ached and felt bruised to the touch. Buster lay beside her, so she picked him up and gave him a squeeze. The bakery was gone. Her apartment was gone. When she inhaled, she smelled fire and burned sugar. There were folded, clean clothes at the foot of her bed. She tossed back the duvet and swung her legs off the bed.

Anna needed a shower. Her hair stank of smoke and ashes. She grabbed the clothes and made her way to the bathroom she'd used growing up. The countertop and cabinets had been redone in granite and walnut after she left home, but the wallpaper was still the same pattern of pink and pale green flowers. Toiletries had been placed on the counter, along with a brand-new toothbrush. Her mama had bought her favorite shampoo, conditioner, and soap. There was also a bottle of fuchsia nail polish that made Anna smile. Her mama would never give up trying to coax her into being more stylish.

After a hot shower, Anna dried her hair and tugged on the new jeans and long-sleeved emerald-green shirt she found on her bed. The house smelled like baked goods, but the idea of her mama baking made her wary because Evelyn could turn brownies into bricks like magic. She left her bedroom in search of her parents. The television in the living room was on a news channel, and the clock on the microwave said it was past one in the afternoon.

The kitchen remodel had drastically altered the kitchen from Anna's childhood memories, but that wasn't what surprised her the most. The countertops and kitchen table were covered in baked goods. Some were sheltered by plastic wrap. Others were cuddled beneath plastic containers. A few sat atop colorful, ceramic cake plates. There was no way her mama could have baked so much in such a short amount of time. Anna walked to the oven and placed her hands against it. It felt cold to the touch.

Evelyn walked through the doorway that connected the living room to the sun porch. "Good morning—or afternoon, I should say. I knew those clothes would fit. That color suits you."

Anna combed her fingers through her hair. "Thanks for the bathroom stuff. And for the clothes."

"Tessa and Lily called this morning to check on you. They're both resting at home," Evelyn said. "I told them you were still sleeping, and they thought I was joking. Lily's exact words were,

'Her body hasn't seen a bed after eight a.m. in at least ten years.'"
Evelyn smiled. "Your dad made me sneak in and check that you
were still breathing like he used to make me do when you were
a baby."

Anna was relieved to know Lily and Tessa were both home
and okay. "Mama, where did all this food come from?"

Evelyn lifted a plastic container and gave it a shake. Cookies
rattled around inside. "Your dad has eaten most of these. They
were good. Not as good as yours, but close enough. These sugar
cookies came from Mrs. Rogers." She pointed as she moved around
the room. "The angel food cake is from Lottie down the street.
Mr. Dixon dropped off the walnut brownies. Dr. Pitts brought the
snickerdoodles. Tracey from the bank made the blackberry cob-
bler." And she continued until she'd itemized every treat.

"But why?" Anna asked.

Evelyn crossed the kitchen to her daughter. "Because they
want to let you know how sorry they are to hear about what
happened."

Anna's throat tightened. "It's not like somebody died." She
reached out and brushed her fingers against a plate full of oatmeal cookies. They warmed her fingertips.

"To them, it's like a death. They loved that bakery, and they
love you. This is their way of letting you know how special what
you did at the bakery was and how special *you* are." Anna's eyes
watered. "Now, don't start crying again," Evelyn said, but her
voice was gentle. "You'll make your eyes all red and puffy, and
it'll completely clash with your skin tone." Evelyn hugged Anna.
"How about some lunch? I have low-fat turkey on multigrain
bread. I'll even add cheese if you want it."

"Hold on now, Mama," Anna said, wiping her eyes. "Are you

offering me a fatty dairy product? There's no need to get crazy."
And they both laughed.

Anna borrowed her daddy's truck and drove to the bakery—to
what was left of it. In the afternoon light, it looked like a scene
from a disaster movie. The area was littered with twisted metal,
burned plastic that had bubbled and formed strange ash-coated
domes, shards of glass that shimmered in the sunshine, and a
yawning hole full of mostly unrecognizable items. Anna's former
life was destroyed. She zipped the old work jacket she'd borrowed
from her daddy because he said he didn't care if she got it a little
dirty. It was at least two sizes too big, but it was warm. Anna
hoped it could keep out the chills brought on by kicking through
rubble.

She slid her hands along the rope strung up by the emergency department and stared into the burned-out bakery. Her
eyes settled on the freezer in the back. It stood alone without the
shelter of the walls that once hemmed it in. Black streaks smeared
the stainless steel and looked like shadows of flames, but the
freezer looked otherwise intact. Against the firemen's advice, and
wearing a pair of yellow rain boots from her high school days,
Anna carefully made her way over to the freezer. The ground
radiated warmth and reminded Anna of a solidified lava flow. She
sidestepped her favorite set of mixing bowls, which had melted
into the shapes of nesting fortune cookies. Anna imagined crack-
ing one open to read the message: *Your life is a wreck. Change
directions.* She looked at what remained of the lovely island her
daddy had specially built for her. The slab of granite had crushed

the wooden frame, and the ceiling had fallen into the middle of the kitchen.

Anna cautiously touched the freezer's handle. The metal was cold, so she wrenched it open. The door swung ajar, scraping debris out of the way. The power was no longer working in the building, but the interior of the freezer was still quite chilly. Anna smiled in the sad sort of way that she'd seen people do on the news when a tornado had demolished their homes. They'd find a framed photo and they'd smile, but they were crying too. She pulled a tub of double dark chocolate chip cookie dough from the shelf and popped off the lid. Then she stepped out into the sunshine and closed the freezer door. She wiped her hand on her pants, which her mama would say was unsanitary, and dug her mostly clean finger into the dough. Anna chewed a mouthful and sighed. For a few seconds, the chocolate eased the ache in her chest. She could breathe around the sorrow without feeling as though she'd swallowed a macaron whole. She breathed in the scents of sugar and cinnamon.

"Afternoon snack?" a voice asked behind her.

Anna turned to see Eli walking up the alley beside the bakery. The soot from the night before was washed from his arms, and he wore a clean shirt advertising the local pizza joint. She offered the tub of cookie dough to him. "Want some? It's only slightly gooey. Still edible. I eat when I'm emotional—it's a terrible habit. I should probably break it, but not today."

Eli smiled, and the sight nearly brought more tears to Anna's eyes. She hadn't been sure she'd ever see his smile again, not after the way he'd left her apartment two nights ago. Anna looked up as if she could see where she once lived, but she saw only blue sky and fat, happy clouds forming shapes. Eli reached out to her, and she took his hand. He maneuvered her over the debris and took the cookie dough tub from her. He stuck his finger into the dough and popped a bite into his mouth.

"How was Jakob's place?" she asked.

"Not bad." He hooked his thumb into the shirt and stretched it out. "He let me borrow his clothes, and, man, are these jeans tight. I'm afraid to bend over or squat because something might burst, and I don't want the bursting to happen on my body."

Anna chuckled. She looked at her car still parked behind the crumbled building. A large chunk of bricks had fallen on her car, crushing her hood like a cartoon anvil. Her front tires looked like someone had held a blowtorch to them. "Guess I won't be driving anywhere today in my car. There goes my escape plan." She heaved a dramatic sigh.

"Looks like someone swapped your tires for tar," he said lightly and draped his arm around her shoulders. "All fixable, though. What we couldn't have fixed was losing you. Good thing that didn't happen."

Anna nodded, but her throat was closing, and tears pricked her eyes. She tried to blink as fast as possible and cleared her throat. "I'm really sorry about everything," she said. Except the kiss.

"Me too," he said, pulling her closer.

"Do you hate me?"

Anna stared at the dancing pizza on his borrowed shirt, and he fisted his hand beneath her chin and lifted her face. "I'm not capable of hating you," he said. "Am I confused? Yes. Do I know what to do next? Not really. But what I do know is that right now you need me, and I plan on staying as long as you need help repairing what we lost."

Anna nodded. "And afterward? What happens then?"

Eli lowered his hand and looked toward the shape-shifting clouds. He pointed skyward. "That one looks like a seagull."

Anna looked up and agreed. It flew toward the ocean on fluffy wings.

"I think it's best that I leave," he said.

"Leave Mystic Water?" she asked.

He nodded. "I need to figure myself out."

Anna nodded because she was afraid to say anything, afraid she might beg Eli to stay with her. She wanted to tell him that she was home when they were together, but she didn't want to sound pathetic. She put her hand on his chest. Her fingers tingled with his warmth, and the heat quickly spread up her arm and pooled in her chest until she was forced to exhale just to make room for all of it. Eli covered her hand with his. Then, he pulled her against him with one arm, holding the tub of cookie dough to the side.

She breathed in the scent of warm sugar cookies and nodded against his chest. "Send postcards," she said, trying to pretend the idea of Eli leaving didn't feel like a glass shard in her chest.

"Where should I send them?" he asked. "The Clarke House or Wildehaven Beach?"

"Wildehaven Beach?" She pulled away from him and looked up into his blue eyes. "Why would you send them there?"

"You love the beach," Eli said. "There's a bakery for sale there."

"But I live here," Anna said slowly.

"For now, but you're not rooted to the ground," he said, running his hand down her arm. "You're free to go."

"Like you?" she asked. She had to change the subject before

she dissolved into a puddle of tears. "About those postcards, maybe fold them into paper airplanes and send them on the wind. I'm sure they'll find me."

Eli grinned. "I'll always find you. No matter where you are, I will always be able to find you."

Anna snorted a laugh. She poked him in the chest. "You sound like Daniel Day-Lewis from *The Last of the Mohicans*."

"Did that up my sex appeal?"

"Definitely," Anna said and couldn't help but grin at his silly smile. He was trying to cheer her up, and it was working. Standing on the edges of the destroyed bakery and apartment, Anna didn't feel as devastated because she still had Eli, and he wasn't leaving her yet. He was going to stay until she was back on her feet, until her life didn't resemble a catastrophe. The sun shone down on them, warming their cheeks. Anna grabbed for the cookie tub and stuck her finger into the dough. Then she leaned her head against Eli's arm and sighed. In that moment, she could almost believe everything was going to be okay.

Anna and Eli spent the afternoon pushing through the debris in search of anything salvageable. At first, Anna found the job depressing, and every little burned item made her feel weepy all over again, but she and Eli decided to make a game out of it. The person who found the most usable items won a free dinner. So far, Anna had a few metal mixing spoons shoved into her jacket pocket, one untouched bottle of chocolate liqueur, and half a dozen cookie cutters. Eli rescued the largest item—a red stoneware baking dish—but Anna insisted size didn't matter, only quantity. She laughed when he raised the dish over his head in victory like a wrestling belt.

"You've got to be kidding me," Eli said, pushing aside what looked like part of her bedframe. "Is this what I think it is?"

Anna stopped rummaging through a pile of rubble. "Did you find my favorite sweatshirt?" she joked.

Eli held up a hand-carved box. The metal lock was slightly warped, but the rest of the box remained unscathed by the blaze. Anna's eyes widened in disbelief. She stumbled over to him and took the box from his hand.

"How did it survive?" she asked, carefully lifting the lid to peer inside.

"Should I say it?" Eli asked, and she met his gaze.

"Magic?" they said together and both laughed.

Anna hugged the box to her chest. It had brought about so much confusion and hurt, but it had also brought her Eli, and she wouldn't take that back even if it meant avoiding everything that had come afterward. She had entertained the idea of destroying the magic sugar before the fire, but now she was thankful to still have her family's gift to share with the next generation.

By dinnertime, when the sun started falling from its afternoon perch and threw horizontal rainbow streaks across the sky, Anna's nose was red, and her fingers were numb and sore inside the work gloves coated with grime and soot. She climbed over the scattered mess where the front of the bakery once stood, and she paused on the sidewalk. She held a cracked cake plate in her hand.

"Think anyone will notice that half of it is gone?" she asked, rotating the plate 360 degrees.

"Nah," Eli said. "You can tell everyone it's a dieter's cake plate. Half the plate means half the calories." He trudged over to her, leaving behind a trail of swirling black clouds. "Shall we call it a night? We can order pizza from this place," he said, pulling out his shirt and reading the upside-down logo, "and have them deliver it to the park."

Anna smiled. "We'll be sitting in the dark," she said. "We could eat in Daddy's truck and pretend when I return it we don't know why it smells like pizza."

Eli carried the salvaged items to the truck and piled them in the truck bed. Anna's stack of reclaimed items was much larger than Eli's. "Looks like I'm buying." He pulled a cell phone out of his back pocket. "Jakob let me borrow his phone. He's using his work phone for the time being," he said as he dialed the number for the pizza place. After ordering, they leaned against the truck grill and looked over the pathways they'd left behind in the rubble.

Two cars pulled up and parked beside them. Mr. Silverstein, who always ordered six cupcakes on cupcake day and swore they increased his happiness, climbed out of a 1970s orange Chevy Camaro. The driver's side door squeaked on its hinges. He gave the door a good shove to close it. The car beside the Camaro was newer and a model Anna didn't recognize. The driver stayed inside with the engine running.

Mr. Silverstein walked over and surveyed the damage before speaking. "Such a shame," he said. "I couldn't believe it when my wife told me. We drove by this afternoon and saw the two of y'all working." He looked at them. "We did some talking, and we figured you'd need a little help from anyone willing to offer it. I noticed your car has seen better days." He jerked his head toward the rear of the bakery. Then he held out his fisted hand to her. "Take this. We don't need it, and we don't drive it. It's just an extra thing sitting at the house."

Mr. Silverstein dropped a set of keys into Anna's hand. "You're giving me a *car*?" she asked. "I can't accept this. Thank you, but I'll get mine fixed." Anna glanced at Eli, who seemed just as surprised by the offer.

Mr. Silverstein shook his head. "I won't accept no for an answer. It's yours." Then he stepped away before Anna could argue, so she hurried to him and threw her arms around his neck and thanked him.

Even in the waning light, she could see he blushed. Anna waved as he rode away with his wife. An easterly wind blew, and Anna breathed in the smells of autumn, reminding her of running through fallen leaves, sitting under blankets roasting s'mores, and carving pumpkins with goofy faces. She tilted her head back and looked up at the stars twinkling in the darkening blue of the sky. Hope floated on the wind and tangled itself in Anna's hair. She reached up and pulled her fingers through the strands, feeling her hand warm.

After finishing most of the pizza, Anna leaned her head against the window and exhaled loudly. "The last slice did me in," she said. "From here on out, three is my limit. No more—definitely no less."

Eli finished off his sixth slice and wiped his mouth. "If I eat one more, these pants will become a hazard. The button could burst off at any moment, ricochet around the cab, and knock us out. Then we'd freeze to death overnight, and they'd find us here in the morning, reeking of pizza and me without my pants buttoned."

Anna chuckled. "You've given that way too much thought," she teased. But she closed the pizza box to prevent him from reaching for another slice. "Precautionary measures," she said as she slid the box onto the dashboard.

She stared down at Mr. Silverstein's keys on the seat between them. She closed her fingers around them and picked them up, then reached toward Eli. "Here," she said. She dropped the keys into his hand, and he looked at her with his blue eyes in a way that made her want to throw her arms around him. The cab filled with the aroma of summertime, all fresh-cut grass and riding with the windows down—freedom.

"Why are you giving me these?" he asked, turning toward her in the seat.

"You'll need a trusty steed to take you on your journey, cowboy," she said, willing her throat not to close up.

Eli nodded and stared out the window. For a few long minutes, they sat in silence. Then Eli stretched his open hand, palm up, across the seat, and Anna placed her hand in his. He twined their fingers together. Energy zinged between their bound hands, and Eli squeezed her fingers as if to show her he felt it too.

"Thank you," he said, leaning his head against the back window and looking at her. He pressed his other hand to his heart. "No matter where I go, you'll always be in here. Always with me."

Anna turned away so Eli wouldn't see how she struggled not to cry, but she didn't let go of his hand, and they stayed like that until the moon was high in the sky and the crickets in Mystic Water sang everyone to sleep.

CHAPTER 20

OOEY GOOEY
BUTTER CAKE

AFTER SPENDING THE NEXT FEW DAYS KICKING THROUGH THE
debris, finding a couple dozen more salvageable items, and
spending time on the phone with the insurance company, Anna
was finally able to sit down and have lunch with Tessa and Lily.
She hadn't been avoiding them exactly, but until that meal she
wasn't ready to talk about what had happened. Her emotions
were still too close to the surface. Still, she had to determine the
best next steps. Strongly encouraged by many and voiced loudest
by her mama was that the bakery must be rebuilt. Anna didn't
disagree, and in fact it gave her something useful to do. So she
focused on coordinating the reconstruction.

Anna walked into the deli on Main Street. She waved to Mr.
and Mrs. Cavelli. Anna scanned the day's specials written in
looping script on the chalkboard and pulled a sheet of folded
paper from her pocket. She'd written down Lily's and Tessa's

orders, and Lily's choice was the special. Mrs. Cavelli came from behind the counter and hugged Anna.

"So sorry to hear about the bakery, honey," she said. "You're going to rebuild, aren't you? It wouldn't be the same without you around the corner."

Anna smiled. "We're definitely rebuilding," she said with a nod. "I think all the insurance quirks should be worked out by the end of the week, which means we can start soon."

Mrs. Cavelli smiled and retied her mustard-stained apron around her curvy figure. "Good," she said. "You need any carpentry help, you let me know. You know our son Richie is a great craftsman. Does beautiful work. Course I'm his mother, and I'm biased, but you ask anyone. They'll tell you he's excellent."

"What can I get you, Anna?" Mr. Cavelli asked from behind the counter. "If you don't order soon, she'll want to set you up with Richie, and I don't think he's your type."

Mrs. Cavelli fisted her hands on her hips. "What's wrong with Richie? He's a handsome boy, and he's a hard worker. Besides, I'm not trying to set Anna up with him. I know she has a boyfriend. You do have a boyfriend, right?" she asked, joining her husband behind the counter. Her large brown eyes looked hopeful.

"Well, I—"

"Now, Rosa, that's none of your business." He grinned at Anna and shook his head. "Anna, what can I get you?"

"Nothing wrong with a mother wanting a pretty young woman for her son," Rosa grumbled under her breath.

Anna smiled and glanced at the list. She ordered a grilled brie and tomato on whole wheat for Lily, a smoked-turkey club on sourdough for Tessa, and an old-fashioned grilled cheese for herself. She grabbed three bags of potato chips while they prepared her order, but when she tried to pay, Mr. Cavelli refused her money.

"Look at it as neighbors helping neighbors," Mr. Cavelli said, and Mrs. Cavelli nodded.

"But I can't let you give me all this food for free. At least let me pay for half of it. I'm feeding Lily and Tessa too," Anna said, pushing her money across the counter.

"When you reopen your bakery, you bake Rosa and me a cake, and we'll call it even," Mr. Cavelli offered.

Anna smiled. "Deal. What's your favorite kind?"

Mrs. Cavelli's eyes lit up. "I love the chocolate peanut butter torte with that cookie crust. I have dreams about it. It makes me feel like dancing." She swayed her hips to the music in her head.

"You got it," Anna said. She thanked them and carried the bags down the street to the park, where she saw Lily and Tessa bundled up in jackets and scarves, stretching out a patchwork quilt in the sunshine. Bright red and brown cardinals bounced from limb to limb in a nearby oak tree, watching them as they arranged their picnic area.

Lily pulled three travel mugs out of her bag, and Tessa folded napkins and anchored them to the blanket with forks. She looked up and saw Anna, and they both waved. Anna plopped down beside them and passed around chips and sandwiches. The breeze carried the scents of melted cheese and hot chocolate.

Tessa fiddled with her potato chip bag and cleared her throat. "Listen, Anna, I need to get this out—"

Sensing exactly where the conversation was headed, Anna lifted her hand to stop Tessa. "I know you're sorry, and you know I'm sorry, but can we table any super-serious conversations for now? I need a breather."

"Yes, of course," Tessa said, exhaling her own relief. She tore open her bag of barbecue chips and flipped off the top piece of sandwich bread. She laid down a layer of chips and then put her sandwich back together.

Her first bite crunched, and crumbs fell onto the napkin in her lap.

"Remember when Tessa went through that phase where she ate only mayonnaise and Bar-B-Q Fritos sandwiches?" Lily asked and sipped her hot chocolate. "Her fingers were constantly orange tipped."

"Did she ever grow out of that phase?" Anna teased.

Tessa laughed and tossed a potato chip at Lily. It caught the wind and landed on Anna's knee instead. Anna popped it into her mouth and said, "Finders keepers."

"At least I didn't go through a ketchup-with-macaroni-and-cheese phase," Tessa said, looking pointedly at Lily.

"That *was* weird," Anna agreed. She drank hot chocolate from the travel mug. The cardinals chirped a song, echoing one another.

A string of brie stretched from Lily's mouth to the bread before it pulled too thin and broke. She wiped her mouth before saying, "Personally, I thought the peanut-butter-and-Doritos phase was the real low point of my food experimentation, but this morning, I made a sandwich of dill pickle slices and cream cheese."

Anna wrinkled her nose, and Tessa made a gagging noise. "I wouldn't be spreading that around town," Anna joked. She finished one half of her sandwich and leaned back on her palms. "Guess you can blame it on the peanut now, though." She glanced over at Lily. "How is everything with you and Jakob and the parents?"

Lily sighed. "Peachy. He's great. *We're* great. Tomorrow the firm is going to make him partner, then after the weekend, we can let the cat out of the bag to everyone and anyone," she said with a devilish smile. "He's been doting on me like crazy, and his mama has done a complete one-eighty. I think the fire really scared them," she said, looking away from Anna's gaze.

"It does put life into perspective," Anna said, glancing up the street at where the bakery used to sit.

"I know everyone's been asking, but you are planning on rebuilding, aren't you?" Tessa asked. "Won't the insurance money help with that?"

"It will," Anna said, "and we're going to rebuild. I'm not sure about the apartment, but definitely the bakery. We might even be able to start as soon as next week."

"What about the Clarke House?" Lily asked.

Anna thought of the sodden contract she'd carried home the night of the fire. It was now dried and wrinkled and sitting on the nightstand in her childhood bedroom. "It's been on my mind but not a priority."

As if reading her mind, Lily asked, "What about Wildehaven Beach?"

"What's in Wildehaven Beach?" Tessa asked, finishing her sandwich.

Anna closed her eyes for a moment and pictured the bakery. She remembered the day she and Eli had visited. "There's been a bakery there forever. Well, at least since I was a little girl. Grandma Bea and Grandpa Joe would take me in there every day when we visited each summer, and the times I went with my parents, we always went to the bakery at least once. The owners are retiring and selling it."

The color faded from Tessa's face. A cloud drifted in front of the sun. "You're not going to buy it, are you? That would mean I'd lose both of you."

"Both of who?" Lily asked, leaning her head back and funneling potato chip crumbs into her mouth. She thumped the edge of the bag to help them slide along.

"Eli told me he's leaving," Tessa said in a quiet voice. She toyed with a string on the quilt. "I don't blame him, really, not after everything that's happened. But I don't want to lose both of you. Even if he stayed, I know I'd still lose him. His heart is with you. I can't continue to ignore that—"

"Tessa—"

"It's okay, Anna," Tessa said. "Really it is. He's been with you every day, helping you. I know he cares about me, but it's not the same way he cares about you. He *loves* you, and I'm sorry I didn't think that love was real. I was wrong. And I'm sorry he's leaving. It's all my fault," she said, blinking away tears.

Anna put down her sandwich and slid closer to Tessa. "Even if I moved to Wildehaven Beach, you aren't *losing* me. I told the same thing to Lily. It's a little more than an hour away, and it's on the beach. You could visit me anytime, but that's null and void now. I'm not going. The bakery here needs to be rebuilt, and it's my responsibility to make sure that happens. None of this is your fault, Tessa. I don't think that for one second."

Tessa swiped at her tears and tucked her hair behind her ears. "But I made that stupid thing that almost *killed* all of us. I burned down your bakery and your apartment."

"True, but you've never been a great baker, so the results aren't entirely surprising," Anna said. When Tessa stared open-mouthed at Anna, Anna gave her a playful shove on the knee.

"You had no idea the dough would turn into a rampaging psycho, and you were trying to help me—"

"I *was*," Tessa agreed. "I didn't know my man was going to be a homicidal dough boy. I mean, why was it so crazy?" Tessa asked through her tears, but her lips were curling up at the corners.

"He was probably furious you made him out of your mama's Italian bread," Lily said. "He looked like someone burned cheese on his head. Plus he smelled like scorched raccoon fur." She leaned her face toward the sun. "That's enough to ruin anyone's day."

"And you know how that smells because . . . ?" Anna asked, nudging Lily's leg with her foot. Lily only laughed.

"I'm really sorry, Anna," Tessa said, folding her hands together in her lap. "I don't want you to leave because of me."

"If I had decided to go, it wouldn't be because of you," Anna assured her. "This is a chance for me to start over. Something good will come out of this mess. But the next time you bake something, you should ask for some assistance." Anna smiled at Tessa.

"I promise," Tessa said and held out her pinky finger. Anna looped hers around Tessa's. "No more men for me. Not for a while."

"Definitely no dough boys," Lily agreed. "Anna, remember the cake Tessa made for your tenth birthday?" Lily asked. "The one she found in the pet magazine?"

"I didn't know it was for dogs!" Tessa said defensively, and all three girls burst out laughing.

Anna slid her new cell phone into her back pocket as she climbed out of her daddy's truck. Baron's car was parked in her parents' driveway, and he sat on the front porch steps. Gray smoke rose from their brick chimney and curled toward the sky. When she walked up, he patted the spot beside him.

"Your mama knows I'm here," he said with an easy smile. "I didn't want her to think there was a lurker on her porch."

The chill of the bricks seeped through her jeans, and she gave a little shiver. "I hope she offered you some of the baked goods from the townsfolk," Anna said. "I swear, if I have to hear her fuss at Daddy for eating another piece of cake, I'm going to go bonkers."

Baron patted his stomach through his thick, fleece jacket. "Proud owner of four peanut butter cookies that were a little on the dry side and a slice of apple pie."

Baron's breath hung in front of his mouth in white puffs before dissipating. Anna wrapped her arms around her knees and looked at the sun hanging over the forest. It would be dark in another hour and too cold to sit outside without a warm drink or being wrapped up like a quilt cannoli.

Baron exhaled loudly, and they both watched the long cloud of white travel toward the roofline. "I stepped outside of the pub that night to take a phone call, and when I saw the bakery glowing like a furnace, I couldn't think. I stared for a few seconds because my mind wouldn't register what my eyes were seeing. Then all I could think about was you sleeping upstairs in your cupcake pajamas, trapped in your apartment. Eli was in the pub, too, and he must have followed me outside. But he saw the fire, and we didn't even speak or ask questions. I didn't care that he was the man I'd seen kissing you at the festival. I only cared that I got to you. We were like one mind working to get into the bakery and save you.

"The whole downstairs was filled with smoke, and I swear I saw something burning and flailing around inside. I refused to believe it was you. We threw a bench through the front window." He paused and shoved his hand into his hair. The scent of the ocean drifted around them, circling them. "I can't even think about what would have happened if I hadn't gone outside. I was still so mad at you, but as soon as I thought you were in trouble, I felt sick with fear." Baron stretched his legs out down the stairs and folded his hands together in his lap. "I wanted to say I'm sorry for being a hypocrite."

Anna looked over at him. His hair was tousled, and his cheeks were pink from the chill in the air. She couldn't deny he was handsome. Part of her still yearned for the comfortable routine they'd had, but she knew there was nothing fulfilling left in that relationship. "What do you mean?"

"I was pissed off when I saw you kissing Eli," he admitted. "It still burns me up. But I kissed a girl when I was in California."

"Valerie?" Anna asked. Thinking of Baron kissing someone else caused an emotion akin to jealousy to slither through her stomach, so she swallowed and breathed in slowly.

Baron's eyes widened. "How did you know that?"

"You called me from a club. She showed up when you were talking to me on the phone."

He shook his head and chuckled. "What an idiot. I felt awful after I kissed her. I knew it was wrong. Then I started thinking about what you said before I left. You were right. I wasn't thinking about us. I wasn't thinking about anyone but myself, and you deserve better than that."

Anna nodded. "Guess that makes us even," she said as she rubbed her hands up her shins, creating friction that warmed her legs.

"Nah," he said. "You were always too good for me, Anna-Banana. Everyone knew that, even me. Now I have to try to find someone to put up with me, and you're free from a selfish jerk."

Baron grinned at her, and Anna laughed. The front door opened, and Evelyn poked her head out. "Goodness, it's too cold for chatting out here. Y'all come inside. I've made Anna's famous hot chocolate, and turkey chili with an extra kick like Anna likes, but heavens, it gives me heartburn. Now, come on in." She closed the door.

Anna stood and stretched. She walked to the front door and opened it. "Wanna stay for dinner?"

Before Baron could answer, Evelyn stepped back into view. "Are you two coming in or staying out? This isn't a barn. You're letting all the warm air out. Baron, I made boxed corn bread. I know how much you love it." She disappeared back into the kitchen.

Anna raised her eyebrows in question.

"How can I say no to your mom's corn bread?" Baron whispered. "Does anyone say no to her?"

"At their own peril," Anna said, and they both laughed. They walked into the kitchen where Anna's daddy sat at the table folding the newspaper. Evelyn ladled spicy chili to the rims of their ceramic bowls.

CHAPTER 21

FORGET-ME-
NOT COOKIES

MID-DECEMBER ANNA SAT ON THE LOW BRICK WALL THE
masons had finished the day before. The new wall framed an
outdoor seating area and garden that had not been possible at
the original bakery. Anna wanted the patio for those months
when customers preferred to sit outdoors. She tapped her feet
against the blue-and-gray flagstones. The masons had created a
three-foot-wide break in the wall so people could step through
onto the patio. Anna was debating whether to add a wrought
iron gate.

The men inside the bakery's new structure hammered and
laughed and laid tiles. Clouds of fine white dust puffed across
the floors and clung to everything. Country music drifted out
through open windows. One of the carpenters hanging cabinets
and shelves in the new kitchen sang off-key and with a twang
so sharp Anna couldn't help but laugh.

She had decided to rebuild the upstairs apartment, but she

eliminated the interior stairs that once connected the two. Now the apartment could only be accessed by an outdoor staircase. She knew she wouldn't live there anymore, but someone else might want to rent it, and she could use the extra money for a vacation, a new pair of jeans, or an industrial-size mixer.

A cool wind blew and toyed with Anna's long hair. She closed her eyes and inhaled. The air smelled of cinnamon and sugar with a distant hint of pine trees, reminding Anna it was only a week until Christmas.

"Every day I'm surprised by how much they've finished," a man said behind her.

Anna opened her eyes and looked over her shoulder. Eli stood on the sidewalk with his hands shoved into his jacket pockets. She'd seen him every day for the past few weeks but only in short spurts, which gave Eli the space he'd asked for. He'd been working odd jobs around town, which was another thing she loved about Mystic Water—the people never hesitated to extend a helping hand. They knew she and Eli were out of work, and while Anna had family in town she could rely on, Eli was a wanderer. The townsfolk called him every day to ask for help putting up shutters or painting a bedroom or planting bulbs for the spring. Eli had become a jack-of-all-trades.

"It's amazing how quickly this has been rebuilt," Anna agreed. "No one can say the people in Mystic Water don't work hard. I imagine by Christmas I could be inside baking again." She could already see the smiles on everyone's faces. She pictured herself standing behind the counter and welcoming them inside on her official reopening day. Her mama would stand among the crowd and beam so brightly the cake plates would throw rainbows of light on the walls.

"Walk with me?" he asked.

His blue eyes carried a faraway look, and she inhaled slowly. Her heart pumped against her rib cage in heavy beats. She followed Eli down the sidewalk toward the park at the end of the street. They walked in silence, and uncertainty spread through her chest like air inflating a balloon.

"I helped Mr. Parker install new faucets in his house yesterday," Eli said as they stepped onto the park's crunchy winter grass. He walked toward a large live oak tree that still held on to its leaves. "His son is opening a brick-and-mortar sandwich shop in the Outer Banks. He also has a food truck for catering and special events."

Anna nodded to show she was listening, but she wasn't sure how to respond. The air felt charged as if a thunderstorm was approaching. She shoved her hands into her pockets to keep herself from fidgeting. Eli stopped walking, and they stood beneath the great oak.

"James, Mr. Parker's son, is looking for a partner—someone who has experience," Eli said. "I talked to him last night for a couple of hours. We have a lot of the same ideas. He seems to really know what he's doing. The sandwich shop idea is what I've wanted to do for as long as I can remember." He smiled ruefully at the sun shining down on them. "Which I suppose isn't all that long."

So this was it. Eli was finally letting go and leaving. Anna couldn't speak immediately. She blinked down at the brown grass, shifted on her feet, and listened to the blades crunch beneath her tennis shoes. Eli had found his dream, and he was following it. She tried to smile, but the motion pulled something deep in her chest, and she felt the sensation of suffocation. Eli put his hand on her arm, and she looked up at him.

"I wanted to tell you first," he said. "I'm leaving this afternoon."

This afternoon. Anna pressed her hands to her chest. She couldn't breathe. She couldn't look him in the eye. She tried to open her mouth to congratulate him, to tell him she was happy, but nothing came out. Eli pulled her into his arms and held her tight. She wanted to be strong, to show her support, but instead, tears filled her eyes, so she squeezed them shut. Her tears were aggressive and needy, and they forced themselves out the corners of her eyes and leaked down the sides of her cheeks. Her breath hitched. Her sadness nearly choked her.

Anna pulled away from him and quickly wiped her cheeks. "I'm sorry," she said, feeling foolish. "I'm overly emotional today. With the bakery and starting over, there's a lot going on. I don't mean to ruin your excitement." She cleared her throat. "It's a great opportunity for you," she added. "I'm sure you'll love it. I love sandwiches. Sandwiches are good. Everybody loves sandwiches. Everyone will love you." Just like she did.

Eli grabbed her hand and grinned. "You're cute when you babble," he said. He wiped a stray tear from Anna's cheek. "It's not easy for me to leave, but it's for the best."

For the best. Anna wanted to wrestle that phrase from the sky and beat it into the ground with a wooden spoon. "For the best" was what people said when something unfortunate happened, like when your college of choice rejected you or your boyfriend up and moved to California without you or your bakery burned to the ground. She nodded.

Clouds covered the sun and tossed Eli and Anna into shadow. A shop door opened down the street, and "Blue Christmas" followed the customer out onto the sidewalk. Eli squeezed her hand and tugged her along beside him as he walked. The park was full of metal, plastic-coated elves, reindeer, gingerbread houses, snowmen, and various Santa Claus figures covered in lights. During the evenings, the park was a festival of colors and Christmas music. They walked around the figures until they reached the parking lot on the far side, where the orange Camaro waited for Eli. Anna noticed a packed bag in the passenger seat.

Anna held out her hand as if to shake his. "Well, good luck to you," she said, amazed her voice sounded steady. Her insides were vibrating in a way that made her feel as though she were caught in a sifter.

Eli raised one eyebrow at her before putting his hands on her cheeks. When he kissed her, it lacked the urgency of their first kiss; the desperate need to connect was replaced with the bittersweet rush of good-bye. She balanced herself by placing her hands on his chest, but still she came undone. She couldn't save herself from falling into Eli, from breathing him in and letting him fill all the waiting spaces. When he pulled away, she felt lightheaded, and her eyes shone with tears.

"I'm going to miss you," Eli said, brushing her hair from her face.

She nodded because she didn't trust herself to speak. They didn't say anything as Eli climbed into the car. She stood and watched him put the car in reverse, and when he drove away, he hung his arm out the window with a final wave. She watched his blue eyes fade from the side-view mirror. She wrapped her arms around her chest to ward off the chill.

"I'll miss you more," she said, and then she walked through the park toward the bakery. Candy canes hanging from the lampposts along the sidewalk swayed in the December wind, which smelled like fresh mint. Her daddy sat on the brick wall holding two to-go cups. He smiled when he saw her and held out a cup. She tried to smile in return.

"Thought you could use some company," he said.

Anna sat beside him and sighed, thanking him for the hot chocolate she could smell through the steam rising from the slit in the top of the plastic lid. "Did you make this?" she asked after a sip. He nodded. "Wow, Daddy, it's really good."

He smiled. "I learned from the best," he said. "Want to take the afternoon off, grab a plate of meat 'n' three to go, and head home to watch old movies? Your mama is off doing last-minute Christmas shopping with Sherry. They're going to some fancy teahouse for dinner."

Anna smiled and leaned her head against his shoulder. "Sounds perfect."

Christmas morning Anna jumped off the couch and slid across the polished wood floor in her gingerbread-man socks. She grabbed the ringing phone just as Evelyn asked, "Who on earth would be calling us on Christmas morning?"

"It's lunchtime," Charlie responded as he tossed crumpled wrapping paper into a black garbage bag.

"Merry Christmas!" Anna said into the phone. She covered the mouthpiece with one hand. "Daddy, could you turn down Dean, please?" she asked. Dean Martin crooned Christmas songs full blast from the stereo system. Charlie put down the trash bag and adjusted the volume.

"Anna, are you there?" a man asked. "It's Mr. Randall." Randall Brown, a local city inspector, was also a good friend of her daddy's since childhood.

"Sorry about that. I'm here," Anna replied. "Merry Christmas, Mr. Randall."

"Sounds like you're having a good day," he said, and she could hear the smile in his voice.

"We're having a great day. How's your family?"

"Everyone is well, thank you for asking," Mr. Randall said. "I went over to do a final inspection on the work at the bakery this morning. It looks good, *real* good. It's all done, all the permits are signed, and the city has approved the building to open for business."

Anna bounced on her toes. "You didn't have to go over there on the holiday. It would have been okay to wait."

"When you have half a dozen grandkids running around in your house," Mr. Randall said, "you'll understand why sneaking out for a while was a welcome time of peace on earth. Oh, and there was a package there for you. I put it inside on the front counter."

"Thank you for all you've done. I'll call if I have any questions."

"Tell your folks I said hello, and y'all have a merry Christmas and a happy new year."

"You too, Mr. Randall. Thank you!" Anna hung up the receiver and smiled at her parents. "The bakery's all done!" she announced.

Evelyn clasped her hands together. "You'll be open by the first of the year," she said. "Let's celebrate over a lunch of pancakes, grits, and scrambled eggs."

"And bacon!" Charlie added.

Evelyn joined Anna in the kitchen and looked for pans in the lower cabinets. While rummaging through an assortment of cookware, she laughed. Evelyn pulled a wrapped package from the cabinet. "Looks like I forgot one for you."

Anna chuckled. "Why did you hide it in the cabinet? It's not like I try to sneak into my presents early." She plucked the red bow from the top and unwrapped the gift. The contents inside slid around, sounding like large puzzle pieces. When she opened the box, she saw a set of cookie cutters. There were outlines for seashells, a sailboat, a dolphin, and a fish. A light breeze whispered through the kitchen, and Anna's mind drifted to the rolling waves.

Evelyn took the box from Anna's hands. "Those are *not* what I ordered," she said with a frown. "I specifically ordered the garden set. It had the cutest little trowel cookie cutter." She exhaled and filled a carafe with water so she could start another pot of coffee. "We can send them back."

Anna reached for the box. "No, I like these." She was staying in Mystic Water, reopening the bakery in January, and buying the Clarke House. These decisions were logical, the path of least resistance in a way. It made sense for her to keep doing what she'd been doing for the past two years, not causing a stir, and going with the flow of what was expected. But staring down at the ocean-themed cookie cutters, a deep longing rose within her. She had toyed around with the idea of buying the bakery in Wildehaven Beach, but that was before Bea's Bakery burned. She'd already used a good portion of her inheritance money as a down payment on the house. There was no changing her mind now . . . was there? Anna stared at the cookie cutters. "How long will it take you to make breakfast? Mr. Randall said there's a package at the bakery. I thought I'd run and grab it so it doesn't sit there all day."

Evelyn glanced at the clock on the wall. "Half an hour at most. You know I like to slow cook my grits, so you have time," she said. "Leave the cookie cutters. I'll package them back up and make sure they send us the right ones."

Anna hugged the box in her arms. "Mama, I like these." She hurried to her room and changed out of her Christmas pajamas. Then she hustled out of the house and jumped into her daddy's truck. As soon as she turned the ignition, the radio blasted her against the back of the seat. The Beach Boys sang about everybody surfing, and Anna lowered the volume. "Dang, Daddy, you were rocking out, weren't you?"

Anna cranked on the heat and drove toward town. She passed driveways with children riding on new bicycles and families tossing around balls in their front yards as though it wasn't too cold for hanging around outside in footie pajamas. Smoke puffed out from chimneys, and the whole town smelled like wood-burning fireplaces and Christmas cookies.

She parked in front of the bakery and climbed out. The streets were empty and quiet. Standing on the sidewalk, Anna smiled at the finished storefront. The bakery sparkled in the noon sunlight. The windows gleamed. The tiled floors were polished and ready for business. Anna stepped onto the patio, and something crunched beneath her shoe. She bent down and picked up a small plastic sailboat. "What are you doing here?" she asked and placed it on the brick wall, imagining for a moment it had fallen out of Santa's red bag of toys.

Anna unlocked the front door and spotted the brown

package on the counter. She tucked it under her arm and locked up the bakery. On the patio a bird squawked at her. A seagull sat on the brick wall. It stared at her, and she stood quietly with the box in her arms. "You're a long way from home, aren't you?" The seagull called again, grabbed the plastic sailboat in its mouth, and flew off. It circled above the bakery and caught a wind current headed east toward the ocean. For a few moments, Anna thought, *Take me with you.*

She climbed into the truck and turned on the ignition to warm the cab. She slid her fingernails beneath the packing tape and popped open the flaps on the box. The smell of the salty air and the ocean rolled out over the edges, filling the cab.

The item inside the box was wrapped first in brown paper, then in parchment paper, and finally in plastic wrap. It was bulky and oddly formed. Anna unwrapped it and found a lump of dough shaped into the form of a body, like a giant gingerbread man. Two blue M&M's were stuck on for eyes, the mouth was a thin red licorice smile, and an indentation in the chest had been made in the shape of a heart. A piece of white chocolate dyed red had been placed into the spot. Anna lifted the attached note and read.

Merry Christmas! Wishing you smooth sailing on your next great adventure—wherever your heart takes you.

Love,

Eli (the Dough Boy)

Anna lifted the bread man carefully from the box and held him in front of her. She smiled despite the ache in her chest and bit into the dough boy's arm. "Tastes as good as he looks," she said to nothing but the empty cab and the candy canes swinging in a Christmas breeze. She leaned her head against the window and stared up at the puffy white clouds. A seahorse drifted across the sky until his shape faded into wisps.

When Anna returned home, Evelyn was still preparing breakfast because Charlie had requested a batch of homemade buttermilk biscuits. Because it was Christmas morning, she obliged him. Anna had premade and frozen batches of biscuit dough and stashed them in her parents' freezer for those times when her daddy needed one of his favorite comfort foods. Evelyn would need another half an hour for the frozen biscuits to bake. That gave Anna time to do a quick internet search. A completely bonkers idea had struck her on the way home. Bea's Bakery had burned right before Halloween, and *no one* in town seemed to have suffered greatly these past two months without cookies, cakes, or Saturday chocolate fests. In fact, everyone seemed to be living their lives just fine. What if—and this was a long shot—the Wildehaven Beach bakery hadn't sold yet?

When the listing for the beach bakery popped up as still available, Anna's stomach fluttered. If she dared follow this train of thought, she would have to back out of the purchase of the Clarke House, put the rebuilt bakery up for sale, and tell her parents about her plans. She questioned her sanity, but the tingly feeling zinging through her body confirmed the beach-bakery dream was still alive inside her heart.

All through breakfast Anna's mind was like a Ping-Pong ball being volleyed from this thought to that one and back again. As she poked the last bite of a biscuit into her mouth, she chewed slowly. She listened to her parents talk about the easiest way to take down the Christmas tree and get it to the recycling yard before the year was over. It was a conversation they had every year because Evelyn insisted on efficiency and a clean house as soon as Christmas passed while Charlie liked to leave the tree up until New Year's Day.

Anna pushed her plate away and folded her hands in her lap. She regretted the extra biscuit because now her stomach knotted, giving her heartburn. She watched her parents for a few seconds more, then she interrupted.

"I've been thinking," she said, her voice sounding weak. She cleared her throat and started again. "I've been thinking. You remember the Cornfoots? They own the bakery in Wildehaven Beach. They're retiring and selling it, and I think—I think I'm going to buy it."

Evelyn snapped her head toward Anna. A tight laugh escaped through her pink lips. Dean Martin sang to his baby, telling her it was cold outside. "What are you talking about? You can't run two bakeries at once. You'll work yourself ragged," Evelyn said.

"I don't plan to run two bakeries, only the one there," Anna said. Her daddy looked surprised, and Evelyn looked like she'd licked a sour lemon. "I'll sell the building here or rent it out if someone wants to open an eatery. I'd already planned to rent the apartment. I can cancel the house contract with Mrs. Clarke—"

"I don't understand what you're saying." Evelyn dropped her green napkin onto her plate and turned in her chair to better see her daughter. Anna inhaled a whiff of overripe cherries. The kitchen light twinkled off the pearls in her earlobes. Her words were slow and deliberate, pulled taut with admonition, when she said, "Please explain what you're saying."

"She's saying she's moving to Wildehaven Beach," Charlie said. He smiled at Anna as though he was proud of her, and Anna's skin tingled with warmth.

Evelyn tossed a glaring look at Charlie before turning her dark eyes on Anna. "Why would you do that? You have the bakery here. It's what you've wanted. Nearly the whole town has helped you rebuild so you can continue the legacy your grandmother started."

Anna exhaled to dispel the guilt her mama could so easily shove into her face. She refused to let it absorb into her skin and taint what she truly desired. "I want to have a bakery," Anna said. "But not here anymore. That's been what *you've* wanted for me. I want something different for my life. I should have been true to myself a long time ago, but I thought I was doing what was right by staying. Now I realize it's time for a change."

The air crackled around the table. A bulb in the pendant light over the island flickered. Charlie slid his chair back as a storm built around Evelyn. Anna clenched her hands together, preparing herself for the conversation she knew would swell into an argument. Anna's heartbeat quickened, and she felt the storm splitting the room in half.

"Is this about that *boy*?" Evelyn asked. "You can't disregard what your grandmother started because some boy ran off. You have a responsibility to this family."

Years of doing what was "right," doing what everyone else wanted, and disregarding her own dreams finally unraveled inside Anna like a ball of yarn bouncing down the stairs. The simple mention of Eli's absence felt like lemon juice on a paper cut. She stood, her body vibrating with energy and frustration, her emotions threatening to explode. The Christmas china rattled on the table. "If you're referring to *Eli*, then you're wrong. This isn't about him. This is about *me*, Mama. This is about me finally doing what *I* want to do. I can continue Grandma Bea's legacy no matter where I am. She'll always be a part of me," Anna argued, pointing a finger into her chest. "I loved her, and she knew it. Leaving Mystic Water doesn't mean I've stopped loving her. And I love you, but I'm not going to stay here in Mystic Water just because *you* think it's what's best for me. This is my decision, and either you can support it or you can't." Anna shoved away from the table and stomped to her bedroom.

She'd never smarted off to her mama, not in all her years growing up. Sure, she'd stuck out her tongue at Evelyn's back, and she'd rolled her eyes a few hundred times, but she'd never gone against her mama's wishes. She'd never disobeyed. Now Anna felt sick to her stomach but also proud of herself. For once, she'd been honest with her mama and with herself. What she wanted was Wildehaven Beach.

A car started in the garage, and Anna walked to her bedroom window. Her mama reversed her car out of the garage and sped off. To where was anyone's guess. Anna had never known her mama to get in a car and drive anywhere without a specific destination in mind.

A few minutes later, Anna heard a knock at her door. "Come in."

Charlie opened the door. "How long has that been festering inside of you?"

Anna sat on the edge of the bed, still facing the windows. "It's been under the surface for years," she admitted. "But I didn't hate it here, so don't think that. I've loved running the bakery and creating for Mystic Water. After Baron left and Eli showed up—and I swear this isn't about a boy—it shone a new light on everything. It made me really think about what *I* wanted."

Charlie sat on the bed beside her. "I'm proud of you, Anna," he said. "It's not easy to stand your ground with your mama. It's simpler to go along with her most of the time, but that's not always the right way to live. It works for us, but maybe not so much for you. We raised you to be strong and independent, but Evie still sees you as a little girl sometimes." He patted her knee. "Go easy on her."

Anna's eyebrows raised. "Shouldn't that be the advice you give her?"

Charlie chuckled. "I will, but what you don't know is that Evie *wanted* to run the bakery."

Anna nearly fell off the side of the bed. "Say what?"

"She did. My mama wanted Evie to continue with the family legacy and take care of the family gift—don't look so surprised. Of course we know about the gift."

Anna's head swam with Charlie's confession. Both of her parents *knew* about the magic sugar? "You never said anything."

"Mama made us swear we wouldn't," Charlie said. "She said you'd come to know in your own time."

"Why didn't Mama run the bakery? If she knew everything, then why didn't she take over?"

Charlie grinned. "Do you even have to ask? Evie can't bake, but, Lord, did she try. She wanted to run the bakery so badly, but she was so awful at it. Mama couldn't let her keep trying day after day. It was killing Evie's self-esteem. She cried so many nights about it too. But then you were born, and we could all see how much you loved baking, and Evie saw you as her little saving grace. If *she* couldn't help the family, then you would. You'd make up for how she had failed the family—"

"Mama didn't *fail* the family," Anna argued.

"I agree," Charlie said. "But try telling your mama that. She's stubborn and hard on herself. Even harder on herself than she is on you. Because she couldn't be good at baking, she strived to be perfect at everything else. That's why she's the way she is now. She didn't want to be found inadequate in any other part of her life."

"She's far from inadequate," Anna said.

"The most competent woman I know. She can do anything," Charlie said. "Except bake." He took her hand in his, a surprisingly gentle gesture he hadn't made in years. "Your mama loves you so much. She's afraid to lose what my family started, but she'll see that you're continuing it. There are no rules that state the family gift has to stay in Mystic Water. She'll come around. Just give her some time to cool down. If anything, I bet she's beating herself up right now for not being able to see what was truly best for you. Now, it's Christmas, so let's not sit around here moping or fuming all day. And tomorrow, you give the Cornfoots a call."

"You support me?" Anna asked.

"I'd support you building a bakery on the moon," Charlie said. "Best cookies in the universe is what I always say."

A couple hours later Anna heard her mama return. She sat on the floor in her bedroom with the contract for the Clarke House in her lap. It was ratty and wrinkled with burned edges, but it had shown Anna the way back to her dreams and doing what her heart wanted. If she hadn't started seriously thinking about her future, which was partly brought on by putting down earnest money on a house, she wouldn't have realized that wasn't the right path. A knock sounded on her bedroom door, and Evelyn walked in without waiting to be invited. She sat on the edge of Anna's bed and motioned for Anna to join her. Anna pushed herself off the floor and eased onto the bed beside her mama. They sat in silence.

"I'm sorry I yelled at you," Anna finally said.

"Honey, that's not yelling," Evelyn said with a small smile. "I yell. You simmer like a pressure cooker, and then you release your steam by yourself. That might be the first time you've ever told me how you really feel." Evelyn pushed Anna's hair from her shoulder. "I've only wanted what's best for you your whole life. I know you're a grown woman now, but I still look at you and see the little girl who was afraid to get on the school bus because she thought people would steal her lunch. And believe me, no one wanted wheat bread and carrots."

Anna chuckled. "Not when they had chocolate pudding and Fruit Roll-Ups."

"I won't pretend that I'm happy about this idea," Evelyn said. "But I do want you to be happy, and if that means having sand in your pants twenty-four hours a day, then I'll support you. I could help you find a cute little apartment with two bedrooms, because you know your dad and I will have to visit all the time just to make sure you're okay. And I could help you decorate it."

Anna smiled as tears glistened in her eyes. "I'd like that." Anna put her arms around Evelyn's neck and hugged her. "Daddy told me about you and the bakery, about how you wanted to run it."

Evelyn huffed. "One of the biggest disappointments of my

life," she said. "I felt redeemed by you, but I see how unfair that was to your own hopes and dreams." Her lips trembled, and Anna squeezed her hand. "I didn't mean to keep you trapped by my own ideas for your life. You don't go bossing me around about how to live."

"I wouldn't dare," Anna said lightly. "Mama, I understand why you were so hard on me about it. But I want you to know that I'll continue Grandma's legacy. I'll keep sharing her recipes and her *magic* with everyone."

"I know you will, honey," Evelyn said. "You've always been a good girl. The very best."

"Thanks, Mama."

Evelyn rubbed Anna's back. "Now, go hug your dad. He's about to burst with excitement for you. I could barely be in the same room with him. It was too contagious."

Evelyn sounded annoyed, but Anna could see the glint in her mama's eyes. Anna smiled, hopped off the bed, and gave a loud whoop. She heard the sound of her mama's quiet laughter as she rushed out of the room calling for her daddy. Merry Christmas, indeed.

EPILOGUE

ANNA BALANCED A BOX FULL OF BUBBLE-WRAPPED CUPCAKE holders on her hip before she shoved it onto the countertop. She unpacked each holder and found a place to shelve it. Then she returned to the front of the bakery and assessed which box she should grab next.

Mint and sage greens ribboned the bakery's walls in fat, vertical stripes. An oversize, whimsical mirror surrounded by a pale blue frame hung from one wall and reflected the ocean in the distance. Blue cake plates of various designs and sizes decorated the shelves. Anna's eyes drifted past the Help Wanted sign tucked into the front window. Her gaze rested on the gray-white sand and the dark-blue waters rolling toward the shoreline.

Her cell phone released a happy tune in her back pocket. She smiled at the picture and name flashing on her screen. She pressed the speakerphone button and placed her cell on the front counter.

"Are you officially a homeowner?" Anna asked.

On the other end of the line, Lily made an excited noise in her throat. "Yes," she said through her car's Bluetooth. "We're moved in. Looks like we've tried to make a fort out of boxes in every room, but I suspect that by the time I get home, Jakob will have at least a quarter of it unpacked. He can't stand clutter."

Anna laughed and waded through the cardboard boxes and crinkled newspaper used as packing material. The mess spanned half of the bakery's front room. "It could be worse. He could be a frantic dad-to-be who insists on reading pregnancy books out loud to you and asking you awkward questions. Oh, wait—he does that too. Jakob used to be so cool."

They both laughed. Anna lifted a box labeled Baking Utensils and hefted it onto her hip. She watched a young woman jog down the boardwalk toward the beach. Early April had arrived with unseasonably warm weather and a spring breeze that made people want to fly kites and laugh loudly. Gulls called to one another and played chase, diving into the waves and skittering across the wet sand.

"We're going to have you over to the Clarke House as soon as it's all sorted," Lily said.

"It's the Connelly House now," Anna said, balancing the box on her hip and shuffling toward the back room.

"It'll probably always be the Clarke House to me. I still can't believe we're actually living in it. Thanks to you."

Anna smiled and knew Lily would host parties in the kitchen with people spilling into the backyard all abloom with lavender and roses. "Thanks to life," she said.

"I left town later than I thought I would. I'll probably be there within forty-five minutes. Want me to bring lunch?" Lily asked.

Anna's eyes drifted to the spot on the wall where the clock would hang, but it was still empty. "Is it already lunchtime? No wonder I feel weak. That would be great. Mama and Daddy won't be here until tomorrow, and my refrigerator is completely empty. You should bring us food unless you want to eat butter and heavy cream."

"Tempting, but no thanks. I'll grab sandwiches or whatever I happen upon. See you soon," Lily said.

Anna disconnected and carried the box to the back island. She sliced through the tape and began unpacking the utensils. She continued this steady process of grabbing boxes and unpacking them for the next half hour. The number of boxes dwindled, and the tiled floor was almost visible in its entirety.

She grabbed a small, unassuming box labeled Postcards and hopped onto the front counter as she opened it. Inside were postcards from Eli. There weren't many, but each was unique, displaying images of lighthouses, seashells, a pair of hugging octopuses, and ocean scenes. He'd also mailed outrageous ones that seemed to be plucked from dive bars or truck stops. Her favorite was an image of the Stay-Puft Marshmallow Man made famous in the *Ghostbusters* movie. On the back, all he'd written was: *It could be worse. I could be fat and gooey and have rolls instead of these rock-hard abs. Love, Dough Boy.* Eli's scrawled messages were short, and Anna had read them so many times, she'd memorized them like cherished bedtime stories.

She slid off the counter and carried the postcards to the back room, where she pinned them to a corkboard. If she couldn't have Eli physically with her, at least she'd have something of his in the bakery to keep her company. She placed the hand-carved box of glittery golden sugar on a shelf above the corkboard to keep the most magical parts of her life close together.

The front door opened, jingling the newly hung bell. The breeze from the ocean rushed inside, and Anna smelled a mixture of briny air and chocolate. She smiled and bounded into the front room, saying, "That didn't take you forty-five minutes. Something smells like chocolate."

She skidded to a halt, her mouth dropped open. Eli stood in the bakery grinning like he had a secret to share. His blue shirt highlighted his tanned skin and bright eyes. He looked better than a perfectly iced chocolate cake. Anna self-consciously reached up a hand and tried to smooth down her hair. She'd been unpacking boxes all day and sweating in the spring heat. She wanted to say something, but she only managed to close her slack jaw and stare at him in surprise.

"Damn, you look pretty," Eli said, still grinning.

Anna's cheeks flushed, and she felt warm all over, like she was lying on a towel in the sun. She pushed her hands down her tank top and fiddled with the hem of her shorts. "I look like a throwaway."

"The best-looking throwaway I've ever seen. I missed you." He maneuvered through the few boxes in the front room, looking at the cake plates on her shelves and the items she'd hung on the walls. "Place looks great, like you. It *feels* like you in here. You were expecting someone?" he asked.

The room smelled like sugar and home. Anna's heart fluttered wildly in her chest because she was so close to Eli again. Her eyes tracked him as he moved. He seemed so calm, so unaware of how his proximity unraveled her.

"Lily," she said and cleared her throat. "She's bringing lunch and going to help me unpack."

Eli moved his hand over his belly. The sunlight shifted on the floor, stretching long beams toward their feet. "How's she doing? Look pregnant yet?"

Anna's body relaxed. She exhaled slowly. Talking about someone else helped to take her mind off the fact that Eli was mere feet away, looking at her, smiling at her. "She does," she answered. "But she's not huge. She'll be one of those lucky women who suddenly looks super pregnant at nine months, but leading up to that, she just looks like she's had a bit too much cheese."

"And Tessa?" he asked. His eyes wandered over the unpacked boxes and then back to her.

Anna looked for a spark in his eyes, for the curiosity that would drive her to think he had missed Tessa too. "She's great," Anna said honestly. "Been dating a pediatrician who moved to town. His name is Richard. We call him Ricardo for fun. He's a nice man."

Eli's expression didn't alter when he said, "Good for her."

She wanted to ask what he was doing there and how long he was going to stay. But she was afraid of what he might say. Instead she asked, "How are the Outer Banks? Do you like working with James at the deli?"

"It's windy," he said with a smile, "but the winter was short. The business took off. James had to hire more workers to keep up with demand. But it's not Mystic Water." He kicked a stray piece of newspaper into the air. They watched it float and descend.

Anna chuckled. "It's better than Mystic Water, I'm sure." She busied her hands by collecting the newspapers and smashing them into one large ball. She looked around for her box of trash bags. She held the ball in one hand and shook out the flat trash bag with her other hand. Then she shoved the paper into the bag.

"Different, not better," he said. "Definitely not better." He gathered newspapers with her. "You weren't there."

Eli's words surprised her and tugged a shy smile from her lips. She held the trash bag open so he could drop in the papers. His fingers brushed against hers—a move he'd made on purpose— and Anna felt a new wave of heat shimmer over her. The air-conditioning unit clicked on.

"What are you doing here?" Anna asked.

"Searching," he said.

"For what?" Anna asked.

But he only smiled and asked, "How have you been?" He took the bag from her hands and placed it beside the counter.

Anna thought of a variety of answers: *lonely, getting by, starting over, excited, happy, missing you, passing time, thinking of you, trying to get over you.* "Busy," she said because it was the least complicated answer she felt comfortable admitting.

He nodded his head toward the back room. "Show me around?"

When he stepped closer to her, Anna's breaths shortened. The temperature rose in the room. The edges of the crinkled newspapers wilted in the wash of heat. Anna pushed her hair behind her shoulders and fanned her face. Eli had seen the kitchen when they visited Wildehaven Beach together months ago, but she stepped into the back room anyway.

"Here's the kitchen," she said. "I kept pretty much everything how it was before. The layout was already efficient. I added those shelves. I need a bit more storage," she said and pointed. Something hanging on the wall caught Eli's attention, and he walked to it. The corkboard. Anna groaned inwardly. Now he would likely think she was obsessed with him. Was she obsessed with him? Did missing him every single day count as an obsession? Probably.

"This is new," he said, and a slow smile stretched across his face, deepening the dimple in his cheek.

"I, uh, decided to hang postcards from friends up there," she said, feeling the heat flush her cheeks. "Only no one else has written me. Yet."

Eli chuckled. "You missed me too," he said without arrogance. He sounded relieved. He pushed one hand through his hair and then patted it down again.

He turned to face her and started to close the distance between them. Anna's head felt light. The pull between them intensified, and she felt her feet moving toward him. Then he stopped moving, and his eyes drifted over her head to the far counter.

"What's that here for?" he asked.

The sugary haze faded from Anna's brain. Eli was an arm's length away, and her fingers tingled at the thought of touching him. But she turned to see what he was asking about. A deli-meat slicer sat on the counter gleaming in the light. She chewed on her bottom lip for a moment.

"It's for slicing meat," she said. A slow burn started up the back of her neck. She tried to rub it away.

"I know what it is. Why do you have it in a bakery?"

Anna started to say that Timothy and Mel Cornfoot had left it for her because they'd found it in their stock room, polished and ready for the right hands, but that would have been a lie. The meat slicer had been an expensive impulse buy at a restaurant supply store.

"I bought it," she admitted, turning to look at his face. "Because I had hope."

Eli stepped toward her. His fingers found hers, and he twined them together. "Hope for what?"

Embers flamed to life inside her. "That you might want to use it," she said, staring at his chest and aching all over.

Eli dropped her hand and walked out of the kitchen. Anna's heart slammed against her chest and then shuddered, making her stomach clench. Had she said something wrong? Was he upset that she'd been stupid enough to want him to come back? She stood alone in the back room for a few seconds before she followed him.

Eli snatched the Help Wanted sign from the front window and spun around. He smiled at her and tossed the sign like a Frisbee across the room. It bounced against the remaining boxes, and he held his hands out to her.

"What do you think about a combination bakery and deli?" he asked, smiling like the Cheshire cat.

Anna's mind burst with possibilities and hope for a future with Eli. "You want to come here?"

"There's nowhere else I'd rather be. I found what I was looking for. *You.*"

Anna's body shivered, and she smiled so wide a laugh slipped out. Then she ran toward Eli, and he opened his arms, catching her and lifting her feet off the ground with a hug. When Eli set her down, he didn't let go. He pulled her against him and kissed her. Anna felt the sunlight on her cheeks, the ocean breeze blowing through her hair. The air was heady with the scents of sugar and spice. She felt like candle wax melting in Eli's flame. She burned from the inside and folded into him. She slid her hands up his back, pressing her fingers against him, clutching him. Eli put one hand on her neck, warming her skin, sending pulses of energy down her spine. Then he moved the hand into her hair. Anna's heart pounded an excited rhythm. Her entire body quivered as though she had laughter trapped inside and it couldn't wait to burst out.

The bell jingled when the front door opened. In her conscious mind, Anna knew she should stop kissing Eli, but her brain asked, *How?* Then it asked, *Why?* Whoever it was could see they were busy, could see she wasn't yet open for business, and could come back later. Or never. Anna wasn't concerned with anything other than the way her lips were tingling and how Eli felt warm and safe and *perfect*.

"Should I come back in fifteen?" Lily asked.

Anna tried to pull away, but Eli held her close. He kissed her cheeks and forehead. Then he kissed down her neck. "Maybe an hour," he mumbled.

Anna laughed and pushed on his chest. He held tight, and she giggled more until he released his grip and smiled down at her.

"You back for good?" Lily asked.

"I'm sticking around," Eli said. "As long as Anna will have me." He grinned.

Anna's face flushed. She couldn't stop smiling even though her cheeks started to ache. She pushed up on her tiptoes and kissed him. Happiness swirled around them like a breeze.

Lily held up two brown bags stamped with the logo from a local taco shop. "I didn't know we'd have company. I only bought two meals. Now that you're sticking around, we'll be forced to share. I volunteer Anna's half." Lily smiled at them both.

Anna rested her hand on Eli's chest and leaned her head against his shoulder, feeling his warmth flush her skin and wrap her heart with heat and love. She thought of the morning she'd first met him and how he'd smiled at her then just as he was smiling now. She thought of the patrons of Bea's Bakery, who had walked into the shop that October morning and seen him—Elijah Guittard—looking like a man who'd strode out of a Hollywood movie: broad shouldered, sun kissed, and blue eyed. He had helped Anna behind the counter like he was born to be her partner. She wondered what they would say if they could see him now.

Some might say he'd hitchhiked hundreds of miles to see Anna again. Others would say he'd appeared like magic. Everyone would agree they'd never seen a man look more in love with any woman than Eli was with Anna.

AUTHOR'S NOTE

I'VE ALWAYS LOVED MAGIC. I FIRST DISCOVERED IT IN FANTASTI-cal stories, like the tesseract in *A Wrinkle in Time*; the Yellow Brick Road in *The Wonderful Wizard of Oz*; and the wardrobe in *The Lion, the Witch, and the Wardrobe*. My imagination took these marvelous tales and ran wild with them, creating my own stories and characters and dreams of faraway lands. As a child, I spent hours in my backyard, taking adventures through pine straw mazes, flying on magic carpets made of quilts, and keeping a lookout for pirates from a perch in the old oak tree.

I started writing down my stories in notebooks, on printer paper, on napkins, on the soles of my shoes. I used the family typewriter to clickety-clack out short stories and poetry, and when I was in junior high, my parents bought me a monster-size Word Processor that printed stories instantly. I could have wall-papered my bedroom with these magical quests.

Years later I understood that magic was not only bound in fantasy stories but also could be found in the everyday. I've seen how kindness can change the course of someone's life. I know the power of love and how it reshapes everything it touches. There is glory in planting a garden and watching it grow. There is so much hope in putting a cake in the oven and seeing it rise into a new creation. These all carry the spark of magic.

One summer after rereading *Frankenstein*, which has its own sort of spooky magic, I thought about how drastically a life could change, for better or worse, by creating a living creature out of cobbled together pieces and a mysterious electrical jolt. Since I'm a self-taught baker, I added a magical twist to this thought and wondered what would happen if a baker made a man out of dough, and the recipe for *The Baker's Man* came to life.

For this whimsical story, I wanted an equally whimsical setting—someplace where anything can happen and usually does. Growing up in a small town in Southern Georgia inspired me to create Mystic Water, which encompasses all of my favorite aspects of my hometown while adding in bits and pieces I've collected in my memory from travels. I wanted Mystic Water to feel like a place you'd want to take a road trip to with your best friends, where you could picture yourself walking downtown eating ice cream, where you could fall in love. I wanted you to feel the magic on the breeze and maybe even like a place you feel *at home*.

Mystic Water is a place of dreams and charm and love. My bags are packed, and I'm ready for that road trip any time you are.

ACKNOWLEDGMENTS

I'M OBSESSIVELY GRATEFUL TO SO MANY PEOPLE WHO HAVE
supported and encouraged both my life and my writing career.

Amanda Bostic—for taking a chance on me and for loving
this little dough ball of a story enough to give it larger wings
to fly. You and the whole Muse team are some of the loveliest,
kindest, and most encouraging people I know. I will always be
grateful for this opportunity to share Mystic Water in a way that
launches me toward my dreams.

My HCCP family—for teaching me, guiding me, and helping
me learn about the publishing industry and how to inspire others
with our books. Mike Briggs for believing in me enough to share
this book idea and for always being excited about the success of
others. Danielle Peterson and Angela Guzman for thinking this
whole book journey is a fabulous idea and helping me pitch the
best possible package I could.

Laura Wheeler—you are literally the kindest editor on the
planet. I don't have words to adequately express how thankful I
am for your gentle guidance and for the way you challenge me to
dig deeper and stretch my creativity past where I think I can. You

brilliantly helped shape this story into something even brighter and more magical than I ever imagined.

Crafting a novel takes perseverance, discipline, lots of flailing, and periodic bouts of staring off into space while questioning life. Having people who pick you up, dust you off, and put you back on the right path are such a gift. These are the ones who read the story, in any stage, and tell you to keep writing your masterpiece. They celebrate with you when it's complete as though the victory is their own. Natalie Banks, Jeanne Arnold, Julianne St. Clair—y'all make this journey full of light and laughter.

Marisa Gothie—everyone needs a friend like you! You are such a gift to authors everywhere, and I'm thankful to have you on my team. Thank you for crafting the book discussion questions for this edition. Anyone looking for a rockstar book club and one of the most voracious readers I know, find Marissa on Instagram @Marisagbooks at Bookends and Friends.

My family—for always telling me to chase after my dreams like someone wearing rocket shoes, for letting me be the fantasy-loving, daydreaming, glitter-tossing kid, and for being my biggest fans and encouragers. Thank you for teaching me to be practical and yet knowing I would probably choose the sparkly rainbow path instead.

Lastly, to all my readers—from more than ten years ago to now—who have fallen in love with Mystic Water and its quirky characters, and who have always asked for more books. Thank you for loving these stories and for sharing the magic with me.

RECIPES

BEA'S BAKERY CHOCOLATE CHIP COOKIES

These classic cookies are one of Anna's childhood favorites. Nothing finds your smile and warms your heart faster than a straight-from-the-oven chocolate chip cookie. The slightly crunchy outside gives way to the gooey, melty center. One bite will have you wholeheartedly believing that everything is going to be okay.

Prep Time: 20 minutes
Baking Time: 20 minutes
Total: 1 hour 40 minutes
Yield: 16 cookies

Ingredients
3 cups bread flour
1 teaspoon baking powder
1/2 teaspoon baking soda
1/2 teaspoon kosher salt

317

RECIPES

1 cup (2 sticks) unsalted butter, chilled and sliced into tablespoon-size pieces
1 cup light brown sugar
1 cup granulated sugar
2 eggs, chilled
2 teaspoons pure vanilla extract
1 cup dark chocolate chips
1/2 cup semisweet chocolate chips

Directions

1. In a large bowl, whisk together flour, baking powder, baking soda, and salt. Set aside.
2. In the bowl of a stand mixer fitted with the paddle attachment, beat cold butter on medium speed, about 1 minute. Add brown sugar and granulated sugar, then beat until incorporated.
3. Add eggs, one at a time, beating about 30 seconds after each addition. Add vanilla. Mix on medium-low speed until the mixture is blended. Turn off mixer, then add the dry ingredients.
4. Mix on low speed just until the dough comes together. Turn off mixer, and fold in chocolate chips by hand using a rubber spatula.
5. Drop the dough onto a parchment-lined sheet tray in 1/2-cup mounds. Place the tray in the freezer and freeze for 1 hour.
6. Preheat the oven to 375°F.
7. Bake straight from the freezer until still slightly under baked in the middle but golden brown around the edges and beginning to brown on top, about 20 minutes.
8. Cool the cookies on the tray for 5 minutes before cooling completely on a wire rack.

TWILIGHT BROWNIES

These decadent brownies help you view life from a higher perspective. They put your heart and mind at peace and quiet your thoughts, letting your creative spirit sparkle through you. Perfect for stargazing.

Prep Time: 10 minutes

Baking Time: 20 minutes

Cooling Time: 10 minutes

Total: 40 minutes

Yield: 9 square brownies

Ingredients:

1/2 cup flour

1/3 cup unsweetened cocoa powder

1/4 teaspoon kosher salt

1/2 cup (1 stick) unsalted butter

3/4 cup sugar

2 teaspoons pure vanilla extract

2 eggs at room temperature

1/2 cup bittersweet chocolate chunks

1 teaspoon Himalayan Pink Salt or flake salt

2 teaspoons turbinado sugar

Instructions:

1. Preheat oven to 350°F. Spray with cooking spray or line an 8-inch baking pan with parchment.

2. In a small bowl, whisk together the flour, cocoa powder, and salt. Set aside.

3. Melt the butter in a medium bowl using the microwave in 20-second increments until just melted, about 40 seconds.

4. Whisk in the sugar and vanilla until incorporated.

5. Whisk in the eggs, one at a time, until smooth.

6. Using a rubber spatula fold in the flour mixture until a few streaks of dry ingredients remain. Add the chocolate and fold a few more strokes to incorporate.

7. Pour the batter into the prepared pan and sprinkle with the flake salt and turbinado sugar. Bake for 20–25 minutes or until a toothpick inserted in the center comes out with just a few moist crumbs. Allow to cool completely in the pan.

DISCUSSION QUESTIONS

1. Each chapter has its own title. How do each of these titles draw you in to the story? What is your favorite title?

2. Magical realism as a genre blends the fantastical with reality. What is your favorite magical element of the story?

3. The people of Mystic Water believe that Beatrice's and Anna's treats are infused with magical powers. If you could eat a sweet treat that would give you a specific talent or offer you a particular feeling, what talent or feeling would you want and what treat would it be from?

4. If you were given a locked box from a loved one, would you be able to wait years to open it? Why or why not?

5. Expectations placed on a person versus following your own dreams is a big theme throughout the novel. Have you ever had a hope or dream that was at odds with

what others wanted or expected? Were you able to find a middle ground between the two? How did you find peace with the differences?

6. Anna faces great disappointment in her relationship with Baron because he does not consider her feelings when he plans for the future. Because Anna tends to put her own feelings second, do you think she would have been happy going to California with Baron if he had invited her?

7. Anna creates Elijah "the dough boy" to fall in love with her. She then worries that he only loves her out of obligation because she created him. As Elijah creates his own life, do you think the love was real or only out of obligation?

8. If you had the opportunity to bake the perfect man, what ingredients would you use?

9. Female friendships are important in this story and very complicated. What did you think of the friendship between Lily, Tessa, and Anna? How do secrets and their eventual reveal affect these friendships?

10. If you were given "magic sugar" to use one time and it would create a desire from your heart, would you use it for yourself or use it to help someone else?

11. Would you ever help your friend create a person? Why or why not?

12. Even though she thought her intentions were good, Tessa made a bold and reckless decision to use the magic sugar. The results were catastrophic. Could you have ever forgiven Tessa? Why or why not?

13. Would you want to visit Mystic Water? What character would you want to meet?

14. Would you read other stories set in Mystic Water? Why or why not?

15. If Mystic Water was adapted for the screen, who would you cast in each role? What songs would you include on the soundtrack?

LOOKING FOR MORE GREAT READS? LOOK NO FURTHER!

HARPER MUSE

Illuminating minds and captivating hearts through story.

Historical Fiction
Women's Fiction
Southern Fiction

Visit us online to learn more:
harpermuse.com

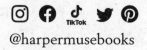

@harpermusebooks

From the Publisher

GREAT BOOKS

ARE EVEN BETTER WHEN THEY'RE SHARED!

Help other readers find this one:

- Post a review at your favorite online bookseller

- Post a picture on a social media account and share why you enjoyed it

- Send a note to a friend who would also love it—or better yet, give them a copy

Thanks for reading!

ABOUT THE AUTHOR

Photo by Matt Andrews

BORN AND RAISED IN SOUTHERN Georgia, where honeysuckle grows wild and the whippoorwills sing, Jennifer Moorman is the bestselling author of the magical realism Mystic Water series. Jennifer started writing in elementary school, crafting epic tales of adventure and love and magic. She wrote stories in Mead notebooks, on printer paper, on napkins, on the soles of her shoes. Her blog is full of dishes inspired by fiction, and she hosts baking classes showcasing these recipes. Jennifer considers herself a traveler, a baker, and a dreamer. She can always be won over with chocolate, unicorns, or rainbows. She believes in love—everlasting and forever.

Connect with Jennifer at jennifermoorman.com
Instagram: @jenniferrmoorman
Facebook: @jennifermoormanbooks
TikTok: @jennifermoormanbooks
BookBub: @JenniferMoorman